Praise for Monica Burns' *Dangerous*

Rating: 4 1/2 Stars "Jane Eyre meets The Mummy...[her] characters are so multidimensional that readers will swear they're based on real people."
~ *Romantic Times BOOKreviews*

"[She] writes lovely erotic romance with plenty of heart and passionate soul."
~ *Michelle Buonfiglio, Romance B(u)y The Book*

"Burns manages to have Constance breaking a few stereotypes without coming off too much like a contemporary character... I find Dangerous is a pretty good read..."
~ *Mrs. Giggles*

"...a powerful, sensually driven historical paranormal that is a testament to Ms. Burns' gift of keeping her readers spellbound. Highly Recommended Reading!"
~ *ParaNormal Romance.org*

"Ms. Burns is masterful at escalating the sexual tension and suspense with her characters. Three generations of murder, stubborn ghosts and an aging matriarch with attitude are the perfect complement to a fantastic love story that is a joy to read."
~ *Coffeetime Romance*

Look for these titles by
Monica Burns

Now Available:

Mirage

Dangerous

Monica Burns

A Samhain Publishing, Ltd. publication.

Samhain Publishing, Ltd.
577 Mulberry Street, Suite 1520
Macon, GA 31201
www.samhainpublishing.com

Dangerous
Copyright © 2009 by Monica Burns
Print ISBN: 978-1-60504-121-6
Digital ISBN: 1-59998-882-8

Editing by Imogen Howson
Cover by Anne Cain

First Samhain Publishing, Ltd. electronic publication: March 2008
First Samhain Publishing, Ltd. print publication: January 2009

Dedication

For my grandmother, Isabel W. Castellano, my first and greatest teacher. Each year, you returned my annual Christmas letter red-lined with edits until I finally achieved my A++ your last Christmas. Thank you for all you taught me, not just the English lessons, but life's lessons as well. True ladies such as you come along only once in a person's lifetime.

Chapter One

London, 1897

"This was a mistake."

Constance Athelson, Viscountess Westbury, swallowed the knot lodged in her throat as she surveyed the crowded ballroom uneasily.

"Don't be ridiculous," Davinia Armstrong scoffed. "You look stunning, and no one is going to recognize you with the mask you're wearing. No queen of the Nile could look as mysterious and alluring as you do right now."

With a skeptical look at her friend from behind the gold-feathered mask she wore, Constance shivered. The filmy silk layers of her costume were designed for hotter climates than the Black Widows Ball. Hosted by a secret and select group of the Marlborough Set, the event's sole purpose was to celebrate one's freedom from mourning and the restrictive social customs that accompanied that state.

It was the first time she'd ever attended the annual ball, even though she'd been officially out of mourning for more than three years. With one more glance around the ballroom, she winced. She must have been out of her mind when she'd agreed to Davinia's suggestion. Even if she met the Earl of Lyndham tonight, she was hardly dressed for a professional interview.

No matter how well versed she was in ancient Egyptian antiquities, her costume did nothing to recommend her as a serious academician. In fact, it did just the opposite, given the way she was being ogled by several gentlemen. She must look like an odalisque ready to submit herself to Pharaoh's whim. Why on earth had she listened to Davinia when it came to her costume? Because her friend could be quite indomitable when she set her mind to it. She tightened her grip on the handle of her fan. A footman walked by with a tray of champagne glasses, and she took one of the flutes off the silver platter.

The moment her friend heard the earl was going to make an appearance at the ball, Davinia had pressed her to attend. Her friend knew how much she coveted the cataloger of antiquities position the earl had available. Although she'd tried to resist, in the end it had simply been easier to give in to her friend's tenacious wheedling.

No, that wasn't true. *Davinia* was the real reason she had agreed to come here tonight. Drinking deeply from the champagne glass she held, she swallowed the bubbly liquid in a quick gulp as Graham's face flitted into her head. She frowned and stirred the air in front of her with the large peacock feather she held. Her late husband would have heartily disapproved of her presence here. Not because of the venue's decadence, although she had no doubt he'd have been less than happy with her attending the ball under any condition. What he would have condemned was her using her gift to protect a friend. She frowned.

"There he is, Constance. Do you see him?" Davinia's fingers bit into her bare arm.

With a glance in the direction of Davinia's discreet nod, Constance spied the man with whom her friend had become enamored. From what she could see of the man's face beneath the slim black mask he wore, it was understandable why Davinia was so enthralled. Oliver Rawlings, Baronet, was a handsome man, but she was certain the man's heart was as black as they came. Just looking at him made her stomach roil.

"Davinia, I know this isn't the time or place, but there's something you need to know about Sir Oliver."

Curiosity darkened her friend's lovely green eyes as she tilted her head in a display of puzzlement. "Something I need to know?"

Uncertain exactly how to proceed, Constance frowned. If Graham were here, he'd be dragging her from the room. But he wasn't here, and she had to help her friend. Inhaling a deep breath, she took the plunge.

"Sir Oliver isn't what he seems."

"What on earth are you babbling about, C⌐⌐⌐⌐⌐⌐⌐⌐" A derisive puff of air parted Davinia's lips.

"The man's drowning in debt, and he's look⌐⌐⌐⌐ with a substantial dowry." There, she'd managed to explain the problem without revealing every horrible detail. Surely, Davinia wouldn't waste her time on a ne'er do well.

"Really, Constance. I'm far from an ingénue. I know all that, but I also know he's in love with me."

Her heart sinking, Constance's fingers tightened on the handle of the peacock feather. Now what? Should she reveal the rest of what she'd seen? Her visions were far from exact depictions of the future. In fact, they were more often like a large puzzle with several pieces missing. Could it be she was wrong this time?

Davinia was one of only a handful of people outside her family who knew about her special talent. More importantly, she'd never actually seen something involving any of her closest friends. Seeing the excitement and hope on Davinia's sweet features made her hesitate. If she interfered now and was wrong...no, she couldn't say anything until she had something more noteworthy to offer up as evidence.

If she tried to explain how she'd seen her friend battered and bruised, Davinia would think her mad. And wasn't she? How could she be so sure it was Sir Oliver who had inflicted the damage? The man she'd seen in her vision had been faceless.

She forced a smile to her lips as she squeezed her friend's hand. "I only want you to be happy, Davinia."

"I am. I'm happier than I've ever been, and it's because of Oliver."

"Then go to him," Constance said quietly as she suppressed her misgivings. Her friend had already made up her mind. There was nothing else she could say to convince Davinia that Sir Oliver was in all likelihood a bad seed.

"Come with me. I want him to meet you." Davinia tugged at her arm with determination.

"Later perhaps. Since I'm here, I should at least make the attempt to discreetly learn if the earl is present and what he looks like."

Her stomach flipped as the words flew from her mouth. She

ᴴd absolutely no intention of looking for the earl. It had been a grave mistake coming here, and she refused to compound the error by introducing herself to the earl tonight.

"Dear heaven, I can't believe I forgot about the earl." Davinia shook her head with regret.

The apologetic note in her voice made Constance smile. It was impossible to find fault with her friend given the happiness sparkling in Davinia's eyes. Perhaps she was wrong about Sir Oliver. She'd been wrong before—rarely. Quieting the small voice in the back of her head, she prayed this would be one of those rare instances.

"Obviously you're preoccupied," she said with a smile. "Go on. Off with you."

Not hesitating, Davinia squeezed her hand and crossed the room toward Sir Oliver. Left alone on the edge of the throng, Constance grimaced at the thought of Lord Lyndham. Ever since Percy had first mentioned the earl's need for a cataloger, she'd been obsessed with the idea of securing the position. Her brother had mentioned the opportunity simply to tease her, never realizing she'd summon up the courage to apply for the position. She'd even surprised herself with her daring. Although why she should be surprised was a mystery to her. The Rockwoods, by their very nature, were impetuous creatures.

At least she'd had the forethought to apply for the position under the pseudonym she used at the British Museum. Using her first initial and her mother's maiden name, C. Stewart sounded every bit the skilled academician *she* really was. Her skills he couldn't question, but her sex in all probability would preclude her from receiving the position. She knew in all likelihood the earl would find it difficult to accept a female as possessing the ability to catalog his antiquities. And meeting the man here—tonight—would most assuredly destroy any credibility she might have on her resume.

She heaved a sigh. Her desire to protect her friend had placed her in a precarious situation. She'd allowed Davinia to coerce her into attending the Black Widows Ball based on her premonitions about Sir Oliver. If not for that reason, she wouldn't be standing on the fringes of the Clarendon's ballroom floor dressed in a costume that was more revealing than most of her nightgowns. Her gaze flitted about the room, and heat suffused her body as she saw she was the subject of an increasing number of male stares.

Good Lord, if she didn't find a dark niche to hide in, she was apt to be accosted on several fronts. She'd been a fool to think coming here would keep Davinia safe. With a soft noise of disgust, she moved toward the doors that opened onto a large glass gallery. The long corridor was cooler than the ballroom, and another sound of irritation parted her lips. She might have been compelled to attend the Black Widows Ball, but giving in to Davinia's demands that she play the role of an ancient Egyptian queen for the night was her own lack of foresight.

The irony of the thought wasn't lost on her. Shivering with cold, she saw what appeared to be a salon at one end of the hallway. Shadows flickering on the partially opened doorway convinced her the room contained a fire burning in an open hearth. Warmth and sanctuary in one place. Not hesitating, she hurried forward, her gold sandals clicking against the marble floor.

Just outside the entrance to the room, a masked couple stood in the shadows, indulging in a passionate embrace. She tugged in a sharp breath as she saw the man suckling the woman's breast. The wickedness of the scene reinforced the decadence of the ball, and it sent a shiver through her. What would it be like to give herself over to a man for just this one night?

Appalled by her thoughts, she swallowed hard. Dear Lord, she should have gone straight home. She slipped quietly past the couple and entered the salon. Closing the door behind her, she locked herself in the room with a quick flip of the key. She'd heard more accounts of debauchery outside the well-lit ballroom during the Black Widows Ball than she cared to admit. The last thing she wanted was to find herself witness to a hedonistic act or worse yet, suffering the unwelcome attentions of a drunken boor. She'd wait here for an hour or two before attempting to leave the ball. By then most of the attendees would either have found suitable accommodations for their trysts or would be too drunk to notice her departure.

The quiet ticking of the mantle clock was soothing to her nerves, and she willed herself to relax as she moved to stand in front of the cheery fire. Hands outstretched to the flames, she closed her eyes for a brief moment as she enjoyed the warmth coating her skin.

Except for the fire, there was little light in the room, and the boisterous sound of the ball was a soft buzz beyond the salon's locked door. The fire crackled as the burning wood popped in response to the heat. From where he sat in the far corner of the room, Lucien Blakemore, Earl of Lyndham, watched the woman as she warmed herself in front of the hearth.

The fire threw her curvaceous figure into stark relief. The soft light passed through the thin silk of her costume to reveal lusty thighs and long legs. Legs that would easily wrap around a man in the midst of lovemaking. His body reacted to the vivid image in seconds. She would never be called a professional beauty, but there was an exotic quality about her that intrigued him. Exotic and original. Just the type of woman he enjoyed.

His musings made him grimace. Damnation, the old woman was up to her tricks again. Somehow, his grandmother had arranged the interception of Lady Billingsly this evening and sent this woman instead. No doubt another attempt to entice him into that damnable state of marriage. She harped on the subject in every single letter she sent him from the country. His grandmother's determination to marry him off had placed him in some rather awkward situations in the months since he'd returned home from Egypt. In the past three weeks alone, the dowager countess had managed to thrust at least four potential candidates for the post of Lady Lyndham in front of him. All from her self-imposed exile at Lyndham Keep.

Unable to help himself, he grinned. She was amazing. Not even a military general could have managed a better-orchestrated campaign than his grandmother. But no matter how much her actions amused him, it didn't change anything. He wasn't about to satisfy his grandmother by playing her games. Marriage was far too deadly a proposition for him.

Clearing his throat, he watched the woman stiffen and whirl around to face him. When she turned, his groin tightened further. Good God, the woman was Isis in her most potent form. The gold silk of her enticing costume caressed every luscious curve of her body, revealing nothing, yet filling his head with all manner of arousing images.

Other than the silk knots holding her dress in place, her shoulders were bare. The soft silk of her bodice plunged downward in a vee accentuating the tops of her soft breasts, and he liked the way the gown flared out over her hips and fluttered around her long legs. Hers was a body for the most erotic of pleasures.

Voluptuous and tempting, her full breasts looked as though they'd fit into his palm quite nicely. What color were her nipples? The notion of parting her bodice to discover the answer sent blood surging through his veins until he was rock hard. Harder than he'd been in months. He wanted to see his hand caressing her breasts—watch her face as she responded to his touch. If he were to dip his fingers into her sweet core, would it be warm and sticky like the honey that flowed so sweetly for the pharaohs centuries ago? It was a tempting thought that tugged at him with relentless persistence. He wanted to plunge into her, feel her spasms as she climaxed over his cock.

Across from him, she stood immobile, assessing him with a wary look. Tension drifted through the air between them, the clock the only sound in the room.

What held her motionless, she wasn't certain. Any other time she would have quietly excused herself from a situation that could easily get out of hand. Especially with this man. Everything about him whispered danger, and her nerve endings sent a wicked frisson dancing across her skin.

Cool, cerulean eyes studied her quietly through a simple black strip of material. It was the mask of a highwayman. The thin, white scar curving its way across his cheek down to his jaw only enhanced the rakish air the mask gave him. The regal line of his nose emphasized the sharp, angular plane of his strong jaw, and there was just the hint of a smile tilting his sensual mouth.

She wasn't certain what historic highwayman he was supposed to be, but he played the role well as he sat there— watching her with a devil-may-care attitude. One boot-clad foot rested on the edge of his chair, his forearm balanced on top of his knee. His other leg was stretched out in front of him in a lazy display of masculine strength. There was a pure, raw

15

sensuality about him that sent every one of her senses into flux. The aura of nonchalance he wore might have fooled others less observant, but she knew it was a deceptive picture. He was a tiger waiting for that exact moment when his unsuspecting prey came within striking distance.

"Isis herself could not have been more exquisite." The low cadence of his voice sent a disturbing shiver of excitement gliding across her skin.

Heat suffused her cheeks as she watched his gaze roam leisurely over her entire body. A flash of arousal flared in his startling blue eyes, and she struggled to swallow the knot swelling her throat. Not even Graham had ever eyed her with such unmitigated desire. In a fluid movement, he rose to his feet and she drew in a breath of surprise. He was as tall, if not taller, than all three of her brothers.

"So, my Egyptian beauty, how shall we pleasure each other this evening?" Again, the silky smoothness of his voice teased her senses.

She tensed. Beneath that seductive tone of his, there was a sardonic note. Dear Lord, did the man think she'd deliberately sought him out? She didn't even know who he was. The thought didn't stop her from imagining her mouth melding with his firm lips, which were now curled in a beguiling smile. With a slight shake of her head, she dismissed the notion.

The last thing she needed was to indulge in an affair. Besides, the man wouldn't last ten minutes when faced with the male members of the Rockwood clan. No, that wasn't true. There was something about him that said he'd be more than a match for her brothers. Butterflies stirred in her stomach as he slowly crossed the room toward her. He had almost reached her when she took a quick step back and raised her hand to keep him at arm's length. Her silent protest didn't stop his forward progression until her palm pressed into his chest.

The moment she touched him, she went rigid. Abrupt and swift, the surreal existence of her visions enveloped her. This time the world she entered was more arousing than anything she could have ever imagined. Erotic and vividly real, the image of her writhing eagerly beneath the stranger stole her breath away.

The moment exploded around her with intoxicating

pleasure. Warm and spicy, his male scent flooded her senses as their bodies melded, and he thrust deep into her with a dark roar. Flexible steel shoulders shifted beneath her hands as she clung to him, her body moving with his as he filled her completely, withdrew, then buried himself inside her again. The intensity of the moment sent her mind reeling from the pleasure buffeting every part of her. His heat permeated her body as her pores rushed to absorb the very essence of him. Tantalized and devoured by his possession, her blood ran hot with need.

The suddenness with which she was thrown out of the surreal experience sent a jolt through her body. Muscles weak with reaction to the wicked imagery, she struggled to remain standing. She stared up at him, all too aware the vision she'd just seen would happen, and nothing she did could prevent it. The simplicity of the knowledge didn't startle her, but the anticipation skimming through her veins did. She wanted his heat burning through her, singeing her until the pleasure she'd just witnessed consumed her.

He studied her with an indescribable emotion glinting in the cerulean depths of his eyes. Slowly, he pulled her toward him, his gaze never leaving her face. A strong hand captured her chin and tilted her head back. Heart pounding with excitement, she waited for his mouth to warm hers.

The moment their lips touched, she melted into him, her eyes fluttering shut. Senses reeling from the pleasure of his touch, she gasped as his tongue laced seductively over her lips. In an instant, his tongue danced with hers in a tantalizing example of the intimacy her gift had shown her. The sharp bite of Cognac tickled the inside of her mouth as she molded herself to his hard, muscular body.

The chill that had encased her earlier was gone. In its place was a fire that stole her ability to think. Everything disappeared in a mist of passion and desire as his mouth teased and tempted her into a wild and abandoned response. Pressed into him so intimately, her body cried out with the need to be possessed by him. She'd never wanted anything so much in her entire life.

In the next moment, strong hands gripped her waist as he put space between them. All too aware of her accelerated pulse and the frantic breaths escaping her lips, she was startled to hear the harsh sound of his heavy breathing as well. His reaction made her believe he was just as affected as she was by their embrace. She watched in silence as he swallowed hard.

"My grandmother didn't send you. Who did? Standish?" The terse note in his voice made her frown.

"I don't understand." She shook her head in puzzlement. "No one sent me."

"Do you really expect me to believe you found me here simply by accident?" he scoffed.

"I do." Setting her chin at a defiant tilt, she sent him a haughty look.

"What woman in her right mind would venture away from the main ballroom dressed the way you are, unless she had every intention of being alone with a man?"

She stiffened at the chastising note in his voice, and heat warmed her cheeks. He was right. Her behavior announced her blatant disregard for propriety. Still, he didn't need to scold her like a child. She lifted her chin to a defiant angle.

"Do not flatter yourself, sir. I wanted to find a safe haven for just a short time. I am not in the habit of locking myself in a room with a total stranger."

"And yet you did just that," he responded softly.

Good heavens, but the man's voice had the ability to reduce her to the state of a tongue-tied debutante. And was that regret she saw in his dark eyes? Regret mixed with desire. Her throat tightened as she saw his gaze slide over her again. Heat returned to her cheeks, and she quickly looked away to prevent him from seeing how much his open admiration excited her. It was difficult to think straight when he looked at her like that.

"It was...it was not intentional, sir."

"Lucien," he murmured as he bent his head toward her. "You may call me Lucien."

"Lucien." She tested the name on her tongue.

She liked the way it sounded. Her eyes locked with his, and her heart skipped a beat at the open desire darkening his features. As his forefinger trailed its way down the side of her cheek, she tried to breathe normally. Impossible. Something about this man sent what little cautionary judgment she possessed dancing off into the wind.

Desire slid through her to coil in every part of her body. It warmed her and sent her blood pounding through her veins. The fierceness of the emotion took her by surprise. In an attempt to collect her wits, she drew in a deep breath. She realized her mistake the moment his spicy male scent flooded her senses.

She didn't move as he bent his head and brushed his mouth over hers. Was it the brandy on his lips or his kiss that warmed her blood? God, if she didn't leave the room right this minute, she might actually lose her head and do something rash and impulsive. She sighed as his mouth grazed her cheek then moved downward to nibble at her neck.

"I think I should go," she breathed.

"Would Isis deny a mere mortal the pleasure of her touch?" he whispered as he trailed his fingertips down her throat and across her bare shoulder.

He leaned into her again to capture her mouth in a hard kiss. Coherent thought deserted her as she melted into him. She knew doing so was a mistake, but she loved the way his hard body pressed into hers. He nipped at her lower lip, playfully tugging at it until she parted her lips to welcome his sensuous exploration of her mouth.

The bite of the brandy she'd tasted on his lips moments ago swept across her tongue and heightened the dangerous male essence of him. She needed to stop this madness. She was playing with fire. Deep inside a small voice encouraged her to linger. Just a few more minutes. Playing with fire didn't mean she couldn't enjoy the warmth of it for a few more moments.

His hand glided over her hip, and a tremor lashed through her. Oh God, she was enjoying this far too much. With a gentle tug, he pulled her tight against him. Through the thin silk of her gown she could feel his thick erection. The tip of it pressed against the apex of her thighs, and her heart thudded against her chest as she acknowledged how much she wanted him. Desire rushed through her as she burrowed deeper into his body. She wanted to feel more of him. It was wrong to want this, but something beyond reason held her in its grip. When his hands slid the knotted material off her shoulders, she didn't even think to protest, she simply gave herself up to the pleasure of his touch.

"Beautiful," he whispered as his tongue flicked out to circle her nipple. "Ra himself wouldn't be able to resist such a tempting sight."

The only response she could muster was a soft moan. Her blood grew thick in her veins as a lethargic heat spiraled through her. Once more, he circled her nipple with his tongue then blew across the dampness of her skin. The sensation made her cry out with pleasure.

Need in its rawest form slid through her, blinding her to anything but the pleasure of his touch. She arched her body backward as he closed his lips around a nipple and suckled her. Immediately, her legs grew wobbly.

Dear Lord, this was the most gloriously wicked thing she'd ever done. Wicked, sinful and decadent. She didn't want it to end. Her muscles were taut and achy, and she whimpered with the need to satisfy the primal longing holding her hostage. His mouth left her breast and slid up to her shoulder. As the remaining silk strap of her bodice fell down into the crook of her elbow, his thumbs rubbed over the pointed tips of her breasts.

Her mouth went dry as she realized she had reached the point of no return. She knew her behavior was appalling, but her vision made her wonder if this moment wasn't meant to be. Moreover, did she have the strength to deny herself something so exquisitely pleasurable? As his mouth covered hers once more, she reveled in the unadulterated pleasure his touch gave her. She'd never known how decadent and delicious Cognac could taste on a man's tongue. She wanted more.

She stroke his cheek, and beneath her fingertips, she felt the ridge of the long scar across his cheek. His hand caught hers, and he turned his head to press his lips into her palm. Passion blazed in his eyes as his gaze met hers.

"Give yourself to me, Isis." Desire made his voice raspy. "Let me show you what heaven can feel like."

The words sent her heart slamming into her chest as he proceeded to pull her finger into his mouth. Dear God, the man's touch was a heady summons to indulge in sin. And it was a wickedly tempting offer that promised a delirious passion. She knew leaving the room was the sane thing to do, and yet every part of her protested the idea of sanity.

"This is madness," she whispered as she looked away from him, struggling with her decision.

"If that's so, then I welcome it. That, and the pleasure I know we'll find in each other's arms."

His words reminded her of the image she'd seen—their bodies entwined together as they indulged in a sinful passion. The vision made her willing to cast all caution aside. In a supplicant gesture she pulled his head down and offered him her mouth.

Instantly, his lips seared hers with a demand she couldn't refuse even if she'd wanted to. Weak-kneed, she braced herself against his chest with her palms, the soft material against her hands a direct contrast to the hard muscles beneath his clothing. A sudden rush of liquid heat made her slick with desire, and she released a soft gasp. The speed with which her body was ready for him astonished her. Graham had never made her feel this way. Hot, needy and aching for release.

The hardness of his arousal pressed into her, and with another catlike stroke, she rubbed her hips against him. Her action ripped a deep groan from his throat, and the sound sent her pulse skidding along at a phenomenal rate. Dear Lord, she'd lost her mind to be acting in such a wanton manner.

Whether it was her vision driving her down this wild and wicked path or something else, she didn't know. Perhaps she was going mad, but she could not imagine a more delicious man to descend into madness with. She wanted to touch him— needed to feel the hot essence of him. Fingertips tingling, she unbuttoned his shirt while her tongue mated with his in a passionate kiss.

Seconds later, her palms pressed into his hard flesh. She breathed in the raw masculinity of him. It had been more than three years since she'd been this intimate with a man. Beneath her hands, his heat penetrated the pores of her skin until she wanted more. It wasn't enough just to have her hands skimming over the hard, sculptured muscles of his chest. She wanted nothing between them. She wanted to experience her vision. She wanted him inside her.

As if he could read her mind, he slowly dragged his mouth away from hers and lifted his head.

With the palm of his hand against her throat, he gently ran his hand downward until his fingers skimmed over a voluptuous breast. He swallowed hard at the desire glowing in her eyes. Their hazel color had changed to a sultry green, and the expression of hunger on her face was enough to drive him to drink.

He hadn't come here to bed a widow fresh out of mourning, but this one had made him forget any intentions he had, good or bad. Her soft flesh filled his hand as he cupped one luscious mound, with his thumb circling a hard peak. Damn, but she was a tempting morsel.

Desire pushed any thought of sanity out of his head, and he lifted her into his arms and carried her to the long divan that faced the fireplace. As he laid her on the backless furniture, the seductive pout of her soft mouth pulled the air from his lungs. Christ Jesus, he'd never seen a more alluring creature. But he wanted to see her without her mask.

He reached out to remove the gold-feathered disguise, but she caught his hand and raised it to her lips. The warmth of her delicate mouth sent need crashing through him the moment she started sucking on his finger. He growled from the pleasure of it. If she could suck his cock as skillfully as she did his finger, he'd find himself well sated. The image pulled another dark growl from him. Her gaze immediately dropped to his taut erection, and she sent him a provocative look as she released her grasp on his hand.

"Undress for me," she demanded in a throaty whisper.

He smiled slowly at the faint flush cresting over her cheeks. It appeared Isis wasn't used to making demands when it came to her pleasure. But she had with him, and her boldness pleased him. As he removed his clothing, he watched her do the same until the only thing she wore was her gold-feathered mask. Following her example, he didn't remove the black silk from his face.

As he studied her in the firelight, his gaze swept over voluptuous breasts down to a softly rounded stomach and then to the dark triangle at the apex of her thighs. Exquisite. He liked how she was curved in all the right places. Exploring every inch of her would be a pleasurable task.

One hand stretched out to him, she silently invited him to

come to her. He accepted without hesitation and lowered himself onto the divan. Unable to keep from devouring her with his gaze, he ran his hand across the roundness of her belly. The tactile sensation was one of downy softness. The aroma of jasmine and lemongrass tantalized his senses. The exotic combination tugged at his groin as he pressed his mouth against her stomach, delighting in the fragrant softness of her. His hand caressed a long, shapely leg before his fingers brushed across the top of her lusty thigh. The quick breath she drew in was filled with a taut need.

"Please," she murmured.

"I have every intention of pleasing you, *yâ sabâha.*"

The desire shimmering in her sultry gaze made his mouth go dry. His gaze not leaving her face, his fingers slipped through her nest of curls. He sucked in a quick breath of surprise as he encountered the slick heat of her passion. She was drenched in cream. Hot and wet, she arched her body upward against his hand with a soft mewl of pleasure. He rubbed the fleshy nub between her slick folds, and she writhed beneath the touch.

"Oh God, please."

Her soft plea tore at him. Damn, she was about to come apart in his arms, and he'd not had a chance to fully explore the delights of her body. But she wasn't the only one wanting immediate satisfaction. His cock jumped as he watched her pink tongue dart out to lick her lips.

Quickly he shifted his body to hover over her. With his erection pressing at the edge of her honeyed core, he reached for her mask. Once again she prevented him from removing the gold-feathered covering.

"No," she murmured. "Tonight belongs to Isis and her mortal lover, Lucien. No one else."

With a nod, he pressed his hips downward and buried himself in her slick heat. The pleasure of it forced a deep groan out of him. God, when was the last time he'd had such a delicious cunny wrapped this tightly around his cock? He couldn't remember. He couldn't remember any woman except her. In the back of his head he heard the warning, but he ignored it. Sheathed inside her tight passage, he lowered his head to suckle on the stiff peak of her breast.

A soft moan broke over his head as his teeth lightly abraded her nipple. The small cry of delight escaping her pleased him. It pleased him more than he cared to admit. Slowly he shifted his hips and eased himself out of her snug sheath. At her murmur of protest, he slid back inside her. Expanding her until he filled her completely with his hard length.

Christ, but she felt good wrapped around him like a snug vise. As she shifted beneath him, he released a dark growl of pleasure. She responded by flexing her muscles around him again. If possible, his cock expanded and hardened against her tightness. God, he'd not enjoyed this kind of pleasure in a long time. Pulling out of her slightly, he kissed away her protest before plunging back into her. His mouth swallowed her cry of delight, and triumph raced through him as he increased the speed with which he plundered her heated core.

As she met his thrusts with equal fervor, he forgot everything but her. Isis was his for the taking, and their mating filled him with a primal need unlike anything he'd experienced before. He rocked his hips hard and fast against her as he stared down at the lushly curved body beneath him. Everything else receded from him except for his awareness of her. The soft cries of her desire as she bucked against him. The exotic floral scent mingling with the musk of her passion. The sweet taste of champagne on her tongue. There wasn't anything about her that he didn't want more of.

Her slick, creamy core tightened around his cock, and he groaned as his ballocks drew up taut at the base of his erection. The faster he drove into her, the more passionate her response. Fingertips digging into his hard shoulder muscles, she clung to him, answering his demand for complete surrender. Seconds later her body shattered around him, her muscles clenching him in hard, rhythmic spasms of intense pleasure. He wanted to prolong the moment, enjoy the sensation, but he couldn't. With a deep, primeval growl, he exploded inside her before slowly sinking down into her soft, full curves.

Chapter Two

The after effects of their joining shivered through her, and her muscles trembled around him. He released a low sound of pleasure against the side of her neck as his firm lips nibbled at her. Satiated and exhausted, Constance murmured a soft protest as he rose from the divan. With a swift kiss to her lips, he smiled.

"The night is still young, Isis. I'm simply going to fetch an afghan I saw earlier."

She watched him cross the darkened room. The masculine grace and power of his movements renewed the desire he'd so deliciously satisfied moments ago. The way he moved emphasized his commanding presence and explained the intense attraction she felt. He reminded her of the statues of Ramesses she had seen when Graham had taken her to Egypt several months after their wedding. She closed her eyes as shame suddenly rolled over her.

In some small way, she felt as if she'd betrayed Graham. Biting her lip, she swallowed hard. What had she been thinking? She'd just given herself to a stranger. She'd been intimate with a man she knew nothing about. Even his face was a mystery to her. She'd always accepted that being a Rockwood meant she possessed an impulsive and audacious nature. But this was by far and away the most outrageous thing she'd ever done. In fact, she was certain she'd outdone all the Rockwood clan with this particular incident. Overwhelmed by the wickedness of her actions, she shot upright and frantically looked around for her costume.

Escape. The sooner she left this man's company, the better. Her fingers absently touched her cheek as she tried to come to grips with the situation she found herself in. The golden feathers of her mask brushing across her knuckles brought a sigh of relief to her lips. The one saving grace in this entire debacle had been her foresight to keep her mask on. He would never recognize her if they met at some dinner party or other social event.

Leaning over, she reached for the gold and green silk of her dress. The warmth of a strong hand covered her fingers, and she jerked with surprise as he gently pulled the garment from her grasp. In an odd gesture of tenderness, he stroked the side of her face with his finger as he sat down beside her.

"You're troubled by something."

"No, I'm just a bit chilly." Even to her own ears, the words sounded false as she turned her head away from him.

"You've not betrayed him, *yâ sabâha*. One cannot betray the dead."

Stunned, she stared into the blue eyes studying her with quiet assessment. Swallowing the knot in her throat, it amazed her how he'd instinctively known she was feeling guilty about Graham. Few other men would have been so perceptive. Even more astonishing was the way he'd addressed her in the Arabic language as his beauty.

The only men she knew who spoke the language were on staff at the British Museum, and this man wasn't one of them. She was certain of that. The scholars at the Museum were much older than this man. With another shake of her head, she reached for the gold and green silks he still held in his hand.

"I really must go. I...what happened here tonight..."

"Was a brief interlude, nothing more."

He finished the sentence for her. The matter-of-fact note in his voice filled her with relief. He did not expect their relationship to continue. To her surprise, a twinge of disappointment nipped at her. Not willing to explore the reason for her reaction, she accepted her costume from his outstretched hand. She dressed quickly, aware he was doing the same. As she adjusted the knotted material on her shoulder, she looked up to see him watching her with an intense look. It was a look that sent a blaze of excitement spiraling through her body.

In the span of a breath, she was in his arms again as he took her mouth in a hard kiss. The uncontrolled restraint of the embrace rocked its way through her. She would never forget tonight or him as long as she lived. For a brief time, she'd experienced a passion that few would ever know. It was worth any guilt or remorse she might feel in the days to come.

As he raised his head and stared down into her eyes, she placed her open palm against his heart. Beneath her fingertips she could feel his heartbeat. It was strong and steady. The sound of it connected her to him until his pulse thundered through her head, assaulting her senses. With the roar came the blood. It was everywhere. Looking down at her hands she gagged as she saw the bright red stains on her skin.

The horror attacking her made her whimper as she stared helplessly about the room she was in. It was a massive library with books strewn all around the floor. Lying close to her feet was the body of a woman. Her eyes were open and vacant. Lifeless. There was a deep gash across her throat that still oozed a trickle of blood. Never in her life had her gift ever thrust her into such a horrible place. Not even her nightmares could compare with this unspeakable carnage.

Then in the blink of an eye, the room shifted around her, and she watched as a handsome man knelt at the woman's side. The look of grief and rage on his face swelled her throat as she suppressed her tears at his pain. In that brief moment, evil wrapped its arms around her. It pulled her into a stranger's body and a knife appeared in her hand. In a fleeting moment of recognition, she knew she'd seen the knife before, but she couldn't remember where. The moment was gone as a flash of light showed the blade descending to slice deep into the man's neck, spraying his lifeblood outward.

With a sharp cry, she raised her hands in an attempt to cover her face. Strong hands gripped her arms, and Lucien's low voice called to her. Her eyes flew open and she stared up at him with trepidation. There was a strange glint in his gaze that unnerved her. Had he been a part of what she'd seen? Was he a murderer? Was that why she'd seen that devastating picture? She shivered.

"Are you all right?"

Bemused and frightened, she nodded. "Yes, I...forgive me—I

must go."

"You're frightened."

"No," she said sharply, and beneath the black silk of his mask, she saw his piercing blue eyes narrow.

Oh God, did he know what she'd seen? No, how could he? She had to get away. Even if he wasn't involved in the horrendous crime she'd witnessed, he was the catalyst that had brought the images forth. Terrible images she wanted to forget. Trembling, she pushed her way out of his arms, and without another word sped toward the door.

Behind her, he uttered a soft oath. Not daring to look over her shoulder, she fumbled with the key before the lock clicked open. The sound of his footsteps propelled her out the door and down the corridor to the brightly lit ballroom. Tonight had ended with a memory she wanted to forget, but knew she never would.

Berkshire

Lyndham Keep, Two Months Later

It was gloomy. No, bleak and desolate was a more accurate description. Against the dreary looking rain clouds, the gray stone walls of Lyndham Keep looked almost menacing. Staring out the carriage window at the massive stone building, Constance shook her head at the fanciful thought. The place hardly looked all that ominous considering the reason for her flight from London.

"It looks like a haunted castle, Mother." Jamie's comment made her turn her head back to her son. The excitement on his face tugged a smile to her lips.

"It does a little bit, doesn't it. Now remember what I told you earlier. You're to be on your best behavior."

"Yes, Mother." His attention span short, he stared back out the window. "Do you think the earl is going to be angry when he finds out you're a woman?"

The question sent apprehension skating down her spine. After a lengthy correspondence, the earl had offered her the position of cataloging his Egyptian artifacts without ever questioning her as to her sex. After all, it hadn't been relevant. Had it?

Jamie was right, what would the earl think when he finally met C. Stewart? Would he send her packing for not belaboring the point that she was a woman? The curiosity in her son's eyes made her flinch as she shook her head in a gesture of uncertainty. She couldn't let the earl even consider the possibility. She had to convince him that he'd based his decision to hire C. Stewart on her credentials and not her sex. C. Stewart had been selected to catalog the earl's Egyptian artifacts because of her skill and knowledge, nothing more.

She had no intention of losing this position. Lyndham Keep was sanctuary. A place to hide until *he* stopped looking for her. She shivered. It had been two months since the Black Widows Ball. What had begun as a glorious night of pleasure had ended on a note of horror. A true Rockwood, she'd succumbed to impulse and only afterward had she realized the folly of her actions. Although the doctors had said she would never conceive again, the possibility had still haunted her. It had been a relief when she learned she wasn't with child, but her connection to the stranger had still remained. Closing her eyes briefly, she remembered the dreams that began shortly after her interlude with the highwayman.

In her dreams, the man who called himself Lucien searched for her. From one drawing room to the next, he hunted for her. The first night she'd brushed the dream off as a remnant of fear from what she'd experienced in Lucien's presence. But as the dreams continued pushing their way into her sleep, something changed.

At first she couldn't understand what was different about each successive dream. Then she realized what it was. With each dream, he came closer to her. At first he'd been a shadowy figure in the distance, but as each night passed, he was more distinct—real. His mask still hid his face, but she knew it was him. The dreams convinced her he was looking for her, and the only way to escape was to leave London.

The thought of telling her family about her predicament had occurred to her, but she'd quickly discarded the notion. The last thing she wanted to do was admit to any of her siblings that she'd gone to the Black Widows Ball. Louisa and Patience would simply be amused by her daring. Unfortunately the rest of the Rockwood clan would be less than amused.

While her sister-in-law would have tried to shield her, not even Helen's sway over her husband would have staved off any inquisition. As the family patriarch, Sebastian would have demanded a full account of her actions, with Percy and Caleb in complete agreement. No, she'd been wise *not* to confide in her family. Her brothers would have suffocated her with a well-intentioned cloak of protection.

She'd even considered taking a house in the country for a few months. It would have strained her household budget considerably, but she'd been willing to do whatever it took to escape the man searching for her. Then the earl had made his decision, and it had been manna from heaven. The joy of being responsible for such a notable collection of artifacts was second only to the knowledge that she could escape London for several months until she completed the archiving of the earl's antiquities collection. By the time she returned, Lucien would no longer be looking for her.

Now, trepidation wound its way through her like a vine of ivy, threatening to choke her as she stared out the carriage window at the large keep they were approaching. Jamie had asked an excellent question. What would the earl do when he found out he'd secured the services of a woman to catalog his prized Egyptian artifacts?

The carriage rocked to a halt, and she tried to ignore the apprehension nibbling at her. It was quite likely she'd be sent straight back to the rail station the moment her deception was discovered. As the coach door opened, she accepted the footman's assistance and descended from the carriage. The massive wood doors of Lyndham Keep rose up like giant oaks, reinforcing the image of an ancient battlement. Standing just outside the door was a slenderly built man who bowed as she climbed the steps.

"Good afternoon, madam. We were expecting a Mr. Stewart."

"I'm C. Stewart. Would you please inform his lordship that I've arrived." Her response made the man's eyes widen, but other than that he showed no other sign of surprise.

"His lordship isn't expected home for at least three weeks, madam, but Lady Lyndham asked to see you when you arrived."

She inhaled a deep breath as she nodded in silent response. With her hand on Jamie's shoulder, they followed the butler into a massive hall. The stone walls rose up at least two levels to wide beams that served to hold up the ceiling. A huge tapestry hung against one wall, while two complete sets of armor framed the entry to a large library. Her heart skipped a beat as she walked past the open doorway of the large book-filled room. The Lyndham Library—from what she could see, the room was every bit as massive as she'd heard. Rumor held the Lyndham Library rivaled Queen Victoria's private collection.

The sound of her shoes clicking on the stone floor mingled with the swish of her bustled gown, the usually soft noise echoing loudly in the great hall. It underlined the sonorous depth of the room. The hair on the back of her neck tingled as she sensed someone or something watching her. Glancing over her shoulder, she saw the figure of a man standing in the shadows near the library door.

An instant later he vanished in a thin stream of mist. Frowning, she inhaled a deep breath. It didn't surprise her to find one or more spirits lingering in a structure as old as Lyndham Keep. The family descended from the time of William the Conqueror. Once more she was reminded of the menacing appearance the keep had presented only a short time ago. With great effort, she controlled the sudden urge to run back to the carriage, dragging Jamie with her. She cast the thought aside. Going back to London was out of the question.

Following the butler, they walked into a room with a ceiling that wasn't quite as high as the main hall. Despite its large size, the room was warm and cozy with its lemon chintz cushions and a roaring fire in the immense hearth. Seated in a wing-backed chair of floral print, an elderly woman eyed Jamie with a look of astonishment before turning her intimidating gaze on Constance.

Powdery white hair piled atop her head in an outdated style, the dowager countess's piercing blue eyes pinned their fierce brightness on her. Blue-veined hands rested on the head of a cane she held. The woman presented the air of a fierce and regal matriarch.

For a brief instant, she saw something vaguely familiar in the woman's expression. Had she met the woman before? She dismissed the notion as Lady Lyndham's sharp gaze settled on her, and her heart sank. There was the distinct possibility the dowager would send her back to London without an opportunity to even plead her case with the earl. Remembering her manners, she curtseyed as she halted in front of the dowager.

"Good afternoon, my lady."

"Harrumph. Jacobs tells me *you're* Mr. Stewart."

Steadily meeting the older woman's stern gaze, Constance nodded. "I am C. Stewart, my lady. I applied for the earl's cataloger position using the initial of my given name and my mother's maiden name."

For a long moment, the woman glared down her sharp, regal nose at her. Determined not to flinch in the face of such a penetrating look, Constance lifted her chin and did not allow her gaze to waver beneath the other woman's crystal-blue gaze. The sudden sound of laughter tumbling from the woman's lips made Constance jump. It wasn't quite the reaction she had expected.

"You have backbone, girl. I like that."

"My lady?"

"You secure this position without disclosing the full truth of who you are, and then you waltz into this ancient hall with a brazen confidence I've not seen in years. And with a child no less."

Constance touched Jamie's shoulder. "If I may, my lady, this is my son, Lord Westbury. Jamie, Lady Lyndham."

At the introduction, Jamie immediately stepped forward and bowed over the dowager's hand to brush the air above her fingers with his mouth. The deep chuckle rippling from the woman's wrinkled throat made Jamie a bit more audacious, and Constance sucked in a quick breath of horror as she saw him wink at the woman.

Another roar of laughter parted the woman's mouth. "By God, boy, you have as much cheek as your mother. Come, sit down. Both of you."

Motioning for them to take a seat in the chairs opposite her regal figure, Lady Lyndham picked up a bell on the table beside her. When the woman shook it, the shrill ring had an edge to it that heightened Constance's already finely tuned senses. With a fierce look of disapproval at her son, she sank down into the chair next to Jamie, uncertain of what to expect next. An inspection by the dowager was the last thing she'd anticipated in coming to Lyndham Keep.

The prickling sensation at her neck made her look over her shoulder as the butler entered the room. A light mist hovered in the salon doorway as Lady Lyndham tossed her hand up in an imperial gesture.

"Tea for three, Jacobs. And bring some of the blackberry scones Cook promised to make today." Without waiting for the man's acknowledgement, Lady Lyndham turned back to Constance. "Now then, C. Stewart. Tell me why you applied for the position my grandson advertised."

Jerking her head around to meet the other woman's piercing gaze, Constance lifted her chin. "It's reputed the artifacts in the earl's Egyptian collection are some of the finest in the world. I've been a student of ancient Egypt since childhood, and I've studied Egyptology with several scholars at the British Museum. As I outlined in my letter to his lordship, I am eminently qualified for the position."

"I see." The woman's eyebrow arched with imperial flair. "And what made you think my grandson would agree to your employment once he discovered the truth about you?"

Constance glanced down at her gloved hands, surprised to see them clutching her beaded purse with desperation. What in heaven's name was wrong with her? She was acting as if she'd just been caught in a lie by one of the nuns at St. Bridget's Academy. Squaring her shoulders, she lifted her head and met the woman's gaze with a steady look.

"To be quite frank, my lady, I didn't even consider that possibility. I had thought to impress him with my work so he would overlook the minor detail of my sex."

"Hmm," the old woman murmured as she nodded her head. "Is this madcap behavior a common one for you?"

The question made Constance wince. The Rockwood disposition for impulsive behavior had always ensured she acted without thinking. But applying for the position of cataloger to the Earl of Lyndham had been driven by more than impulse. She'd needed salvation.

"It is true that my family is known for their impetuous natures, but I am confident my knowledge will serve the earl well."

Jacobs entered the room with a tray of china. The cups rattled lightly as he set the tea on the table next to Lady Lyndham. Ignoring the man, the old woman arched an eyebrow at Constance.

"How do you take your tea, girl?"

"Two lumps, my lady."

With a bob of her powdery white head, Lady Lyndham poured the hot liquid, added the sugar then handed a cup to Constance. The piercing blue of her gaze swung to Jamie. "It appears that Jacobs has brought you a glass of milk to accompany your scones, young man. I take it that will be satisfactory."

"It will indeed, my lady." Jamie's blasé tone of voice made Constance grimace. He had never been his father's son. Jamie's personality had displayed his Rockwood lineage from the first moment he could sit up. The dowager didn't seem the least bit put off by Jamie's cavalier response. Constance breathed a sigh of relief, determined to chastise her son when the moment presented itself.

"So, you want to catalog that rubble my grandson brought back from Egypt. Did you really think he would overlook the fact that you're a woman?" The dowager's voice held a distinct thread of amusement.

"Not exactly, my lady." She studied the tea in her cup for a second before looking into Lady Lyndham's discerning gaze. "I believe my work will show me qualified for the task. I've heard the earl was not happy with his last appointment to this post. I am confident my skills as a cataloger will more than satisfy his lordship—enough to overlook any other unsuitable qualities I may possess."

Lady Lyndham set her cup down and eyed her with a look that reminded Constance of a watchful bird of prey. It was a look she'd received from her brothers on more than one occasion in an attempt to intimidate her. She did not drop her gaze. Harsh frowns from her brothers had never frightened her, and Lady Lyndham's scowl was no different. The woman's dour expression changed suddenly as she looked at Jamie then back at Constance.

"Westbury," the woman said sharply. "Is that the same Westbury who upped and died of some fever in Cairo a few years back?"

The stark question caught Constance off guard, and her heart lurched painfully in her breast. Graham's death had been sudden and unexpected, leaving her to raise Jamie on her own. If she had been able to make any sense out of her dreams in the days before they left for their second visit to Cairo, she would have insisted that they not go. But she hadn't, and Graham had succumbed to dysentery despite all her efforts to save him. Aware of the dowager's arched look of impatience, she nodded.

"Lord Westbury was my husband."

"If I recall, that would make you a Rockwood. One of Matilda Stewart's clan," the dowager said as she took a sip of her tea. "I've heard your aunt is as formidable as your grandmother was."

"You knew my grandmother, my lady?"

"I did. Catherine and I debuted the same year. A fiery woman—that Scots background I suppose. Broke a few hearts before she upped and married Magnus MacDonald. You look like her, and from what I've seen, you're just as impulsive as she was."

"It is a propensity for which the Rockwoods are known, my lady. But we stand by our impulsive natures," she said with a touch of pride.

"Uncle Sebastian says she's almost as bad as Aunt Louisa when it comes to stumbling into trouble." Jamie's precocious comment shot a bolt of horror through Constance. Had her son taken leave of his senses? Leaning over toward him, she caught his hand up in hers, her tight grip making him send her an uneasy look.

"First you will apologize to her ladyship for being so rude, and then you will wait for me in the hall."

Thoroughly chastened, her son stood up and bowed toward the dowager countess. "My sincerest apologies, my lady. If you will excuse me, I'll leave you and my mother to finish your tea."

Amusement twinkled in the old woman's eyes, but the dowager countess did not smile as she gave Jamie a sharp nod.

"Make certain you stay out of trouble in the hall, my lord. This keep is haunted, and I'd hate to see you anger any of our resident ghosts."

Constance suppressed a groan at the woman's words. In most children, such a warning would be more than sufficient to keep them on their best behavior. But Jamie was an unusual child. Anything sounding remotely of the supernatural had him racing down paths even seraphim refused to walk. The excitement on his face made her lean toward him again.

"Remember, my lord, you are to wait for me in the main hall."

She saw the way his eyes clouded with disappointment, and with a gesture of dismissal, nodded toward the door. When he had left the room, she turned back to the dowager countess, aware of the other woman's curious gaze.

"I must ask your forgiveness for my son's capricious nature, my lady. He's young and rarely stops to think."

"Harrumph, I imagine he comes by it naturally." Amusement sparkled in the sharp blue eyes watching her. "How often must *you* account for your own hasty decisions?"

Why, the woman was actually chiding her for disciplining Jamie. She bit back a smile. Like his father, Jamie had the ability to charm people simply by looking at them. It was a trait that would serve him well in the House of Lords when the time came for him to take his father's seat. Aware the old woman wanted an answer, she smiled.

"I must account for my impetuosity more often than I care to admit, my lady."

The dowager arched an eyebrow at her, and Constance found herself liking the old woman in spite of her abrupt mannerisms. And despite the age difference, Lady Lyndham reminded her a great deal of her Aunt Matilda.

"I should send you home, Lady Westbury." Indecision threaded Lady Lyndham's voice. "I'm certain my grandson will be less than pleased at your deception."

"My deception will be moot once he recognizes my skills are more than equal to the task he needs performed."

"Harrumph." Lady Lyndham's thin mouth tightened into a firm line, but there was a distinct twinkle in her gaze. "How did you find out about this librarian post?"

"My brother Percy mentioned it in passing, and the earl's decision to secure my services was an answer to my prayers."

"Prayers, eh? Well, girl, if I were you, I'd reserve judgment on that point. You've yet to meet my grandson, who is quite likely to toss you out on your ear for deceiving him."

"I did not deceive anyone, my lady. I simply allowed his lordship to form his own opinion."

The woman barked with laughter as she shook her head. "We'll see how the boy reacts to that when he arrives. In the meantime, I suppose it will do no harm to let you at least attempt to do the task you were charged with."

A rush of elation surged through her at having overcome what she was certain had to be a major hurdle. The dowager countess was clearly not someone to be trifled with, and to have passed the woman's rigorous inspection increased the odds of convincing the earl that she was capable of the position.

"Thank you, my lady."

"Oh, don't be too hasty in thanking me. You've yet to meet my grandson. Although I admit it's an occasion *I* do not wish to miss." Her blue-veined hand picked up the bell again and gave it a sharp ring. Almost immediately, the butler appeared in the room. "Jacobs, place Lady Westbury in the Blue Room. As for the young Lord Westbury, he can stay in the nursery with Lady Imogene under Nanny's care."

Jacobs nodded his answer and waited patiently as Lady Lyndham turned her attention back to Constance. "Once you've settled in, you may begin your task in the library. We dine at eight, and I do not tolerate tardiness."

Aware she'd been dismissed, Constance stood up and offered the woman a brief curtsey, then followed Jacobs out of the room. Emerging from the salon and into the main hall gave her the sensation of clouds passing over the sun. There was a chill here that made her hair stand on end. Lyndham Keep had seen more than its share of anguish, and its effect on her senses made her uneasy. She quickly suppressed the emotion as she saw Jamie staring up at the second-floor landing. Following his gaze, she saw the face of a young girl peering down at them.

The moment the butler started up the stairs, the girl leaped back and disappeared from view. With Jamie in front of her, they climbed the massive staircase. Carved from mahogany, the spindles in the banister were fine examples of detailed and exquisite workmanship. It was a beautiful staircase, but something in the air made it feel dark and dense.

When they reached the second floor, Jacobs led them down a long corridor of stone archways and portrait-laden walls. The dismal atmosphere resembled something out of a Dickens or Brontë novel. The only light illuminating the hall came from a tall window at the end of the corridor. Pressing against her, the darkened hallway made her long for the bright, airiness of her own home.

The thought vanished as she remembered why she'd fled London. No, Lyndham Keep would suit her just fine, dark corridors and all. Jacobs stopped in front of a door and opened it for her.

She entered a serene-looking room that was much brighter than the hall it bordered. The butler moved to the fireplace and, using a flint, lit the fire in the grate. When he finished, he bowed in her direction.

"I'll have your trunks brought up immediately, my lady. Do you require anything else at the moment?"

"No, thank you, Jacobs."

"Very well, then I'll take his lordship up to the nursery, my lady. It's on the next floor and easy enough to find."

With a nod, Constance eyed her son's remorseful expression. Smiling, she lifted his chin so he could see her face. "We'll talk later. In the meantime, *no* ghost hunting. Is that understood?"

As if realizing his penance was over, he grinned. "Yes, Mother. But may I explore just a little?"

"Perhaps later, hmm."

His wry grimace made her laugh as he turned and followed the butler out of the room. As the door closed behind them, Constance reached up, pulled out her hatpin and removed her hat. Sticking the pin into the large ribbon bow in the back of the headgear, she set it on a nearby dressing table and surveyed her surroundings. The room was large with furniture reminiscent of medieval times. The clawed feet on the dresser and wardrobe were repeated on the bed and chairs with intricate carvings on the legs and posts.

She crossed the room to the window and pushed aside the curtains to look out over the keep's grounds. Despite the gloomy sky brooding above the earth, there were brilliant signs of spring's arrival. Green buds were unfurling on the trees, and the grass lining the lawn was the color green that always accompanied the season.

Something told her the grounds would be lovely when spring was in full bloom. Just as lovely as the banks of the river Nile were after the annual floodwaters had receded. Excitement skittered through her. She was going to have access to one of the world's most valuable collections of Egyptian antiquities. Or at least she would until the earl returned home.

The dowager countess had been far from reassuring about the earl's reaction to her presence at Lyndham Keep. Shoulders lifted in a slight shrug, she sighed. She'd eluded her masked lover, and that's all that mattered. A shiver pricked her skin as she remembered the horror of the vision she'd had that night. Refusing to dwell on it, she turned away from the window, her gown rustling quietly against the wooden floor until she reached the large carpet in the middle of the room.

A sudden noise stopped her in her tracks. It was a soft sound, and she strained to hear it. She was uncertain what it was at first until she recognized it for faint sobbing. There was great sorrow in the sound, and in seconds an icy chill engulfed her body. Her breath small clouds in the cold air, she waited for the spirit to show itself. Instead, the sobbing stopped as quickly as it had begun, and the temperature in the room grew warm again.

The memory of the spirit she'd seen earlier made her frown. Although she and the earl had never met, she'd heard numerous stories about his family. Never one to put much stock in gossip, she now wished she'd been a little more attentive to the stories she'd heard. She thought there had been something about a murder, but she couldn't remember for sure. Hushed whispers of all sorts of mayhem accompanied old families of the nobility. Even the Rockwoods had their share of murderers and thieves.

The fire popped loudly in the hearth, and she jumped at the sharp sound. Grimacing at her nervous behavior, she shook her head. It was time to get to work. The sooner she started cataloging the collection, the more she'd have done by the time the earl came home. And the further along she was with her task, the less likely the man was to throw her out of the keep.

℠℞

Slapping her hands to shake off the dust coating her skin, Constance stared at the crates stacked in the makeshift storage room adjacent to the keep's library. There were still so many of them. She'd taken on a monumental task, and the notion of it made her heart sink. It had been almost three weeks since her arrival, and in that time, she'd worked hard to be as thorough and efficient as possible in her cataloging efforts. The question was whether her work would suitably impress the earl when he returned home. For the first time, she realized the light from the room's windows had been fading for some time. She needed to return to her room to freshen up or she'd be late for dinner.

With one more brush of her dirty hands, she returned to the library. The moment she entered the room, the usual prickling sensation crawled across her skin. From the first time she'd entered the library she'd sensed something terrible had happened here. She wasn't certain what, but pain and sorrow permeated the room to the point that it often made it difficult for her to concentrate. It was one reason why she worked in the adjacent room rather than here in the library.

Despite her efforts to convince herself that working in the storage area gave her more convenient access to the crates of antiquities, she knew better. Eager to leave the library, she hurried across the large carpet that covered most of the beautifully polished oak floor. She had only taken a few steps when her skin grew icy cold. Coming to an abrupt halt, she exhaled a breath to see it become a small cloud.

"Whoever you are, I don't frighten easily," she said in a firm, dispassionate voice.

The moment her words rang out into the room, the air around her warmed to normal room temperature. Exasperated, she shook her head.

"Not so brave when someone snaps back, are you?" she muttered.

"I am far from being frightened, my dear."

Unable to help herself, she yelped in surprise and whirled around to see a handsome man watching her with a look of curiosity.

"Damnation." His eyes widened with astonishment. "You really can see me."

Gathering her wits, Constance brushed a stray lock of hair away from her brow as she glared at the spirit. Under normal circumstances, ghosts didn't speak to her. Here apparently was one of the rare exceptions.

"Yes, I can see you."

"Excellent. I'm Nigel, by the way, and you are?"

"Constance," she said with a quick shake of her head.

"You're a pretty little thing. I suppose he's already told you that." There was a familiar note in the man's voice, and she frowned.

"I'm afraid I don't understand."

"My brother. I suppose he's told you—" The ghost's smile collapsed into a grimace as he faded swiftly into thin air.

Quickly stepping forward, Constance stood in the area where the ghost had been, but there was no cold spot of any kind. Over the years, she'd come to recognize many things about the spirits she had contact with. The stronger personalities were the ones best able to manifest their energy into making themselves visible or even moving objects in the physical world. But it was a short-lived ability because of the vast amount of energy it took. This ghost had one of the strongest vibrations of any spirit she'd ever encountered.

Strong enough to speak—and that had only happened to her one other time. The bittersweet memory of her mother made a knot of tears swell in her throat. She clenched her fists to push back the sadness and buried the memories deep below the surface.

Whatever the ghost wanted from her, it would be some time before he made another appearance. Turning back toward the door of the library, she gave a violent start at the sight of Lady Lyndham in the doorway. A second later, light illuminated the dowager countess's features as she moved into the room, her cane softly thudding against the carpet.

"Is talking to thin air another of your eccentric behaviors, Lady Westbury?"

Heat burned her cheeks at the skeptical tone in the dowager's voice. It was bad enough she'd arrived at the keep by dubious means, and now she'd been caught in a conversation with someone no one else could see. Not an easy thing to explain. Straightening her shoulders, she nodded her head as she relied on the explanation she'd used since she was a young girl.

"I'm afraid so, my lady. I must confess that I often talk out loud. People find that far more comforting than if I were to tell them I was conversing with the spirits." Deliberately smiling at the woman, she watched amusement cross the dowager's face.

"I like you, Lady Westbury. You've a freshness that this decrepit tomb hasn't experienced in years."

"Thank you, my lady. You're most kind."

"Nothing of the sort." Lady Lyndham snorted. "If I'd taken a dislike to you, you would have been out the door the first day."

"I thought as much," Constance murmured with a smile.

"Harrumph." The dowager countess uttered the disgruntled sound with great emphasis. "Did you now?"

"If you'll excuse me, my lady, I should go and change or I'll be late for dinner." She waited for the woman to respond, but Lady Lyndham seemed lost in thought as she stared around the room.

"I can't remember the last time I was in here." The dowager's whisper was faint as her gaze focused on the spot where the ghost had been only moments before. "Not since…"

Constance watched as the woman barely shook her head. There was a forlorn air about the woman that resembled the grief she was all too familiar with. Stepping forward, she gently rested her hand on the elderly woman's shoulder.

"Are you all right, my lady?"

"What?" Lady Lyndham looked startled as she glanced over

her shoulder at Constance. "I must have been daydreaming again. A codicil to growing old. Come, I want to leave this dreary place."

Puzzled, Constance offered her arm as the woman waved a hand toward her. Together they walked slowly toward the library door, the dowager relying on the sturdy cane that seemed almost a part of her. As they stepped into the hall, Lady Lyndham came to a halt, her shoulders hunched over as she rested both hands on her cane.

"Tell me, how is it going with my grandson's artifacts?" There was a distinct twinkle in those fierce blue eyes, and Constance laughed.

"They are exquisite and overwhelming. I had no idea of the magnitude of the task itself. I know I've accomplished a great deal, but it looks quite insignificant when compared to what is still left to do."

Nodding, Lady Lyndham pinned her with a cool look of assessment. "Does that mean you're going to give up?"

"I am a Rockwood, my lady. We do *not* give up."

"I had hoped that was the case." The woman chortled with a raspy laugh. "It will do my grandson good to meet an intelligent woman who's strong enough to stand up to him."

"But surely he has you to do that, my lady." Constance smiled as the woman stared at her in amazement before bending over her cane and coughing out her laughter. As the dowager's laughing fit subsided, she lifted her head and sent Constance a chiding look.

"Don't make this old woman laugh like that again. It does the body ill."

"I am sorry, my lady." The notion of having caused the woman discomfort made her grimace with concern.

"Oh stop looking like that. I might be old, but I'm not in my grave yet. Run along now. If you'll recall, I do not tolerate late arrivals for supper."

With a nod, Constance turned away and hurried toward the stairs. As she reached the midpoint of the staircase, she looked back at the dowager countess. The woman was still watching her, and there was a look of satisfaction on her face. Confused by the woman's odd behavior, Constance continued up the staircase to her room. The entire house was a conundrum haunted with troubled spirits and dark mysteries.

Chapter Three

With a powerful gait, Anubis trotted up the long drive to Lyndham Keep. Keeping his touch light on the reins, Lucien smiled at the way the large horse shook his head. His gloved hand patted the animal's thick, muscled neck.

"You smell those oats, don't you, boy?"

Almost as if he understood the question, the animal tossed his head again. Laughing, Lucien nudged the horse into a slow gallop as he rode toward his ancestral home. In the late afternoon light, the ancient fortress looked far from welcoming. He eyed the massive structure with resignation. Lyndham Keep had never really been home. Too much death resided behind the gray walls.

There were times when he simply wanted to raze it to the ground. But doing so would never wash the blood away. It would always be with him. Scowling at his thoughts, he urged Anubis to go faster. He'd come back to the keep simply to ensure that Stewart was archiving the collection correctly. If the man's work was satisfactory, it would enable him to begin planning another expedition back to Egypt. The sooner the better. He rarely slept well when he was home.

As Anubis pranced to a halt in front of the keep, the massive doors swung open. Jacobs stood outside the wide doorway, while a footman ran out to take the horse's bridle. With one last pat to the animal's neck, Lucien dismounted.

"See to it that he has a good quantity of oats after you cool him down, Tony." Pulling off his gloves, he strode through the open doorway and handed his riding crop and accessories to the man following him into the keep. "Where's my grandmother, Jacobs?"

"I believe she's in the main salon, my lord. She had tea a short time ago," the servant said with quiet regard.

There was no need to look at the butler's face to know that his grandmother was taking a short nap in her favorite chair. Jacobs had been with the family almost since the time his grandmother had come to Lyndham Keep as a young bride. The man knew exactly when and how to appease the dowager countess. Smiling, he nodded his understanding. "I'll look in on her a little later. For the moment, I want a bath and some fresh clothes."

"Very good, my lord."

Eager to refresh himself after a long train ride and the subsequent ride from the Nottingham station, Lucien crossed the stone floor toward the staircase and glanced into the library. From the main hall he could see through the library into the small reading room he'd converted into a storage area for his antiquities. The sight that greeted him made him come to an abrupt halt. In the room just off the library, a woman stood at one of his crates, examining the markings of a piece of pottery.

Stewart hadn't mentioned anything about a wife, and even if the man had, he had no business letting unskilled hands handle delicate artifacts. Wheeling sharply toward the door, he strode through the library and into the storage area.

"Who the devil are *you?*" Instantly he regretted his sharp tone as the woman cried out in surprise and almost dropped the jar she was holding. Recovering from her fright, she sent him a brief glance of annoyance before gingerly setting the pottery back into the straw-filled crate. He noted the tender care she took in nestling the item back in the packing material.

"I told you before, I don't frighten easily, and I'd appreciate it if—" With a sharp jerk she turned to look at him as if suddenly realizing he wasn't the person she was expecting.

To his surprise, she paled considerably as she met his gaze. Fear glimmered in her eyes before it vanished, making him think he'd been mistaken. Narrowing his gaze at her, he watched her expression become wary as her eyes met his. No, he'd not made a mistake. She'd simply buried her fear beneath a serene expression. The woman was most definitely afraid. But why?

"It wasn't my intent to startle you, but the only person who should be handling these artifacts is Mr. Stewart."

A small silence drifted between them as he saw her swallow nervously and avert her gaze. "You're Lord Lyndham?"

"I am." He nodded abruptly. "And you are?"

"C. Stewart."

The soft words took several seconds to register with him as he stared at her. But the C. Stewart he'd corresponded with was a man. Did the woman think to convince him otherwise? He'd conversed and questioned Mr. Stewart vigorously in three different letter exchanges. How could this woman be C. Stewart?

"C. Stewart is a man," he muttered fiercely.

"No, my lord. You simply found it convenient to think that I was a man."

He glared at her as he struggled with the fact the woman had hoodwinked him. And she was most definitely a woman. She had a pretty face, full breasts and a lush figure that echoed the promise of a Titian nude. Even the husky sound of her voice had a soothing effect on his irritation. It brought back memories of Isis and their fateful meeting at the Black Widows Ball. This woman's voice possessed the same sultry sound as his Egyptian goddess.

Damn it, when was he going to get Isis out of his head? For more than two months he'd been employing every method possible in his search for the woman, only to come up empty-handed. Was he so desperate to find his mysterious lover that he was beginning to imagine another woman sounded just like her? He found this irrational need to find Isis exasperating. Worse, the Stewart woman's deception only heightened his irritation.

Clasping his hands behind his back to conceal his clenched fists, he strode back into the library in an effort to think clearly. In the close confines of the storage area, her soft honey-sweet scent had filled his nostrils and made it difficult to focus. He turned his attention away from her tantalizing smell to address the matter at hand.

With her qualifications, her sex wouldn't have prevented

him from hiring her. But he couldn't abide being lied to, and he hated being made to look like a fool. She'd done just that by not disclosing everything about herself. Furious with her deception, he paced a small area of the carpet like a caged lion. Aware that she'd followed him into the library, he came to a halt and turned sharply to face her.

"You lied to me," he snapped.

"I did *not* lie. I can hardly be blamed for your assumption that I was a man. I truthfully outlined my qualifications for you, and you commissioned me to do a job." Her head assumed a regal tilt as she glared at him.

The movement shifted the room's light on her head, revealing golden highlights in the mass of chestnut hair gathered on top of her head in the popular American fashion. On her it should be loose and tumbling down her shoulders. The fact he'd even thought such a thing increased his ire as she faced him defiantly.

"You should have made it known you were a woman."

"Why? There was no request to do so in the advertisement."

The logic in her argument angered him all the more as he took a step toward her. He noted she didn't back away from him. It gave him a grudging respect for her fortitude in the face of his anger. It wasn't often someone could withstand his intimidating manner. In fact, the only woman ever to do so before was his grandmother.

"Damn it, woman, I thought you were a man."

"Well as you can see, I am not." Exasperation laced her sensual voice and his body instinctively responded to the sound.

God, what the hell was wrong with him? Just the mere sound of another woman's sultry voice was stirring his lust into a frenzy for the phantom lover who'd escaped him. The only thought he seemed capable of anymore was Isis's seductive body beneath his, her long silky legs wrapped around him as he plunged into her creamy hot core.

The image tightened every muscle in his body. Angered by his hunger for a woman he couldn't find, he whirled away from the Stewart woman. He expressed his fury by slamming his fist into a stack of books on top of a nearby table. The explosive sound reverberated through the room with the force of a tree cracked in two by a lightning bolt. Silence hung between them as he froze.

"I shall pack my things and leave in the morning." The quiet sound of her voice was like the gentle rain that washed away the fury of a wild storm.

With a sharp nod, he didn't look at her as she left the room. The moment she was gone, he pressed his palms into the edge of the table and stood hunched over the book-laden surface.

Had it started?

Was this what Nigel and his father had battled when the curse first afflicted them? When was the last time he'd lost his temper like that? Two days ago. When Nate Bilkens had told him the trail was cold and finding Isis was next to impossible. Losing control wasn't something he did often, and to lose his temper twice in less than a week was almost unheard of for him. But it wasn't unheard of for a Blakemore to become crazed over a woman.

Frustrated, he straightened and crossed the large room to one of the arched windows that rose from the floor to the ceiling. Staring out through the glass, he studied the gardens that had been his mother's pet project. The gardeners who had worked with her on the design and plantings still worked on the estate, and they were faithful to her vision. Nothing had changed in the garden since he was a boy.

With a grunt of disgust, he closed his eyes. He'd probably frightened the Stewart woman out of her mind with his anger. Well, she shouldn't have applied for or accepted the position under false pretenses. He stared out the window once more. Perhaps that was a bit harsh, but the woman had known damn well her sex could be an issue, otherwise why had she hid it?

As he turned away from the window his gaze fell on a table filled with a neat display of artifacts. Reviewed and cataloged, they were carefully laid out on a layer of fabric. Curious, he walked over to the table and examined the note cards accompanying each individual piece. The information and detail on the cards was worthy of a senior staff member in the museum's Department of Egyptian and Assyrian Antiquities. Even Director Budge would be impressed with this woman's work. Where had she gained such detailed knowledge?

He picked up one card after another, reviewing the depth of information provided for each artifact. It was impressive work. Generally, women didn't have access to the same education that men did, but the Stewart woman clearly had enjoyed the benefit of expert teachers willing to impart their extensive knowledge to her.

Although times were changing, educational opportunities for women had always been limited. Women stepping outside the boundaries of normal society wasn't something he objected to, but for a woman to extricate herself from the confines of current trends was unusual. Still, meeting a well-educated woman was a pleasant experience.

One of the things his studies about ancient Egypt had taught him was that women had played an integral part in the now-extinct civilization. Their role in society had not been one of second-class citizens, rather they'd had rights comparable to men. It was an idea he supported, but rarely encountered in England, although the number of women demanding the opportunities long reserved for the male population was growing.

Returning the last card back to the table, he stared down at the display with thoughtful consideration. In his anger, he'd insulted the Stewart woman. It was obvious she had not been lying about her credentials. An enigma, the woman puzzled him. Even more puzzling was her reaction to his arrival.

When he'd first stormed into the library's side chamber, her initial reaction had been more of annoyance. It was as if she'd already made his acquaintance, and his interruption had irritated her. Then the moment she'd turned to look at him fully, fear swept through her. She'd hid it immediately and quite well, but he'd recognized it just the same. Why was she afraid?

With a growl of irritation, he shook his head. It didn't matter. Nor did it matter whether she had acquired her education in the usual manner or if she was self taught. The woman's knowledge was exactly what he needed for cataloging his artifacts. The only problem now was whether he could convince her to stay and finish what she'd started.

ℬↃ☾ℬ

Constance clung to the bedpost as if gale-force winds were buffeting her body. Fear wrapped a layer of ice over her skin as she struggled to control her roiling stomach by breathing in long, deep breaths. How in heaven's name had she managed to come to the one place she would never have visited if she'd known what she did now?

Lucien—the highwayman—the earl. They were the same man.

The Earl of Lyndham was her lover from the Black Widows Ball. There was nothing she'd ever been more certain of in her entire life. She could only be grateful he'd not recognized her. And he hadn't. She was certain of it.

But she had known who he was the moment she faced him. It wasn't just his brilliant blue eyes, the scar on his cheek or the sound of his voice. It was everything about him. The male scent of him, his movements and the way every nerve ending in her body responded to his presence. Even though they'd spent only an hour or so together that night at the Clarendon, her body had recognized him almost as quickly as her eyes had.

One cheek pressed to the wooden spindle of the bed, she closed her eyes. She'd thought she was safe here, so far away from London. Over the past three weeks, she'd managed to put every thought of Lucien out of her head. Her days had been pleasurable ones, cataloging the earl's artifacts and exploring the estate with Imogene as her and Jamie's guide. More importantly, her nights had been devoid of dreams—dreams about *him*.

Think. She needed to think rationally and calmly. If she allowed her fear to control her, he might suspect something. He didn't know who she was. She had to remember that. There was nothing to be afraid of as long as she kept her head. Still, the sooner she and Jamie were gone from this forbidding place, the better. A shiver skimmed down her back as she moved away from the bed and dragged her trunk out from beside the large wardrobe that held her clothes.

"He is not a murderer."

Barely suppressing her scream, Constance spun around

too quickly, and lost her footing to fall backward over the trunk. The misty image of the ghost shimmered in the dim light of her room. It was the first time she'd seen him since that day in the library more than a week ago. Scrambling to her feet, she turned back to her trunk, deliberately ignoring her ethereal visitor. She didn't care what the ghost said. The earl had blood on his hands. Her vision had shown her that much. Pulling a dress out of the wardrobe, she didn't even have the opportunity to fold it when an invisible force ripped it from her hands.

"Lucien is not the one with blood on his hands." There was a fierce anger in the ghost's voice as the dress went flying back into her wardrobe and the door slammed shut. "He is not a murderer."

Whirling around to face the spirit, she sent him an angry look. "I don't care what he is. I'm not staying."

"*Help him.*" The anguish in the ghost's voice weakened her resolve, but she shook her head.

"You don't understand—" The sudden speed with which the ghost moved toward her tugged a small cry from her throat.

In that instant, she knew he intended to show her his past. She had no time to prepare herself as Nigel melded his thoughts with hers and everything went dark. The darkness frightened her. It was filled with despair and deep sorrow. Someone sobbed softly, and the sound rippled through the dense pain that pressed against her flesh. Her heart ached at the wounded cry, and she tried to reach out in the darkness, but it abruptly evaporated. She immediately longed for the darkness again. Anything to escape the library and its terrible images.

Her stomach lurched at the carnage in front of her, and she swallowed hard, trying not to retch. Just like the last time, there was blood everywhere. Inhaling a deep breath, she suppressed her fear at the images in front of her. It was only a vision. She couldn't be harmed here. There was a reason Nigel's spirit wanted her to witness this horrible sight.

Throat slit in one long deep cut, the woman she'd seen in her previous vision lay dead on the keep's library floor. She knew it was the library because she recognized the bank of windows that lined the far wall. On the blood-soaked carpet beside the dead woman was the body of a man. As she stepped closer, she flinched at the glazed look in his startling blue eyes.

She recognized him as the grief-stricken man from her earlier vision who'd discovered the dead woman. There was almost a look of surprise on his lifeless features.

Blood sprayed the furniture and floor as if the murderer had taken special pleasure in creating such a grisly display. Then she saw it. The knife. The dead man clutched it in his hand as if refusing to give it up even in death. This man had killed the woman. For a fraction of a second, she vehemently denied the idea. He'd loved this woman. There was something terribly wrong with the entire picture before her. The denial was fleeting as she realized there could be no other answer. The man had killed the woman. He'd killed her with a vicious, sickening brutality. Pain wound its way through her body, assaulting her with a physical blow she recognized as overwhelming grief. The ghost's emotions engulfed her until she felt every moment of anguish he did. Startled by the thought, she stretched her hands out in front of her. The coat sleeves and hands she saw were that of a man. Nigel as he had been when he was alive. She had become him in the vision. He was showing her the past in the only way he knew how—through his eyes.

Despair lashed through her with the sharpness of the blade her father held.

A shrill scream of sorrow echoed out behind her, pulling her back into the scene as she whirled around. The dowager countess and a young boy stood staring at the scene of butchery in front of them. The shocked horror on their faces made her race forward and shove them back out into the hall. She pulled the library door closed then turned to catch her grandmother as the woman fainted. Gently easing the woman to the floor, she screamed for Jacobs. Her brother stood a few feet away, shock etched across his pale features.

"Lucien, come here." She stretched out her hand toward the boy who didn't move. "It's all right, lad, come here."

With a muffled cry the boy ran forward and wrapped his arms around her neck, his sobs breaking her heart. The sting of her own tears burned her cheeks as she rocked the boy in her arms and gave way to her own grief.

Eyes closed, she sobbed wildly from the horror of it all. The pain ripped through her, tearing at her like a wild animal gnawing at her flesh. From far away, she heard a thunderous banging noise and Jamie calling out her name. Weak with exhaustion, she opened her eyes just as her bedroom door flew open.

In a daze, she saw Lucien dash into the room followed by Jamie and the dowager countess. Staggering to her feet, she fought to remain standing, but failed. She felt no fear when the earl's strong arms lifted her up and her hand settled over his heart. No visions of murder lashed out at her this time. Beneath her fingertips, only a solid heartbeat thrummed against her nerve endings. She had misjudged him. Exhausted, her eyes fluttered shut as she sank into a peaceful darkness.

₭₯

Lucien stood at the salon's fireplace, one hand braced against the mantle as he stared into the fire crackling softly in the hearth. She was here. Isis was under his roof. She'd been here for almost three weeks. All the while he was frantically searching the whole of London for her, she'd been here.

The moment he'd broken into her bedroom and seen the stricken look in her hazel eyes, he'd recognized her. Her gaze had been just as dark with horror the night she left him so abruptly. He'd been a fool not to realize who she was sooner. No. His body had recognized her from the start, but his head had ignored all the clues.

The soft beat of a cane thudding against the salon carpet interrupted his thoughts. He turned and moved forward to escort his formidable grandmother to her favorite chair.

Satisfied as to her comfort, he returned to his spot at the fireplace. Picking up the snifter resting on the mantle, he took a deep draught of the amber liquid it contained. The fiery drink burned his throat, reassuring him he was still with the living. Too often the keep had a way of making him think he was dead. Tossing the last of the brandy over his tongue, he set the glass down and turned to meet the concerned look on the dowager's face.

"Should we arrange for Doctor Martens to pay a call?" he asked in a quiet voice.

"No," she replied with a shake of her head. "She's sleeping now. I'm sure she'll be fine in the morning."

"What the hell happened to her?" Hands clasped behind his back, he frowned in puzzlement.

"I'm not sure. The boy said he heard her talking to someone and when he tried to open the door, he couldn't do so."

"The door was simply locked," he said tersely.

"Are you so certain of that?" His grandmother shook her head in silent disagreement. "I should have known better than to put her in Nigel's old room."

The bemused note in her voice made him stiffen. Any time his grandmother mentioned his brother, she usually experienced a period of forgetfulness. For all her formidable personality, Aurora Blakemore was far frailer than she would ever admit. Hoping to keep her in the present, he changed the subject.

"I take it the boy is hers?" he asked, waiting patiently as the dowager countess slowly focused her gaze on him.

"The boy?" She shook her head for a moment until her eyes brightened. "Ah, yes. Jamie. A lovely boy, and very much like his mother. Quick witted and charming."

"Is there some reason you didn't bother to send word to me about the fact that Mr. Stewart was really Widow Stewart with a child in tow?"

"Actually, Stewart is her mother's maiden name. She's Constance Athelson, Viscountess Westbury."

"Westbury," he growled.

"Did you know him?"

"No." He shook his head. "I simply remember he died in Cairo before his expedition even set out for Abydos. Dysentery, I believe.

It had been Standish who'd financed the Viscount Westbury's final expedition, although the doomed man had never gotten out of Cairo. The poor bastard had died shortly after reaching Egypt. If she was Westbury's widow, the odds were Standish had sent her here to find the papyrus. Was that really why she was here? Had she come to the ball that night in hopes of seducing him to give up the papyrus?

It didn't matter. He had no intention of giving it up to her or anyone else. The ancient document was far too valuable. It contained one half of the map leading to the tomb of Sefu, high priest of Abydos. Legend had it that when a particular statue of Isis was joined with its mate, a statue of Seth, it would reveal the second half of the map. Finding those statues would possibly lead to the tomb. Not an impossible feat, but it had been an improbable one until his last trip to the desert.

As for Westbury's widow, he'd be wise not to trust her. Letting her leave would be the sensible thing to do, but for the first time in recent memory, he didn't want to do anything sensible. He scowled at his grandmother as he realized she'd diverted him from his original question.

"You've still not answered me. Why didn't you send word to me that C. Stewart was in fact, a woman?"

"I did consider it, but in truth, I like her. I wanted her to have the chance to prove herself." There was just the hint of a sly curve to Aurora's mouth, and he pinned her with a stern look.

"I see, which tells me that you saw this as an opportunity to meddle again. Just like you have for the past six months."

"I hardly call it meddling. I simply want to see you happy, boy. It's high time you married."

Aurora's cane swung outward as she pointed the walking stick in his direction, the blue veins on the back of her hand made more prominent from the strength of her grip on the falcon cane head. He grimaced and shook his head.

"Yes, and there's been a Blakemore at Lyndham Keep since ten seventy-six, and it's my responsibility to see to it the family name doesn't die out." The chilly sarcasm had the effect he expected.

Aurora slammed her cane down on the coffee table, the tea service rattling loudly. Powdery white hair slightly askew, she sent him a scathing look down her regal nose.

"It is your responsibility," she said fiercely.

"We both know why I'll never marry, Grandmother." He rolled his shoulders in a nonchalant shrug.

"Your brother knew he had a responsibility to the family."

The sharp, critical note in her voice cut through him. He

knew his grandmother loved him, but Nigel had been her lifeline. He'd held them together as a family that horrible day. It was something Aurora had never forgotten, and when Nigel had fallen victim to the curse, Lucien had never thought to see his grandmother recover from the shock. She had, but at a cost. Her once-sharp faculties were now dimmed as her mind would wander periodically during times of stress or when she grew tired.

Perhaps the hardest part to deal with was her refusal to believe the curse existed. Everything he said fell on deaf ears. Nothing he said convinced her otherwise. The decision never to marry had been made the terrible day his parents had died. His choice had only been reinforced with Nigel's death.

Vivid memories flashed before his eyes. Once again he stood frozen in the library doorway witnessing the results of his father's bloody handiwork. His decision had been an easy one. It was at that moment he'd known he would never marry. Never risk the possibility of loving someone only to destroy them in the end. A muscle twitched in his cheek as he met his grandmother's piercing gaze, refusing to yield to her wishes.

"Blast it, Lucien, you're as stubborn as your mother was."

"But I am still my father's son."

He delivered the icy words as brutally as possible, and guilt lashed out at him at the way she flinched. It wasn't pleasant to be so cruel to her, but it was time she realized he would not change his mind. Over the past thirty years, every Blakemore male had succumbed to an unknown madness, prompting them to murder anyone in their midst at the time they were overcome by the curse. That their victims had been loved ones simply emphasized the dangers of falling in love.

The memory of his recent fits of anger was even more reason not to give in to his grandmother's wishes. As it was, he needed to guard against being alone with anyone, particularly his grandmother and Imogene. Eventually, he would need to hire someone to serve as a deterrent against his harming anyone.

Aurora's shoulders slumped with defeat, and with a sigh, he crossed the room and bent over her. His touch gentle, he took her hand and squeezed it tenderly.

"I'll not be a willing participant in the bloodbath the men in this family have inflicted on their loved ones, Grandmother. Even a marriage of convenience would require some form of affection to be tolerable, and the risk of harming any woman I married is too great."

"How can I convince you there is no curse, my boy?" Aurora shook her head. "I don't understand what drove your father and Nigel to do what they did, but it wasn't a curse."

"For a woman who believes in the supernatural, I find it ironic you refuse to acknowledge the likelihood of my doing exactly what my father and brother did." He heaved a sigh. "I cannot allow myself to fall in love. It would be irresponsible of me to do so."

She didn't answer for a long moment. Then with a slight nod, she lifted her gaze to meet his.

"Your happiness is paramount to me, Lucien. Even more so than a Blakemore heir. However a child *would* make my victory sweeter."

"Victory?" He arched an eyebrow at her.

"You must understand I'll not admit defeat. I simply intend to regroup." Despite the determination in her voice he heard the disillusion there as well.

"I know," he said with a slight smile. "If it helps, I think you managed to execute a brilliant strategy of attack over the past few months. I doubt there's a military man anywhere to match your ability to outflank an opponent."

The weak smile his words brought to her lips sent a chill through him. For the first time, he recognized the true fragility of her appearance. If she were standing and a harsh wind blew across the room, it was doubtful she'd be able to withstand its force. Even the deep blue material of her gown created the image of fragile vulnerability with its stark contrast to her pale skin.

She'd aged in recent months, and she seemed more delicate now than he had ever seen her. Aurora had always been a tower of strength, vivacity and fire, and the lack of spirit reflected in a pair of blue eyes that matched his own worried him. For the first time, he saw her for what she was—a tired, old woman.

"Come, I think you've experienced enough excitement for today. I'll have Jacobs arrange for you to eat in your rooms this evening."

Nodding wearily, the dowager accepted the support of his arm as she stood up. "I think that's an excellent idea."

"In the meantime, I'll dine with Imogene and young Lord Westbury in the nursery. I think my niece will enjoy playing hostess at supper, and I'll enjoy spending some time with her. It's been too long since I've done that."

"She's missed you a great deal." Some of her energy returning, his grandmother smiled. "Be prepared for her to inundate you with questions about Egypt. The child is convinced you'll take her there one day. She takes after you, not her father."

"Then I'm certain to enjoy the meal in the company of someone who will be enthralled with my stories."

As they left the salon and headed toward the stairs, a streak of satisfaction sped through him. Dining with Imogene and the young Lord Westbury would give him the opportunity to learn more about his mysterious goddess. And when the opportunity presented itself, he intended to indulge himself with the woman who had haunted his dreams for almost three months. Marriage might not be in his future, but there was no harm in enjoying the pleasure of Isis's company or her delectable body.

Chapter Four

Staring at her reflection in the vanity table's mirror, Constance quickly arranged her hair on top of her head. Out the corner of her eye, she saw the trunk still sitting in the same spot it had been when everyone had rushed into her bedroom earlier.

The memory of Lucien crashing through the door pulled a quick breath past her lips. He'd burst into her room with the same powerful, tiger-like movements she remembered from their one night together. Solid and strong, he'd lifted her into his arms as easily as he had that night. In his arms, she'd been safe. An overwhelming wave of relief had swept over her when her hand had settled over his heart. She realized now the vision she'd seen that night at the Black Widows Ball had not been his. For some reason, he'd simply been the conduit through which she'd seen those horrible images.

With a frown, she shook her head. Her visions were seldom clear to her. They were more like puzzle pieces. Small bits that ultimately formed a larger picture. Putting them together in a cohesive manner could be difficult at times, but this puzzle was far more complex than anything she'd been shown before.

Ever since that night at the Black Widows Ball, her gift had been sending her clues through her dreams. She had thought the man in her dreams was Lucien. Now she wasn't so sure. The dreams could have meant a number of things, and she'd allowed her fear to blind her to the possibilities. Frustrated, she hit the vanity top with her fist. There were no coincidences. Everything had a place and purpose in the universe. Even her presence here at Lyndham Keep was part of the puzzle. She could not believe her presence here was an accident.

But if the man in her dreams hadn't been Lucien, who was he? Complicating matters was what the ghost had shown her this afternoon. The murder scene was the same as the one from her first vision, and yet different. That night at the Clarendon she'd witnessed someone else murdering Nigel and Lucien's father. And she was certain the murdered man was their sire. It was the only way to account for the overwhelming grief she'd been subjected to in the surreal experience.

The only thing she found truly puzzling was the knife. Why would it be in their father's hand if he'd been murdered like his wife? Unless someone had placed the knife in the dead man's hand to make the scene look like a murder-suicide. The alternative was her first vision had been wrong. Either possibility was disconcerting.

Then there was the unusual murder weapon. This time she had seen it clearly for what it was. It was a blade often used in ancient Egyptian magic rituals, although the handle in the vision was not the normal design she'd seen at the Museum. It was grotesquely fashioned, almost evil-looking in its design. She shivered.

Whoever had murdered Nigel's parents had done so with a barbarity that frightened her. Nigel's grief had been heart wrenching. Even now she could still feel the pain of his sorrow. What would the earl say if he knew his brother was still here in the keep? The strong and poignant emotions she'd experienced in her vision told her the relationship between the two brothers had been a close one. The earl had turned out to be as strong willed as his older brother. He was a law unto himself.

"Lucien." His name echoed softly in the room, but she ignored the soft sound.

As she studied her reflection, the memory of their intimate encounter sent hot color sailing into her cheeks. How could she possibly remain here? If he discovered who she was, he'd think she'd deliberately sought him out. A soft rustling whispered nearby, and she stiffened. Glancing about the room, she gave a shake of her head. Whatever spirits inhabited the keep, they seemed determined to make her stay.

"*Help him.*" The whisper was more insistent this time.

"How can I help him, if I don't even know how I'm supposed to help?" The sharp-edged question hovered in the air, but there was no response.

Frustrated, she sprang to her feet to pace the carpeted floor. What was she going to do? Lucien might not have recognized her, but staying at the keep could be the most dangerous thing she'd ever done. She'd given in to impulse the night of the Black Widows Ball, and it wasn't something she wanted to repeat, no matter how deliciously wicked it had been. The memory of that night filled her thoughts and flooded her senses as she halted her restless prowling.

Closing her eyes, she was in Lucien's arms again, and the sensations were strong and powerful. Behind the mask she'd worn that night she'd ceased to be Constance. Instead she had been Isis, goddess of fire and passion. She'd given more of herself to Lucien that night than she'd ever given in her marriage. Shocked, she shook her head. No, that couldn't be true. She had loved Graham. How could she have held anything back from her own husband?

But she *had* kept a piece of herself hidden from Graham. He had loved her in spite of her gift, but he'd never been comfortable with it or her use of it. It had been his quiet disapproval that had stood between them. Keeping her gift buried so deep beneath the surface would have eventually taken its toll.

Now, the thought of exposing herself like that again, even for a brief affair, made her decidedly uneasy. A small gasp parted her lips. She was so concerned about how the earl would react to her unique talent, that she was treating the notion of an affair with him as if it were a commonplace event.

For her it was anything *but* ordinary. She understood why most of the Set conducted love affairs outside of their marriages of convenience. Everyone needed to feel loved, but what she'd shared with Lucien was beyond anything in her experience, even with Graham. The raw intensity of it made her ache for his touch again. Her breath hitched as her skin tingled from the memory of his caress. Her special talent had taught her the art of discretion. Would it be such a terrible thing if she were to give in to temptation?

Flustered by the idea, she dismissed it immediately. It didn't matter. Her gift would guarantee she'd earn the man's scorn. The Earl of Lyndham wasn't the type of man to believe in ghosts or spirits. No doubt he'd denounce anyone who professed an ability to see or talk to the dead. He was a man of action, a scholar, and her gift was as far removed from science and the academic world as it could be. And since he no longer wished to retain her services, all her angst was moot.

With one last glare of frustration at her reflection in the vanity table's mirror, she left her room. The hall carpet deadened the sound of her shoes as she walked, her gown a mere whisper in the cold, stone corridor. At the main stairwell, she hurried upward toward the nursery. Jamie was probably worried about her, and she wanted to reassure him. On occasion her gift made her appear disoriented, but she'd always managed to explain away the incident. This time her experience had been far more debilitating.

Explaining her gift to her son was something she'd not done yet. Every time she considered doing so, something stopped her. She knew Graham would not have approved. She stopped outside the nursery door, surprised to hear loud laughter coming from within. Quietly opening the door, she stared at the sight of the Earl of Lyndham stuck in a comical pose. Shoulders hunched upward, he had one arm crooked so his hand was at a ninety-degree angle to his forearm, while his opposite hand was at the same angle, his palm facing upward. He resembled a terrible imitation of an Egyptian hieroglyphic.

Seated in front of him, Imogene and Jamie were laughing with boisterous glee, encouraging him to do more. Complying with their demands, he quickly changed his position and became a one-legged bird about to take flight. The ridiculous pose forced her to suppress a laugh, and in that moment, a pair of cerulean blue eyes met hers. The penetrating look he sent her pulled her body as taut as a violin string, and she found it difficult to breathe.

Had he finally guessed? Did he realize who she was? No, he couldn't have. Their time together that night had been too short. A small voice reminded her how easy it had been for her to recognize him. She refused to consider the possibility. It was an absurd notion. She was being far too arrogant to think the man even remembered or cared about the woman he'd been with for such a brief moment. Averting her gaze, she saw Jamie leap to his feet and run toward her. His arms wrapped around her waist, he hugged her tightly. When he stepped back to look up at her, he eyed her with a worried expression.

"Are you all right, Mother?"

"I'm much better, thank you, my darling." She bent over and kissed his cheek. "There's nothing to worry about."

"Have you eaten?" Lucien's deep voice was a stroke of seduction teasing her senses as she realized he'd moved to stand at her side. Muscles wound tight with tension, she shook her head.

"I had thought I would eat downstairs, but I wanted to visit Jamie first."

"Ah, then it's fortunate you came here before going to the dining room. My grandmother was tired, so I sent her to bed. Imogene is playing hostess for the evening's meal." His hand captured her elbow and pulled her toward a nearby table. "We've already eaten, but there's plenty left to satisfy even the heartiest of appetites."

Beneath his touch, her skin grew warm until it sent a wave of heat washing over her entire body. Unable to look at him without remembering the past, she sat at the table. The presence of Imogene at her side offered a welcome relief from the strain of being so close to Lucien.

"I'm glad you're feeling better, my lady."

"Thank you, Imogene." She smiled at the dark-haired girl. "The meal looks delicious. Did you make the selections yourself?"

"Yes, but Jamie helped. He insisted on having strawberries and cream for dessert. He said you would like that."

"Jamie knows me too well," she said with a laugh. "Strawberries are my favorite fruit."

"Uncle Lucien likes them too. So be careful that he doesn't steal them all from you." Imogene grinned at the man who had seated himself opposite Constance at the table.

"Incorrigible imp." Lucien grinned back. "Off with you now. Go play that game I brought you from Cairo with young Lord Westbury."

Dark curls bouncing against her shoulders, Imogene hurried back to the fireplace where Jamie was rolling some dice in front of a pegboard with odd sticks. Turning back to the table, Constance saw that Lucien was busy preparing a plate with roast chicken, baby new potatoes and carrots, which he set in front of her. Suddenly aware she was hungry, she picked up a fork and lifted a bite of chicken to her mouth.

She ate in silence, while Lucien's steady gaze slowly escalated her level of discomfort. Midway through her meal, when she could no longer endure his gaze on her, she laid her fork down and sent him a direct look.

"Is there something wrong, my lord?" The sharpness in her voice was easy to hear, but she didn't care. He was unnerving her considerably.

"My apologies, Lady Westbury, I was simply trying to remember where we've met before." His words sent ice sliding across her hands as she stiffened.

She didn't like the small smile touching his firm lips. It was unsettling. One minute she was certain he hadn't recognized her and the next she was terrified he had. Uncertain how to respond to his observation, she simply stared at him in silence. Seconds later, his attention shifted toward the door across the room, and she exhaled a silent breath of relief at being free of his dark, penetrating gaze.

Turning her head, she saw Nanny Burke enter the nursery's main room. The short, rotund woman wore a cheery expression, and Constance had liked the woman from the first night of Jamie's stay at the keep. Nanny Burke's charges were well loved and cared for.

"Well now, my darlings. Did you enjoy your meal with his lordship?"

As the woman spoke, she glanced over in the direction of where she and Lucien were sitting. A look of delighted surprise on her plump, cheerful face, the woman hurried forward as the earl rose to his feet.

"Master Lucien! I had no idea you were still here with the children."

With a laugh, Lucien moved forward to envelop the woman in a big hug. "Well, Nanny, you're still as beautiful as ever."

"Pshaw! Go on with you now," the woman scoffed, but her face revealed how much she loved the compliment. Her hands on his biceps, she held him at arm's length and frowned.

"You've lost weight."

"Have I? I hadn't noticed," he said with an amused chuckle.

"You can't fool me, Master Lucien, I always could see through that devil-may-care attitude of yours. Pining over a woman I'll wager."

Heat warmed her body as Lucien sent her a quick glance over his shoulder.

"Perhaps, but that's a confession you'll not hear from me."

"You always did like to keep your secrets." With another laugh, the older woman wagged her finger at him as he grinned.

Turning away, she uttered several sounds of encouragement as she urged her young charges to say their goodnights. Protesting loudly, Imogene and Jamie did as they were told. Together they bid Constance and Lucien goodnight before being shuffled off to bed by the good-natured nursemaid. As the children left the room, Constance realized there was no longer a buffer between her and Lucien. The thought propelled her out of her chair with lightning speed.

She froze as she realized he had anticipated her movement and blocked her path. Leaning forward, he reached around her for something on the table. He was so close, she could breathe in the spicy leather scent of his cologne. Rich and earthy, it teased her senses with its tangy aroma. As he straightened, his mouth came close to her ear, and she trembled at the fire that skimmed through her veins to spread heat throughout her body.

"Leaving so soon? I thought we might talk a few moments." The murmur of his voice tightened the coil of tension inside her.

"I...I have packing to do."

"Ah, a minor detail I should have addressed already."

He didn't look at her, but focused his attention on the strawberry he held in his hand. With deliberate movements, he brushed off the top of the berry and removed its green leaves. When he finished, he raised his gaze to meet hers, a seductive smile curving his mouth. The white of his teeth were a sharp contrast to the bright red fruit as he bit into it. For such a simple action, the effect was highly erotic. Her chest tightened as he finished off the strawberry.

"After you left the library this afternoon, I reviewed the

cataloging you've done so far with my collection. Your work is most impressive."

Surprised, she tipped her head to one side, uncertain she'd heard him correctly. "I beg your pardon?"

"Your attention to detail in cataloging each artifact is excellent. Even more impressive was the knowledge included with that detail. It's of a caliber I've only seen at the British Museum."

Pleasure mixed with skepticism as she sent him a dubious look. "Thank you."

"Naturally, it made me realize that I couldn't possibly allow you to leave without completing your task."

"I don't think that would be a good idea," she said quickly as a knot swelled in her throat.

"Why not?" He shrugged. "What's changed other than my opinion of your work?"

Something about the innocent note in his voice set her nerves tingling, and she shook her head. "My own opinion of the work has changed, my lord. I'm no longer convinced I'm right for the position."

"I see. And is there a particular reason for this change of heart?" Leaning forward again, he picked up another strawberry from the bowl on the table.

His close proximity was a fire sweeping over her skin. Struggling to ignore the wild sensations stirring in her, she fought to consider his words carefully. What had changed? Nothing and everything. The man might not be a murderer, but there were secrets in this dark structure he called home. Secrets she wasn't sure she wanted to delve into. Normally, the spirits she encountered didn't affect her adversely, but the ghosts and the grief in the keep were a powerful combination of energy. If she stayed, she would have to battle that on a daily basis. No, that wasn't the reason. She was lying to herself. *He* was the reason why staying would be so dangerous.

"I can offer you nothing specific, my lord. Simply my instincts. Now if you'll excuse me, I'll say good night."

Without waiting for him to speak, she flew toward the door. In a flash he followed her. Before she could even touch the doorknob, his large hand was braced against the door, holding it shut. Heat engulfed her as he towered over her, his chest pressing gently, but firmly, into her back. The intimacy of the position made her pulse rocket out of control. Warm lips nuzzled the side of her neck, and she struggled not to give in to the hedonistic pleasure cascading over her. He made her feel out of control, and that made him more dangerous than any man she'd ever met.

"Turn around and look at me, Isis." The hoarse command pulled the air from her lungs as her body went rigid against his.

He knew. He knew who she was.

Unable to move, she trembled as his hand cupped the side of her neck then slid downward across her shoulder. It was a lover's caress. She didn't resist as he forced her to turn and face him. With her back pressed against the door, she looked up into his blue eyes. Desire flared in his gaze as he trailed the tip of his finger across her cheek before tracing the edge of her jaw.

"Do you have any idea how difficult it is to find a beautiful widow in London?" There was just a hint of irritation in his voice as his penetrating gaze locked with hers.

Her heart skipped a beat. He really had been looking for her. Her dreams had not lied about *that.* The knowledge filled her with a sense of delight. Instantly, she swatted the emotion aside. Why had he been looking for her? Wetting her dry lips, she shook her head.

"Since it's not my habit to look for beautiful widows, I wouldn't know." She was pleased that her voice held just the right note of amusement so as to disguise her agitation.

"It's damned difficult," he bit out between clenched teeth. "But I find it interesting how you managed to find me so easily."

"Find you so easily!" she sputtered. "I did no such thing, you arrogant beast."

"No?" he sneered. "And I suppose you expect me to believe you don't know Malcolm Standish either."

Infuriated by his assumption that she found him so irresistible as to deliberately seek him out, she glared up at him. The blazing anger in his gaze made her try to push herself free from the way he had her pinned to the nursery room door. It was a futile effort.

"Frankly, my lord. I could care less what you believe," she

puffed angrily as her hands shoved at his unyielding chest. "I don't know anyone named Standish, and I most certainly did *not* try to find you. I had no idea Lyndham Keep was yours. If I had, I wouldn't—"

His eyes narrowed as she abruptly closed her mouth. "You wouldn't what?"

"This conversation is ridiculous. I wish to return to my room to pack my belongings." She flinched at the determination in his gaze. She'd said too much.

"*Answer* me."

"I wouldn't have come here," she snapped.

"You wouldn't have come here," he murmured, almost as if he were speaking to himself.

She experienced a brief moment of relief as she realized he wasn't curious about why she would have stayed away from Lyndham Keep. His hand cupped her chin while his thumb rubbed across her lower lip. The action sent a stream of lava coursing through her veins straight to her nether regions. Sweet heaven, it was happening all over again.

With just one touch he had stirred a fire inside her. His mouth beckoned to her, and she struggled not to lean into him. Oh God, what was it about this man that made her respond to his touch so quickly?

"My lord, I—"

"Lucien. I want to hear you say my name again." It was another command and she tried to stifle the thrill of it. She didn't like anyone telling her what to do, but there was something about his dominating manner that excited her.

"Lucien, please. I must pack."

"No, Isis. I want you to say it like you did before." Desire darkened his blue eyes as his mouth hovered over hers. "I want to hear you cry out my name in the heat of passion."

She shuddered as his hand curled around the back of her neck and pulled her head toward him. Powerless to resist, she molded herself to his hard, muscular body as her mouth parted beneath his. In that split second, fire engulfed every one of her senses. Passion flowed hot and heavy through her as she gave in to the need gripping her body.

Her tongue mated with his with a ferocity that stunned her, but she held nothing back as his large hand slid over her bare shoulders to trace the line of her bodice down to her breasts. God, how she wanted him to suckle her again. She craved him, hungered for him with the same intensity she'd experienced that night at the Clarendon.

The desire to feel his skin against hers spiraled through her, and her fingers quickly undid the buttons of his shirt. She splayed the material open so she could caress the warm steel of his chest. Touching him wasn't enough. She wanted to taste him too. She broke away from their kiss, her mouth edging its way along the line of his jaw, then down his throat to where his heart pounded against his breastbone. Breathing in his delicious spicy scent, her tongue flicked out to taste him. He was hot and tangy.

Dear Lord, she wanted him more now than she had that night. What power did he wield over her to make her so willing to forget everything but the sensation of his touch? Hot and wet for him, she ached for his possession. Remembering the way his thick, hard length had filled her, she slid her hand downward as she continued to taste the hardness of him.

The moment her fingers brushed over his rigid length he jerked with surprise. She wanted him—needed him inside her. With the palm of her hand, she rubbed him through his trousers. A deep growl rumbled out of his chest as he pushed his hips forward against her hand.

Strong hands pulled her upright as he sought her mouth again. Base emotion skittered through her as another rush of heat dampened the area between her thighs. Clinging to him, she moaned softly, taking pleasure in the shudder that ripped through her body. The delight coursing through her only increased the ache he'd created inside her with his touch.

Incendiary kisses singed her lips before heating her skin as his mouth glided across her cheek toward her ear. The moment his teeth nibbled on the soft flesh of her ear lobe, she whimpered a sigh of pleasure.

Cupping her face with his hands, he found her lips again, his tongue probing the warm cavern of her mouth in a raw imitation of what he intended to do with her in the near future.

Damn, she tasted good. Even better than that night at the Clarendon. Her mouth was sweet and warm like fresh honey. Was she as hot now as she'd been then? Roughly, he pressed her against the door with his body, while his hand hitched her skirt up enough for him to stroke a warm thigh. She was just as luscious as he remembered. A gasp parted her lips, and he swallowed it as his fingers slid through wiry curls to find her sweet cream. Christ Jesus, she was drenched with passion. His thumb pressed on the button of her sex, and she arched her hips toward him with an eagerness that made him growl in anticipation. Her eagerness excited him, and the way she was rubbing his cock made him painfully hard with an ache that only her hot cunny would ease.

He slid one finger inside her. Immediately, she jerked against him, her body tightening with delicious spasms of arousal. He remembered well the way she'd clenched around him that night, and he needed to have her do so again. Slick desire coated his fingers as her musky heat mixed with her exotic perfume. It created a sultry scent that flexed his body with a pull that was undeniable. Damn, but he wanted to taste her cream on his tongue. Warmth grazed his cheek as her hard, fast pants of excitement parted her soft mouth. She was hot velvet against his hand as he continued to stroke her in the same way he intended to do when he buried himself between her legs.

"Oh dear God. Lucien."

The plea in her voice nearly undid him. It was the heartfelt cry of passion he'd demanded of her just moments before. God help him, but he hadn't needed a woman this badly in his entire life. He stiffened as the thought gave him the sensation of having been doused with icy water. Stunned by the realization that he was out of control, he twisted away from her and put several feet between them. Glancing at her over his shoulder, he grimaced at the way his body responded to her.

Framed against the door, her face glowed with desire, and her mouth was rosy from his kisses, while her eyelids were half closed from her aroused state. She was a delicious temptation that urged him to cast aside all restraint and carry her off to his room where he could immerse himself in her lush curves.

No. Doing that at this moment in time was far too reckless.

It was one thing to desire, but to do so without control was far too dangerous. He needed to maintain a tighter hold on his emotions when he took her to his bed. And there was no doubt in his mind that he would have her again. He simply could not afford to lose his head when he did so. Something he was close to doing at this very moment.

He'd been blind to everything around him when he was caressing her. Pleasure was something he could only afford if he kept his head. From across the small space that separated them, he watched her slowly gather her wits. Dismay and embarrassment darkened her lovely eyes as she looked at him. Clearing his throat, he took a step toward her before reminding himself of his resolve. Patience. If he touched her now, he'd be lost, and that was far too risky. He refused to give in to the emotions that had driven his father and brother into the abyss.

"You have a way of going to my head, *yā sabāha*," he muttered as he shoved his hand through his hair.

"I think...think I should go to my room." Eyes large in her face, she averted her gaze from him as he studied her.

"I'll walk you there."

"*No.*" Her expression was closed and unreadable as she shook her head fiercely. "I'm more than capable of finding my own way."

Stepping forward again, he paused as she darted to one side and opened the door. Almost as if she feared he might stop her, she didn't take her gaze off him as she fled the room. The moment she was gone, he was encased in a morbid silence that set him on edge.

He needed a drink.

The thought propelled him out of the nursery with a forceful stride, the door slamming shut behind him. He winced at the loud noise. Nanny would have his head if he'd disturbed the children's sleep. Quick and sure, his steps carried him downstairs to the one room in the keep that had always troubled him.

Candlelight illuminated a large portion of the library, and a small fire crackled in the grate. The horror he'd witnessed here on his twelfth birthday had taunted him night and day for years. It had taken him almost seven years before he could even cross the threshold of the room, let alone stay in it for any length of time. After Katherine's murder and Nigel's death, he'd remodeled the library in one final attempt to rid himself of the past. It had failed, but he no longer feared the room.

Going to the sideboard, he poured himself a healthy dose of whiskey then tossed it down in one gulp. Just as quickly he refilled his glass and drank it in quick succession, the liquid burning its way down his throat. It had been a long time since he had imbibed so freely.

With a grunt of restlessness, he grabbed the neck of the decanter and took a seat by the fire. Perhaps if he drank himself into a stupor, he'd be free for a short time. Free of the pain that haunted him every day. There was so much of it.

Grim images rose up out of the dark corners of the room to mock him with their grisly horror. The sight of his parents slaughtered like cattle. Katherine's brutal murder at the hand of his brother. The terrible sound of Nigel's scream as he threw himself from the North Tower in atonement for killing his wife. The sight of Imogene as a toddler crying for her mother, and the grief that had weakened his indomitable grandmother.

He splashed more amber liquid into his glass, ignoring the droplets that hit his trousers. Drinking had never provided him any solace, but it would deaden the anguish threatening to push its way through his body. Perhaps it would allow him to forget Isis. No, that wasn't her real name. She was Constance Athelson, Viscountess Westbury.

The thought of her here, in his home, filled him with mixed emotions. The entire time he'd been searching for her, she'd been at Lyndham Keep, right under his nose. He wasn't surprised she'd denied knowing Standish. If she was working for the bastard, she sure as hell wouldn't admit to it.

But her anger when she'd expressed no knowledge of the man had been genuine. He was certain of that. Either she was an exceptional actress or she was telling the truth. And then there was that momentary slip of the tongue about her never coming to Lyndham Keep if she'd known he was the owner. She'd been quite adamant on that point. He winced. The blunt remark had stung, and he didn't like how it had substantially pricked his ego.

Her desire to avoid him wasn't all that unexpected. They'd

shared an illicit moment, and no doubt she'd gone against everything she'd been raised *not* to do. But it was the small note of fear hovering in her voice he found so puzzling. Then there was her surprise when he'd confronted her in the library upon his arrival today.

He remembered how she'd gone pale the moment she'd gotten a good look at him. Clearly, she'd recognized him straight away, but her fear confused him. Much like an ancient script in need of deciphering, she was mysterious and evasive. She was a puzzle he wanted to solve.

Of course, he could be reading more into her reaction than he should. It wouldn't be the first time a woman had found his scar unappealing. He touched his cheek, his fingers sliding over the rough bumpy line that marred his skin. The long white mark was a reminder of his narrow escape five years ago.

Escaping his destiny was the one thing he couldn't do. That was clear now. Tonight he'd wanted to possess Isis completely. Hold her captive until he'd had his fill of her. But fulfilling that need could have easily come at a cost. Already his ability to keep his anger in check was being tested. If his desire were suddenly to evolve into something else—

Weary of the darkness that wove an insidious path through his head, he took another long draught of liquor. He no longer wanted to think or feel. He only wanted to silence the memories. But most of all, he wanted to suppress the image of a beautiful pair of sparkling hazel eyes on the face of a temptress. And he needed to forget a seductive smile that beckoned him to push all caution aside.

With a groan, he stared into the fire, his vision growing blurred as the alcohol slowly worked its magic. Eventually, he sank deeper into his chair, and his head dropped toward his chest. He tried to watch the dancing firelight, but his vision shifted, and when logic told him the two fires he saw were really only one, he closed his eyes and slept.

The corridor he walked along was dark, and he felt very small. Ahead of him a light blazed. He didn't want to go toward it, but something compelled him forward. The closer he got to the light, the more terrified he became. Horror engulfed him as something pushed him from behind.

Instantly, he knew where he was. The library at Lyndham Keep. His father lay sprawled on the floor beside his mother. The scent of death filled his nostrils, choking him with its foul stench. The blood sickened him. Splattered over the carpet and the furniture, the life force had spread its way across the floor, forming huge dark stains. Life's essence ebbing out of his father and mother. His father's lifeless body twitched suddenly before rising to turn in his direction. As his gaze met his father's soulless look across an ever-growing chasm of darkness, a shout of horror rushed out of him.

Shooting upright in his chair, Lucien gasped quick breaths of air, his heart beating with a fury that threatened to explode in his chest. He sprang to his feet and wheeled about to survey the room. Empty. His fingers raked through his hair in a hopeless gesture. He'd not had a nightmare like that in years. A shudder racked him and he jerked at the knock on the library door.

"Come," he snarled.

Jacobs quietly entered the room. "Forgive me, my lord, but I wanted to ensure you were all right."

"I'm fine, thank you, Jacobs."

"Very good, my lord. Is there anything else I can get for you this evening?"

Lucien found the question ironic. The one thing he wanted, no one could get for him. No one could relieve him of the demons he carried inside him. They waited with baneful patience, ready to take hold of him the moment he relaxed his vigilance. He uttered a harsh laugh.

"No thank you, Jacobs. Go on to bed."

"Yes, my lord." The butler bowed and turned to leave the room.

"Jacobs." He frowned at the way his tongue didn't seem to function properly. "In the morning, do not let Lady Westbury leave the keep without my blessing."

"My lord?" The note of shock in the retainer's voice was clear, and he winced at the man's unspoken objection.

"You heard me, Jacobs," he growled with irritation.

The butler stiffened, but nodded his head before he left the library. Alone once more, Lucien looked around the dark room. The candles had long since burned down to stumps, and the fire in the hearth barely lit the area where he stood.

In the darkness, he thought he saw a movement, and he peered into the shadows. For a moment, he could have sworn he saw Nigel watching him with a look of annoyance on his face. Shaking his head, he waved the image away with his hand. He was drunk. But not drunk enough to dismiss the pain that constricted his heart at the thought of his brother. He missed him. Missed all of them.

His pain exploded in a fit of fury as he dashed the empty decanter he held into the dying fire. The crystal shattered into tiny fragments against the stone façade. Stumbling around his chair on unsteady feet, Lucien headed out of the library. As he lurched through the doorway, he thought he heard someone whispering behind him. He did not turn. The ghosts of the past would have to wait for another opportunity to torment him.

Chapter Five

Constance awoke to the sound of sobbing. Why did the spirit insist on waking her at this time of the morning every day? Each morning, just before dawn, the weeping started and never ended until she got out of bed.

"For the love of God, please let me sleep," she protested as she rolled over onto her back. Although the sobbing didn't stop, it softened to a mere whisper. A sigh of relief parted her lips. Thank God. She was exhausted and had hardly slept at all through the night. Draping her arm across her eyes, she groaned. What was she going to do?

Last night she'd been helpless to resist Lucien or his touch. If he hadn't stepped away from her, she would have eagerly given herself to him over and over again. She'd craved his caresses with a desperation that stunned her. Even now her body ached for him. Ached to have him stroking her to a fevered pitch until she shattered against his hand. The memory of how he'd teased her into an exhilarating climax sent heat skimming across her skin.

He'd pleasured her in a way that blinded her to everything but the sensations wending their way through every part of her body. Even after he'd released her, it had taken her a moment to regain her senses. When she did, she was mortified. It was one thing to have an affair, but quite another to do so outside her son's bedroom.

Not even the fact Lucien had called her *yâ sabāha* again could ease the embarrassment of her wanton behavior. Even more alarming was her wish that they'd been somewhere else more private. Leaving Lyndham Keep was no doubt the prudent thing to do before she became embroiled in an affair she knew could easily consume her. But there was something about the earl that tugged at her heart.

The memory the ghost had shown her the day before was a haunting one. Even in the vision, she'd seen the echoes of the man Lucien had become in the grieving boy. It was the thought of that boy and the deep sorrow etched on his young face that made her hesitate to leave. She'd never been one to desert those in need.

Graham had often teased her about her desire to mend the world's problems. But Graham had drawn the line at her using her gift to help others. People would think her mad, he'd always said. The real world functioned on tangible facts, not dreams of things that might be. She'd met few people who would have disagreed with him.

All her siblings, with perhaps the exception of Sebastian, had some clairvoyant abilities. It was a Stewart trait passed down over the generations. Although the gift predominantly touched Stewart women, it also appeared in some male members of the family. Aunt Matilda rarely spoke about the Stewart gift of clairvoyance, and then only under the auspices of a family history lesson. But she'd understood the stories for the warnings they were. Stewarts throughout history had always had the ability of the sight, but most of them had paid a terrible price for their special gift.

Some had been burned at the stake. Others stoned to death. The last Stewart to use her gift had been thrown into an asylum. Hearing Aunt Matilda share the poor woman's plight had made her cautious about whom she took into her confidence when it came to her gift.

What would the earl say if she suddenly mentioned she'd been speaking with his dead brother? The question was laughable. The earl's reaction would be like the one she experienced in boarding school. Lonely and missing her family, she'd wanted friends so desperately that when Elizabeth Chasefield had befriended her she was elated.

Her excitement was quickly crushed when her new friend betrayed her by telling everyone about her gift. Horrified, the headmistress had summoned Sebastian to fetch her immediately. It had been a lesson in humiliation and pain. It had taught her not to share her secret with anyone.

She'd even kept her secret from Graham until he proposed. Accepting his offer without telling him everything would have been dishonorable. To Graham's credit he had reassured her the Stewart gift would not affect his love for her. But deep below the surface of their relationship, her precognitive abilities had always been a chasm between them.

And while Graham had never been so cruel as to openly deride her, his silent disapproval had pained her as well. No, the only thing Lucien would believe was that she qualified as a candidate for the asylum.

Frowning, she scrambled out of bed and pulled on her robe. With the sash tied snugly at her waist, she hurried toward her trunk and threw open the lid. She couldn't stay. It was as simple as that.

"He won't let you leave, you know."

The sound of Nigel's deep voice made her yelp. She whirled around to face him, her hand pressed against her breast as if that would steady her frantic pulse. Glaring at the spirit, she walked back toward the vanity table, making certain she gave him a wide berth. She had no wish for a repeat of yesterday's incident.

"Isn't there some other way you could announce your presence? Like rattling some chains or moaning?" she snapped.

She eyed him with irritation as she gathered several items from the vanity table before turning around to return to the trunk. As she secured the vials in the interior tray of the luggage, she grimaced as his laughter filled the room. The ghost shimmered in the early morning light as she wheeled around and sent him a cold look. He arched his eye brows and offered her a careless shrug of his translucent shoulders.

"My apologies for my abrupt arrival, but I only thought to spare you the effort of packing."

"Then you're wasting your energy, something we both know you have little of."

"*Touché.* Still, you should know that Lucien has left orders that you're not allowed to leave the keep."

"He can't keep me here," she exclaimed. The moment she spoke she knew the statement was false. Lucien's staff would do as they were told, and no one would fetch a carriage to take her to the train station.

"I see you understand the situation."

"All I understand is that you're as arrogant as your brother."

Angry, she turned away from him, slammed the lid of the trunk closed then stalked to the window. In silence, she stared out over the gardens her room overlooked. Although winter's cold edge had given way to spring, it was still winter in the keep. Somehow, she doubted even summer's heat could drive out the pain and grief that chilled this ancient fortress.

"My wife often told me the same thing." The wistful note behind his words made her turn in surprise.

"Your wife?"

"Katherine." He whispered the name with a reverence that touched her heart. "She always said I was far too arrogant."

"You loved her."

"Of course I loved her," he growled. "I didn't believe in the curse like Lucien does."

"Curse?"

"Don't tell me you've never heard of the Blakemore Curse," he scoffed. "My brother believes the curse is why our father murdered our mother before killing himself."

She frowned for a moment as she searched her memory for any mention of such a story. There was nothing she could recall, and she was certain that anything like a curse would have made for excellent gossip amongst the Set. Shaking her head, she watched the spirit's image fade then brighten. It was clear his energy to maintain his form was lessening.

"You're weak."

"Yes, and I don't have much time. Neither does Lucien. I want your promise you'll help him."

"What do you mean Lucien doesn't have much time?" She breathed in a sharp breath of dismay. If something happened to Lucien— She immediately closed the door on her thoughts. She refused to contemplate what her reaction meant.

"Your promise, madam. I will have it."

Fear streaked through her as she nodded her head. "I promise. Now tell me what you mean when you say that Lucien doesn't have much time."

"If you don't help him, he'll die."

Frustrated, she closed her eyes and exhaled a noise of disgust. "You keep insisting I have to help him, and yet you refuse to tell me how. There's little I can do to help when you're so bloody cryptic. Tell me what has to be done."

For a moment, the ghost looked taken aback. The surprise on his face was slowly replaced by a perplexed look. "But I thought you knew. Isn't it why you came to the keep?"

"I came to Lyndham Keep to catalog Lucien's—your brother's antiquities collection."

"Then how can you say you don't know how to help him?"

"Were you this obtuse when you were alive?" she snapped with exasperation. "Simply because I came here to do a job doesn't mean I know how to help Lucien."

"But aren't you Isis?"

Embarrassment set her skin on fire as she stared at the ghost in openmouthed dismay. Wheeling away from the apparition, she stared out the window again as she struggled with the knowledge that the ghost had— Horrified, she banished the notion to the back of her mind.

"You haven't answered my question," he said in a bullish tone of voice.

Furious the spirit had been privy to a moment of intimacy between her and Lucien, she grabbed a book off a nearby table and threw it at the spirit. It traveled straight through him to crash into the front of the vanity table. A startled look on his face, the ghost shook his head.

"Madam, whatever's upset—"

"Upset? I'm not upset, I'm incensed that you would spy on me—on Lucien—during a moment of...a moment of..." She couldn't finish the thought.

"A moment of... Good God, madam. I am not a voyeur to my brother's intimate affairs," he roared.

The affront on the ghost's face made her blush, and she turned away from him, grateful he'd not witnessed the intimacy between her and Lucien. The ghost's outrage was like a sharp fingernail across the back of her neck. Spirits often retained many of the emotions they'd experienced in their earthly form, and Lucien's brother obviously possessed a deep sense of honor and integrity. She'd insulted him, and he was furious.

"I'm sorry," she murmured, but the tingling across the back of her neck had dissipated. He was gone.

Frustrated, she expelled a breath of irritation. Once again, her conversation with the spirit of Lucien's brother had simply raised more questions and given her fewer answers. Logic. She needed to apply logic. It was the one thing her brother Sebastian prized above all others, except for perhaps Helen and their children. A sudden longing for Melton House and its chaotic warmth welled up inside her.

She adored all her brothers, but Sebastian had always been the rock everyone in the family could cling to. He'd been the one to come to Egypt to help her settle Graham's personal affairs and escort her back to England. And Sebastian had been the one to teach her how to apply logic when searching for an answer to a problem.

Logic. She needed to approach this conundrum without emotion and with a simple review of the facts. Sitting on the bed, she considered everything she knew. First there was the murder in the keep's library. It had been Lucien and Nigel's parents she'd seen lying dead.

Someone had killed the couple in a brutal fashion, then made it appear to be a murder-suicide. Whoever had done such a horrible deed had used a ritualistic blade she'd only seen used in Egyptian magic ceremonies.

The blade resembled a cross. Generally, the handle depicted a god or a pharaoh. But the blade she saw was of a design unlike anything she'd ever seen. The handle was grotesque in form, and it was as evil-looking as the deed it had committed. She frowned. What else did she know?

The collection. Somehow, the antiquities in the library were part of the puzzle too. Nigel had also mentioned her being Isis. But not Isis in the sense that Lucien thought of her. Nigel had meant something else, but she didn't know what. Did he somehow think she was connected to the antiquities in the library? What else did she know? The curse. Nigel's ghost had mentioned the Blakemore curse.

She closed her eyes as she struggled to remember his exact

words. *Of course I loved her. I didn't believe in the curse like Lucien does.* Yes. That's what he'd said. Not an illuminating comment, but it was more than she'd had before her ghostly visitor had called. The question was, how was she supposed to help Lucien? Even more important, what did he want from her? She heaved a sigh. There was only one way to find out. She needed to stay at Lyndham Keep until she'd done whatever the universe had sent her here to do.

ℤ℥

As she crossed the threshold of the library, she waited for the familiar edge to assault her nerve endings. Today the room's vibration was simply a soft breeze across her skin compared to the usual sensation of ants scurrying about on her arm. Grateful for the reprieve, she took the opportunity to survey the room itself. It was the first time she'd taken the time to do so since she'd arrived at Lyndham Keep. Most of her time had been spent in the adjacent room cataloguing the collection.

The heavy drapes over the tall windows had been pulled all the way back to let in the morning light. Sunshine streamed through the glass, warming the dark wood of the furniture. Inexplicably her gaze was drawn to the area where Lucien's parents had been murdered. She frowned. Now that she was focusing on the library for the first time, she realized it had changed. The room was different from what she remembered seeing in her visions.

Turning her head, she surveyed the large room with puzzlement. What was different? When the answer came to her, she wasn't really surprised. It had been completely made over. The fabrics on the chairs, the oval-shaped rug, the tables— everything that had been in the library at the time of the murders had been replaced.

A sudden frisson slid across her skin, and she briefly closed her eyes. They barely knew each other, and yet her body instantly recognized his presence. The sensation unnerved her. She'd never experienced this type of physical connection with Graham.

"Good morning." The deep note of his voice sent a

pleasurable chill sliding down her back. "I trust you slept well?"

Slowly she turned to face him. He stood just inside the library door, his expression remote as his eyes met hers. Dark and dangerous was the first thing that came to her mind as she studied him. She remembered the silky feel of his black hair against her fingers, and the touch of his firm mouth. The blue of his eyes made her think of the deep and mysterious loch at Callendar Abbey, the Stewart family home. Tension emphasized the thin white scar that ran down his cheek toward his jaw, making her uncertain as to his mood.

She nodded her head in greeting. "I slept soundly, thank you."

The lie rolled off her lips as she met his probing gaze. Assessment glittered in his eyes as he studied her in silence for a tense moment. Then with a leisurely stride, he moved deeper into the room. He brushed past her as he headed toward the table of artifacts she'd finished cataloging. Heat ricocheted across her skin as his arm bumped lightly against hers. Swallowing hard, she watched him pick up a small mirror that a noblewoman had used thousands of years ago.

"Amazing, isn't it?" he murmured. "A small piece of history that's more than two thousand years old."

The note of awe in his voice drew her to his side, and she pointed to the indentations on the handle. "I'm certain there were jewels of some sort on the handle here."

"I think you're right." He nodded as he peered more closely at the handle.

The magic of her work took hold of her, and her fingers covered his as she made him turn the mirror over. Instantly, her body hummed with exhilaration. Startled by the sensation, she jerked her hand off his to point toward the inscription on the metal.

"The markings...were...they were hard to make out, but I believe this was a wedding gift to a woman from her husband."

He didn't speak for a moment, but simply stared at the artifact he held. Laying the mirror down, he sent her a indecipherable look.

"This is exceptional work, Lady Westbury. I'm looking forward to your opinions on several pieces that you've yet to unpack." His autocratic statement made her frown.

"I don't recall agreeing to stay, my lord." She winced at her reply.

It was hardly the appropriate response given her recent decision to remain at the keep. But then she couldn't let him think she was eager to stay. He might misinterpret her reasons for remaining. She watched him pick up a small vial that had once been used to store perfumed oil.

The close proximity of him was making every nerve ending in her body scream for his touch, but she was afraid to move. If he were to realize how much his presence disturbed her— She crushed the thought before it could materialize as she struggled to breathe normally. Replacing the vial, he turned, and the space between them vanished as he bent his head toward her.

"Do you really want to pass up this opportunity?" The husky note in his voice sent her pulse skittering along at an accelerated pace, as his hand swept across the side of her neck.

Suddenly finding it difficult to breathe, she stared into his dark eyes, and trembled at the desire blazing there. Without thinking, she leaned into him until her lips brushed over his. A low growl rumbled in his chest as he wrapped her in his warm embrace.

In an instant, a delicious heat swept her up into a vortex of passion.

Unable to suppress her desire, she gave herself up to the bliss of being in his arms again. His mouth nipped at hers until she eagerly parted her lips for him. Spice and bergamot washed over her senses as she breathed in the sheer maleness of him. Dear Lord, he smelled wonderful.

As his tongue swirled around hers, she shuddered at the possessive nature of his kiss. She should be stopping this madness, but he was impossible to resist. Her fingers slipped through the silk of his black hair as she pressed her body into him. The sensitive nub between her legs screamed for his touch, and instinctively she ground her hips against his in an imitation of what her body was crying out for.

Through her skirt, his erection was hard and full against her thigh. Unbidden, the memory of an erotic papyrus she'd studied recently filled her head with wicked thoughts. What would Lucien do if she tasted him like she'd seen illustrated in the ancient scroll? Would he like her mouth on him? The thought of pleasing him in such a way pulled a quiet whimper from her as she reached for him.

As if aware of her intentions, he captured her hands and pinned them behind her back. He bent her backward slightly so her throat was exposed. Roughly, his mouth moved downward to where a layer of ruffles hid the open vee that plunged down to her breasts. The moment his mouth caressed the slight swell below her throat, she moaned softly.

Christ Jesus, she tasted like the desert. Hot and sweet on his tongue. With one hand, he parted the frothy ruffles at her throat to reveal the shadowed valley of her breasts. Beneath his fingertips her jasmine-scented skin was as soft as the petals of the flower itself. He drank in a deep breath of her fragrance as his mouth brushed lightly across the top of her breasts. Eager to taste her, his tongue flicked out to stroke her skin and she gasped.

Once again he sampled her, before his tongue slid into the valley between the rounded curves of her breasts. With slow, deliberate strokes, he imitated the carnal act they both wanted. The sweetness of her made his cock ache. Bloody hell, he wanted her. Needed her.

He pulled her into the small room off the library. The moment the door closed behind them, she ran her palm across his erection. He groaned and caught her hand to push her away from the hot weight pressing against his stomach.

"Lucien, please," she whispered against his mouth as she gently nipped at his lower lip. "Let me touch you. I want to please you."

Her voice was a siren call that was impossible to resist, and he didn't stop her as she quickly unbuttoned his trousers. As she released his engorged length he drew in a ragged breath and welcomed the velvet heat of her hand wrapping around him. Unable to help himself, he groaned at her touch.

"Damn, that feels good," he muttered as he leaned back against the door and closed his eyes. Her fingers tightened around him, the fire in her touch biting into his iron-hard rod as she stroked him. "That's it, *yā sabāha, yes.*"

Hot and firm, her fingers slid over him. It was the unexpected warmth of her moist mouth that made him grab the door frame with a sharp jerk as he suppressed a loud cry of pleasure. His eyes flew open, and he looked down to see her tongue flick out and curl around the tip of his erection before she took him back into her mouth. Captivated, he watched her take in the length of him. A second later he jerked as her tongue swirled around his rod.

One hand braced against the door, he cupped the back of her neck to gently hold her in place as he slid his cock in and out of her mouth. He watched in fascination as she took every inch of him without protest. Christ Jesus, he loved the way she was sucking on him.

His gaze never wandered as she gripped him with her beautiful lips. Soaked in the heat of her mouth, he struggled to remain upright as she increased the rhythm of her strokes. God, she was incredible. No woman had ever sucked him like this before. His body throbbed from the heat of her touch, and he groaned as she looked up at him with her mouth wrapped tightly around him.

Her tongue laced its way around him one more time. Then with a quick movement she took him all the way into her mouth and her fingertips brushed against his ballocks.

"God, yes, Isis. Yes," he rasped.

A familiar surge lunged through his engorged length and before he could move, he exploded in her mouth. As she drank his seed, she continued to use her mouth to pleasure him. Shuddering, he closed his eyes.

Bloody hell, but that had to be the most incredible experience he could ever remember. Had Westbury taught her how to suck on a man's— His thoughts slid to an abrupt halt as he struggled not to envision her with her husband. Harsh and swift, his blood boiled at the thought of her with Westbury or any other man.

He wanted to obliterate her thoughts and images of every man she might have ever been with. With a quick movement, he jerked her upright to face him. The startled look on her face barely registered with him as he met her wide-eyed gaze. She was his and his alone, and he'd kill the first man who came near her.

The primeval nature of the emotion was brutal and harsh in its potency, and the force of it lashing through him made him freeze in his tracks. These were the thoughts of an irrational man. A mad man. He'd never had thoughts about a woman like this before. Where the hell was his self-control?

Her soft floral scent drifted across his senses, and he almost gave in to temptation before clenching his jaw. No, he needed to keep his wits about him. The little he had where she was concerned. The thought made his fingers fumble with the buttons of his trousers as he adjusted his clothing. Clearing his throat, he met her troubled gaze and frowned as her cheeks flushed with pained embarrassment.

"I apologize, my lord," she whispered in a stilted tone as she turned her head away.

The humiliation in her soft words slashed at him like a hawk's talon. Damnation, she thought he found her behavior appalling. If anything she'd nearly driven him mad with her erotic touch. He caught her chin with his fingers and forced her to look at him.

"Giving me pleasure does not require an apology, *yâ sabāha.*"

Hazel eyes flickered with an undefined emotion as her gaze met his. When he released her, the silence between them filled the small room. Clearing his throat one more time, he shoved a hand through his hair. Christ, he'd not felt this awkward since his first woman.

He watched her as she turned away from him to fiddle with the contents of a nearby crate. Her rigid shoulders betrayed her tension, and there was a vulnerability to her profile that filled him with a relentless need to protect her. Keep her safe from everyone, including himself. Bloody hell, he needed to get out of here. He was mad to even think such a thing.

"I've estate business to attend to," he growled as he clasped his hands behind his back. "I'll leave you to your work."

Without waiting for a response, he lunged out of the small storage room and into the library, leaving Constance to stare after him in mute confusion. He was all too aware of her gaze on his back as he crossed the floor of the library. Deliberately, he pulled the door closed behind him as he entered the hall. The quiet snap of the door latch made him exhale the pent-up energy surging through him. Damn.

He'd just made one of the worst mistakes he'd ever made in his entire life. There was only one thing left to do. He needed to return to London—tonight. The moment the thought entered his head, he smashed it aside. No. For three months he'd been searching the city for her. He wasn't about to let her go that easily. He simply needed to maintain control of his emotions and the situation would handle itself.

Restraint. A simple word that had applied to him when he'd walked into the library and greeted her. He had been fully in control of his senses for several minutes. It wasn't until her hand had guided his in turning that damned mirror over that he'd been forced to admit his control was an illusion. With a grunt of disgust, he strode through the hall and out the front door for his morning ride.

Goliath, a large roan stallion, chomped restlessly at his bit as Lucien accepted the reins from the stable hand. The animal wheeled sharply as he swung himself into the saddle and he welcomed the stallion's struggle. With a vicious nudge of his heel, he urged the horse into a gallop.

The sunshine warmed him as Goliath raced away from the keep toward the estate's pastureland. Bent over the horse's neck, he rode furiously in whatever direction the animal wanted to go. Fences came and went as they raced across fresh, green fields.

Eventually, the stallion tired and slowed from a hard gallop to a slow walk. Relaxing in the saddle, Lucien stared out over the lands that were his. A sarcastic grunt of disgust broke past his lips. The estate was his until the day he ended his own life and that of anyone he loved. But he wasn't going to let that happen. He refused to be like Nigel and dismiss the Blakemore curse. It was real. He'd witnessed the results one time too many.

First his great-grandfather, then his father and finally Nigel. The madness that destroyed them all ran in his blood too. He would not make the mistake his father and brother had made. Love of a woman had pushed the two of them over the edge. He vowed it wouldn't happen to him. He refused to give way to emotions that would awaken the insanity inside him.

The reins cut into his fingers as he tightened his grip on

the leather straps. Cruel and horrifying images from the past rose to taunt him. They mocked his determination not to repeat the crimes of his father and brother. With a stoic cynicism he'd developed the day he'd seen the lifeless bodies of his parents on the library floor, he pushed back the memories of the bloodbath flooding his head.

Grimacing, he shook his head. With his last breath he would resist the madness that drove the Blakemore men to wreak murder and mayhem on the heads of those they loved. He could easily avoid that fate if he remained emotionally detached from his passionate Isis. All it required was for him to maintain control of his senses when he was near her.

With a snort of disgust, Lucien closed his eyes as he recalled how easily she had distracted him with her sweet lips. He'd been so bewitched she could have demanded anything of him and he'd given it gladly. And God help him, but when she'd taken him into her mouth—

The memory made him grow hard in the blink of an eye. He wasn't accustomed to this type of temptation. In fact, he couldn't remember a single instance of any woman making him as hot as Westbury's widow did.

Constance Athelson, Viscountess Westbury—her name conjured up the image of a prim schoolteacher. It reflected none of the passion simmering beneath her composed features. Her fire was that of Isis, goddess over all Egyptian gods. He growled with frustration. No, it was for the best if he thought of her as Constance. That would make it easier to control his lust for her whenever she was near.

A gentle breeze stirred the thick, wiry mane against Goliath's neck before it brushed across his fingers in a light caress. Like the invisible wind, Constance was equally elusive. Beneath that serene expression was a woman with mysterious depths.

She also harbored a secret of some sort. The manner in which she'd left him that night at the Clarendon Hotel had convinced him of that. Whatever had frightened her had made her run from him as though the hounds of hell had been biting at her ankles.

He grew still in the saddle. She'd been afraid that night at the Clarendon, but her fear had only shown itself in the last few moments of their time together. What had happened to make her so afraid? Concentrating on the last moments before she fled, he tried to remember if he'd said or done something that might have alarmed her.

Just before she'd raced from the room, he'd kissed her. By most standards it had been an ordinary kiss of passion, but when he'd started to release her, a strange expression had come over her features. He frowned as he remembered her look.

It had been an expression of shock. He'd seen excavation sites collapse and kill men, and those who'd survived had been in shock afterwards. Constance's features had reflected the same look of trauma. She'd been immobile for several moments until he'd given her a slight shake. At that moment, she'd cried out and lifted her hands as if to ward off an attack of some sort.

When her gaze had focused on him it was as if she'd seen a monster. Worse, her expression of horror had twisted his gut in a way he didn't like. Whatever her thoughts were in those fleeting seconds, they'd managed to terrorize her. She'd been hell bent on putting as much distance between them as she could. Her flight had caught him off guard, and before he could stop her she'd disappeared, leaving him to begin searching London for her. A fruitless search because she'd been at Lyndham Keep.

"*Bloody hell.*"

Goliath shied at the loud oath of frustration, and Lucien turned his attention to keeping the stallion from leaping forward. Rubbing his hand over the animal's neck, he calmed the horse. Satisfied the stallion wouldn't bolt, he focused his thoughts on Constance once more.

There was no doubt in his mind that she was afraid of something. And whatever she was afraid of it involved him. That was the most perplexing thing of all. Yesterday, when he'd confronted her in the library, he'd attributed her loss of color to her deception in securing her post. Now he wondered if there wasn't another reason for her pallor.

"*Lucien.*" The cheerful shout echoed out over the pasture, causing him to turn his head.

The sight of Major Duncan Fenwick riding toward him brought a grin to his lips. He'd not seen his old friend and neighbor since returning from Egypt. Beneath him, Goliath shifted restlessly at the approach of the other horse. Holding the reins with one hand, he offered his other to his friend as Fenwick came to a halt at his side.

"Duncan," he exclaimed as the two of them shook hands. "It's been a long time."

"How the devil are you? Your grandmother told me you'd returned from Alexandria more than six months ago, but somehow we've managed to miss each other here and in London."

"I'm afraid I've been kept busy trying to outwit my grandmother's obvious attempts to marry me off."

Laughing, Duncan turned his horse around so they could ride in the same direction, and gave Lucien a friendly slap on the back. "She'll never give up, old man. Why not give in and make her happy?"

"I'll never marry." He nudged Goliath forward into a sedate walk.

"Never is a long time, Lucien. What about an heir?"

"The Blakemore line will die with me," he muttered fiercely. He intended to deny the fates another bloodbath. Better he lived a life of solitude than fall in love and become a raging, murderous madman.

"I hope you haven't told Aurora that. At her age, news of that sort could have an adverse effect on her health." Duncan sent him an arched look.

"My grandmother knows how I feel. She simply refuses to give up trying to change my mind." He smiled. "I'm willing to wager she could outfox your best military strategist."

"I know better than to take that bet." Duncan shook his head with a smile. "I haven't forgotten how she managed to nearly thwart my efforts to secure support for that textile bill in the House of Commons."

"Grandmother mentioned in her letters to me that you'd been elected MP. Congratulations." He laughed at the grimace on Duncan's features. "So how are you adapting to political life?"

"It's been interesting, especially when Aurora decides to interfere."

Unable to help himself, Lucien laughed again. "You need to learn how to get on her good side, Duncan. Why don't you come for supper tonight? I can help you mend your fences with Grandmother, and I have some artifacts I brought back with me from Egypt that might interest you."

"I accept," Duncan said with a pleased smile. "By the by, I understand you have a female Egyptologist working for you."

Startled by the comment, Lucien tightened his grip on his reins. The action made Goliath toss his head angrily. How the devil had Duncan found out about Constance? He'd not even known she was a woman until his arrival yesterday.

"Yes. Her name is Lady Westbury."

"Westbury." Duncan frowned. "Isn't that the name of the chap who died in Cairo a couple of years ago?"

"The same." His terse response made his friend turn his head to look at him.

"If I recall correctly, Westbury was involved with that Standish fellow. The one who's been trying to buy that papyrus your family's held for years."

"She's Westbury's widow."

"Interesting."

"You say that as if there's a mystery here," he said in a cool tone.

"Well I admit to finding it a bit odd that a *woman* is cataloging your antiquities." Duncan sent him an inquisitive look. "We both know it's a highly unusual occupation for a female."

"I didn't know she was a woman when I offered her the post. I relied on our correspondence and the references she provided me. None of them referred to her feminine aspects. In fact, it wasn't until yesterday that I discovered the truth."

"I thought you would have sent her packing. I know how you despise being lied to." Duncan smiled at him.

"Actually, she didn't really lie. She simply didn't inform me that she was a woman. Despite the extraordinary means by which she secured her position, I decided to retain her services. I find her knowledge exceptional, and her work is precisely what I need to ensure my antiquities are categorized appropriately."

"And what about her relationship to Westbury?"

"Get to the point, Duncan." Irritated, he narrowed his eyes as he met his friend's contemplative gaze.

"From what you've told me, Standish is a devious sort. You don't suppose he's hired Lady Westbury to steal the papyrus do you?"

"Anything's possible, but I don't think the lady in question is a thief," he said firmly. "And she's already denied knowing Standish."

"I take it the lady is quite attractive?"

"What the devil is that supposed to mean?"

"It means the lady was married to a man who was partners with Standish, and she acquired her post in a somewhat devious manner. It leaves the impression that Lady Westbury has the strong potential to be trouble for you when it comes to that papyrus."

Irritated by his friend's astute observations, he glared at the other man. "And you think I've not already considered those possibilities? I'm not a fool, Duncan."

"I know you're not, which tells me there's more to your Lady Westbury than you're telling me." There was a glint of mischief in the other man's eyes as he chuckled.

"Damn it, man," Lucien snapped. "She's my employee, not my mistress."

His friend's obvious amusement was all the more annoying because his statement was already half a lie. When Duncan pulled his horse to a sudden halt, Lucien experienced a sense of relief that his friend's attention was no longer devoted to teasing him about Constance.

"This is as far as I go, my friend. If I don't hurry, I'll be late for my appointment with Terrence Moore. But I'm looking forward to supper this evening. The usual time?"

"Yes, eight o'clock. And remember, Grandmother is a stickler about punctuality." With the subject of Constance receding into the background, he laughed at Duncan's pained expression. His friend had only been late to supper one time and had been paying the price ever since.

"I'll be early," his friend muttered as he shook Lucien's

hand then turned to ride away. Just before he prodded his horse with his heels, he grinned. "And I want an introduction to the esteemed Lady Westbury. She sounds like a very interesting woman."

With that parting shot, his friend rode off, leaving him to grit his teeth in frustration. If the man thought to vie for Constance's attentions, he was mistaken. He intended to see to it that Lady Westbury had little time to socialize with Major Duncan Fenwick.

As for the papyrus and its clues to the location of Sefu's tomb, the only way Constance was going to find the damn thing was if she dared to enter his room. And if she was that bold, he'd be certain to keep her so well occupied, she'd have no time to search for Sefu's papyrus.

Chapter Six

Lucien turned toward the salon doorway as his grandmother entered the room. The soft thud of her cane against the thick Moorish rug on the floor tapped out a simple rhythm as she walked. Beside her, Edward Rawlings served as her escort, his manner solicitous as he seated her in her usual chair. Pleased to see his father's childhood friend, Lucien stepped forward as the older man turned to look at him.

With avuncular familiarity, Rawlings took a quick step forward and embraced Lucien in a hearty hug. Pushing him back, the older man's large hands grasped Lucien's shoulders as he grinned.

"It's high time you returned to the keep, Lucien. Aurora's been as prickly as a hedgehog waiting on you to leave the pleasures of London behind. How are you, my boy?"

"Quite well, thank you, Edward."

"Aurora tells me you've brought back a new treasure stash of Egyptian antiquities."

"I did, and did she tell you that I found an unusual statue of Isis?"

"*No*, she failed to mention *that* fact," he said as he shot a brief look of exasperation over his shoulder at the dowager countess. "So tell me—is it the one? Have you found the goddess?"

"I'm waiting on my antiquities librarian to study the piece and give her opinion, but I think this statue might be the one."

Rawlings's grin widened as he clapped his hands together. "Capital, my boy. Capital."

"The two of you are acting like schoolboys over this ridiculous statue." Aurora glared at them down the length of her regal nose. "Surely you don't really think you could have found the right one."

Lucien turned his attention back to his grandmother and shrugged. "We'll know soon enough whether the statue is a fraud or not. I trust Lady Westbury's opinion in the matter."

"I say," the older man said with surprise. "Lady Westbury? Are you telling me your librarian is a woman?"

"Yes, and quite competent I might add. She's extremely knowledgeable." He'd barely finished his sentence when a flash of color caught his eye and he turned toward the door. As Constance entered the room, he heard Edward choke back a cough of astonishment.

"Good God, Lucien—" the older man leaned toward him, "—don't tell me *she's* your cataloger."

It was easy to understand the older man's reaction to Constance's arrival. She looked exquisite. Suddenly feeling the urge to drink a stiff whiskey, he wheeled away and strode to the sidebar against the far wall. Standing in the doorway of the salon, she'd not only taken Edward's breath away, she'd made it difficult for him to breathe as well.

God, he'd been mad to ask her to stay. An ironic thought given the Blakemore tendency to madness. It was becoming clear how difficult it was going to be to keep his wits about him whenever he was anywhere near her. Struggling to regain control of his senses, he poured himself a stiff drink. He didn't need to look at her to remember how lovely she was.

Swaths of pleated folds crossed just below her breasts, rising upward to cup her soft, full shape. The sleeves of her gown barely crested her shoulder as the bodice dipped to a low vee. The peach silk of her gown emphasized the soft golden tones of her complexion. Unlike the milk-sop women he'd seen in London, Constance's skin had a creamy, sun-kissed glow to it. Even the dusky sheen of her high cheekbones added to her exotic charms. She looked radiant, and every muscle in his body was tugging him in her direction.

Amber liquid splashed into his snifter one more time, and he threw the fiery drink down his throat. It burned its way to his stomach, but it gave him something to focus on besides *her.*

Slowly turning around, he watched in silence as his grandmother introduced Constance to Edward.

"Constance, let me introduce you to an old friend of the family, Edward Rawlings."

"Rawlings? Are you by chance related to Sir Oliver Rawlings?" Constance frowned slightly as she asked the question.

"My son." Pride filled the older man's voice. "The Queen bestowed a title on him for his archeological contributions to Britain. Have you met him?"

"No, although I believe he's an acquaintance of my friend, Mrs. Armstrong," she said quietly.

"Ah yes, Oliver mentioned her in one of his letters." Edward bowed over Constance's hand. "If she's as lovely as you, then my son will be a lucky man."

The flattery brought a smile to her lips, and it irritated him. She'd never smiled at him like that. From across the room, his gaze met hers and her smile faltered. Blast, one would think him an ogre the way she was staring at him. Nodding a curt greeting in her direction, he moved forward to where the others stood.

"Good evening, Lady Westbury."

"My lord," she murmured with a brief nod.

There was a breathless quality to her voice that aroused savage urges in his body. Clenching his teeth at the way his body responded to her, he cleared his throat. "How is your work progressing?"

As he waited for her to respond, he watched the pulse throbbing on the side of her neck reflect the quickening of her heartbeat. The sight fascinated him, and he steeled himself not to reach out and run his fingers over her soft skin. He saw her swallow quickly, and a streak of satisfaction whipped through him. Despite her serene manner, she was far from calm in his presence.

"Yes, dear lady," Edward said warmly. "How did you leave Lucien's precious collection? I understand from him that you're quite the authority."

"I'm grateful his lordship finds my skills adequate enough to catalog his collection," she said quietly as her gaze flickered toward him before focusing on the older gentleman. "Actually, I was able to accomplish a great deal today. I studied and cataloged fifteen more items in the collection."

Astonished, Rawlings's bushy white eyebrows went up in a skeptical arch. "That many in one day?"

"Several items were quite similar and required less study than most of the other pieces."

"And did you find anything of particular interest?" Lucien clasped his hands behind his back as he sent her a steady look, well aware of what her answer to his question would be. Earlier in the day, he'd placed the statue of Isis in plain view for her to find. Now he was curious to know her reaction.

"You know I did, my lord." Pique mixed with excitement as she scowled at him briefly. "It's extraordinary."

"Harrumph. So what is it that you've found, girl? A one-of-a-kind object or is it that ungodly statue of Isis?" The dowager countess's voice was querulous as she interjected her questions into the conversation.

Surprised, Constance sent his grandmother a curious look. "You know about the statue, my lady?"

"Of course, I do," she snorted with derision. "It's been the obsession of every Blakemore for more than three generations."

"Hardly an obsession, grandmother." Lucien arched an eyebrow in irritation. "A keen interest, perhaps."

"It's an obsession. It has been since your great-grandfather supposedly gained possession of the first statue." There was a bitter note of pain in the dowager's voice as she glared at him.

"The first statue, my lady?" Constance sent his grandmother a puzzled look.

"A statue of Seth, the god of Chaos." Disgust tipped the woman's mouth downward. "Without it, the Isis figurine is simply another artifact."

"I don't understand." Confusion marred Constance's lovely face as she turned toward him.

His gaze locked with his grandmother's as he shook his head in a gesture of annoyance. There had been too many times in the past when she'd expressed her disapproval of his searching for the statues. She blamed the death of his grandfather on the Seth statue.

Aurora had convinced herself his grandfather and great-grandfather had argued bitterly over the statue until the father had murdered the son. It might have been a plausible argument with the exception of one thing.

There was no Seth statue. At least not one anyone had ever found. His grandmother wanted to believe her father-in-law had accidentally killed her husband in a fit of anger before taking his own life out of grief. Getting her to believe the Blakemore curse had been the real cause of their deaths was an impossible task.

If there was one thing Aurora Blakemore was, it was stubborn. Once she made up her mind about something, there was nothing anyone could do to make her think differently, short of providing her irrefutable proof she was wrong. Still watching his grandmother, he offered Constance a brief explanation about the statue's history.

"Family legend has it that my great-grandfather returned from Egypt with a statue of Seth that he received as a gift from the family he was staying with in Cairo. Supposedly, when the statue was interlocked with its mate, a statue of Isis, it unlocked a secret compartment that contains part of a map to the tomb of Sefu, high priest of Seth."

"Bah!" The dowager countess cracked her cane on the floor, causing Constance and Edward to start with surprise. "The statue of Seth doesn't exist any more than the labyrinth does."

"And yet the markings on the Isis statue I found are identical to the ones described in the papyrus my great-grandfather brought home from his trip to Egypt. A rather *odd* coincidence, wouldn't you say, my lady?" His gaze locked with hers until she looked away.

"At least Nigel had the good sense not to run off in search of a myth," she snapped in a waspish tone.

The unexpected surge of rage whipping through him took every ounce of self-control he possessed not to respond to his grandmother's words. She never missed an opportunity to bludgeon him with guilt for spending so much time away from Lyndham Keep. He understood why she did it. It was her way of reminding him how much she'd lost, and that she didn't want to lose him as well. Normally her words didn't elicit any emotion in him. But tonight, for some inexplicable reason, her comment infuriated him.

He enjoyed his expeditions. They were far more enlightening than any London social he'd ever attended. More importantly, he was tired of Nigel being held up to him like a martyr. Especially when his brother had taken leave of his senses the day he chose to murder Katherine and kill himself. The tension tightening every muscle in his body made him ache, and it was a great relief when Jacobs announced Duncan's arrival. Turning sharply away from his grandmother, he watched his friend cross the room toward their small gathering.

Bowing over the hand of his hostess, Duncan smiled. "Lady Lyndham, thank you for tolerating my company this evening."

"You're a scoundrel, Major Fenwick, and you know it. What Lucien sees in you is beyond me, but at least you're on time this evening." Despite her crisp tone, there was a twinkle of amusement in Aurora's blue eyes.

With a laugh, Duncan shook his head. "I doubt I'll ever be late to one of your functions again, my lady."

"I would expect no less." Aurora gave him a sharp nod as Duncan turned away from her to accept Edward's hearty handshake.

"Major Fenwick, a pleasure to see you again. I was delighted to hear that Lucien had invited you to supper this evening."

"Always a pleasure, Mr. Rawlings. How is your son doing with his business investments in Cairo and Istanbul?"

"Quite well, I believe." Edward frowned slightly. "He seldom visits me here in the country, so it's difficult to know from one month to the next how he's faring."

With a nod of understanding, Duncan turned toward Constance, and the glint of appreciation in his friend's eyes stirred a beast inside Lucien that he instinctively suppressed. Bowing, Duncan took Constance's hand and kissed the tips of her fingers as Lucien introduced them.

"Lucien tells me your knowledge of ancient antiquities is exceptional, Lady Westbury. I'm interested to know if he's actually managed to bring back anything of real value from his sojourn in the desert."

The smile curving her mouth sent a charge of electric current through Lucien. Damn. That was twice tonight she'd exhibited the full radiance of her charms on a man other than him.

"I believe it's quite possible his lordship has indeed returned with at least one noteworthy treasure." Soft and sultry, her voice made Duncan lean into her.

The primitive urge to put himself between the two of them was so strong, Lucien's jaw cried out from the way he ground his teeth together. Damnation, he needed to control these irrational emotions. Given his family history, they would only lead him down the path to hell.

Even though the woman was an enchantress, he had no intention of giving way to anything but lust where she was concerned. But watching her smile at everyone except him darkened his mood. Why the devil did she avoid even looking at him? The note of surprise in Duncan's voice intruded upon his thoughts.

"Rockwood. You're Percy Rockwood's sister?" A smile of delight accompanied the pleased astonishment in his friend's voice. "Percy mentioned one of his sisters enjoyed studying antiquities, but he never mentioned how lovely you were."

Laughing, Constance shook her head. "You're too kind, Major Fenwick, but your gallantry is most appreciated."

Blast Duncan to hell. The man had always been popular with the ladies, and now he had something in common with Constance. It was becoming decidedly unpleasant listening to the two of them converse as if they were old friends. The last thing he wanted was Duncan showing up on his doorstep every day with the eagerness of a besotted suitor. He grimaced at the thought as his friend turned toward him. Amusement curled Duncan's lips upward as he arched an eyebrow at him.

"That's a devilish scowl, Lucien."

"I wasn't aware I was scowling," he said through clenched teeth. Duncan simply grinned as he shook his head. The smug expression of perception on the other man's face intensified his fierce glare.

"So where is this artifact you wanted to show me?" Duncan

asked. "Do we have time before our meal to view this ancient marvel?"

Eager for a distraction, he nodded sharply. "It's in the library. I think you and Edward will find it most interesting. Grandmother, do you wish to come?"

"No," she said with just a trace of her earlier irritation. "I prefer to stay here until Jacobs announces supper."

"As you wish." He bowed in sharp acknowledgment of her reply then led the way out of the salon and into the library where the statue stood on the long table with the other cataloged artifacts. After his morning ride, he'd visited the library. Constance had been absent, but he'd deliberately pulled the statue out and placed it in clear view for her to find. Now, as he entered the library, he saw she'd moved it to the center of the table.

The coolness of the gold beneath his hands had always surprised him when he held the heavy statue. It was exquisitely molded in the form of Isis, goddess of fire and love. The detailed etching on the face showed incredible workmanship. Even more interesting was the hieroglyphic inscription etched into the side and base of the statue. The translation depicted Isis waiting patiently to take the god Seth to her bosom to avenge the murder of her husband, Osirus.

Turning around, he handed the statue to Edward. The older man's hands shook slightly as he accepted the beautiful artifact. "By God, boy. I think you've found it. This must be the one."

"Do you see anything unusual on the side?" Lucien pointed to the small indentation on the side of the statue.

Constance stepped closer to peer at the statue the older man held, her body a hair's breadth from Lucien. The sweetness of her scent floated beneath his nose, and he struggled not to lean forward and drink in a deep breath of her perfume.

"Good heavens," she exclaimed. "I was so busy translating the inscriptions, I didn't even see this. It looks like a hole for a pin to slide into. A locking mechanism of some sort."

"Exactly!" Edward said with excitement as he looked up at Lucien. "It's just like the papyrus describes, my boy! This is the one. Now if only we had the other statue. It must be here in the keep somewhere."

Rawlings handed the statue to Duncan, and Lucien shook his head at the older man's enthusiastic statement.

"Unfortunately, I'm going to have to concur with Grandmother. I don't think the labyrinth exists, and if the Seth statue were in the keep, someone would have discovered it by now. You know full well we've searched every nook and cranny in this godforsaken place."

Edward shook his head fiercely. "No. I can't believe that. It's here, Lucien, I know it."

"What is this labyrinth you're talking about?" Constance looked at Lucien directly, her lovely hazel eyes filled with curiosity.

Steeling himself not to be swayed by her charms, he cleared his throat. "It's said the builders of the keep included an elaborate set of passageways behind the walls. More than a dozen entrances were said to have been skillfully hidden throughout the fortress, allowing the first Blakemores to come and go undetected by enemies storming the castle. But any knowledge of the hidden entrances was lost long ago, if they ever even existed. As I just told Edward, I'm inclined to agree with my grandmother that the labyrinth is simply a family myth and nothing more."

Duncan nodded as he handed the statue back to Edward, who resumed his study of the object with an almost obsessive look in his eyes.

"I'm going to agree with Lucien on this, Rawlings," Duncan said firmly. "We've all hunted for an entrance into the labyrinth, but no one's ever found one. In all the years Nigel and Oliver played here as children, and all the time Lucien and I did the same, none of us found any evidence of a labyrinth."

"Nigel?" Constance's quiet query made him stiffen slightly.

"My brother. He died several years ago."

"I'm sorry," she murmured as she averted her gaze. "That must have been a difficult time for you."

Not about to delve into the pain-ridden past, he shook his head. "Sympathy is unnecessary."

"I say," Edward exclaimed as he peered intently at the

bottom of the statue. "Look at this! Is this another pin hole, Lady Westbury?"

Constance immediately turned toward Rawlings and stretched out her hands to take the statue the older man was offering to her. She smiled at him as her hands wrapped around the gold artifact, which was now warm from being handled so much. An instant later, the statue grew ice cold in her palms. She tried to let go, but her fingers remained wrapped around the statue, frozen in place.

The familiar sensations of her surreal gift abruptly flooded her senses. As the room spun around her with increasing speed, her stomach lurched unpleasantly. This time she was simply an observer. It was impossible to tell where she was. In the darkness, there was no sense of time or place.

Suddenly, a light flickered in the black night. She was in a room made of nothing but stone. Devoid of decoration, the room was lit only by a single branch of candles. Shadows loomed large against the wall as two men argued. The silence was almost deafening as she tried to hear what they were saying, but there was no sound at all. The darkness obscured even their faces, and she could only see their shadows painted on the stone behind them as the light illuminated and reflected their bodies onto the wall.

Anger contorted their figures as they shouted at each other. One was taller and portly. He gave her the impression he was the oldest. It was reflected in the way he argued. There was a stately, restrained demeanor to his movements. He displayed his fury with slower, more sharply defined gestures than the other man.

The younger of the two was far more flamboyant in his gestures. His was the posturing of a man in his prime. He would turn and walk away from the taller man in obvious frustration, before he turned around to argue another point.

She was so focused on the two men that she didn't see anything else at first. She heard it. It was a soft sound, but it was the only noise to break the silence. Fingernails scraping across a mahogany table could not have been any louder. Then she saw it. A third shadow on the wall.

It was small and moved swiftly toward the younger man.

There was no warning, only the sudden shock of one man frozen in mid-sentence, his arms outstretched almost as if in surrender. The shadow behind him was merely a shape with only an Egyptian blade glinting in the candlelight as it plunged into the man's back.

Horror filled the man's silent death scream, and she nearly sobbed with the desire to hear it piercing her ears. But it didn't. The only noise breaking the silence was the terrible hiss of the blade slashing into the man over and over again.

As the dying man slid toward the floor, the candlelight sketched out his features with startling clarity. It was enough time for her to recognize the dying man, and she cried out in surprise. The man crumpled to his death, leaving two shadows illuminated on the wall. The older man shouted his fury and leaped forward. But with a single strike, the smaller shadow slit the older man's throat in one swift stroke.

His movements quick and efficient, the murderer calmly rolled his last victim over onto his back. From a pocket in his coat, the shadow retrieved a second Egyptian dagger and casually dipped the blade in the dead man's blood. Revolted by the murderer's utter disregard for his victim, she shuddered and prayed for the vision to end. Seconds later, the newly bloodied blade was tucked into the hand of the old man. It was impossible to see the shadow's face, but she could feel his satisfaction. He was pleased with his handiwork, and it sickened her. With one last look around him, the shadow doused the candles with a single breath.

The darkness swallowed her whole again and she struggled not to feel any fear. Trembling, she fought down the panic threatening to overwhelm her. It was a vision, nothing more. There was nothing to be afraid of. Slowly, the darkness ebbed away and her body grew warm as a strong hand gripped her waist and held her close to a hard chest. Lucien. Even with her eyes closed she recognized his scent, his sinewy muscles. There was a sudden chorus of concerned male voices as the silence evaporated into a loud cacophony of noise.

"Constance." The rough edge to his voice brushed over her. "Damnation, woman, answer me."

"Good God, what the devil is wrong with her?" Edward's voice was easy to make out and she shuddered at his close proximity.

He had died. She'd seen Edward Rawlings die. No. It had to be someone else. The man in her vision had been much younger. There had to be some other reason she'd witnessed this scene. She drank in a sharp breath of air as her eyes fluttered open, and she stared up into Lucien's cerulean blue eyes. A flash of emotion flared in his gaze before he replaced it with a calm detachment.

"Are you all right, Lady Westbury?"

Aware that she needed to explain her sudden incapacitation, she raised a hand to her brow in a confused gesture. "I'm sorry. I must have fainted for a moment. It happens to me sometimes. The doctors have never been able to explain it."

Still caught tightly against Lucien, she absorbed the heat of his body. As she lowered her hand, it came to rest on his shoulder, and she waited for him to release her. He did so immediately, but his withdrawal was slow—almost reluctant. She sucked in a quick breath as she realized she didn't want him to let her go. For a fraction of a second, his fingers tightened against her waist, and his eyes narrowed with a flash of emotion that sent a rush of excitement through her.

"Are you certain you're all right, dear lady?"

Edward Rawlings's voice broke the tenuous connection between her and Lucien as she moved out of his arms. Smoothing the material of her skirts, she turned toward the older gentleman and smiled. "Yes, I'm fine. I apologize for troubling each of you."

"Nonsense," Major Fenwick scoffed gently. "You have nothing to apologize for. We're simply delighted that you're all right."

"Yes, Duncan is right. You have no need to apologize." Lucien's breath warmed the bare skin of her shoulder. It was a reminder of how close he still was to her.

She avoided looking at him for fear her face would reveal the sudden need skimming through her body. The need for his touch was so strong she was certain everyone could see it in her expression. As Jacobs coughed quietly in the library doorway and announced supper, she breathed a sigh of relief.

Edward Rawlings quickly stepped forward and offered her his arm. "If you feel up to joining us for supper, my lady, I would be delighted to take you into the dining room."

The older man's pleasant expression made her falter slightly. The resemblance was so startling, and yet she knew the man in her vision couldn't have been Edward Rawlings. None of it made sense. She shivered. Whose death had she just witnessed? Only time would answer that question. Accepting Rawlings's arm, she forced a smile to her lips and allowed him to escort her to the dining room.

�)�

With supper finished the small party moved to the salon. As he entered the room, Lucien saw Constance bend solicitously over his grandmother.

"Are you well, my lady?" she asked with a gentle touch of the dowager's blue-veined hand. "Would you like me to have Jacobs bring you a cup of tea?"

With a wave of her hand, Aurora frowned. "Thank you, no, Lady Westbury. I'm a little tired this evening, but I was hoping I could persuade you to play the piano for me. I love music, and we so seldom entertain."

"Unfortunately, I don't play the piano, my lady. That talent was reserved for my oldest brother, Sebastian."

"Good Lord," Aurora exclaimed. "Do you mean to tell me you didn't learn how to play the piano? Every woman of good breeding knows how to at least stroke the keys of the blasted thing."

"I'm afraid I banged on the keys too loudly for Sebastian, and he bought me a violin instead. I'm sure there were times when he deeply regretted that act, but I have a passable talent for the instrument, it seems."

Her dry note of humor forced Lucien to bite back a smile. Why did he think there had been moments when she'd deliberately played badly?

"I want to hear you play." The command in Aurora's voice said the dowager refused to take no for an answer.

"Oh, but—"

"Not another word. Is the instrument in your room?" Aurora vigorously rang the bell she always kept on the table beside her. Constance nodded as Jacobs hurried into the room. "Jacobs, send someone up to Lady Westbury's room to retrieve her violin."

Armed with instructions, the butler left the room as the gentlemen joined her and Lady Lyndham in the salon. Seeing Jacobs scurrying out of the room, Mr. Rawlings grinned as he approached the older woman.

"It appears Jacobs is on another mission. What have you sent him to do this time, Aurora?"

"I sent him to fetch Lady Westbury's violin. I wanted to hear some music this evening, and she doesn't play the piano. However, she apparently knows how to play the violin."

"The violin?" Major Fenwick smiled at her. "It's one of my favorite instruments."

"How can you have a favorite instrument when you're tone deaf?" Lucien snapped.

Grinning, Duncan shook his head. "I'm never tone deaf when a beautiful woman is involved, Lucien."

With a grunt of disgust, Lucien turned away from his friend and walked to the sidebar. He'd been drinking more than usual tonight, but it eased the pain inside him. All during the evening meal, he'd been witness to Duncan's and Edward's flirtations with Constance. With each passing course of the meal, his mood had darkened as he battled with the demons clamoring at his doorstep.

Brandy splashed into a crystal snifter. One glance at the amount in the glass convinced him to double the quantity. He poured it down his throat in a long gulp. A strong hand settled on his shoulder, and he turned his head to see Edward eyeing him with an intent look.

"What the devil are you doing? I've not seen you drink this much since Nigel—in years."

"Leave me alone, Edward."

"I'd be happy to, my dear boy, but I'm afraid you're forgetting that Duncan is flirting with your lovely Lady Westbury."

Anger lashed through him as he shot a quick look over his shoulder to where Duncan and Constance were standing at the piano, their heads close together as they discussed what music she would perform. It made him crave another drink. He reached for the decanter, but Edward's hand fell on his wrist.

"Don't be an ass, Lucien. If you want to drive the woman away from you, you're doing an exceptional job."

"I don't know what you're talking about," he muttered as he shook off Edward's light touch. But he refrained from picking up the decanter.

"No? Then I'll tell you. If it were possible, Duncan and I would have died a thousand deaths tonight from the looks we received from you at the supper table."

Despite the knowledge that Edward was right, he glared at the older man. "If my looks made you uncomfortable, then perhaps you're feeling a touch guilty at flirting with a woman half your age."

His dangerous snarl made Rawlings shake his head in disgust. "I enjoy Lady Westbury's company. And I think you would too, if you'd forget this ridiculous curse and savor life. Both of us know how short it can be."

With that, Edward walked away from him. Turning around, he surveyed the scene in front of him. Duncan said something witty as he sat in a nearby chair. The remark pulled a laugh from Constance as she tucked her violin under her chin. He ached with jealousy that he'd not been the one to amuse her. Aurora and Edward, seated next to each other, offered her their full attention as with a smile she pulled the bow across the violin strings.

Watching Constance move as she played the violin was excruciating. There was so much passion in her movements it was almost unbearable to watch. He wanted to sweep her off her feet and carry her up to his bedroom where he'd make love to her repeatedly throughout the night.

The need to do so snarled deep in his soul and possessed him with the fury of a wild animal. Bitterly, he fought down the raging beast inside him that was growing more powerful every day. His craving for the woman was quickly becoming unmanageable. If he lost control of his desire for her, God only knew what he was capable of doing. And looking to God served no purpose, for God had abandoned the Blakemores to their curse a long time ago. With a muffled noise of frustration, he stormed from the room, uncaring of what anyone thought of his abrupt departure.

Chapter Seven

Constance crossed the floor of her bedroom to look out over the keep's gardens. Splashes of varying hues of pink, red and yellow dotted the flowerbeds, while the trees swayed gently in the soft breeze. Today promised to be a glorious day. Even through the windowpanes she could feel the sun warming the air outside. It was perfect for an afternoon picnic, something she'd promised Jamie several days ago when he and Imogene had returned to the house after playing in the garden.

A lone figure on horseback streaking across the pasture in the distance made her heart skip a beat as she tried to make out the rider. She sighed with frustration as she accepted the fact it wasn't Lucien. It had been more than a month since the dinner party and his abrupt departure from the salon.

The memory of that morning in the library returned to haunt her, and heat flushed her skin at the manner in which she'd seduced Lucien—pleasured him. There had been little doubt that she'd pleased him, but the awkwardness that followed had made her wish she'd never come to Lyndham Keep.

Despite his reassurance he'd found her adventurous touch enjoyable, she still experienced doubt over her impulsive behavior. What on earth had possessed her to even contemplate performing such an intimate act on him? The erotic papyrus text of the Mystical Rites of Isis had been little more than a flicker in her head one minute, and in the next she was pleasuring him with an act she was certain no woman of society would know about. It was certainly nothing she and Graham had ever discussed, let alone done in the privacy of their bedroom.

Oddly enough, the thought of doing such an act with anyone else but Lucien made her flinch. For some strange reason, when she'd kissed and stroked him so intimately, it had seemed perfectly natural. Her fingertips touched her mouth at the memory.

Had he really found her actions acceptable? It was hard to believe given his quick departure the next morning. He'd left for London at the break of dawn without even saying goodbye to his grandmother or Imogene. She found that surprising because she'd seen how fond he was of the dowager countess.

When she'd heard he was gone, she'd experienced a mixture of relief and disappointment. She had hoped his absence would make matters easier for her, but she'd been wrong. With each passing day, she found herself listening for his voice or his footsteps in the main hall.

Irritated she was even thinking about the man, she grimaced and shook her head. Even Nigel's spirit had decided to remain silent during Lucien's absence. Now she regretted her decision to help solve the mystery surrounding Lucien and his family.

There was still little to glean from the visions she had. Everything was a crazy patchwork of clues. She'd tried for days to piece them together in a coherent fashion and had failed. Exasperated with her train of thought, she knew the best way to solve the riddle was to let it go and simply focus on something else. Determined to do just that, she left her room and went downstairs to resume her daily task of cataloging the antiquities in the library. On her way she stopped in at the kitchen to arrange for a lunch basket for an afternoon picnic.

The morning passed quickly as she immersed herself in deciphering two bas-reliefs she'd had several of the footmen remove from their crates the day before. Lost in beauty of the intricate detail of the artwork, she jumped violently when a hand touched her shoulder. Whirling around, she stared into Lady Lyndham's amused expression.

"Forgive me, my dear, but I did try to capture your attention several times." She smiled. "The only other person I know who can become so absorbed in these artifacts is my grandson."

Still recovering from the surprise of the dowager countess's appearance, Constance simply nodded her understanding as her heartbeat escalated at the mention of Lucien. Laying her tools on the workbench, she dusted off her hands.

"Forgive me, my lady. I often lose track of time and place when I'm working."

"That is plainly evident." The old woman smiled broadly. It lightened her aged face considerably. "However, I have two young scamps eager to go on a picnic, which they tell me you've arranged."

Glancing at the watch pinned to her dress, Constance grimaced. "I completely forgot the time. I'll come straight away."

With a nod of her white head, the dowager countess headed toward the door before coming to a sudden halt. As the elderly lady stopped, Constance saw the mist forming next to her. The figure shimmered in the air next to Lady Lyndham, and Constance suppressed a gasp as she recognized the man she'd seen in her vision the night of the dinner party.

Even though she was elderly, Lady Lyndham's hearing was excellent and she turned her head sharply toward Constance. "You feel it too, don't you?"

Not about to lie to the woman, she nodded. "Yes, my lady."

A look of sorrow touched the ghost's face as he reached out to touch the dowager countess's shoulder. As his hand brushed against her, Lady Lyndham uttered a soft cry.

"William? Is that you, my love?"

The man nodded his head at Lady Lyndham's tremulous query as he once again tried to touch the woman's cheek. The intensity of love on his features was painful to watch as Lady Lyndham closed her eyes and tilted her head toward the invisible energy of the ghost.

Watching their silent interaction, Constance bit back tears at the love and pain on both their faces. The ghost turned his head toward her, the silent plea in his gaze heart wrenching. Quickly, she shook her head no. How could she explain to Lady Lyndham that the man she'd called out to was standing next to her?

"William, please. Give me a sign that it's you. Please my love. I miss you so much." The heartfelt plea nearly broke Constance's heart as the dowager countess touched her cheek, her hand brushing through the spirit's shimmering shape.

Once more the ghost looked in Constance's direction, his gaze now an autocratic demand. She recognized the expression as one she'd seen on Lucien's face on more than one occasion. Her decision made, she inhaled a quick breath then released it in a soft whoosh.

"He's here, my lady," she said quietly. "He's standing right next to you."

The dowager countess turned her head sharply to meet Constance's steady gaze. "You can see him?"

"Yes, my lady." She nodded slowly as the older woman's face filled with hope and disbelief.

"Then describe him to me," Aurora demanded hoarsely. "And take care with your words, Lady Westbury. I will know if you're lying."

Swallowing the sudden wave of fear that swept over her, Constance squared her shoulders. "He's taller than you, my lady. Tall and lithe in form. His hair is dark, like the color of coal. I believe he has brown eyes, although it's difficult to tell."

"You could be describing any number of men, Lady Westbury," Aurora snapped. "Tell me something specific. Can't you talk to him?"

"I'm sorry, my lady, he's not strong enough to communicate that way." Constance spread her hands helplessly at her inability to give the woman what she wanted to hear.

"Of course not," Aurora sneered. "Why would he when we both know ghosts aren't real?"

The ghost's face grew angry as he wagged his finger at the elderly lady. Despite his inability for anyone to hear him, he was arguing with her fiercely. With a glare at Constance, he grimaced with frustration as she shook her head in confusion. The ghost's ire grew as he desperately looked around for something.

An expression of satisfaction settled on his face as he floated across the room and pointed to a bootjack beside the French door leading outside. Confused, she shook her head.

"I don't understand."

"What are you babbling about, Lady Westbury?" The cold

anger in Lady Lyndham's voice sent a chill through Constance.

She recognized that note of disdain and disbelief. She'd heard it often enough when people had learned about her gift. Befuddled by the ghost's behavior, she heaved a vexed sigh as the ghost moved to a statue of Alexander's horse, Bucephalus. With an apologetic grimace, the spirit pointed to the rear of the horse. Thoroughly confused, Constance shook her head.

"What are you trying to say?"

The ghost pointed at the bootjack and then the rear of the horse repeatedly before pointing to Lady Lyndham. Baffled by what the spirit was trying to say, she met the older woman's cold gaze.

"He's pointing to the bootjack and then the horse, my lady. Do either of these mean anything to you?"

"Certainly not." The old woman turned away and started to walk out of the room, her cane beating a sharp tap of anger against the floor. "In fact, I've grown weary of all your posturing, Lady Westbury. You obviously take me for a fool."

At that moment, a tingling sensation tickled her throat. Thinking she was about to cough, she raised her hand, but not quickly enough. "Jackass."

Horrified, she clamped her hand over her mouth as the dowager countess came to an abrupt halt before slowly turning around to face her. Constance shook her head with dismay.

"I'm terribly sorry, my lady. Please forgive me. I don't know what prompted me to say such a thing."

"William." Heartfelt emotion filled the single word as Lady Lyndham closed her eyes and a small smile tilted the corners of her mouth.

Turning toward the ghost, Constance saw him return to the dowager countess's side, an expression of satisfaction on his transparent features. Tenderly, William reached out to brush his fingertips across Lady Lyndham's face, and her smile brightened.

"He's really here, isn't he, Constance?"

"Yes, my lady. He's here." Her voice hitched at the love and longing emanating from the woman and ghost.

"He always said for me not to be a stubborn jackass when I

was objecting to something he wanted me to do." Lady Lyndham's voice was soft, almost ethereal, as she spoke with her eyes still closed. A broad grin tilted the corners of William's mouth as he nodded.

"He's agreeing with you, my lady."

"He would." Aurora laughed. "My husband always liked to be right, didn't you, my dearest love."

The dowager countess opened her eyes to look around her, trying to see what she couldn't. Already Constance could tell William's energy was fading, and she bit her lip. "I'm sorry, my lady, but he's growing weak. I don't think he'll be here much longer."

"No, William. Don't leave me. There's so much I want to say to you. Don't go." The anguish in the older woman's voice tore at Constance's heart.

She watched as William drew close to his wife and gently tried to brush at the tears streaming down wrinkled cheeks. The movement was done with such love and tenderness that Constance turned her head away simply because it was such a private act of adoration. Swallowing hard, she blinked her eyes rapidly, trying not to cry.

An instant later she knew the ghost was gone. A sob poured out of the dowager countess's throat, and Constance hurried to her side, afraid the woman would collapse onto the floor. With a gentle yet firm hand, she guided the elderly woman to one of the nearby chairs. Kneeling at the woman's feet, she rubbed Lady Lyndham's cold hands for several seconds in an attempt to warm her.

"Forgive me, my dear, for doubting you. I've been disappointed so many times before, I just..." Aurora's voice died away as she closed her eyes. With a gentle squeeze of the old woman's hand, Constance bit back tears at the pain and sadness darkening Lady Lyndham's face.

"I understand, my lady. It's not easy to believe in something one can't see, hear or touch." Constance sighed with regret. "I wouldn't have even acknowledged his presence at all if I hadn't been so startled by his resemblance to Mr. Rawlings."

"Ah yes, the likeness between the two of them was always striking. They easily passed for the brothers they were. Half-brothers that is."

Constance stared at the woman in amazement. Once again, another piece of the puzzle had fallen into place. The problem was, she wasn't sure *where* it belonged. Lady Lyndham smiled at her.

"Edward was born on the wrong side of the blanket."

"Oh, I see," Constance murmured. The explanation made perfect sense now. In her vision, she'd witnessed William's death, not Edward's. But who was the older man? And the murderer's identity? Who was he and why had he killed? She shook her head in confusion and Aurora uttered a soft laugh.

"I suppose it does seem odd, doesn't it. The bastard included as one of the family. William and Edward were inseparable as children. They were as close as two brothers could be. Even after William and I were married, Edward remained a part of the family. In William's mind the only thing that separated the two of them was that Edward's mother, Maibe, was his father's mistress."

"What a beautiful name."

"She was Egyptian. William's father brought her back from Cairo with him. As I understand it, the old earl stayed with Maibe's parents when he visited Egypt on one of his expeditions."

"She must have loved him very much to leave her homeland."

"I suppose. She deeply resented William, though. She thought Edward should have been the one to have the Lyndham title." The dowager countess shrugged as her lips twisted in a bitter smile. Then with a deep sigh, she gave a small shake of her head. "Enough of the past. It's long dead and buried. As for you, my dear, I don't know how to thank you."

"There is no need to do so, my lady. If it brought you some measure of peace, I'm glad," Constance said with a smile.

"It's eased my mind greatly, Constance. You have no idea how many times I thought William might be with me, but was never certain of it until today."

"I'm certain he's visited you many times, my lady. I could tell he misses and loves you very much."

"Do you really think so?" Lady Lyndham clasped her hand

in a tight grip.

"Yes, my lady. I do. "

"He was never one to share his emotions easily. Every time I thought he was near I'd asked him for a sign it was him, but he never answered. I always thought it was my imagination. But he's been here all this time. He's never left me."

The catch in the woman's voice made Constance squeeze her hand in understanding. As if remembering something, Lady Lyndham frowned. The dowager countess cupped her chin and forced her to look directly at her.

"You mustn't tell any of this to Lucien." The insistence in the woman's voice chilled her.

"But if—"

"No. He won't believe you," Aurora snapped fiercely. "In fact, he'll be furious. He'll accuse you of pandering to my *hallucinations*. If there's one thing Lucien despises more than being lied to it's spiritualists and mediums."

Ice sluiced through her veins at the words, and she struggled not to cry out from the pain lashing through her. Why did it matter so much what Lucien believed? She didn't want to answer the question, but the way her heart ached told her it mattered a great deal. With a nod, she rose to her feet.

"I understand, my lady. I'll not reveal what happened here today."

"What is it, child? You look ill." Lady Lyndham grasped her hand. "Why, you're as cold as winter. Is this what happens when you have contact with the other side?"

Not about to divulge the source of her chill, Constance simply nodded. Better to let the woman think it was a reaction to the ghostly encounter rather than suspect the truth. Alarmed at the direction of her thoughts, she gently withdrew her hand from Lady Lyndham's.

"I'll be fine, my lady. If you'll forgive me, I should find Jamie and Imogene. I did promise to take them on a picnic."

"Of course," Aurora said with a puzzled note in her voice. "Thank you again, Constance. You've given me a peace that has eluded me for years. I can never thank you enough for that."

Nodding, she fled the library. In the main hall, she caught

the glimpse of a misty shadow near the salon, but she blocked it out. No. She didn't want to see any more ghosts. She didn't want any more visions. All she wanted was to be like everyone else. How many times had she expressed those thoughts to her sister Patience?

The cold stone of the hall matched the temperature of her hand as she paused to fight back tears. She was a fool to think there was any man who would care for her without being intimidated by her gift. It was too much to ask of anyone. Even Jamie. She swallowed hard. That was why she'd not told her son about her gift. Not because Graham would have disapproved.

She finally recognized the excuse for what it was. Fear had kept her from telling Jamie about her gift. Fear of losing his love and having him stare at her in horror. She blinked back tears at the realization. The usual tingling skated across the back of her neck, and she stiffened.

"No. Go away. I won't look at you, and I won't talk to you," she said with quiet vehemence. "Leave me *alone*."

Not even turning her head, she raced down the hall toward the kitchen. The warm aroma of baking bread drifted out into the corridor, and she stopped to wipe her cheeks dry. She had no intention of trying to explain to her son or anyone else the reasons for her tears.

Satisfied she was sufficiently poised, she forced a smile to her lips and entered the large cooking center to find Jamie and Imogene waiting impatiently for her. Grateful for something to divert her attention from the pain twisting her heart, her smile became genuine at the rowdy reception the two children gave her.

"Are the two of you ready for our little expedition?"

"Expedition?" Jamie exclaimed with enthusiasm. "What expedition?"

"Well I thought we'd venture past the gardens out into the pasture where you can search for Roman denarii and other artifacts."

"Were there really Romans at the keep, mother?" Jamie's voice held a skeptical note.

"I'm not sure about the keep, but I know they had several

legions based in this area. It's more than possible they might have dropped items to mark their stay here."

With a wild whoop, Jamie danced about the kitchen to the amusement of Cook and the scullery maids. Imogene shook her head and rolled her eyes as if to say her companion was far too excitable. Her heart lighter than when she'd first entered the kitchen, Constance laughed as she led the two out on their great adventure.

∞(∞

The sun was warm as Constance sat on the edge of the large blanket Cook had packed in the picnic basket. The remains of lunch were scattered across the soft spread, and she watched Jamie leading Imogene out into a field littered with stones and rocks of all shapes and sizes. They were involved in an exuberant discussion and she smiled at the way Imogene refused to go along with whatever it was Jamie wanted to do. With a shrug of disgust, her son turned and followed Lucien's niece off in the opposite direction. Chuckling, she shook her head. Jamie would never admit it, but he was already infatuated with Imogene.

The sound of a galloping horse pulled her attention away from the children, and she turned her head to see a lone rider approaching. Fear and hope burrowed its way through her at the thought Lucien had returned. Scrambling to her feet, she lifted her hand to her brow to shade her eyes. When she realized the rider was a stranger, her heart sank with disappointment.

The man slowed his horse to a trot, and a trickle of fear slid across her skin as he drew closer. There was something about the man she recognized as familiar, but she couldn't place what it was. Pulling the horse to a halt, the stranger dismounted.

Short and stocky, he had the swarthy complexion of a man accustomed to being in the sun. The desert sun. The comparison struck her as odd as he removed his hat and bowed in her direction.

"Lady Westbury. At last I have the honor of meeting you." The smoothness with which he delivered his greeting made her question the sincerity of his words.

"Do we know each other, sir?" Again fear tracked its way across her skin, leaving chill bumps in its wake. The black depths of the man's eyes made her think of a lifeless pool of brackish water.

"I confess, we were never introduced, my lady, but I was good friends with your late husband."

At the mention of Graham, she grew still. Something wasn't right. How had this man found her, and why would he approach her in the middle of a field? Swallowing the uneasy feelings rising inside her, she sent the man a questioning look. He bowed slightly.

"Forgive me, my lady. My name is Malcolm Standish. I was one of the investors who funded your husband's last expedition into Egypt."

The man's name made her frown. She recognized the name, but she couldn't recall Graham ever mentioning the man. Suddenly, she remembered where she'd heard this man's name before. Lucien had accused her of knowing a Malcolm Standish. When he'd charged her with being in collusion with the man, there had been a wild fury in his voice. Clearly Standish was a man to avoid unless she wanted to face Lucien's anger. Even if Lucien's fury weren't a matter of concern, her instincts warned her to stay away from this man.

"As I'm sure you know, Mr. Standish, my husband is dead. He has been for more than four years now."

"And I'm sorry for your loss, my lady. I should have paid my respects to you long ago. I have no excuse for such a lengthy delay."

"Perhaps you would care to explain why you've sought me out now? And I'm curious as to how you knew where to find me."

"Yes of course," Standish said with unexpected eagerness. "Everything in due course, my lady. I've come here to ask for your help."

"My help?" She glanced over her shoulder to ensure that Jamie and Imogene were still in sight. Her senses were now tingling with an edge that was growing decidedly uncomfortable.

"Precisely, my lady. I'm here to offer you whatever you ask

in exchange for your assistance in finding a statue." The man's words heightened her discomfort and she shook her head.

"I'm sorry, but I'm not sure how I can help you."

"I understand that you're working for Lord Lyndham. The gentleman in question took something that belonged to my...my family. It's of great sentimental value and we want to retrieve it."

"Has it occurred to you to discuss this matter with Lord Lyndham? I'm not in any position to speak for his lordship, and he's far from likely to listen to anything I have to say about your problem."

"Oh I've approached Lyndham," the man in front of her snarled softly, reminding her of the hyenas she'd seen in the Zoological Park in London. "The man refuses to discuss anything with me, which is why I am willing to offer you whatever you wish in exchange for your assistance in finding my statue."

"How can it be your statue if it's not in your possession, sir? I've not know the Earl of Lyndham for long, but I'm certain he isn't a thief."

Standish's face contorted into a mask of hate that sent fear flying through her body with the speed of a hawk in its dive. Determined not to yield to her fear, she didn't move as he took a step toward her.

"What you think isn't important, but you will help me find the statue I'm looking for. I won't allow you or anyone else to stop me from regaining what belongs to Seth."

Still frightened, she refused to let the man bully her. "I can't help you, Mr. Standish."

"Oh, but you will, Lady Westbury." The man once again imitated an angry hyena as he grabbed her by the arms and gave her a hard shake.

Familiar sensations flooded her senses as she recognized the onset of another vision. Panicked by the fact she was alone and at the mercy of the man holding her, she tried to stop the images from pulling her out of her reality. Her efforts failed, and her body went rigid as she was dragged into the shadows of a small shrine.

A fire lit the wall behind Standish, and he faced a man

whose back was to her. As with her last vision, there was no sound, and she stared at the two men dressed in ancient Egyptian priest robes. In the firelight, she saw Standish accept a familiar blade from the man whose face remained a mystery. With her mind she tried to make the stranger turn to face her, but she sensed a powerful evil in the man.

Suddenly, she knew he was aware of her presence. How was that possible? Never in her visions had someone sensed her. The stranger lifted his hand and admonished her with a wag of his finger. Then with breathtaking speed, his hand closed in a fist before he opened it and threw a ball of light directly at her. For the first time in her life, she realized her visions were not places of safety. Terrified, she fought to deflect the fiery ball of light racing toward her. Hands raised, she forced herself out of the surreal plane back to reality. Standish was glaring down at her as her eyes fluttered open.

"You'll get me that statue or you'll be sorry, Lady Westbury. Remember what I've told you. I want that statue. I'm staying at The Barking Dog in the village. I'll be looking for your message that you've found what I want."

Confused, she shook her head. Even if she wanted to, she couldn't give the man what he wanted. The only statue he could possibly be referring to was the statue of Isis. Did Standish have the other statue? The one Lucien and his family had been searching for?

The pounding sound of a horse at full gallop filled her ears, and Standish released her quickly as he turned to face the oncoming rider. Even from a distance, she recognized Lucien, and a wave of relief washed over her. Lucien would deal with Standish.

Drained from the strength of her vision and the fear that had engulfed her, she watched with lethargic detachment as Lucien wheeled his horse to a stop and dismounted. Dazed, she saw him head toward Standish with a wild look of fury on his dark features. The scar on his face was stark white against the darkness of his skin. Without speaking a word, he stopped in front of Standish and dropped the man with a single punch to the jaw.

"I'm giving you five minutes to get off my estate, Standish. If you're still here after that, I'll kill you." The quiet normalcy of

Lucien's voice made the words echo with the deadliness of a viper. It was impossible not to recognize a man close to the edge of losing control.

Getting to his feet, Standish touched his with a slight grimace as he examined the blood on his fingertips. With surprising speed for a man of his build, he moved toward his horse and bolted into the saddle. With a cruel smile, he nodded his head toward her.

"I appreciate your assistance, Lady Westbury."

Appalled by the implication that she was working with the man, she took a step forward only to have Lucien block her way. Standish yanked viciously on the reins of his horse, turning the animal back toward the village. As he rode away, Constance stared up into Lucien's implacable features.

"It seems you have a habit of lying, Lady Westbury." The suppressed fury in his voice reminded her how much he hated being lied to.

"I have not lied to you," she said quietly. "I've never met Mr. Standish before today."

"And yet he conveniently happened to stumble across you, *here* on the Lyndham Estate."

"I have no idea how the man knew where to find me, but he did. The question you should be asking me is why."

"We both know the answer to that. The man wants the papyrus my great-grandfather brought home from Cairo almost forty years ago."

Confused, she shook her head. "No, he didn't mention anything about a papyrus."

"You lie." Lucien jerked her toward him, his voice dark with an emotion that set her senses on fire. "But God help me, I want to believe you."

His large hands squeezed the softness of her shoulders as he bent his head toward her. The maleness of him filled her nostrils, and she welcomed the dark heat that threatened to consume her as his mouth barely grazed her cheek and moved toward her ear.

"Tell me why I should believe you, Isis? From the first moment we met, you've hidden behind a veil of secrecy, and I'm determined to unearth your secrets."

Overwhelmed with a need to touch him, she focused on the fact that her son and Imogene were only a short distance away as she struggled not to cup Lucien's face with her hands and bring his lips to hers. With a sharp shove at his chest, she broke free of his hold and stumbled backward several steps.

Warily she stared at him, the need gripping her body reflected in his brilliant blue gaze. Her breathing hitched at the desire burning in his expression, and she fought the urge to throw herself back into his arms. Dear heaven, but the man was a potent force. She needed to remember what Lady Lyndham had said. Lucien would despise her for the gift she possessed. Like other skeptics, he would label her mad. The thought of his doing so was painful, and she refused to consider the reason why.

"I haven't lied to you, my lord," she said stiffly. Addressing him so formally made it easier to put emotional distance between them. "I have no idea how Mr. Standish found me, but he wants a statue he says you stole from his family."

"What statue?" Lucien snapped, the desire in his face still evident, although his anger had not diminished.

"I don't know. He insisted I help him, and when I refused, he threatened me."

The change in Lucien was instantaneous. The stillness of his rage alarmed her, and she immediately stepped back from him. He looked as if he wanted to kill someone. "How did he threaten you?"

The moment he asked the question she knew she wasn't capable of answering. She'd not heard anything else the man had said once he'd touched her. The strength of her waking dream had made her deaf and blind to the events in this reality. But she couldn't tell Lucien that. She couldn't explain that somehow the man she'd seen with Standish in her vision wanted to harm Lucien. She hadn't realized that until this moment. But she was as certain of that as she was that Lucien would condemn her for the gift she was using to help him.

"How did he threaten you, Constance?"

"I don't remember. I must have fainted again," she whispered as disbelief crossed his face.

"Another convenient explanation, my lady. Somehow I

think you offer up that particular excuse whenever you want to avoid telling the truth."

He whirled away from her, and his long stride carried him toward his horse. She watched him leave with an anguish that was almost crippling. Instinctively, she knew he wasn't capable of rational thought right now. He was too furious. There was something about Malcolm Standish that made it almost impossible to reason with him.

"Lucien please, I'm telling you the truth. I don't remember what the man threatened me with. I only know he wants this statue of yours, and he wants it badly enough to pay me for it. If I'm lying to you, why would I tell you what he wanted from me?"

The knuckles of his hand were white as he gripped the withers of his horse. The tension holding him rigid showed in the way his coat stretched tightly across his broad, muscular back. His silence and his stance convinced her that he was trying to decide whether to believe her or not. Wanting only to persuade him as to her innocence, she moved toward him then stopped as he swung himself up into the saddle.

"I'm taking you back to the keep. If Standish really is a threat to you, it's not safe for you to be out here. I'm better able to protect you inside."

"I have no need of your protection. In fact, I don't need anything at all from you," she snapped, furious he was unwilling to believe her.

He nudged his horse several steps forward until he could lean down toward her. Cupping her chin with his hand, he studied her with a forbidding gaze. "You might not need anything from me at this moment, but I can assure you of one thing Isis. One night very soon, you'll be pleading with me to fulfill your every need."

His mouth suddenly captured hers in a rough kiss, and the fiery touch stirred a liquid heat inside her. In the next instant, he released her, a strained expression on his face as his mouth thinned into a harsh line.

"We're returning to the keep. *Now.* Collect your things while I fetch the boy and Imogene." Digging his heel into the side of his horse, he rode off toward the children, leaving her behind.

The children had walked some distance from the site of their picnic, and as he rode toward them he tried not to consider what might have happened to her or the children if he'd not found them. Even if she were involved with that bastard Standish, she clearly had no idea what type of man he was. His hand rubbed the scar on his cheek. Standish wouldn't hesitate to use force if he thought it would get him what he wanted.

If Constance had truly recognized how dangerous the man was, she would never have come out here with the children. She loved her son too much to put him in harm's way, and her behavior with Imogene had already shown him that she had great affection for his niece.

So what was he to think now? Had she really experienced another one of her spells or was she lying to him about Standish? He'd been too angry about Standish to even consider her pleas a few moments ago, but despite his best judgment, he believed her.

It wasn't just the sincerity of her words. It was the memory of the expression on her face as he'd ridden up that made him believe her. Just like the last two times she'd experienced one of her episodes, her face had the look of someone in shock.

And what the devil were these spells of hers? He'd heard of people suffering from epileptic seizures, but what little he'd read didn't resemble Constance's experiences. Grimacing, he expelled a harsh sigh of frustration. He was a fool. When he'd arrived home a short time ago, he'd been eager to see her.

For more than a month he'd thrown himself into gambling and drinking unlike anything he'd ever done before. He'd even considered bedding several whores, but when the time had come, he'd sent the women on their way. None of them smelled the way she did. None of the women in London had a sultry voice that wrapped its heat around him like hers.

In short, he'd not been able to empty his head of her. He'd stayed away from her as long as he could. But once home, the need to see her, hear her voice, breathe in the sweet scent of her perfume had filled him with an eagerness he knew was dangerous to feel.

And yet, he'd allowed himself to consider that she might be

pleased to see him as well. The moment Jacobs had told him where she'd gone, he'd set off to find her. When he'd first caught sight of Constance, he'd immediately thought Duncan was with her. The territorial surge of primeval emotion flowing through him had been unsettling.

Even more troubling was the white-hot rage that engulfed him when he'd realized it was Standish with her. Killing the bastard was something he'd contemplated on more than one occasion, but today, the raw power of his fury had proven almost uncontrollable. He had wanted to choke Standish until the man's face turned a mottled color of blue.

The ferocity of his rage had almost blinded him to everything. Those few seconds of action were more of a blur than a memory, and he still didn't understand what had kept him from killing the man where he stood. Now, as he reflected on the incident, the depth of his anger chilled him.

There were rarely any initial signs of the Blakemore curse, or at least none that he knew of, but the results of the curse were undeniable. The subsequent bloodbath was further evidence of the rage that lay just beneath the surface of the Blakemore men.

Worse yet, despite all his best intentions, he was finding it more and more difficult to keep his distance from Constance. Even his trip to London had done nothing to diminish the power of his craving for her. So he'd returned home with the intent to harness his demons, while satisfying himself in the lushness of Constance's delectable body. But if there was one thing he was learning about his beautiful Egyptian goddess it was how stubborn she was.

Glancing over his shoulder, he saw her angrily throw a piece of food out into the grass for some animal to eat. Perhaps her anger was a good thing. If she was angry with him, it was unlikely she'd be willing to come within ten yards of him, making it easier to keep his hands off her.

His gaze narrowed as she suddenly turned to stare after him. The moment she realized he was watching her, she tipped her nose into the air and whirled away from him. It was a challenge. And when had he ever passed up a challenge, even if the stakes were exceedingly dangerous?

Chapter Eight

Lucien was still contemplating how best to handle this latest situation with Constance, when he heard a familiar shout. Imogene, a wide smile on her face, was flying toward him at a dead run. As she reached his horse, he leaned down and swung her up to sit in front of him. Wrapping her arms around his neck, she kissed his cheek and hugged him tightly.

"You left without saying goodbye," she accused with a scowl.

"I had urgent business in London, poppet. I would have told you goodbye if I'd had time." Guilt bit into him as he realized his need to escape had hurt his niece.

"Well, it's all right. At least I had Jamie to play with. I like him very much."

"I'm glad."

"He's special, you know. He can talk to ghosts."

Raising a skeptical eyebrow, he watched Jamie heading toward them at a leisurely pace. Clearly the boy wasn't in any hurry to return to the keep. "And what ghosts does the young Lord Westbury claim to have seen?"

"He's talked to Papa," Imogene exclaimed. "Isn't that exciting? Jamie told me that Papa is very proud of me."

Stiffening, he frowned at Imogene's look of happiness. Christ Jesus, the child believed the boy had talked to Nigel. Clearing his throat, he sent his niece a steady look.

"Listen to me, poppet. I'm afraid young Westbury is teasing you and not in a nice way."

"No he's not," Imogene denied with a vehement shake of her head. "Jamie wouldn't lie to me."

"Wouldn't lie about what?" Young Westbury's tone was belligerent as he stared up at Lucien.

"Uncle Lucien doesn't believe you can talk to Papa." Imogene's voice was filled with a note of disgust.

"Why not?" Jamie asked as he looked up at him with a puzzled expression.

"Because there's no such thing as ghosts," he replied firmly as he looked at first his niece and then the boy.

"Then why can I see him?"

Lucien pondered the boy's question for a moment as he offered the lad his hand and pulled him up onto the horse's hindquarters. The boy was emphatic in his ability to see Nigel, but it was impossible.

The day his parents had died was the day he'd stopped believing in anything except for what he could touch, see and hear. His grandmother had always believed in ghosts, and even confessed to having felt his grandfather's presence on numerous occasions. But he knew better.

He couldn't count the number of times his grandmother had paid some charlatan to talk to her dead loved ones, only to be disappointed time and time again. One of the primary reasons his grandmother believed in the spirit world was because she didn't want to believe in the Blakemore curse.

She didn't want to accept that his great-grandfather had committed filicide before taking his own life. She didn't want to think her own son and grandson had fallen victim to the curse as well. Instead she tried to reach beyond the grave to talk to those she loved. An impossible notion, even if life after death existed.

He nudged Napoleon into motion. The boy didn't strike him as a liar, so what would provoke the child to tell such an outrageous story? He frowned as the horse carried the three of them back to where Constance was still busy gathering the remains of their picnic.

"You didn't answer us, Uncle Lucien. If ghosts aren't real, how can Jamie see Papa?"

He didn't like how the simple question befuddled him. He

131

couldn't accuse the boy of lying, especially when the child was convinced he'd seen Nigel. Still, he couldn't let Imogene continue to believe the boy could talk to her dead father.

"Well, sometimes we want something to be true so badly we begin to think it's true."

"I saw him." Jamie muttered with the stubborn nature of his mother.

Unwilling to alienate the boy, he shook his head. "Since we're in disagreement over the matter, lad, I propose a compromise. The next time you see my brother, ask him where the statue is. If he gives you an answer, then I'll be more than willing to change my mind on the subject. Is that fair?"

"Quite, my lord."

He suppressed a grin at the boy's affronted tone. So like his mother. His gaze settled on Constance angrily stuffing a blanket into the basket that had carried their lunch. There was a mutinous expression on her face, and he frowned. Mending his fences with her was going to be a considerable challenge. As Lucien brought Napoleon to a halt, Jamie slid off the horse and hurried to his mother's side. Imogene abandoned him as well as she broke free of his hold and slipped down to the ground.

"Mother, I talked to Imogene's papa, and his lordship doesn't believe me." The boy sent him a disgruntled look of disgust over his shoulder as he touched his mother's arm.

As her son spoke to her, Constance sent the boy an absent-minded nod and continued to load the picnic basket. But when her son's comment actually seemed to register with her, she froze in mid-action. The tablecloth she held slid from her hands as she whirled around to face the boy. Grabbing her son by the shoulders, she stared down at him with a stricken look on her face.

"What are you talking about, Jamie?" She gave him a slight shake.

"Imogene's papa. I talked to him, Mother," Jamie said with a bemused look on his face. "Was that wrong?"

At the boy's words, Lucien saw Constance pale considerably. Her gasp was a sound of sheer panic as her fingers bit deeply into Jamie's shoulders. The moment the boy cried out in pain, he quickly dismounted. Before he had two feet on the ground, she'd released her son. What the devil was wrong with her? The boy had simply succumbed to an overactive imagination. Puzzled by her reaction, he stepped toward her, but she darted back out of his reach.

"We'll discuss this when we return to the keep, Jamie. Now, apologize to his lordship for your rude behavior."

"But mother—"

"Do it *now*, Jamie," she choked out in a harsh tone.

"I don't think the boy meant any—" He halted his objection as she showed him the palm of her hand in a sharp command of silence.

"Forgive me, my lord, but do not try to tell me how to discipline my son." Once again she focused her attention on the boy. "Apologize. *Now*, Jamie."

The sharp edge in her voice made the words sound like a whip cracking through the air. Pale and shaken, she possessed an air of fragility that worried him. But it was the stunned expression on the boy's face that made him frown. It was clear the boy had rarely, if ever, been spoken to by his mother with such sharpness.

Lucien's gaze returned to Constance's blanched features. Tension tightened the corners of her full mouth, and her body was taut with suppressed emotion as she waited for the boy to speak. This wasn't about the boy telling tales, this was something else altogether. She cast him a quick glance, and fear flickered in her eyes before she looked away.

The odd behavior baffled him, and his eyes narrowed as he recalled he'd seen her act like this once before. Everything about her behavior reminded him of that night in London. Her nervous state was almost as tangible as it had been at the Clarendon, and like before, her expression was closed off to him.

"My apologies for my behavior, my lord." The boy's voice was polite despite the glare he directed up at his mother.

"Thank you." The tension in Constance's voice eased considerably, but her fear remained a strong undercurrent. "Now return to the keep. We'll discuss this matter shortly."

Without even glancing in his direction, she picked up the picnic basket and began walking toward home at a pace he could only define as frantic. With a nod at Imogene and Jamie, he silently urged them to run ahead. They needed no further invitation to race past Constance, who was stalking her way through the pasture. Leading his horse forward, he caught up with her in several quick strides. With his hand on her arm, he brought her to a halt. This close to her, the sweet scent of jasmine was maddening.

"Release me, my lord," she snapped as she tried to jerk her arm out of his grip. Her strength was no match for his, and he held her easily.

"The boy was simply confused, Constance. There was no reason to be sharp with him like that."

"Confused? Don't you mean he's a liar just like his mother?" The bitter note in her voice didn't surprise him, but it was the fear flickering in her eyes that made him frown with frustration.

"Damn it, you know that's not what I meant."

"I see, then you think Jamie is simply confused, whereas I'm a liar." She twisted his words in a way that made him grit his teeth. The direction this conversation was taking was definitely not to his liking.

"Bloody hell, Constance, that's not what I meant either," he muttered harshly. Dropping Napoleon's reins to the ground, he pulled her closer, ignoring the basket that banged against his knee, and shrugging off the possibility the children might look back. "I don't think you're a liar. I believe you when you say you never met Standish before today."

"I'm so pleased that you've been able to clear your conscience, my lord," she sniffed with a condescension designed to cut him to ribbons. "Now release me."

Infuriated by her stubborn refusal to discuss the matter, he freed her and took a quick step backward. She sent him a final glare before wheeling away from him and hurrying after the children. Driving a fist into his palm, he grunted with anger. The woman was more secretive than a pharaoh's tomb. Those large hazel eyes of hers had held a definite gleam of fear, and he was determined to find out what she was so afraid of.

80C3

Constance pulled Jamie into her bedroom and sat him at her dressing table. Worried, she paced the floor, well aware that her son was watching her with angry puzzlement. She'd never considered the possibility that Jamie might possess her gift. Even though her brother Percy's gift equaled hers and Patience's, it had never occurred to her that Jamie would have the same gift. No, she'd considered the possibility. She'd simply hoped he'd be spared the burden.

Coming to a halt, she turned to look at Jamie's stubborn expression. He was hurt and angry. She'd never spoken so fiercely to him before, and she understood his confusion. In two quick steps, she knelt in front of him. Clasping his hands in hers, she blinked back tears of regret.

"Jamie, did you really see Imogene's father?" She immediately recognized the stubborn tilt of his head. If there was anything of her looks that he possessed, it was her expressions. "Please, darling. I need to know exactly what you saw."

"I saw Imogene's papa, and he talked to me," Jamie said with a pout.

"Oh, God." Bowing her head, she pressed her forehead against her son's hands.

"What is it, Mother? What's wrong?" The note of fear in his voice made her lift her head to look at him through the tears in her eyes. Hastily she brushed the wetness off her cheeks.

"Darling, you know how sometimes I have moments when I don't know where I've been?" She waited as he nodded his head with a puzzled look. "That's because I can see things just like you. It's just that sometimes, I have dreams while I'm awake."

"Is that what happened to you the night his lordship came home?"

"Yes," she said quietly. "I'm so sorry, Jamie. I should have said something to you sooner. I think deep inside I was hoping you wouldn't have the gift. And then today, when you came to me and said the earl didn't believe you'd seen Imogene's father, I panicked. You see, we can't let the earl know about our gift. He doesn't believe our gift is real."

"But Imogene believes." Jamie said with a frown.

135

"I know that, darling, but not everyone will believe. It's very important for you to understand you can only tell people you truly trust. Even then the people you trust might be uncomfortable with your special talent."

"Imogene isn't."

"I understand that, Jamie, but her uncle doesn't feel the same way. There are a great many people like the earl, who won't believe we can see and talk to the dead, my darling. They're often frightened by our special gift. Sometimes that fear can make them say and do things that will hurt us. They might say we're mad or call us liars."

"Like Lord Lyndham did today?"

"Yes, darling, like his lordship did today," she murmured, remembering the pain that had twisted her insides when Lucien had accused her of lying.

"Is it all right if I still tell Imogene when her father comes to see her?"

"Oh, Jamie," she sighed, her heart torn between protecting him and easing the heartache of a little girl. "I don't know. If Imogene were to accidentally say something to Lord Lyndham...I don't think it's a good idea."

His face wreathed in serious contemplation, he frowned and nodded his head. "All right, I'll not say anything to Imogene if her father comes to the playroom again."

Gently touching his cheek with her fingertips, she smiled. "I'm sorry I didn't tell you about all of this sooner, darling. I was afraid to."

"I know. Father said it might be hard for you to tell me you can see dead people."

Startled, she pulled back from him slightly. "What do you mean?"

"Father visited me a long time ago. Or at least I think he was my father. He told me that he'd not been very understanding about your gift. He said he was sorry for that."

Stunned, she sank back on her heels and stared at the boy in front of her. Graham had visited their son. The idea was so unbelievable, she didn't know what to say or think. With a laugh, she shook her head. It would be just like Graham not to apologize to her directly, but to do it through Jamie. He'd always had a difficult time admitting he was wrong. Leaning forward, she hugged her son tightly.

"I'm glad he came to see you, Jamie. I'm sure he's proud of you."

"He said I was to take care of you."

"Your father never did think I could take care of myself without someone else's help," she said with a laugh. Climbing to her feet, she pulled Jamie up with her and bent over him to give him another hug. "Now then, why don't you find Imogene and let her know you're not in trouble. I'm sure she's worried about you."

With a nod, Jamie raced toward the door then slid to a halt before turning around and running back to her side. Wrapping his arms about her waist he squeezed her tight. "I'm glad you told me that you can see things too, Mother. I don't feel all alone now."

Her heart aching with love, she kissed the top of his head then laughed as he protested and wheeled about to race from her room. Watching him leave, she swallowed the knot in her throat as she recalled how Lucien had watched them both as she'd listened to Jamie explain how he could see Nigel.

It had taken every ounce of willpower not to panic more than she already had. The look on Jamie's face when she'd ordered him to apologize had filled her with such guilt. Remorse gripped her as she remembered Jamie saying he no longer felt alone. She should have talked with him a long time ago. If she had, then he would never have mentioned his ability to see Nigel.

Brushing the tears from her cheeks, she recalled the confusion on Lucien's face as she had made Jamie apologize. She winced at the memory. Her fear of discovery had made her overreact. If only Lucien hadn't sought her out. No, she was glad he had ridden out to find her. If he hadn't, she wasn't sure what might have happened to her or the children. Malcolm Standish was a dangerous man.

Despite her best efforts not to be frightened, the nightmarish images of her vision had only reinforced her opinion of the man. Lucien's arrival had filled her with an overwhelming relief. Even the ferocity of his anger hadn't frightened her.

The murderous expression on his face as he'd dismounted and approached the other man had told her there was something more between them than just the statue Standish had insisted she help him find.

With Standish gone, her heart had skipped with pleasure at Lucien's return. It wasn't until that moment she realized how much she'd missed him. But her happiness at seeing him again had vanished in a brief instant. When he had accused her of lying, it had been as if he'd branded her with a hot iron.

Now, with Jamie's confession about Nigel, she feared it was only a matter of time before Lucien discovered she possessed the same ability. Only with her, he wouldn't find it so easy to brush aside as if it were a childish prank. He would have to make a choice whether to believe her or not, and Lady Lyndham had made it perfectly clear what Lucien would believe.

If only she could understand what all of her visions meant. There were still too many pieces of the puzzle missing, and the images she'd seen when Standish had grabbed her shoulders had been the most frightening. The man with Standish had known she was there. How was that possible? It was something that had never happened to her before. And the flash of light he'd thrown at her. Was it a weapon her vision had disguised for some reason?

Frustrated, she grimaced and shook her head. This wasn't the first time she'd been unable to make any sense of her visions. Better she focused on something else for the moment. She would eventually figure out what the images meant. There was still time before supper to catalog several new artifacts, and occupying herself with Lucien's collection would take her mind off this troubling puzzle.

Moving toward the door, she suddenly remembered the book she'd been reading the night before. There were several references in it that she wanted to compare against the collection. Turning around, she went to the nightstand where she'd laid it last night. Puzzled, she stared at the empty spot where she'd left the book.

She looked over her shoulder at the vanity table to see if she'd moved it, but it wasn't there either. Baffled, she moved toward the vanity table and knelt to look under the front drawers of the furniture, fully expecting to find the book shoved underneath. Exasperated, she scrambled to her feet empty handed.

"Blast!"

The sound of her aggravation echoed through the bedroom as she returned to the nightstand and opened its two drawers, hoping she'd absently stored the book there for safe keeping. But it simply wasn't there. Determined to find it, she quickly dropped to her hands and knees and lifted the heavy bed skirt that brushed the floor. Edging her way along the side of the large canopied bed, she peered into the dimly lit area beneath the mattress.

A dark shape caught her eye. Smiling with triumph, she reached for the book. When it suddenly moved and ran across her hand, she screamed. Jerking her hand out from under the bed, she screamed again as a small mouse ran along the edges of her skirt and darted across the room. The rodent scurried along the edge of the wall until it disappeared behind the wardrobe.

Intense fear made her muscles rigid and inflexible as she struggled to stand up. Few things frightened her, but a mouse could render her almost incapable of movement. Unable to halt her sobs of terror, she clutched at the bedpost and tried to pull herself upright.

The door of her room banged open as Lucien strode in like an avenging angel. At the sight of him, she shuddered as he quickly pulled her to her feet. The nerve endings on her skin screamed in protest at even his touch, and she twisted away from him in a violent move. Despite having seen the mouse run behind the wardrobe, she snatched up her skirt, frantically searching for any sign of the creature.

"Tell me what's wrong," Lucien demanded as he reached out to touch her shoulder. Smacking his hand away, she uttered another small scream as her skin crawled with the memory of the rodent racing across her hand.

"A mouse...I was...it ran over my hand...it went...under the wardrobe." Her words were small gasps between sobs of fear as she tried to explain her behavior.

In an instant, he caught her up in his arms, sweeping her off her feet. The relief from having her feet off the ground was instantaneous, and she closed her eyes with another sob as her arms slid around his neck. Tears still streaming down her cheeks, she buried her face in his shoulder as she clung to him. His mouth brushed against her hair as he gently kissed the side of her brow.

"It's all right, *yā sabāha*. You're safe. I won't let anything harm you."

The quiet strength in his voice soothed her, and the solid warmth of him was a welcome haven against the terror flooding her body with shudders. As the moments passed, her fear lessened and, with her face buried in the strength of his shoulder, it was impossible not to breathe in the deliciously spicy scent of him.

The sudden rush of awareness that cascaded over her senses sent liquid fire through her body, heating her from the inside out. Inhaling a ragged breath, she realized she needed to put distance between them for the sake of her sanity. She wiped first one cheek then the other dry as she lifted her head.

"Thank you, but I believe I'm well recovered from my fright. You can put me down now," she murmured as she swallowed the urge to trail her fingers along the scar that slashed its way down his cheek.

"You're certain?" Concern, mixed with something else, flashed in his brilliant blue eyes. Dragging her gaze away from his, she nodded her head.

"Yes. I'll be fine."

Gently, he lowered her to the floor, his hands burning through the material of her gown to warm her waist. "I'll see to it that one of the footmen comes up to find the mouse and dispose of it. It's rare the keep ever has one, let alone that it reaches the second floor."

"Thank you," she said with a nod, as she stepped back from him. "I would feel much more comfortable not having to watch where I walk."

For a fraction of a second, his hands resisted letting her go, betraying his desire to keep her in his arms. All too aware of her own needs, she squashed the emotions his touch aroused in her, forcing herself to turn away from him. She could not allow herself to come to care for a man who would reject an important part of who she was.

Remembering the book she'd been hunting for, she moved back to the nightstand and glared at the empty spot where she had left the book. Where the devil was it? She knew she'd not taken it downstairs with her to breakfast, and this was the first time she'd returned to her room since then.

"You were looking for something?"

Lucien's quiet question made her turn her head to look at him. Even despite his concerned demeanor, there was a dangerous edge to his appearance that dried her mouth. He hadn't changed out of his riding clothes yet, and she swallowed hard at the effect he had on her senses.

The polish on his boots gleamed in the room's late afternoon sunshine, and his fawn breeches outlined his muscular thighs and legs. She remembered all too well the hard, flexible steel of his legs against hers the night they'd—

The memory of their lovemaking forced her to press one hand to her throat as she wheeled away from him. He looked dangerous because he was. There was nothing safe about Lucien at all when it came to protecting her heart. From the rakish scar on his cheek to his penetrating eyes, the man was a potent, mesmerizing force of raw masculine power.

Desperate to stem the desire suddenly sinking into every one of her pores, she made an effort to act as though she were still searching for her book.

"Yes, I was looking for a book Graham gave me on the story of Seth and Horus. It had some drawings I wanted to compare with the statue of Isis." She grimaced as she remembered the other items she'd misplaced recently. "It's the third item I've lost this week."

"What other items are you missing?" Tension pulled the corners of his mouth tight, and his eyes glittered with an indecipherable emotion. The look on his face feathered a chill across her skin. What had she said to make him so incensed? She averted her gaze, uncertain what to make of his reaction.

"I can't find a hairbrush my brother gave me for my sixteenth birthday and a brooch Jamie gave me this past Christmas."

"Did you report the items missing to Mrs. Clarke, the housekeeper?" The dark note in his voice unnerved her.

"No, I'm sure they're here somewhere," she said with a wave of her hand as she turned her head to survey the room once more. "I just can't recall where I placed them."

Having searched all the likely places for the book, she suddenly realized how heavy the silence was in the room. Heat spread across her back, and she was certain it was because of his intense gaze. As she turned to face him, her heart skipped a quick beat as she realized he'd moved closer to her.

The distance between them was less than an arm's length, and she froze, fascinated by the stray lock of black hair that had slipped down to caress his forehead. Before she could stop herself, she reached out to brush it back off his face. Shocked by her daring, she jerked her hand away from him as if she'd been burned.

His jaw clenched with tension, a muscle twitched in his cheek as his gaze met hers. The air in the room had suddenly become thick and hot, and warmth flooded her cheeks as she struggled to breathe normally.

"Do you know why I came back from London, *yâ sabâha?*"

His words were a soft growl, and she swallowed hard at the way his voice slipped an invisible rope around her, tugging her toward him. A familiar hunger swept through her, raw and powerful. It settled deep in her nether regions until she ached with a need she knew only he could fill.

Every time they'd touched, she'd been consumed with an unquenchable fire. A fire he created inside her with just one look. One caress. Even now she could feel the heat of it moving toward her, enticing her. Sweet, merciful God, she was mad to even want to be in his arms. He would reject her the moment he discovered her secret, and she didn't think it was possible for her to keep her heart intact before or after that moment.

In the next instant, his hand caught her chin, and his thumb rubbed across her lower lip. The intensity of his look made her swallow hard, which was almost impossible to do since her mouth had gone dry several minutes before.

Frantic to break the spell she was under, she tried to breathe normally as she forced herself to step away from him. Skirting him, she moved toward her vanity when his arm wrapped around her waist and stopped her. Startled, she cried out softly as he pulled her backward and into his chest. The solid breadth of him pressed into her back, and she shuddered as his mouth caressed the edge of her ear lobe. Oh God, the man had simply to touch her and she was incapable of thinking straight. Strong hands held her motionless against him as her breathing grew more ragged with each passing second. The low growl caressing her ear made her legs trembled as she fought to hold herself still against the warmth of him.

"I came back for you," he rasped. "I came back because no matter how much I drank or gambled I couldn't forget the scent of you, the heat of you, the fire of you."

"Please, Lucien—"

"Come to me tonight, *yâ sabâha*. Let me pleasure you as you did me that day in the library. Let me worship you with my mouth, my hands, my entire body."

She wanted to melt. There was no other description she could think of to describe the effect his seductive words had on her. Incapable of thinking clearly, she succumbed to his mesmerizing voice and nodded. Strong fingers bit gently into the soft flesh of her shoulders as his mouth caressed her neck in a light kiss.

"Until tonight, *yâ sabâha*."

Releasing her, Lucien walked quickly from the room, almost as if he thought she might have a change of heart. A change of heart? What she needed was to have her head examined. It had been madness to agree to visit his room tonight. She'd been behaving licentiously with the man since their first meeting. Although her behavior shocked her, affairs among the Marlborough Set were daily occurrences. Her actions would not be viewed as shocking unless she was indiscreet.

A widow could have a dalliance as long as she didn't become pregnant and didn't make a spectacle of herself. The weeks after her first tryst with Lucien had only confirmed the doctor's diagnosis as to her ability to conceive a child. As for making a spectacle—her special gift had taught her the value of discretion. But neither of those things worried her half as much as the way she craved Lucien's touch. One thing was certain: she was proving just how rash and impulsive a Rockwood could be.

Chapter Nine

Hands braced against the fireplace mantle, Lucien stared down into the flames of the small fire. Above his bent head, the clock chimed the quarter hour before eleven. He'd sent her a note before dinner, instructing her to join him at half past ten. Where the devil was she? Had she changed her mind? No, only fear would make her change her mind, and she was too stubborn to admit she might be afraid of him.

Roughly pushing himself away from the mantle, he growled his displeasure as he turned around and studied the room. The only thing missing was Constance, his bewitching Isis. One hand rubbing the back of his neck, he paced the floor.

Why did he even care she was late? More than fifteen minutes late, a small voice reminded him. He flexed his jaw in self-disgust. He'd bedded women before, why should Constance be any different? Tonight he'd prove his fascination with her was little more than his cock craving the heat of her cunny. He grimaced.

Crudity where Constance was concerned seemed like an insult. She wasn't deserving of it, and yet he knew it was just one more way of keeping distance between them. The realization irritated him. He wasn't in danger of losing his head over the woman. He simply wanted her body. Emotion didn't even enter into the equation. All he wanted was to satiate his lust and get her out of his system. When he'd done that, his body would stop hounding him for one more taste of her.

Blast it to hell. What was keeping her? He'd waited long enough for her as it was. The woman simply enjoyed keeping him on tenterhooks. He was certain of it. But not tonight. He wasn't going to wait any longer. Tonight he was going to seduce

Constance and purge her from his system. He'd promised to worship her body, and he intended to do just that. The woman was going to find herself seduced unlike anything she'd ever experienced or imagined. Wheeling toward the door, he started across the room.

It was time to fetch his elusive Isis. If she wouldn't come to him, he'd go to her. To hell with the preparations he'd made.

He was only a foot away from the threshold when a quiet knock echoed in the room. With a sharp jerk, he pulled the door open.

Framed by the doorway, she was a vision in ivory lace and silk. Two gaslights some distance down the corridor threw her profile into relief. He couldn't remember any woman who'd ever tempted him the way this one did. The warning shot in the back of his head went ignored. All he wanted was one more night with her. That should be more than enough time to rid himself of this intense craving she stirred in him.

Her lovely mouth was tilted in a small pout of uncertainty, and she looked skittish enough to flee back to her room. But he wasn't going to let her run. He stretched out his hand to her. Hesitation flitted across her features as she darted an anxious look down the dimly lit hallway. "No one will see you come or go, *yâ sabâha*. I instructed Jacobs to keep the staff confined to other parts of the keep until midday."

Relief crossed her features for a brief instant before her eyes widened in horror. "Dear Lord, do you mean the servants will know that..."

"No," he said as he gently pulled her into the room. "Jacobs knows I often have trouble sleeping, and I occasionally request to be left undisturbed until I ring."

"Oh."

The concern on her face disappeared completely, leaving a soft glow of what he could only define as anticipation. He swallowed hard as her expression taunted him with temptation. Hell, he was ready to bed her now and to hell with the special arrangements he'd made for her seduction. She shouldn't be denied pleasure just because he wanted her out of his system.

His fingers bit into the wooden doorframe at the thought. Christ Jesus, what was wrong with him? Tonight meant nothing. The door closed with a quiet snap of the latch. Why the soft sound sent tension rolling through him, he wasn't sure. No, he knew why. He just didn't want to admit it. For several long seconds, he debated sending her back to her room.

"Lucien?"

The question in her voice twisted his gut. Sending her away accomplished nothing. No, he would stay the course and seduce her in the manner he'd intended. Giving in to the temptation of bedding her immediately said he had no control of his emotions where she was concerned. He refused to admit such a possibility. Tonight was about pleasure and nothing more. Deep inside he thought he heard the sound of maniacal laughter. Dismissing the notion, he turned around and met her luminous gaze.

"Do you trust me, *yâ sabāha*?"

She arched her eyebrows as she considered the question for a moment. Then with a nod, a smile curved her lips. "I'm not really sure why, but yes. I know you would never hurt me."

The irony of her words was not lost on him, and he flexed his jaw as a dark tension assaulted his body. Exerting the control he'd learned over the years, he buried his turbulent emotions deep.

"Then turn around."

She frowned in puzzlement for a moment before she did as he ordered. With her back to him, it was impossible to keep from leaning forward to kiss the nape of her exposed neck. She shuddered at the touch, and he reveled in the knowledge his caress could elicit such a strong, physical response from her.

Quickly removing the hairpins from her hair, he watched in fascination as the silky chestnut tresses fell down over her shoulders and back. He'd never known a woman's hair to smell so wonderfully exotic—so tempting. A lock of hair curled round his finger. Would she be willing to go along with what he had planned? Reaching into the pocket of his trousers, he pulled out a black silk scarf. With a quick movement, he whipped the dark cloth over her eyes, blindfolding her. Startled, her hands flew up to the silk material in silent protest, but he stayed her with his hand.

"Trust me," he whispered firmly.

"I trust you, Lucien." The acceptance and faith in her voice threatened to unleash the darkness still lurking beneath the surface. He swallowed hard and forced himself to focus on pleasing her. Purging his soul would happen soon enough.

"Tonight, Isis, I'm going to show you pleasures unlike any you've experienced before. I'm going to caress you, drink from you and make you cry out for my touch."

She quivered beneath his hands as he circled her then caught her hands in his and pulled her toward the center of the room. Unable to resist, he allowed himself the quick pleasure of leaning forward to nibble at a delicate earlobe before moving to the silky skin of her throat.

"Tonight isn't just about pleasure, *yâ sabāha*, it's also about the senses. Tell me what you hear," he murmured. Beneath his lips, he could feel her pulse jump with excitement as she tipped her head to one side and strained to listen. He waited as she listened to the soft sound of their breathing and the fire crackling in the hearth.

"The fire?"

"Excellent, *yâ sabāha*," he whispered. "That sound represents the fire we're going to experience tonight. I intend to brand you as mine. Mine alone."

He smiled with satisfaction when his words made her breath hitch and her mouth parted in a soft *moue*. The keen expectation in her expression below the strip of black silk pleased him more than he cared to admit. He frowned slightly before discarding the niggling concern darting through his head. It was natural to enjoy her eagerness as it would be with any other woman. And he intended to satisfy her anticipation in ways she would never forget. He would give her a night to remember unlike any other. He'd mark her in such a way that it was his touch she longed for—his and no other man.

"And what do you smell, my tempting Egyptian goddess?"

"Strawberries," she said with a soft laugh. "I smelled them the moment I entered the room."

"Correct."

Her laughter was a gratifying sound, and he smiled. For once, he was the one who'd made her laugh, not Duncan. A twinge of disquiet tugged at him as he acknowledged how much he enjoyed pleasing her. Pushing the thought aside, he untied the blue-corded ribbon holding her robe closed at the neck. The moment he slid the lightweight garment off her shoulders his chest tightened as air fled his lungs.

The robe had been a willing accomplice in hiding the sheer nightgown that clung to her full figure like a second skin. The sight had him hard in mere seconds. Iron hard. Damnation. He didn't think he'd ever seen a more exquisite sight than the soft roundness of her breasts.

His mouth watered at the thought of licking and sucking her nipples, which he could see were stiff peaks jutting out through the transparent cream fabric of her gown. No, not yet, he needed to maintain control. The slower he proceeded, the more certain he could be that tonight was about lust and nothing more. Maintaining control meant his emotions weren't involved. Unable to help himself, he trailed his fingers along the line of her breastbone down between her breasts then under the lush beauty of one firm globe. Christ Jesus, she was lovelier than he remembered.

Quickly taking a step back, he tried to control the desire beginning to rage inside him. Moving toward a nearby table, he retrieved a strawberry from a bowl. When he turned around to face her, the full force of her exotic beauty barreled through him. Her gown hugged her voluptuous breasts before edging down to caress her softly rounded belly as the fabric draped its length over a full, sensuous thigh. The dark mauve of her areoles sent his pulse racing, and the small triangle of curls between her legs made him swallow hard.

God help him, but the woman was a siren. And all the more powerful because she had no idea how erotically sensual her body was. Returning to her side, he slowly wet her lips with the taste of the berry he held in his fingers.

"Open your mouth, *yā sabāha*," he said as he slid the red fruit across her bottom lip.

Half of the berry entered her mouth and she bit into the dimpled temptation when he told her to. Even beneath the blindfold, he could see the look of pleasure the fruit gave her as she slowly relished its taste. Leaning into her, he breathed in the scent of strawberry as he popped the remainder of the berry past her lips.

"You have a touch of juice at the corner of your mouth," he murmured before his tongue licked the droplet off her skin.

The touch made her entire body tremble, and he didn't stop her as she reached up to explore his face with her fingers. He grew still at her caress. The tenderness in her soft touch tightened his throat, and he swallowed hard. A sudden longing for something he knew better than to even dream about rose up inside him. With a violent mental blow, he crushed the thought. Instead he lowered his head and captured her mouth in a teasing caress.

"You're ripe and succulent, just like that strawberry," he murmured as he enjoyed the sweetness of her lips.

The pulse at the side of her neck pounded a frantic beat beneath his fingers. Eager to taste the warmth of her skin, he pressed his mouth against the fluttering beat. A soft moan whispered out of her, and the sound sent elation shooting through him. Before the night was through he'd have her doing more than simply moaning. He wanted to hear the aching need in her voice when she pleaded with him for release.

Impatient for the sound of that husky plea, he trailed his mouth across her shoulder and down her arm. For a fraction of a second he paused at the stiff peak of her breast. The silk of her nightgown was stretched taut over the tight tip of her. It betrayed her heightened awareness, and instead of suckling her, he continued to blaze a fiery path down her arm. Her whimper of protest filled him with satisfaction.

"Sweet heaven, Lucien, surely you're not going to tease me like this all night." She blindly stretched out her hands to him.

"This is far less of a torment than what I've suffered these past several months, my sweet." He fought to keep his tone light. Admitting the depth of his torment would only give her power over him. "Months of aching for you. Nights needing you, but the only release my cock had was my hand and images of you."

She gasped at his words as a pink blush filled her cheeks. Coming upright, he rubbed his thumb across the plump fullness of her lower lip. "My words shock you."

"A little," she said. He saw her throat bob as she swallowed hard.

"Shall I describe the fantasies I had about you every time I grasped my hard rod?" Slowly, he traced his finger along the edge of her bodice where the lace met her jasmine-scented skin. "Fantasies of me licking the insides of your thighs then sucking on that tender little nub of yours. Sucking on you until you drench my tongue with your hot cream."

The pink color in her cheeks darkened to a rosy hue as her mouth formed a wordless cry of shock. He watched her carefully as his finger slid down toward the shadowy valley between her breasts. She might have found his comments shocking, but they excited her as well. The slight flare of her nostrils and her shallow breathing were enough to tell him that. He reached for the ribbons of her nightgown, then used the tips of the silk fasteners to tease her skin as he unlaced her bodice.

The almost-transparent garment slid off her shoulders and floated downward to pool at her feet. The dark mauve hue of her rigid nipples made his mouth go dry as he lightly rubbed his thumb over one stiff peak. She jerked at the touch.

"Lucien—"

"Hush, sweetheart. Just let me look at you," he rasped.

She was beautiful, and his groin tightened with an urgency that troubled him. Christ Almighty, was he going to be able to finish this seduction? His body grew taut with tension as he fought the need to take her without another word. No. He needed to resist the temptation—remain in control. It was the only way to manage this insatiable need she created in him.

With a feather-light touch, he slid his fingers down over the tips of her breasts to her waist. His mouth longed to suckle her, but he resisted the impulse. Instead, he blew gently across each nipple until she reached out for him. Capturing her hands in his, he forced her to cup her breasts.

"I want you to touch yourself, *yâ sabāha*. The whimper parting her lips made his cock jump. "Stroke those lovely nipples of yours."

A violent shudder ripped through her, and he gripped her waist to hold her steady. She slowly obeyed his command, and he watched in fascination as her fingers tentatively circled the stiff peaks of her breasts.

"Tell me how it makes you feel, my sweet."

"I...wicked. I feel wicked." Desire made her voice husky.

"I like watching you being wicked." He knelt in front of her and pressed his lips to the silky smoothness of her rounded belly. "But I want more."

"More?"

"I want to taste your cream, *yâ sabâha*."

She moaned at his statement and swayed toward him. The soft musky scent of her desire tantalized him as he cupped the round swells of her bottom and tilted her hips toward him. Leaning into her, he slipped his tongue through her damp curls and circled her sex.

"Oh dear God."

An instant later, a small gush of cream slid across his tongue. Eagerly he welcomed the hot essence of her into his mouth. She was sharp and tangy. He wanted more. With a gentle stroke of his fingers, he parted her slick folds then swirled his tongue around the tender bud of her sex. She called out his name in a quiet plea, and pleasure lashed through him. He intended to make her cry out like that over and over again tonight.

Her hips shifted slightly as she whimpered with need. Encouraged by her response, his teeth gently clamped down on the tender bud of her sex as he slowly slid one finger into her tight core. Almost immediately, her body clenched around him in a tiny spasm, but it wasn't enough. He wanted her to shatter completely over his tongue. Slowly, he pressed another finger up inside her, caressing her insides with delicate strokes. She trembled like a leaf in the wind, and he pulled back from her slightly. Looking up, he saw her mouth working as if to speak, but she didn't make a sound.

"You like that, *yâ sabâha*, don't you? You like my fingers dipping into that hot cream of yours."

"Ye...yes," she gasped with a nod.

"Tell me what else you like."

"I... I don't..."

"You do know. Tell me."

"I like...the way you were sucking on me."

A deep red color crested in her cheeks as her hoarse

whisper filled the air above his head. He smiled with satisfaction.

"And I like sucking on you."

Leaning forward again, he resumed massaging her sex with his tongue while continuing the rhythmic stroke of his fingers inside her. The deep moan pouring out of her throat excited him as her fingertips bit into his shoulders. Seconds later, a tremor shook through her until her insides tightened like a silk vise around his fingers.

God Almighty, he wanted her wrapped around his cock now. He wanted to feel her cunny flexing tight around his hard erection, clenching him until he exploded inside her. The sultry bite of her flooded his mouth, and he took pleasure in knowing it was his touch that had made her explode across his tongue.

Her cream had tasted hot before, but *damn* she tasted even better this time. With every kiss, caress and taste of her, he'd expected to ease the need gnawing at him inside. But the opposite was true. Each time he touched her simply increased his desire. Pressing a kiss to the inside of her thigh, he ached to bury himself in her slick, wet core.

Throwing his head back, he looked up to see her lovely mouth forming a soft circle as she drank in short, sharp gasps of air while the shudders wracking her body eased. Slowly, he rose to his feet, his body literally sliding up over her naked skin.

The heat of her pressed into him, and he grimaced at the way his body responded to her. Bloody hell, he needed to just fuck her until they were both spent, and then he'd take her again and again until he ended this damnable lust she stirred in him. As if she could read his mind, she pressed herself against his erection, and he bit back a groan.

The soft skin of her buttocks dimpled slightly as his fingers bit into her, and he tugged her tight against his hips. It was a possessive gesture. A signal he wouldn't let her leave him. But she didn't want to escape. It might be sinful and wicked, but she wanted him. The desire coursing through her was more powerful than anything she'd ever felt for any man, including her husband. She heard him pull in a deep breath as he rested his forehead against hers for a moment.

"You go to my head, *yâ sabâha*."

She couldn't see his face from behind the blindfold she wore, but the hoarse, oddly tender, note in his voice made her quiver in his arms. She went to his head? The man had no idea what he was doing to every one of her senses. If she were wise, she'd make certain he didn't find out. He would use the knowledge to bend her to his will. His mouth brushed across the side of her neck, and small shivers of pleasure raced across her skin.

God, she wanted him to suckle her again. The thought of his mouth on her made the tips of her breasts grow taut with need. When his lips finally tugged her nipple into his mouth she trembled at his caress. Sweet heaven, the man was a mind reader. His fingers returned to the sensitive spot between her legs, and her hips bucked beneath his stroke. Oh dear Lord, if he kept this up she wouldn't be able to remain standing. She swayed, grateful for the strong arm wrapped around her waist. Her arms dimpled with goose bumps as his fingers parted her slick folds once more. Pleasure whipped through her and she whimpered at his touch.

"Oh, God, Lucien."

"Remember I told you tonight was about the senses, *yâ sabâha*. Tell me what you're feeling right now."

"On fire...I'm on fire." Her body screamed with an exquisite need for more of his touch. "Please, Lucien, I want you."

"And I want you, *yâ sabâha*."

The black silk covering her eyes heightened her other senses, and she felt the warmth of his breath on her cheek. She raised her hands and cupped his face, the rough stubble scratching at the pads of her fingers. She tried to pull his head down to meet her lips, but he resisted her without any effort. As if to punish her for daring to distract him, his fingers pressed relentlessly against the tight nub of flesh between her legs. He increased the pace of his stroking, and she found herself riding a crest of sensation that was decadent, exquisite and dangerous.

"Lucien, please," she gasped.

"Please what, my sweet?"

"Oh dear Lord, I don't think..."

The fevered pitch inside her rose quickly to assault her nerve endings, and she uttered a cry of delight as she exploded once more. As she shuddered against him, Lucien gripped her hips and knelt to lick at her with his tongue again. The sinful nature of his touch only intensified the rivers of sensation cresting over her body.

Inside her, a fire raged out of control. Untamed, it threatened to consume her completely. Her hand flailed in the air as she tried to touch him in the darkness. When she found his shoulders, she braced herself against his strength.

"Lucien, please, I don't think I can remain standing for much longer."

The soft chuckle tickling her thigh echoed with triumph, and she reached for the blindfold. In an instant he was on his feet to stop her from removing the silk scarf. His hand was warm against her skin.

"I don't think quite yet, my lovely Isis."

"Dear God, Lucien, I don't deny how much I'm enjoying this, but I need to sit down."

"And sit you shall, my dear, but there are still two senses we haven't yet explored." The delight in his husky tone made her smile.

"Then let me see you," she demanded, delighting in this game they were playing.

"Hmmm," he said softly, the smile of satisfaction in his voice easy to hear. "No, I think touch is the next sense I want you to experience."

"Touch?" She laughed. "Isn't that what we've been doing?"

"I think it's time you touched *me*."

She heard him step away from her followed by a soft rustling sound. Stretching out her arms, she took a tentative step forward. A quiet laugh to the side of her made her turn as though she were playing blind man's bluff. Seconds later, her hands encountered a hard, bare chest. Pleasure parted her lips in a sigh.

"You feel as wonderful as I remember."

Almost as if her words had surprised him, the muscles of his hard chest tightened then flexed under her caress. His body was warm, supple steel against her palms. There was a raw power in the way his sinewy muscles tightened at her touch. She slowed her exploration of him to savor the sound of his ragged breathing. He liked the way she was touching him. She smiled. Her touch didn't just please him—it aroused him. Taking her time, she continued to map his chest with her hands, her fingers lightly grazing the flat tip of his breasts. He hissed in a sharp breath at her touch before he reciprocated and stroked her taut nipples with his thumbs.

She pressed her breasts into his touch, the pleasure of it mixing with the joy she found in memorizing the hard line of his body. The taut muscles in his chest gave way to bare skin across his waist and abdomen. The flat planes of his stomach tensed as she moved her hands downward. And breathed in a breath of pleasure.

He was completely naked.

The soft rustling she'd heard a few moments ago had been him undressing. Tentatively, she slid her hand down to his groin. The moment her fingers glided over the tip of his hard erection, his solid length jumped at the light touch.

The guttural sound he made was a primitive, primeval sound. It said he found her touch intense and pleasurable. A tremor shot through her. Her caresses aroused him. He wanted her as badly as she wanted him. She tightened her grasp around his hard, thick erection. Beneath her thumb, a wet bead of desire seeped out of him, and she smeared it slowly over the tip of his phallus.

"Is this what you meant when you said you wanted me to experience the sensation of touch?"

She could hear the womanly note of power in her question and she smiled with the expectation of hearing him laugh. Instead he stiffened against her. Even blind she knew his expression had darkened. Had she angered him? Placing her palm against his heart, she willed her gift to show her what he was feeling, but she saw nothing. The air between them was heavy with unspoken emotion, and she knew he was struggling to control whatever demons she'd aroused in him.

"Not quite," he said roughly.

As he swept her up into his arms, she released a small cry of surprise. Blindly, she reached out, and her fingers brushed across the taut planes of his cheek. His teasing mood had evaporated under the stress of battling an inner beast. The savage tension reverberating off him didn't alarm her. If anything, it made her want to ease the pain and conflict she sensed in him. She recognized the folly of such an emotion, but she couldn't suppress her desire to ease his suffering.

Without any warning, he dropped her unceremoniously onto his bed, and she cried out once again. She reached up to remove her blindfold, then gasped as he roughly pinned her hands over her head, while his hard muscular frame pinned her to the mattress.

The darkness suddenly driving him should have frightened her, but it didn't. Her instincts told her she was safe with him. If anything, his dominating manner only heightened the desire flooding her body. She was at his mercy and no longer in control. The sensation excited her. Unable to help herself, she sobbed a sharp breath of expectation. God, she wanted him. Needed him inside her. She shifted her hips upward, trying to encourage him to take her.

"Not yet, *yâ sabâha.* I want you pleading with me to thrust into that hot little honey pot of yours. I want to hear you begging me to fuck you."

Although she was still unaccustomed to the coarse language, his tone of voice was what shocked her. The turbulent emotions layered beneath the words were dark and raw.

"Say it," he growled. There was a saturnine edge to his voice, and it betrayed the battle he waged against some inner turmoil.

"I...I want you."

His body flexed with tension against hers, and in response she tingled with need. He wanted more from her. He wanted her complete surrender. His teeth roughly abraded her nipple almost to the point of pain. Still unable to see his face, she could only imagine the ferocity of his expression as he nipped his way up to the side of her neck and then her earlobe.

"Tell me you want my cock." Blinded not only by the silk over her eyes, but by need as well, she shuddered at the sardonic, compelling command.

"Oh dear God," she whimpered.

"Admit how badly you need me, Isis."

"Lucien, please. I want—"

"I know what you want, *yâ sabâha*. But until you tell me what I want to hear, you'll stay just like this—hot, unfulfilled and whimpering with need."

Her body jerked as the tip of him pressed against her damp curls. Immediately her muscles grew taut, silently pleading with him to enter her. How could he deny her like this? Deny himself? And she was certain he wanted her as much as she wanted him. He'd pushed her to the edge of insanity, and now he seemed determined to continue torturing her. She released a soft moan of frustration.

"I don't understand."

"I think you do. You want me buried inside you—ramming into you until that hot little cunny of yours milks cum out of me."

"Yes, please, Lucien," she sobbed. "I want you inside me."

"I want your *cock* inside me." The savage darkness in his voice made her swallow hard, and she winced. His fingers tightened on her wrists. "Say it, now."

"Please...I want...I want your cock inside me."

Never in her life had she ever used such coarse language. It sent an illicit thrill down her spine as it rolled off her tongue. A split second later Lucien thrust himself deep inside her. Primal and exquisite, the hard stroke forced a sharp cry of pleasure from her. He filled her completely, his erection stretching and expanding her until she wanted to weep from the joy of it. Every nerve ending in her body was on fire, and she tried to shift her position beneath him when he didn't move.

"For the love of God, Lucien." She twisted slightly against his powerful hold. "You're tormenting me."

Her insides tightened and flexed around his hard thickness as he moved just a fraction. She wanted more, but he seemed hell bent on denying her the release she needed so badly.

"Am I?"

"You...know...you...are," she panted.

"Your torment is *nothing* compared to the hell I've endured

157

for more than three months," he rasped as he dragged his mouth across her shoulder and down to her breast. "I've ached for you, hungered for just one more taste of you."

Restrained anger filled his harsh tone, but something else echoed under the surface. Desperation? She shuddered as his mouth singed her with each word he uttered. Never in her life had she ever been so hot and needy—not even that night at the Clarendon. Raw and powerful, the craving for his touch clawed at her until she could think of nothing but the blinding ache tearing through her body.

After an endless moment of intense need, he moved inside her. She'd expected to feel relief. Instead, she trembled with a stark hunger for more. God, if only he would move faster. She wanted him to take her with the same wild intensity he had that night at the Black Widows Ball. Slowly he eased himself out of her then pressed back into her snug sheath. If she could only caress him, perhaps she could entice him not to draw out this hot, leisurely seduction.

Desperate, she tried to tug her hands free of his strong grip. It was a futile effort. Her punishment for trying to break free was the wet, hot sweep of his tongue around the tip of her breast. The lazy movement illustrated how powerless she was against his relentless strength. She could do little more than sob as he slowly slid back into her. It was a maddening pace, and no matter how hard she tried, she couldn't make him increase the rhythm of his strokes. Her insides clutched at him in desperation as a whirlwind of blistering need raced through her.

"Lucien! For the love of God, *please.*"

"I've given you what you asked for, Isis." His voice echoed with desire as his breath blew hot flames over her skin. "I've buried my cock inside you."

"But I want more. I want...I want..."

"Say it." The harsh command was a dark growl as he plunged back into her.

"Oh God, Lucien, I want you to fuck me."

A gasp of shock blew past her lips as she recognized the base level her need had reduced her to. She had little time to dwell on the knowledge as a deep groan rolled out of him, and he withdrew then pumped back into her with a powerful thrust.

"And I, *yâ_sabāha*, want you to see me fuck you."

Darkness became light as Lucien whipped the blindfold off her eyes, and she blinked. Hovering over her, his strong features were dark with desire and a grim triumph blazed in his gaze. Her eyes adjusted to the soft candlelight and widened in surprise as she looked past his shoulder. In the ceiling of his bed canopy, mirror tiles reflected the decadent image of their entwined bodies on a large bed of red silk sheets.

Her gaze jerked back to his as he began to slide in and out of her at a faster pace. It was decadent—wicked—sinful. She'd never felt such intense pleasure before, and her eyes fluttered shut.

"No," he rasped sharply. "Look at me. At us. Tonight there are no masks. Only Isis and the man who possesses her."

Startled, her eyes flew open to meet his intense gaze. The desire reflected in his dark eyes was all consuming and potent. In the candlelight, their reflection in the mirrors captured her attention once more. It was wickedly erotic to see him burrowed between her legs, his strong sculpted buttocks arching up and down as he drove into her with heavy thrusts.

She knew she shouldn't enjoy watching his strong, naked body moving over hers, but she did. She loved it. Wanting more of him, she bent her legs and opened herself wide to give him better access to her. The moment she did so, he groaned and lowered his head to kiss her hard. The pressure building inside her made her arch upward into his kiss with a demand of her own.

The first ripple of sensation she felt was breathtaking. Inside her, his hard length jerked against the tiny spasm lacing through her. Still driving into her, his body demanded and pleased at the same time. Tiny spasms followed the first, and in one split second she shattered beneath him.

As she cried out in pleasure, he plunged deep into her with one last stroke. The wild roar breaking from his lips matched hers in intensity as he throbbed inside her. For several long moments, their bodies flexed together in the ebbing tide of their lovemaking until a languid warmth filled her limbs. Looking up at him, she noted the possessive gleam in his eyes.

He'd done exactly what he'd said he would do. He'd branded her—spoiled her for any other man. She closed her eyes against the ramifications of that knowledge. No matter what else happened between them, this night would be a precious memory of incredible passion. As the weight of him settled into her curves, Lucien captured her mouth in a hard kiss. A kiss of possession.

In a fluid movement, he rolled off her to lie flat on his back. Satiated, she sighed softly as a warm silence hung in the air between them. She turned her head to see he'd closed his eyes, and she relished the opportunity to study him.

Not only was he handsome, but there was great strength and power in his features as well. Slowly, her gaze slid down over his body. Hard and sinewy, he possessed a devastating masculine appeal that both alarmed and excited her in one fell swoop. What would it be like to wake up each morning with this man at her side?

Appalled at the direction of her thoughts, she closed her eyes against the reflection of the two of them lying side by side in his bed. Sweet Mother of God, how could she even contemplate such a thought? The moment he learned about her ability, she'd be subjected to his ridicule and scorn. It was madness to entertain such an arrangement. Biting her lip, she realized how ridiculous all of it sounded. She'd just made love with the man—there could be no other arrangement more intimate than that.

"You were late."

Steel edged his quiet statement as he remained on his back with his eyes closed. His observation startled her for a moment until the context of his words sent warm pleasure flowing through her. She'd kept him waiting, and he hadn't like it. He'd been impatient for her to arrive.

"Yes, your grandmother delayed me."

"My grandmother?" He turned his head and fixed his startling blue gaze on her.

"I walked with her to her room when she retired for the night."

Rolling onto his side, he traced the line of her jaw with his thumb. "She likes you very much."

"Yes, I like her too. She's so sad and lonely. If I'd realized sooner, I would have—"

Constance inhaled a sharp breath and turned her head away from him as she realized she'd almost revealed her dark secret.

"You would have what?" The curiosity in his voice increased the tension holding her body hostage.

She forced a smile to her lips, but kept her gaze averted as she tried to make light of her blunder. "I don't know, I suppose nothing. It simply makes me sad to see people in pain."

As if he could read her thoughts, he brushed his lips over her ear lobe.

"That's not what you were going to say," he murmured. "But I'll discover your secrets soon enough, *yâ sabāha.*"

Slowly she turned her head toward him, her eyes meeting the probing look in his gaze. Alarmed by the determined set of his mouth, she desperately tried to think of a way to divert his attention. The thin white scar that traced its way across his dark cheek prompted her to run her forefinger along the disfiguring mark.

"How did you get cut?" she asked softly as she studied the healed wound with a sympathetic eye. It must have hurt dreadfully given the length of the scar.

At her question, he stiffened. His fingers captured hers and he pulled her hand away from his face. "I made someone angry."

"It must have hurt a great deal." She adjusted her head on her pillow as she peered at the scar more closely. "It wasn't a normal knife blade, was it?"

His eyebrow arched as he sent her an amused look. "If by that you mean it was incredibly sharp, you're correct."

With a quick twist of her body, she pushed herself up on one elbow and leaned into him. The scent of sandalwood tickled her nose as she noted the way the skin had distinctive marks that indicated the cut had been made by an unusual knife.

"No, I mean it looks like the edge of a blade the priests of Seth used in their rituals. Their blades always had the shape of the serpent with small curves winding back and forth in the form of a snake. It usually leaves a mark like yours."

161

An odd expression crossed his face as he reached up to touch the scar. Then with a quick movement, he climbed out of bed, leaving her to stare after him in surprise. Red sheets clutched to her chest, she sat up and watched him walk toward the fireplace. His body was a fluid mix of power and grace as he crossed the wooden floor.

"You're angry with me."

"No," he said with a shake of his head, before looking over his shoulder. "I simply have no wish to spend the rest of the night discussing the past when I can enjoy the delicious curves of your body, Isis."

Heat swept over her skin before it settled in her cheeks. With an amused smile, he turned back to the fireplace and reached for a poker. The predatory beauty of his movements made it impossible not to watch him.

The strong line of his back raced downward to the firm, muscular buttocks she'd admired in the mirrors over his bed. More beautiful than the finest Michelangelo sculpture—she marveled at his mesmerizing physique. As he stoked the fire, the sinews of his arms flexed with power, reminding her how it felt to be locked in his solid embrace.

When he faced her again, he arched an eyebrow at her as if he were able to read her thoughts. Embarrassed that she'd been ogling him, she fell back into the mattress then rolled onto her stomach, her head turned away from him. The man would have an inflated ego if she continued to admire him so openly.

It wouldn't do to have him think she was so engrossed in him that she couldn't think straight. Especially when it was the truth. Frustrated by her inability to keep her emotions detached where he was concerned, she closed her eyes with a beleaguered sigh. Their arrangement wouldn't last, and when they were finished with each other, what would become of her heart?

Warm hands swept the hair off her back before he began kneading her shoulders in a manner that was the most relaxing thing she'd ever experienced. Unable to help herself, she uttered a small noise of pleasure. His hands stopped for a moment as he reached for something on the nightstand. Seconds later, she gasped as a cool liquid dribbled over her back. His firm mouth feathered a kiss on the top of her shoulder.

"It's simply oil I brought home from Alexandria," he said with amusement. "The shopkeeper assured me it would enthrall any woman I used it on."

The words clutched at her chest like a vise, and she went rigid against his hands as he spread the oil over her back. Dear God, had he used this on another woman? The idea of him with another woman sent anguish burrowing into her as she suppressed a tremor of pain.

The palm of his hand spread the oil across her back, and the faint scent of jasmine wafted its way into her nostrils. Swallowing hard, she squeezed her eyes shut as she fought the urge to weep. Why had she come here tonight? She should have known this would happen. That night at the Clarendon she'd witnessed their lovemaking, why couldn't she see a glimpse of the future where he was concerned? It would make it so much easier to simply walk away from him.

His hands suddenly grew still against her back as he leaned forward to kiss the top of her shoulder. "The shopkeeper called the oil Isis. I've not used it on any other woman, *yā sabāha*, nor do I intend to do so."

The overwhelming relief melting its way through her made her suck in an audible breath. She immediately wished she hadn't. It revealed more than she wanted to. Acutely aware of the fact, she didn't speak, but her body relaxed as he worked the oil into her skin. Jasmine tickled her nose once more as his hands moved downward to knead her buttocks with gentle, firm strokes.

Pleasure rippled through her at the knowledge this moment was for her and her alone. The oil would not touch any other woman's skin. It was a heady thought. She sighed again as his hands glided downward to massage the back of her legs. Seconds later, his teeth gently nipped at her buttocks.

The provocative caress forced a breath of surprised excitement from her. Wicked and delightfully sinful, his mouth nibbled its way to the small of her back as his hand slid between her legs to find her sensitive spot. The gentle pressure on the small bud of flesh sent a blissful moan floating past her lips as she squirmed under the delicious touch.

Satisfaction echoed in his soft chuckle as he circled the nub with his finger. The caress made her insides clench with need, and she arched her buttocks into the air to push back against his touch, eager for more. God, she loved the way he made her feel. Hot, needy and desirable. The rough edge of his knee pushed her legs apart in a masterful move. His free hand slid across her stomach as he forced her to curve her body upward at a higher angle.

The moment his thumb ceased pleasuring her, she groaned her protest. How could he tease her so wickedly only to deny her a release? A split second later, he pulled her to her knees and buried himself inside her. The action made her cry out with a mixture of astonishment and ecstasy as he slid deep into her. It was a new experience for her, and the pleasure was sharp and intense.

As he retreated, she instinctively tightened her muscles in an attempt to keep him inside her. In the blink of an eye, he was buried deep inside her once again. Another cry flew out of her as his body moved to meet hers with long leisurely strokes that made her want to weep with need.

The sensations holding her prisoner were acute as she rocked backward to meet the hedonistic call of his body. With each thrust, he increased the pace until he was driving into her with a force that pulled a deep groan from him.

The scent of jasmine and her passion filled the air, and his eyes closed as her body squeezed him with small contractions. Her buttocks were soft and round against his palms as he slammed into her with a need to possess her in the most primitive way possible. With every thrust into her, his body shouted for more. He wanted to absorb every part of her until she was his completely.

Her musky scent mixed with the exotic fragrance of the oil, and he groaned at the way his body responded to even the slightest nuance of her. She looked like a penitent worshipper on a red silk altar of decadence. The image sent blood surging through him, making him harder than he ever thought possible. Christ Jesus, she was tight. Remembering the taste of her cream over his tongue made him growl with need as tiny spasms grabbed at his erection.

The low moan echoing from her was one of raw passion, and his body responded with a wild frenzy of strokes. In seconds, she exploded over him, her sweet cunny clenching around him with a demand that he explode as well. His body obeyed as he thrust into her one last time and a shout of release poured out of his throat.

Arching away from her, he welcomed the fierce climax that made his cock throb as her body continued to clench and massage his erection. Time stood still as she shuddered under him for several minutes. The sensations of their climaxes slowly subsided, and as she sank down into the bed, he followed her.

The moment they were no longer joined as one, his body renewed its ache for her. It was a familiar sensation. He'd lived with it for some time now. Throwing himself down on the mattress beside her, he stared up at their reflection in the mirrors above. The crumpled silk sheets surrounding her created the perfect frame for the sensuous curves of her delicious body.

She turned toward him and curled up close to his side, a satiated expression on her face as her eyes drooped sleepily. "You, my lord, are incredibly wicked."

The soft words tugged a smile to his lips. "I'm happy to oblige, my lady, but I confess I had excellent incentive."

"Incentive?" she asked as her eyes widened with puzzlement.

Sending her a wicked look, he settled a hard kiss on her lips. "I've never seen a sweeter derriere, and taking you the way I did afforded me the added pleasure of seeing my cock covered in your hot cream every time I slid in and out of you."

"Lucien," she gasped loudly. The shocked expression on her face was quickly replaced by a deep blush as she shook her head at him in silent dismay.

Amused, he ran one finger over her shoulder and down her breast to circle a nipple that had grown hard and stiff. "Which offends you more, *yâ sabâha*? The fact that I find your bottom erotically pleasing or my language?"

"I have to *choose*?" There was still a scandalized look on her face, but it was the note of laughter in her husky voice that made him grin. Bending his head toward her breast, he flicked his tongue over her nipple.

"Then you're willing to please me if I decide to take you in that manner again."

"Yes," she sighed as he tugged gently at her nipple with his teeth.

He watched her closely as he swirled his tongue around the stiff tip of her breast. The moment her hazel eyes darkened with desire, he pulled away from her and blew a steady breath of air across her skin. The mewl escaping her tugged pleasantly at his groin.

"Then tonight you'll please me over and over again, Isis," he murmured as he captured her mouth in a deep kiss. A long moment later, he lifted his head to study her luminous features.

The womanly smile curving her lips set off a firestorm of protest in the back of his brain, but he ignored the outcry. Tonight he wanted to lose himself in the potent charms of an Egyptian goddess.

Chapter Ten

The mantle clock chimed quietly five times, and Lucien could see the first gray light of dawn peeking through the slit in the bedroom curtains. Nestled against him, Constance murmured softly in her sleep and snuggled deeper into his side. One arm wrapped around her, he lifted a lustrous lock of chestnut hair and wound it around his forefinger. Beneath the sheet, her body was outlined in all its lush proportions. His gaze slid downward to the curve of a full breast and on to the gentle flare of her hip.

Passion surged through him again as his fingers lightly traced the area where her hip met a lush thigh before brushing across the upper part of her calf. His groin tightened as he grew hard with need. He closed his eyes. Bloody hell, he'd fully expected his desire for her to abate once morning had arrived.

How could he have misjudged the situation so badly? With a grimace, he shook his head as he tried to form a plan. He'd been a fool to think one night of passion would quench the hunger he'd endured for so long. All he'd succeeded in doing was to feed the demons possessing his soul.

Last night he'd wanted nothing more than to consume her, devour her until she was part of him. Looking down at her soft features, he burned with the need to rouse her from sleep and slake his thirst inside the tight velvet heat of her one more time. The thought filled his head with images of her writhing beneath him, and he suppressed them with a deep groan.

Slowly, he removed his arm from around her and replaced the sheet that had slipped off her as she rolled away from him in her sleep. Climbing out of bed, he pulled on his robe and cinched the cloth belt about his waist with a sharp jerk of his fists. Frustration forced his hand through his hair in a rough gesture as he grabbed the back of his neck and stared at the wood floor.

Disgusted at his lack of restraint where Constance was concerned, he suppressed the dark growl seeking to fill the silence with unrestrained fury. The raw emotion of it reminded him how tenuous his position was. If he'd steered clear of her before last night he wouldn't be in this predicament. He'd thought he could harness his desire for her. Master his emotions when it came to her. He'd failed miserably. Primitive and insatiable desire had been the sole force driving him to take her time and again last night. That type of need couldn't be satisfied in one night, and for the first time he realized just how dangerous a game he was playing.

With a glance over his shoulder, he looked at her. The sheet had slid off one side of her as she'd shifted in her sleep. Red silk framed a full breast, the edge of the material barely brushing against her nipple. In an instant his mouth went dry, and he quickly turned away. Even looking at her made it difficult to think straight.

Had his father and Nigel experienced this crushing need? This uncontrollable desire? Nigel had never believed in the Blakemore curse. Surely his brother had experienced some irrational thoughts before he murdered Katherine. Why hadn't anyone seen what was happening to his brother? Or perhaps it had happened too quickly in his brother's case. The pain and fury of Katherine's betrayal must have been overwhelming.

Why hadn't *he* seen the signs that morning?

Guilt twisted its sharp blade in his heart. He, of all people, had known his brother best. Even he'd failed to recognize Nigel's slippery descent into a hell that had left him and Katherine dead. How could he have failed to recognize the madness taking hold in his brother?

And what of the vow he'd reaffirmed the day they'd buried Nigel and Katherine? The oath never to become so captivated by any woman that he might arouse the same beast inside him. What of that? He hadn't simply broken that vow, he'd shattered it last night every time he'd made Constance his. No, that wasn't true. He'd broken his vow that night at the Clarendon when he'd begun his search for her.

Closing his eyes, he tipped his head to one side then the other in an effort to release the tension in his neck. He still didn't have a solution to his problem. Worse yet was the knowledge that Constance had already begun to realize the power she wielded over him. As each hour had passed last night, her smiles had become more seductive and empowered. It had been almost as if she realized how much her presence affected him.

It was a power he couldn't afford to give her. Doing so might easily bring him to his knees where she was concerned. *That* he couldn't allow. He couldn't permit himself to develop any feelings for Constance. Loving her was impossible.

No, not impossible, but it was far too dangerous. He refused to surrender to the beast dwelling inside him, but most of all, he refused to put Constance in harm's way. God knows he didn't want to push her away. There wasn't anything he wanted more than to be free of the Blakemore curse. Free to care for her, but he couldn't.

He had to protect her, and the only way he knew how to do that was to put an emotional distance between them. If he'd been thinking more clearly last night, he would have sent her back to her room without touching her. He'd been a fool to think he could bed her again and remain unaffected. Now he needed to guard her from harm, and that meant hurting her. Guilt whipped through him at the thought, and he grimaced. Better to injure her emotionally than to take her life in some blood-red mist of passion and madness. A soft sigh from the bed interrupted his thoughts, and he turned to look at her.

"Lucien?" Constance's sleepy voice whispered across the room.

Still half asleep, she had sat up, resting her weight on one elbow. As she swept a cloud of hair back off her face, he couldn't help enjoying the ripe, sensuous look of her. Her face shimmered with the sleepy, sultry look of a woman who had been thoroughly made love to.

Unable to move, he contented himself with watching her as she grew more aware of her surroundings. When she spotted him standing in the middle of the floor, she smiled. It was the smile of a siren. Inhaling a sharp breath, he didn't move as she wrapped herself in the sheet and walked toward him. No

Egyptian queen could have been more beautiful. The knot in his throat threatened to choke him.

The worst was yet to come as the sheet slipped from her fingers, and she pressed the warmth of her sweet curves into him. Passion assailed him with the ferocity of a wild desert storm while the hot softness of her waist heated his palms. His mouth slashed over hers in a kiss that was hard and savage.

The decision to drive her away from him was a blurred thought in his head as he cupped her breast and bent to suckle her. The taste of her was sweet and intoxicating. As he circled his tongue around a taut nipple, a mewl of pleasure feathered its way over the top of his head. In that instant, rational thought returned, and he pulled away from her.

"It's getting late. You need to return to your room," he said gruffly.

"I know," she murmured as she caressed his cheek with one hand.

Her gaze focused on the sunrise beginning to peek through the bedroom drapes as a mournful tilt touched her sweet lips. Impulsively, he turned his head and kissed her palm. Eyes closed, he cupped her hand with his, holding her fast against his mouth. She raised her other hand to touch his face.

"What is it, Lucien? What's wrong?" Apprehension threaded her voice as he looked at her.

In the first blush of dawn he'd never seen a more beautiful sight. Nigel would have labeled him insane for letting her go. There was no doubt about his impending insanity, but there were considerable doubts where her safety was concerned. His brother hadn't heeded the signs of the beast within, but he knew better. It was only a matter of time before the anger and jealousy he'd been experiencing where she was concerned would erupt in a nightmarish repetition of death.

"Lucien?"

"Last night will not be repeated."

The coldness of his words sliced through the air, and he wanted to bite his tongue off as the color drained from her face. The pain furrowing her brow slashed at his heart, and he fought to keep from pulling her into his arms. Christ Jesus, what had prompted him to be so cruel? He didn't take his eyes off her as her expression became dispassionate—closed to him. As she turned away from him, he battled the demons encouraging him to go to her and beg her forgiveness. He'd be a fool to do such a dangerous thing.

Silence filled the room as she quickly retrieved her nightgown. With her back to him, she slipped the garment over her body, hiding her lovely curves from him. There was a restrained dignity in her demeanor as she donned her robe and moved toward the door. Immediately, he took a step toward her before conquering the urge to stop her from leaving.

It served no purpose to explain why he was pushing her away. More importantly, he wasn't certain he'd be able to fight her if she were to realize the strong hold she had over him already. As she grasped the doorknob to leave the room, she hesitated.

"I trust, my lord, I can count on your discretion about this...this interlude."

"For God's sake, Constance. I know I'm a bastard, but give me credit to act as a gentleman should."

In a flash, she whirled to face him. The icy look she sent him made him stiffen. He'd expected her to be hurt, not angry. What the devil was going on in that beautiful head of hers? Steeling himself for a display of typical female anger, he narrowed his gaze at the sight of the cold, lifeless glint in her hazel eyes.

"A gentleman?" she said softly. "No, my lord, I would not consider you a gentleman. In fact, I wouldn't dare to speculate what you are. It's impossible to identify that which doesn't exist."

Thunderstruck by her frost-ridden retort, he didn't move as she left the room. When he recovered, anger flowed hot and furious through him at his reprehensible behavior. The last thing he'd meant to do was hurt her, and he was certain her reaction had been born of pain and humiliation. He'd done what needed to be done, but he hated how the entire mess twisted at his gut. God, when in the hell had he evolved into such a consummate libertine?

$\infty$$\infty$

Constance hurried through the dimly lit corridors toward her bedroom. How could she have been so blind to his true motives? Her stomach roiled at the memory of her behavior last night and since she'd first met him. The intimate acts she'd performed with him were ones few women would admit to having knowledge of, let alone actually perform.

Queasy from the thought of her wanton actions, she stopped and pressed her forehead to the cool stone of the wall. Worst of all, she'd taken great pleasure in every sexual act. With Lucien, she'd allowed layer after layer of protective emotional barriers to be stripped away until there was only one obstacle still left to be cleared. Then to have him treat her like a common whore he'd hired for just one night had been not only humiliating, but more painful than she had ever dreamed possible.

She was finally beginning to understand how deeply she was entangled in his life. If she hadn't been, his actions would have simply humiliated her, not drawn blood. And he had wounded her. Her heart ached with a dull throb that assaulted every inch of her body.

Hot tears pressed against her eyelids, but she refused to give way to them. The man wasn't worthy of her tears. He wasn't worthy of her. She bit her lip. It was easy to think that, but believing it would be far more difficult. A soft sound tightened her muscles with tension. The last thing she wanted was to be caught in the corridor in her nightclothes, even if she was only a few doors away from sanctuary.

Pushing herself away from the wall, she took one step toward her room when she spied a dark flash of movement in the corridor. Startled, she waited for the familiar sensation that always accompanied the presence of a spirit. When the hair on the back of her neck didn't stand on end, she frowned. If it wasn't a ghost in the corridor then it meant someone else was out and about.

Dear Lord, if someone saw her— Shrinking back against the wall, she remained as still as possible. As the shape moved again, she watched it suddenly vanish into the wall. Seconds later there was a barely perceptible click. If most of the household hadn't been asleep, she doubted she would have even heard the quiet sound.

She allowed several long moments to pass before she dared to move. Certain the corridor was empty, she hurried toward the spot where she'd seen the shadow disappear into the wall. She frowned as she ran her hand over the rough stone surface. There was nothing on the wall to even suggest there might be a door. So what had she seen?

She stared at the gray stone in a bemused fashion. The shock of Lucien's rejection had made it impossible to think straight. She'd imagined it. It was a self-defense mechanism her brain had set into motion to divert her attention from the pain clawing at her insides. It was the only explanation, given she'd been mad enough to even think Lucien might actually— She slammed the door on the traitorous thought. A searing fire began to replace the numbness in her chest as tears forced their way up into her throat.

Sanctuary her only thought, Constance raced toward her room. Only when she was behind the closed door of her bedroom did she allow the tears to flow. Hot and steady, they burned her cheeks as she sank to the floor. One hand pressed against her heart to ease the pain slicing through her, she cried until there were no more tears left to shed.

How could he? How could he have made love to her so passionately only to discard her with such callous abandon? And how could she have let him? Staggering to her feet, she crossed the floor to the window. Dawn had grown into the first rays of sunshine, and she tugged the drapes open in an attempt to wash away the bleakness assaulting her soul.

One hand pressed against the glass, she inhaled a ragged breath. What was she going to do? She couldn't stay. It was impossible under these circumstances. She would go home. Home to the warmth of Melton House. Sebastian and Helen would welcome her and Jamie with open arms. Yes, that's what she would do. She turned toward the wardrobe, but before she could move, a whispering sound drifted through the air.

"You promised." The disembodied voice hung in the air, soft and yet firm.

She closed her eyes in dismay. Why had she ever made such a promise, and to a ghost no less? Why did she always have to try to help others with her gift? Perhaps Graham had been right. Maybe using her abilities was wrong. Whether it was right or wrong, she'd given her word. The fact it was to a ghost was beside the point. She was doing it for Lucien too.

God, she was a fool to even care what happened to him, but it was impossible to forget the image of him as a young boy at the scene of his parents' grisly deaths. Chewing on her bottom lip, she crossed the floor to the wardrobe and pulled out one of her more practical dresses. She would seek solace in her work, and perhaps a few hours spent in the gardens with Jamie and Imogene. The children always made her laugh with their antics, and laughter would help to ease the pain in her heart.

Dressing quickly, she moved to the vanity and gasped. The drawer where she kept her personal journal had been pried open. Fear shot through her as she remembered the intimate details she'd included in the book. With a frantic movement she yanked the drawer wide open and grew dizzy as she stared at the empty drawer.

Sinking down onto the dressing table's small stool, she stared in disbelief at the vacant spot where her journal had been. The churning in her stomach eased at the same moment her anger boiled to the surface. It was bad enough that someone had stolen from her, but for someone to take something so personal infuriated her.

What could anyone want with her personal diary? God help her if the thief were to show it to Lucien. But it wasn't just her intimate thoughts about Lucien that were in the journal. The diary included dozens of notes on the antiquities collection she was cataloging for Lucien. Notes she'd recorded when she'd awakened in the middle of the night with some revelation about one of the artifacts.

Losing that information meant she had to go back and reexamine half a dozen pieces she had thought completed. It would set her back by almost a week. The thought of adding one more week to her stay here at Lyndham Keep suddenly seemed like a cruel trick of fate. Burying her face in her hands, she shuddered. She should have known better than to record the notes in the diary, but she'd kept forgetting to bring up a workbook simply for her late-night record keeping. Furious, she slammed the drawer shut. Whoever had taken her journal would regret doing so the moment she found them.

෫ල෭

Constance set the pottery bowl she'd been studying down on the workbench then added another detailed note on the bowl's artwork onto the catalog card. A beautiful piece, the bowl had required extensive cleaning to reveal its meticulous craftsmanship. Satisfied with the work she'd done over the course of the morning, she laid her pen down and stretched her aching back.

The sudden frisson across her neck made her muscles flex and draw up tight in her back. With a quick glance over her shoulder, she saw Lucien in the doorway of the workroom, an unreadable expression on his dark, brooding features. Without warning, her body immediately responded to his presence. Her heartbeat doubled, her skin became hot and her palms grew damp. Every part of her cried out with awareness at his presence.

Quickly and brutally, she reminded herself of his earlier treachery. If that weren't enough to convince her of his deplorable character, she needed to remember her secret and his opinion about people with abilities like hers. Even without this morning's painful revelation, she knew he could never accept her for who she really was. He'd shown his true nature, and trusting him was something she dare not do again. She turned back to her work, picked up the pottery bowl and set it on the overflow table she'd erected in the storage room.

Without another glance in his direction, she retrieved the next artifact from the crate. Seated once more on her wooden stool, she picked up her tool brush and lightly dusted off the beaded necklace she held, keeping her back to him.

"Is there something I might help you with, my lord?" She made sure to keep her voice even and polite—devoid of any emotion. There was silence for a long moment, and she thought perhaps he'd left, except her neck was still tingling.

"I didn't expect to see you here after…" His words trailed off into silence.

"Are you asking me to leave, my lord?"

Bent over the necklace, she struggled to keep up the

175

pretense that she was working. Although she'd managed to keep her voice cool and emotionless, the battle raging inside her was exactly the opposite. The thought of leaving Lyndham Keep, leaving him, cut through her like a sharp blade. Alarmed, she desperately sought to crush the reaction. Sweet heaven, how could she be so oblivious to who and what he was? She closed her eyes for a brief moment to steady her emotions.

"Damn it, *no*. I'm—for Christ's sake, I can't talk to you when you have your back to me," he barked angrily.

Slowly turning around, she sent him a steady look. "Is there something you wanted to discuss with me, my lord?"

The harsh line of his jaw was rigid, causing his scar to become a taut line of white lightning slashing viciously down his cheek. When he suddenly exploded in a furious motion of pent-up energy, she jumped as he lunged into a fast-paced prowl across the floor of the small room. Each time he passed where she was sitting, the delicious scent of sandalwood tantalized her senses.

Dear Lord, why did he have to smell so wonderful? Look so dark and dangerously attractive? It wasn't fair. She didn't have the same effect on him. Wincing, she bit the inside of her cheek. She didn't want to have any effect on the man. She simply wanted him to leave her be. Suppressing a sigh, she looked away from him. She was lying to herself and she knew it.

"I'd like for us to come to an understanding." The words seemed twisted out of him as if he were suffering under a great weight. She immediately squelched the sympathy that threatened to take hold inside her.

"An understanding, my lord? Is there something about my work that you prefer me to do differently?"

"To hell with the collection," he growled. "I'm talking about last night."

"I don't think there's anything left to be said, my lord. I understand the arrangement quite clearly. Last night will not happen again."

Oh God, how was she able to keep her voice even and detached when all she wanted to do was scream at him? Lash out at him for the pain and humiliation he'd inflicted on her. She watched as he shoved his hand through his hair and halted his pacing.

"I have compelling reasons why last night can never happen again, *yâ sabâha*."

"I'm sure you do, my lord. However, you'll forgive me for not caring."

"Damn it, Constance, I'm trying to explain why I did what I did."

"I'm sorry, my lord, but you seem to be under the mistaken impression that I care. If you are harboring some notion that I am in any way devastated by your behavior, please don't."

"My comments appeared to affect you deeply enough this morning," he said with a grim look. The expression tightened his features into a dark mask of anger.

"Appearances are often deceiving, my lord. If I felt anything at all, it was regret for giving myself to a dissolute degenerate," she said with cold deliberation.

The words hit their mark as she saw him jerk in reaction to her insult. His eyes narrowed with anger as he clasped his hands behind his back as if to keep from throttling her. "I'll grant you that insult, *yâ sabaha*, but know this, what I did this morning *was* for your protection."

"My protection? From what? This Blakemore curse of yours?" Her control slipped as a sliver of bitterness crept into her voice. "You must take me for a fool, my lord."

"What the devil do you know about the Blakemore curse?" His quiet question was like velvet over steel. It held a deadly note that sent a chill racing across her skin.

Flustered, she tried to remember exactly where she'd heard about the curse. Her first memory of it was when Nigel had visited her. Her mouth went dry. Surely she'd heard about the curse from someone other than a ghost. Lifting her chin slightly in an act of bravado, she glared at him.

"I must have heard something about it in passing."

In two steps he closed the distance between them. A grim expression on his face, he shook his head. "No, Constance, I don't think so."

"Where else would I have heard of this perceived family affliction?"

"Where indeed." His gaze bored into hers with an icy anger that made her swallow a knot of fear. "Somehow I don't think you heard about the Blakemore curse at a social engagement."

"I don't remember where I heard it," she snapped. God, if he were to pry the truth out of her, what then?

"Perhaps Malcolm Standish thought the information would be useful to you."

"And perhaps your grandmother confided in me." Furious that he would bring up Standish's name, she didn't stop to think about the impact her retort might have.

"My grandmother?" His eyes narrowed to dangerous slits, as his mouth became a thin, harsh line of anger.

Flinching slightly, she averted her gaze. She might not have told an outright lie, but she was doing nothing to clear up the misconception. She didn't care—let him think what he liked. The man seemed determined to link her with Malcolm Standish, and it infuriated her.

"And did my grandmother elaborate on our family's bloodied history?"

"I know enough," she whispered as she remembered the visions that had haunted her since she'd first met him.

"Ah, but perhaps she omitted some small tidbit. After all, she does want to see me married off."

"Family history or not, no woman in her right mind would have you," she said with an artificial smile of sweetness. Fury darkened his gaze as he reached out and cupped her chin with his hand. The touch was like a branding iron, the heat of it scorching her skin.

"Shall I tell you about the Blakemores and their curse, Constance? Shall I tell you what I'm certain my grandmother left out? The Blakemores have a long history of blood lust. With each generation the male members of the family go on a murderous rampage that is barely describable in words. First there was my great-grandfather who committed the vile deed of filicide. To hear my grandmother tell the story, they were arguing over the Seth statue when my great-grandfather lashed out at his son, accidentally killing him. Filled with remorse, my great-grandfather immediately took his own life. The only problem with this story is there was no statue of Seth found with them. Next was my father. His blood lust was far more terrible. Not content to simply murder his wife, he butchered her in a savage, brutal manner—slaughtered her like an animal."

Tension had drawn his mouth into a thin line of pain, and her heart wept for the agony he still suffered from his memories.

"Don't, Lucien, I—"

"Surely you want to hear all the details, my dear. My father didn't just slit my mother's throat," he said in a voice devoid of emotion as he lightly trailed his finger across her own throat as if it were a blade. The effect was chilling.

"He splattered the library with her blood. Thank God he had the courage to slit his own throat. As for my brother, he was a little less blood thirsty when he murdered his wife. Nigel simply broke Katherine's neck before he had the decency to throw himself off the ramparts."

"I did not murder my wife." Furious outrage laced Nigel's voice as he materialized behind his brother.

The sight of him over Lucien's shoulder made her stomach lurch with dismay. Oh God, what was he doing here? He couldn't have picked a worse moment to show himself. Desperately, she fought to keep her attention on Lucien and not his dead brother.

"Tell him I didn't kill Katherine."

She averted her gaze from Nigel's angry expression, and shook her head in hopes that the ghost would understand her silent refusal. Things were already spiraling out of control, and she had no desire to arouse Lucien's suspicions further. With a sudden move, Lucien completely removed the small distance between them.

"You disagree. But know this, *yâ sabâha*—I have no illusions as to my fate. It is only a question of when—and I refuse to put you in harm's way."

With his lips pressed close to her ear, his words were a dark whisper that reflected a pain she had already witnessed in her visions. But it was the depth of emotion in his voice that made it impossible to remain unaffected by his torment. Caught against the warmth of him, she drank in the scent of spice and sandalwood as she instinctively touched his cheek in a gesture of comfort.

"Damn it, the boy needs his head examined. Tell him Standish wants the Seth statue."

"No," she snapped in response to the ghost's demand before realizing what she'd done. In an instant, Lucien jerked away from her as if he'd been burned. Horrified she might have unwittingly revealed her secret, she met his cold, dispassionate gaze.

"I agree, my lady." His face was an inscrutable mask as his voice chilled the air. "Avoiding temptation is the wisest choice of all options."

Spinning around, he strode out of the workroom, leaving Constance to stare after him with a sinking heart. In his own way he'd been trying to apologize, and he'd misinterpreted her outburst to Nigel's prodding as discouragement. Angry she turned toward the ghost.

"Did anyone ever tell you that you have *less* than impeccable timing?"

"Why didn't you tell him any of what I said?" Nigel asked with intense displeasure. "He needs to know there's no curse."

"Even if that's true, how do you propose I convince of him of that?"

"I'll tell you what to say."

For a moment, she simply stared at the dead man facing her. Was it possible for a ghost to be delusional? Shaking her head, she glared at him.

"If you think I'm about to tell Lucien I can see and talk to you, think again. He believes people who see and talk to spirits are charlatans."

"And yet he can believe in this ridiculous curse."

"I'm not so sure he isn't right. What else can account for all this blood and mayhem in your family? It can't be coincidence."

"Whatever it is, it's not that bloody curse," he snapped with angry confusion. "My memory is faulty, but I *know* I didn't kill Katherine."

Nigel's bewilderment was no greater than her own. Since early this morning, the whole world had suddenly turned upside down on her. Closing her eyes, she inhaled a deep breath and willed herself to relax. Although Lucien's brother was no longer mortal, he could still be a wonderful source of information if she could help him focus.

It wasn't unusual for a spirit to have memory lapses. For some reason, time didn't exist when a person died. It would explain Nigel remembering some things vividly and others less so. In most cases, it was the result of his memory recording only those images that were of major importance to him at the time.

"Nigel, please. To help you and Lucien, I need more information. When you lose your temper you waste your energy, and we both know what that means."

He nodded sharply as frustration furrowed his brow. Satisfied he was acting rational again, she tipped her head to one side as she studied him carefully. "I'm going to ask you a question you won't like, but tell me why you're so certain you didn't kill your wife."

Outrage hardened Nigel's features as he glared at her, but he didn't explode with anger as he might have earlier. With a dignified bob of his head, the ghost glanced away from her.

"We'd had a fight, and I left Katherine crying in our room. When I came back—" A stark expression of grief slashed across Nigel's face as he turned away from her. "When I returned, she was lying dead on the floor. I don't remember much of that moment except the horror of losing her. Katherine was everything to me. All I can remember with clarity is that someone had broken her neck. The next thing I remember is the labyrinth."

"The labyrinth," Constance murmured. "Lucien and Lady Lyndham said it doesn't exist."

Waving his hand in an almost dismissive manner, he nodded as he suddenly paced the floor. "I never thought it existed either, but it does. I've been in it. The problem is, I can't remember *how* to get into it again."

"How do you know you were in the labyrinth?"

"Because I was chasing Katherine's killer. I chased the bastard all the way to the North Tower where we struggled. Clearly, I lost the fight." There was a bitter note in his voice.

Startled, she shook her head in disbelief. "You were both murdered?"

"Yes."

"But by whom, and why?"

"I don't know," he growled in a manner reminiscent of Lucien. "I can't remember what the bastard looked like. Everything about him is nothing but shadows."

Impossible. That's what it was. Impossible. How was she supposed to help Lucien if his own brother couldn't remember who his enemy was? It was just one more tiny piece of the puzzle. And like before she didn't know which way to turn.

"Nigel," she said in a pensive tone, "this man who murdered you. Is there anything about him that you *can* remember? The way he dressed, how tall he was, his voice? Anything?"

With a violent sound of disgust, he shook his head. "*No.* God knows I wish I could. I only know he wants the statue of Seth."

"But you said Standish was the one who wanted the statue."

"Yes, yes," Nigel exclaimed in frustration. "Standish works for the bastard, or at least that's what I think. Everything is such a jumble, it's hard to be certain of anything."

"But Lucien said the statue isn't here. He's not even sure it ever was."

"My brother is wrong. It's here. It has been all along, and it's the key."

She uttered a sharp noise of irritation as Nigel's figure shimmered in the light of the workroom. "Blast it, man! Don't say something like that and then just disappear on me."

"I see now why I confused you with Isis when you first came to the keep." Nigel directed a rueful smile in her direction as he faded away.

As the ghost vanished in a fine mist, Constance slammed her fist on the workbench in anger. This was the second time he'd done this to her, and she didn't like it one bit. The dead man had the decidedly unpleasant habit of disappearing just when he was about to reveal an important tidbit. Equally disturbing was the way he'd suddenly materialized in the middle of her conversation with Lucien.

It had been an unsettling moment having both brothers berate her at the same time. Although she couldn't really classify her exchange with Lucien as a reprimand. If anything it had been his attempt at an apology. And it had been exactly that—an apology. He might not have begged her forgiveness, but his regret had been heartfelt.

Had his behavior this morning really been for her protection? There seemed some merit in the notion given the heart-wrenching manner he'd described the mayhem she'd already witnessed in her visions. And she'd be a fool not to admit his explanation made his actions far easier for her to bear. Still, she wasn't ready to trust him yet.

Although it was difficult not to do so given his attempt to apologize. Still, it didn't change anything—or did it? She nibbled at her bottom lip for a moment. The man had definitely been remorseful. In fact, he'd even used that special endearment he had for her. What if the Blakemore curse wasn't real? Nigel had said he and Katherine had been murdered. But that didn't explain Lucien's parents or his grandfather and great-grandfather. Then there was everything else she'd encountered during her stay here at the keep.

Heaving a sigh, she shook her head. If ever there were a more troubled family than the Blakemores with their dark history, she'd yet to meet them. But could she fulfill her promise to Nigel? What was she supposed to save Lucien from? Himself perhaps? That would make sense given his frame of mind. If the curse didn't exist, the torment Lucien was inflicting on himself was enough to drive any man mad. It was the memory of that small boy staring into the library at the horrible scene of his parents' deaths that was so haunting. She couldn't abandon that boy, and deep in her heart she knew she wanted nothing more than to free the man from the demons lurking deep inside him. And when she'd freed him? What then? What indeed.

Chapter Eleven

"Tell me, Edward, what's this I hear about Oliver and Colonel Armstrong's widow? Is the boy finally going to settle down at last?"

Lucien was the last one entering the salon as his grandmother questioned Edward Rawlings. The conversation was like a fly buzzing near his ear as his attention settled on Duncan talking to Constance near the terrace doorway. Damn the man's hide for showing up unannounced again.

He knew bloody well why his friend was here, and it wasn't to discuss county politics either. No, the man had come to see Constance. It was the fourth time this week alone. Thank God Edward had decided to pop in as well. The older man had sat next to Constance this evening, preventing Duncan from monopolizing her attention throughout the meal as he'd done for the past three nights.

"So I take it he's quite serious about the lady?"

Edward shrugged. "I sometimes think the only thing that boy is serious about is his damned Egyptian Society. Apparently there was a bit of a commotion with the British Museum just last week about some artifacts that went missing."

The mention of the Museum caught Lucien's ear, and he dragged his gaze away from Constance to look at the older man. Edward's son had always been known for being a bit wild, but this was the first time any possibility of real scandal had ever touched him. Oliver and Nigel had been closer in age, so a friendship hadn't developed between Lucien and his cousin.

Growing up, Oliver always had a way of setting one's teeth on edge. Perhaps it was the pompous attitude he possessed, especially when it came to discussing and classifying Egypt's treasures. Despite his dislike of the man, he'd never tolerated any of the Set's snide comments made in his presence. He despised people who were polite to the man's face, while behind his back did nothing but express horror at his Saracen ancestry and the swarthy complexion of his skin. That was the one thing he could safely say didn't bother him about Oliver. No, his reasons for disliking the man went much deeper than that.

Worse still, he had to endure the man's company simply to avoid wounding Edward with Oliver's betrayal. A perfidy he'd not even revealed to his grandmother. It was the only reason he went out of his way to endure Oliver's presence and his pretentious discussions on the worship ceremonies of various Egyptian gods and goddesses. Curious to know more about what Edward's son had gotten himself involved in, Lucien frowned.

"Are they actually accusing Oliver of something?" he asked.

"No, no." Edward waved his hand as he took a puff on his cigar. "The boy has an alibi for the time in which the items were taken from the Museum."

"Alibi?" Aurora snapped. "What the devil has he been accused of?"

"Well, there have been no formal accusations you understand, but Budge did question him about the disappearance of the items. Fortunately the two of us were having supper with Mrs. Armstrong at the time the items went missing. Seems a night watchman must have startled the thief as there were several precious items left untouched."

"I don't understand," Aurora said in an astonished voice. "You mean someone broke into the Museum and didn't take anything of value?"

"Apparently so." Edward's brow furrowed as he nodded. "Budge told me the day I left London that the only items missing were several religious artifacts for one of the lesser-known cults around the time of Ramesses."

Lucien frowned. "What sort of items were taken?"

"An ancient text and several relics. Nothing of real value, other than for us intellectuals," Edward said in a miffed tone.

Clucking her tongue, Aurora took another sip of her coffee.

"Well at least the boy is clear of any scandal. Perhaps this lady friend of Oliver's is making him more steady."

"Time will tell, but the boy could do far worse. Mrs. Armstrong is a lovely woman." Edward took another puff of his cigar as he turned to Lucien. "Speaking of beautiful women, Lucien, your lovely cataloger seems to have captured the Major's heart."

Rawlings nodded toward the terrace doorway. Turning his head, Lucien stiffened as he realized Constance and Duncan had moved outside onto the flagstone patio. What the devil was the woman thinking by going out there with Duncan? Not acknowledging Edward's comment, he headed toward the liquor cart to quickly pour himself a brandy. Certain his grandmother and Edward were occupied in conversation, he moved closer to the French doors in an effort to keep Duncan and Constance in eyesight.

"Really, Lucien, you're acting as if Constance were in some sort of danger." Aurora's cup clattered in its saucer as she glared up at him. "Do sit down."

"I agree, my boy," Edward cleared his throat. "Lady Westbury is in excellent hands with the Major."

Muttering an oath of frustration, he threw himself into the chair opposite his grandmother. Even then he couldn't stop himself from tipping his head to one side just to watch the couple standing on the patio. The sound of Constance's laughter made him grit his teeth. More than two weeks ago she'd laughed like that with him. Giving her delectable body to him with a passion he knew he wouldn't find elsewhere.

Damn it, he should never have turned her away. Stiffening, he swallowed hard. What the devil was wrong with him? He'd done the right thing, hadn't he? Of course he had. It was a necessary step for her protection. He'd ended the affair for her safety. And tonight was a glimpse into the future. The sight of her with Duncan had awakened the beast within him. He'd already imagined more than a dozen ways to end his friend's life. Each successive idea more bloody than the last.

Even keeping his distance might not be enough when it came to keeping her safe. God, he needed to leave Lyndham Keep, and yet he couldn't bring himself to do so. If he was doomed to go mad, then a glimpse of her or a whiff of her exotic scent when she passed him in the hallway would make his descent into hell a little easier to bear.

"So are you going to tell us what's troubling you?" There was just a bit of a smug satisfaction in his grandmother's voice, and it annoyed him.

"Nothing's wrong, Grandmother," he said tersely as he saw Duncan dip his head intimately toward Constance.

The sound of Edward's deep chuckle made him glare at the older man, while Aurora took another sip of coffee and eyed him with an amused look. "I agree with you, Edward, they do make a handsome couple, don't they?"

"What the hell is that supposed to mean?" Lucien growled.

The cup she held rattled noisily as she set it back into her saucer and put her coffee on the tray at her side. "It means you're a bloody fool."

"Your grandmother's right, Lucien." Edward blew out a puff of smoke from his cigar and nodded. "It's obvious you have feelings for the woman, why do you persist in this ridiculous notion of the Blakemore curse?"

"Because I've yet to come up with any other explanation for six deaths."

Edward shrugged in defeat. "You've your mother's stubborn nature, boy."

At the mention of his mother, vivid memories of her flooded his head. He rarely allowed himself to think about her or his father. It was too painful. Closing the box on those thoughts, he returned his attention to the open French doors. What the hell were they talking about out there?

"For heaven's sake, Lucien. If you care for her, then tell her." Aurora heaved a disgusted sigh.

"She deserves better than the dark, depraved madness existing within these walls. It's not possible," he snapped.

"What's not possible, Lucien?" Duncan's cheerful voice echoed from the patio doorway.

Jerking his gaze toward his friend, he glared at the other man before turning his head toward Constance. She was looking especially lovely tonight. The dark ivory satin of her gown suited her coloring. Her hazel eyes met his for a brief moment before she averted her gaze.

God help him, he wanted to drag her out of the salon and up to his room where he'd douse himself in her exotic scent and her sultry heat. His mouth went dry at the image filling his head. Remembering Duncan was waiting for an answer, he shrugged.

"It's impossible winning an argument with my grandmother."

"Ah, we're in sound agreement on that fact." Duncan laughed as he turned toward Constance. "I must be going, my dear, but I hope you'll think about my offer."

The words sent Lucien's fingers digging into his palms as he hid his clenched fists behind his back. Bloody hell, had Duncan proposed to her in such short order? Jealousy lashed through him, and he tugged in a quick breath of air.

He watched a flush crest Constance's cheeks, and the tension coiling in his body created a dull throb in every muscle. In silence, he watched Duncan extend his goodbyes to first Aurora and then Edward. A moment later, he turned toward Lucien with an outstretched hand.

"I enjoyed myself, Lucien. Thank you for having me."

"Good night, Duncan," he said as they shook hands. He didn't care that his voice was colder than an icicle. He wanted the man out of his house and as far away from Constance as possible.

With a glance in her direction, he saw Constance frown at his abruptness. Well, how did the woman expect him to react when another man was attempting to lay claim to her? Clearing his throat, Duncan expressed his thanks to Aurora one last time before leaving the room. With his departure, the silence in the salon hung thick and heavy around his head. His grandmother coughed slightly, and Edward rubbed his hands together as he looked at first Lucien and then the women.

"Well then, I believe I should be trotting off as well." Edward stepped forward and kissed Constance's hand then Aurora's as he said his goodbyes. Turning to Lucien, he snapped his fingers.

"By George, I knew there was something I'd forgotten to mention to you. I happened to see Standish in the village the other day." Edward grimaced at the statement. "Seems he's convinced himself the Seth statue is here in the keep somewhere. I suggest you be on your guard for any of his tricks. God knows what lengths he'll go to just to find the damn thing."

Unable to prevent it, his gaze flashed over to Constance's frozen features. There was a look of fear there, and he frowned. As if suddenly aware he was watching, her expressive features became unreadable. Returning his attention to Edward, he nodded.

"I knew the man had taken lodgings at the inn, and I assumed it was because of his interest in the statue."

"Still no thoughts as to where it might be?"

Edward reached into his coat pocket to retrieve another cigar. For a fraction of an instant, Lucien thought the older man's voice held a troubled note. But his fears were allayed as Edward lifted his head and smiled. From the man's avuncular expression, his question had been one of curiosity and nothing more.

"None, but you'll be the first to know considering you invested a considerable sum of money in the expedition that brought Isis here."

"I did, didn't I," Edward said with another chuckle. "But then I had every faith in the skills and experience of the expedition leader."

Reluctantly, he smiled at Rawlings's jovial comment. "And your faith in my abilities is appreciated."

"All right then, I'm off. Lady Westbury." He nodded toward Constance then leaned down to kiss Aurora's cheek. "Good night, Aurora. A pleasure as always."

With a quick shake of Lucien's hand, the white-haired man left the salon. Watching him leave the room, he heard his grandmother set aside her coffee cup one last time.

"I think I'll turn in for the night. Constance, will you walk with me?"

"Of course, my lady." The speed with which she agreed to his grandmother's request served to reignite his irritation.

He didn't want her to go. He wanted to know what Duncan had proposed to her. And if it was marriage— Clasping his tightly fisted hands behind his back, he directed a sharp nod in his grandmother's direction. The old woman rose to her feet at a slow, dignified pace before stepping toward him. She offered her cheek to him, and he brushed his mouth over her papery-soft skin in a gentle kiss.

"Goodnight, Grandmother."

"Goodnight, Lucien," she said with a tender pat on his arm.

Constance moved to his grandmother's side and offered her arm to the older woman. With a quick look in his direction, she murmured a quiet goodnight then escorted his grandmother out of the room. When they were gone, he slammed his fist into the hard back of a nearby chair. Bloody hell, he was in for a sleepless night.

He turned his head toward the liquor cart. A decanter of brandy would remedy that. If he was going to allow a woman to drive him mad, he might as well let her drive him to drink too. Crossing the floor, he poured himself a glass of liquor and drank it in one gulp. The burning sensation was reminiscent of his craving for Constance—hot and fiery. Taking the decanter with him, he crossed the hall into the library. There was no better place to face his demons than in the hell where they'd been spawned.

SO)CB

Constance awoke with a jerk. Sleepily, she rubbed one eye with her palm as she sat up in bed. She'd thought someone had been knocking at her door. Waiting a moment, she shook her head before sinking back into her pillow and closing her eyes. The sound came again. Bolting upright in bed, she frowned. It was an odd noise. More like a chisel tapping on stone, and it was coming from behind her headboard.

Scooting out of bed, she turned up the gaslight of her bedside lamp before padding across the cold floor to stoke the fire. The sound returned, only it had moved along the wall. Confused, she wrapped a shawl around her shoulders and picked up the lamp to examine the wall more carefully. The tapping on the wall came to a sudden stop before there was a scuffling sound lower to the ground that quickly moved away from her toward the corner of her bedroom.

After several more moments, the noise echoed in her room again, only it was much softer and as if it were coming from some distance away. Thoroughly bemused by the strange sounds, she returned her lamp to the bedside table and sank down onto the mattress to stare at the stone wall. Could the noise have been made by one of the keep's numerous ghosts? She frowned. If it was a spirit, then why hadn't she experienced any of her usual tactile sensations? No, there had been nothing of a ghostly nature about the sound. Something else had created the noise. But what and how?

One hand supporting her chin, she mulled over the strange happenings for several moments, but reached no conclusion. Frustrated, she glared at the wall as if it would offer up its secrets. When it didn't, she hopped to her feet to pace the floor. Lyndham Keep was filled with more secrets and spirits than any ancestral home she'd ever visited. And it refused to reveal any clues to help her find her way through the maze of riddles she was trying to untangle.

When her journal had disappeared more than a week ago, she was certain it had been taken by one of the household staff. After reporting the theft to the housekeeper, she'd waited for the woman to find the thief and return her journal to her. But Mrs. Clarke's investigation had turned up nothing but one innocent staff member after another, while her journal had remained missing.

Where was Nigel? Why hadn't he reappeared? Perhaps he was waiting for another inopportune moment. She grimaced as she came to a halt in front of the fireplace and stoked the coals again. If that was what the ghost was waiting on, then it was doubtful the opportunity would present itself anytime soon. Ever since the morning after their night of passion, Lucien had avoided her with amazing agility. Whenever she entered a room, he was just leaving. The only time she saw him or heard his voice was at dinner and the occasional evening in the salon.

When he did deign to acknowledge her presence, it was in a polite, but distant manner. But the eyes were windows to the soul, and she had on occasion caught him staring at her with that penetrating gaze of his, his desire for her blazing in his blue eyes. And Duncan's recent visits didn't seem to please him at all.

Tonight especially, Duncan's presence had appeared to stir up deep emotions in him. With each passing day she was finding it easier to read his moods, and tonight he'd been furious at Duncan's presence. She stiffened as she stared at a small flame that suddenly flared out of the coals. Could he be jealous? Immediately, she dismissed the notion. She was too close to losing her heart to the man, and hoping he was jealous would only lead her further along a path of heartache. Her gift and his torment created a chasm between them that couldn't be bridged.

Despite her best efforts, it was difficult not to remember the pleasures of that night in Lucien's room. The memories made her nipples peak and harden beneath her nightgown. She bit her lip at the need to feel his hand on her again. Her body ached everywhere for him. Slowly, she slid her hand down toward the apex of her thighs. Even now, she could feel his fingers stroking her, touching her with a hot intimacy.

She shuddered, craving his touch with a rush of hunger that threatened to consume her. Would he turn her away if she went to him now? She didn't even need to ask such a question. Based on his behavior tonight, he would gladly take her into his bed. In the salon, the possessive look in his eyes had been stark and vivid. Seeing her with Duncan had infuriated him.

No, he wouldn't turn her away from his bed tonight, but she was certain he'd reject her once their passion was spent. His belief in the Blakemore curse was too strong for him not to. It controlled his every action. He was already beginning to question having her remain at Lyndham Keep. And if she didn't solve this puzzle of the Blakemore curse soon, he would send her away before she could learn the secrets clouding the air of the keep.

The thought of him sending her away pierced her like a sharp blade. She'd never known such longing before, and the pain of it was a physical ache that gnawed at her. With a quick glance at the clock on her dressing table, she heaved a sigh. Two in the morning and she was wide awake. It wasn't an unusual occurrence these days. For a week now, she'd awakened in the middle of the night unable to sleep.

After the first few nights, she'd given up tossing and turning to sneak downstairs to the salon and play her violin. It gave her an outlet for her restless cravings. Music had always soothed her. It had become a panacea for any time she was troubled. Tonight it would work its magic again.

Throwing her robe on, she hurried from her room. The gaslights in the hall had been turned down low, but there was plenty of light to illuminate her way. The first night she'd crept downstairs she'd expected any number of things to happen, including another incident like the one she'd witnessed the morning after her night with Lucien. But the corridors had remained quiet and peaceful during her nightly visits to the salon.

At the foot of the main staircase, she hesitated as she thought she heard a sound coming from the library. When there was no repetition of the noise, she entered the salon and closed the door behind her. Seconds later, she picked up the violin off the top of the baby grand piano.

The wood of the instrument heated her hand with the same warmth Lucien's caress had aroused in her. The memory of his hand on her skin sent a sweet tremor through her. If she was to be held hostage to her passion then she'd play out the emotions in her music. With a deft movement, she tucked the violin under her chin.

The familiar curve of the chin rest warmed and soothed her skin as she grasped the bow's frog in her fingers. Eyes closed, she slowly caressed the instrument's strings with the bow. It was a musical imitation of Lucien's hands sliding across her skin. The heat of his imagined touch expanded and tingled across every inch of her body as she feathered the bow back across the strings. The violin's haunting notes heightened the slow, teasing image of his dark hands stroking her body until her senses hummed with awareness.

Her nipples grew hard at the erotic images flying through her mind, and in desperation she focused all her attention on the difficult sonata she was playing. It was a useless attempt. The memory of Lucien licking her nipples until she was writhing beneath him was too delicious to clear from her head. With each note her bow pulled from the strings, it reminded her of the passion she'd shared with Lucien.

The memory of watching the two of them in the mirror over his bed sent her heart and fingers racing. What had begun as a slow arc of sensual notes quickly erupted into a flurry of sound that echoed the heat flooding her body. The bow danced across the strings of the instrument, and her breathing grew ragged as the pace of the music increased.

She had always loved this particular piece, and had played it many times with Sebastian accompanying her on the piano. But tonight she understood the meaning of the sonata. It was a cry of desperation. It represented the need and hunger of two lovers. And in her mind, her hands caressed Lucien, touching him, arousing him until he groaned with need. Need for her.

With each lyrical phrase she coaxed from the violin, her body reflected a hunger she knew only one man could satisfy. Each powerful note she played pulled every one of her nerve endings taut until they wept from the haunting music flowing out of her soul.

The violin's notes became an extension of her emotions, and the melody evoked the tactile sensations of Lucien stroking her skin. God, she wanted to feel his touch again. She wanted his hands and lips on her—caressing her, tempting her. It was a craving that quickly peaked. She pulled another fiery passage of notes from the violin, her movements sharp and frantic as the bow flew back and forth. The fierce intensity of the music sent desire charging through her body

Dear God, her playing only seemed to increase her hunger for Lucien. The beat of her heart crashed against her breast, matching the violent pace of the sonata, while a fire burned in her belly. If only she could exhaust her emotions in the passion of the piece.

The bow darted its way across the strings in her attempt to quell the desire the music evoked in her. Fierce and exquisite in their composition, the strains of the sonata blazed their way through the room. Sweet heavens, she wanted to weep from the way the melody forced her to cajole note after note from her instrument with renewed fervor. It if were possible for a violin to cry it did so now, and the music she played swelled around her, caressing her like a lover. It was a poor substitute for Lucien's embrace, but it was all she had.

She sucked in a fresh breath and her body arched in surrender to the emotion in the music. The notes escalated into a frenzied arpeggio and tension sailed through her as she envisioned her body responding wildly to Lucien until they were both satiated. Her fingers raced across the fingerboard at the intoxicating image. Each note flying out of the violin represented a kiss, a touch, a thrust of Lucien's powerful body into hers. With several frantic strokes of the bow, she pulled the final furious passage out of the violin. An instant later, she uttered a soft cry of release and felt the familiar rush of liquid heat between her thighs.

Ragged breaths escaped her lips, and she sagged into the soft curve of the baby grand piano. Her heart pounding, she allowed the emotional outpouring of her frantic musical display to wash over her. Eyes closed, she imagined herself caressing Lucien's hard muscles one more time, tantalizing him—teasing him into a frenzied pitch of need. A need that ended with wild, hoarse cries of excitement as they rode their desire to the ultimate peak. She shuddered at the image.

"Most impressive, my dear lady."

With a jerk, Constance opened her eyes to see Nigel watching her from the darkened corner of the room. Setting her violin and bow down on the piano, she glared at the ghost.

"Must you do that?" she snapped. "It's disconcerting when you simply appear out of nowhere like that."

"My apologies. I'm afraid I have little control over my comings and goings."

"Just like you have no control over knowing where I can find the statue, I suppose."

"Not exactly, but I do remember where one of the entrances to the labyrinth is, although I doubt you'll be pleased."

"Where is it?" Trepidation hitched her breath as she saw the rueful expression on the ghost's features.

"My brother's bedroom," he muttered.

"What?" She starred at him in disbelief. "Of all possible locations, that's the *only* one you can remember?"

"I am sorry. If I could remember where another entrance was, I would tell you, but at the moment, this is the best I can offer."

"And exactly how am I supposed to search his bedroom?" she snapped.

Nigel bent his head as he cleared his throat. Rigid with horror, she shook her head vehemently. "*No.* Not again. You can't ask it of me. I don't think I could bear it."

"Exactly *what* couldn't you bear, my lady?"

The familiar low growl in her ear made her cry out in surprise. Wheeling around she took two quick steps backward as she looked up into Lucien's dark features. His gaze scraped over her with contempt as he moved forward to search the area where Nigel was standing. When he found nothing, he whirled around to face her, a cold rage tightening the muscles of his jaw.

"Where is he?"

For a moment, she simply stared at him in puzzlement. "I don't—"

"Standish, my lady. Where is he?"

"If you're suggesting I was talking—"

"Suggesting?" he snarled. "I'm not suggesting anything. I know what I heard, and I want to know who the hell were you talking to just now?"

"I...no one..." she stammered, unable to think of a reasonable explanation, especially when she had no idea how much he had heard. What had he heard? Obviously her last comment or he wouldn't have referred to it when he'd pressed his mouth to her ear just a moment ago.

"I'm going to ask you one more time, Constance. Who were you talking to?"

"No one," she lied. Telling him the truth would only make matters worse.

"You, my lady, are a liar," he ground out harshly.

"I wasn't talking to Standish," she snapped. "I have no idea where the man is, nor do I care."

"I heard a man's voice, Constance. I couldn't understand what he was saying, but I know he was here."

"No, that's not possible." She stared at him in shock. How could he have heard Nigel? He couldn't have.

As he stepped toward her, she shrank back at the fury on his face. His hands clamped on her upper arms to hold her in place. Something about his demeanor said he'd reached the edge of his patience.

"Tell me, how much is he paying you?"

"Wh...what?" she stuttered as she tried to understand how Lucien could have possibly heard his brother's voice.

"Standish. What's the bastard paying you? Did he pay you extra to slide between my sheets? If not, I'll be happy to correct that oversight."

"He's not paying—" Her outrage evaporated into horror as she met his contemptuous gaze, the full impact of his statement washing over her. Swallowing her humiliation, she tilted her chin in rebellious anger. "Believe what you will of me, my lord. I was not talking with Standish."

Brilliant blue eyes narrowing, he studied her for a long moment. The look of assessment on his face told her he was carefully weighing her words. She'd not lied to him in stating she wasn't talking to Standish, but she'd not denied talking to someone either. The expression on his face showed he'd finally deduced that fact, and his mouth was a harsh line of determination as he pinned her with his penetrating gaze. She shuddered beneath his look, her breathing ragged.

"If not Standish, my lady, then who?"

"I...no one...I told you I have a habit of talking to myself," she said desperately as she fought to fight her way out of the corner his words were backing her into.

"Most convenient," he sneered. "Avoid an outright lie simply by claiming you fainted or were talking to yourself."

"Somehow I don't think it would matter whether I told you the truth or not, you'd still call me a liar." Glaring up at him, she pushed against his chest in a futile effort to break free of his grasp.

"So you admit you were talking to someone."

"I admit no such thing."

"Then perhaps you'll explain whose bedroom you're supposed to search."

His icy words were like a blast of winter air as she stared up at him. Dear God, he must have heard her entire conversation with his brother. Or at least her responses. She swallowed hard at the emotion blazing in his eyes. How could she explain without revealing everything? A shudder rippled through her at the thought.

"Let me go."

"Who was he, Constance? Your lover?"

With a dark growl, he jerked her forward into a tight embrace. In an instant, the heat of him sank into her skin until she was convinced she would melt from the fire burning inside her. Astonished, she shook her head in disbelief.

He thought she had a lover. Someone other than him. Why would he think that, unless—he was jealous. It would explain everything, his behavior over the past few nights when Duncan came to visit and his reaction now. Was that the reason? Uncertainty flared inside her as she met his fierce gaze.

"The only lover I have is you, Lucien. There is no one else."

Her soft whisper made him go rigid as she met his gaze steadily. Indecision crossed his face, before he uttered a groan that sounded as if he'd pulled it from deep within his tormented soul. An instant later, his mouth captured hers in a harsh kiss.

Filled with dark passion, it was a kiss that demanded complete surrender, and she eagerly yielded to his touch. Deep in the recesses of her mind, logic screamed she was a fool for giving in to her desire. In doing so, she was only begging for heartache. But it was too late. Her heartache had begun the first time they'd touched.

Arms wrapped around his neck, her fingers spiked through his silky black hair as his thumb circled her nipple. She drew in a sharp breath of pleasure at the way his touch sent heat flowing to her nether regions. Lost in her desire, she pressed her hips into his. God, she wanted him. Needed him. He had only to speak and she would give him whatever he asked. Gently, his fingers tweaked her nipple as he nipped at her neck. Another moan spilled from her throat.

"You're mine, *yâ sabāha.*"

"Yes," she sighed as his mouth brushed over hers in a light kiss.

"I'm the only man who excites you." Gently his mouth tugged at her earlobe before grazing the edge of her jaw toward her mouth.

She moaned again, her body crying out for his possession.

"Oh God, Lucien, please, I want you."

"Then give me his name." The whisper feathered its way across her cheek to her ear, and in the back of her head a warning screamed for her not to answer. But not soon enough.

"It was Nigel."

The moment she spoke her blood ran cold. Oh God, what had she done? He'd deliberately seduced her to get the answer he wanted. And she'd given it to him. Caught up in the throes of desire, she'd not taken care with her words. He shoved her away from him, his eyes hard and glittering with anger. The abruptness of his retreat made her sway where she stood as she stared at him in horror.

"Nigel," he ground out. "And his last name, Constance. I'll have that too."

"Oh God, don't ask it of me," she pleaded. Trembling, she shook her head as she stared into his angry features. His expression was unrelenting, and she knew he'd hound her until she told him the truth.

"His last name." The fury in his voice made her wince.

"Blakemore," she whispered in a voice so low she could barely make out the word herself. He didn't move for a long moment as he stared at her with a frosty gaze that seared her skin.

"Do not mock me. My brother is dead." Bitter and cold, his words lashed out at her with the fiery sting of a whip.

"I know," she said as she bent her head to avoid his cold gaze. He wasn't going to listen to her. It would have been difficult enough to make him understand if he'd not already been angry with her. Trying to convince him now was going to be impossible.

"You know." His contempt was a steel trap clamping down on her heart. "Then naturally, you know it's impossible to speak to the dead."

"For some people, yes." She swallowed the knot of fear in her throat. It was easy to tell from his demeanor that he believed she was lying again. Bowing her head, she stared down at her clasped hands. Her knuckles were white from the strength of her grip.

"Ask him if he remembers Professor Hodge."

Constance's head jerked up at the sound of Nigel's voice. He had materialized next to Lucien, and she uttered a soft sound of consternation. She shook her head at his autocratic demand, but like his brother, Nigel's expression was implacable. Squaring her shoulders, she looked directly into Lucien's cold eyes.

"He wants to know if you remember Professor Hodge."

Lucien's body jerked violently before he recovered and folded his arms across his chest. A muscle twitched in his cheek, tugging at his scar. "Take care, Constance, you're playing a dangerous game."

Beside him, Nigel's mouth contorted with anger as he smashed his hand into his open palm. The action made him shimmer slightly as if he were about to disappear. Determination lined his features as he glared at his brother.

"Ask him if he remembers the nickname we gave the Professor?" Nigel's command held the same steely note Lucien's had. Caught between the two of them, she shook her head in protest. "Damn it, woman, ask him."

Shivering, she closed her eyes for a brief instant before taking a deep breath and doing as Nigel had instructed. "He...your brother...he wants to know if you remember the nickname you had for the man."

"Suppose you tell me," Lucien sneered as his lips thinned with anger.

"Wooly Bear, because he looked like one of our toys by the same name." Nigel said as he watched Lucien's face. Quietly, she repeated the name.

Pain flashed across Lucien's face, only to be replaced in a split second by a fury darker than he'd already displayed. The rage filling his features washed over her like an icy bath, and she quickly stepped backward out of reach. She'd expected a cool, mocking disdain when he learned about her gift, not this all-consuming wrath.

"Get out," he growled in a raw rasp of sound.

"Damn him." Nigel shouted his fury then vanished into thin air.

Alone in the face of Lucien's rage, she stretched out her hand to him. "Please, Lucien, try to understand, I—"

"Leave now, Constance." The savage note in his voice made her jerk her hand away from him. "Leave while I am still in control of my temper. If you stay, you do so at your own peril."

Blue eyes glittering with scorn, he raked his gaze over her, and the contempt in his face sent a physical tremor of pain sailing through her. How could she make him understand she wasn't lying? What could she do to make him see she had no control over her gift? Couldn't he see how much she feared for his safety? How much she loved him?

The revelation lashed out at her with the force of an explosion. Shock stiffened her body, making it a supreme effort even to move. Step by step, she stumbled toward the salon doorway and tried to smother the sobs rising in her throat. As she raced from the room, only two thoughts churned in her head. Escape, and the knowledge that she loved a man who despised her.

Chapter Twelve

Lucien didn't move as Constance fled the salon. The coals in the hearth glowed red as a flame sparked upward, throwing the shadow of her retreating figure onto the wall. It reminded him of the erotic vision he'd witnessed moments ago as she'd played the violin in the near darkness.

He'd stood in the shadows watching her, unable to move. The way she'd played had twisted his emotions into a knot of need and desire. Every note she'd pulled from the violin strings had given her the look of a woman in the throes of one climax after another.

The music swelling around her had only served as a reminder of the passion they'd shared. But when she'd arched backward and played the instrument with even greater abandon, he'd thought he would go mad. Surely he couldn't be blamed for wanting just one more taste of heaven.

His fist crashed into the hard leather of a wing-backed chair.

He was a fool.

She'd deceived him.

A wild fury surged through his blood until it gripped every one of his muscles. He fought against it, struggled with the desire to go after her and drag the truth out of her in ways he didn't dare imagine. Lies. All lies. First the deception about her true identity and her husband's connection to Standish, denying she knew the man, and yet he'd found them together that day in the pasture. Now *this*. Using his brother's name to try to convince him there hadn't been a man in this room with her.

Those beautiful lips of hers spewed out lies as easily as a serpent did its venom. God, he'd wanted to kill her a moment ago. And not just because she'd lied to him. No, that wasn't what had provoked his fury.

It was the thought of her with another man that had set fire to his anger—stoked the flames of his fury until he could barely think straight. Christ Jesus, it had started. He'd been tumbling over the precipice and didn't even realize it. Chilled by the thought, he sank down into a nearby chair.

From that first moment he'd seen her luscious curves outlined in the firelight, he'd been determined to have her. Driven to find and possess *his* Isis, the woman behind the mask she'd worn that night at the Clarendon. And it had brought him to this. The beginnings of madness.

Head buried in his hands, he shuddered at the rage still seething inside him. It was a demon he wasn't sure he could control. But he had to find a way of doing so. He needed to know who she'd been talking to. Standish was still staying in the village, and the man wasn't simply on holiday. He was up to something, and it had to be related to the statue of Isis.

He reached up to trace the long scar on his cheek with his fingers. Standish had been intent on killing him that day in the desert when they'd fought over the rights to the tomb of Aramun, a priest of the Seth cult. The man probably would have succeeded in slicing up more of him if his men hadn't arrived to escort Standish off the site at gunpoint.

As a boy he'd searched for the Seth statue diligently, determined to find it. But over time, he'd come to believe the icon was a myth. Then he'd discovered the statue of Isis in Aramun's tomb, and he'd been forced to reconsider. Now, with Standish being so close by, it increased the odds that the Seth statue did exist.

The question was, did Standish already have it, or did he think it was here in the keep? Without the other half of the map, anything the statues gave up would be useless in finding Sefu's tomb, and he'd hidden the half he owned—in his bedroom.

Springing to his feet, he paced the floor. Bloody hell, she *was* working with Standish. The man had told her to search for the papyrus in his room. Why else would she protest searching his room? Why indeed? Perhaps she found being in his bed a far worse fate than his anger.

The thought of her coming to his bed simply out of avarice only served to increase his fury. In the next instant, he remembered the fiery passion they'd shared. The sweetness of it. No, he couldn't believe she'd come to him simply as a matter of necessity. Was Standish threatening her, forcing her to do his dirty work? God, he was still making excuses for her.

And how had the man gotten into the keep? He'd not seen anyone near her, and he'd not detected any movement while she was playing. Shaking his head, he came to an abrupt halt near the piano. With a frown, he stared at the carpet beneath his feet. Whoever she'd been talking to had surprised her. What was it she'd said? Something about being disconcerted. Yes that was it. Her visitor had been unexpected.

If she wasn't expecting someone, how had they entered the room? Lifting his head, he peered into the shadows at the wall behind the piano. The large tapestry covering the gray stone wall had been there since childhood and longer. Of that he was certain. Quickly moving toward the gaslight on the wall sconce, he turned up the flame then focused his attention on the tapestry.

The weight of the material made it difficult to pull the tapis back from the cold, gray stones so he could study the wall behind it. Other than the outline of where the large sandstone blocks butted against each other, there was no indication of a hidden door.

He let the material fall back against the wall, the heavy thud echoing in the silence. Even if there were a hidden door behind the tapis, no one could have come and gone without disturbing the decorative hanging. The entire time he'd watched Constance play her violin the tapestry hadn't moved. Whoever had been in the salon with her had to have departed some other way than a hidden door behind the tapis.

Slowly walking along the length of the wall, he carefully studied the junctures of each stone, searching for a possible hidden door. Something. Anything to explain how Constance could have a conversation with her mysterious visitor one minute only to find the visitor had vanished into thin air. But more importantly, an explanation for how she knew about

Professor Hodge.

He recalled her standing in front of him, boldly declaring she could speak to Nigel. Did she think he would believe such an outrageous story? She must think him a fool. And yet she'd sounded so sincere. Damnation, he needed to stop making excuses for the woman. She'd lied, and he was going to prove it.

With renewed vigor he continued to search along the wall. When he reached the corner where the outside and interior walls met, he uttered a grunt of anger. Nothing. Damn it, no one could have come in and out of the room without him seeing something. How the devil had the bastard done it? Could she have been telling the truth?

"Christ Jesus, of course not. She was lying," he raged to an empty room.

Wheeling about, he stared at the violin lying on top of the piano. It was a suitable instrument for her fire and passion. Watching her from the doorway a short time ago, he'd never seen anything more beautiful in his entire life. Just the way her body moved in time with the music had aroused him until he'd wanted nothing more than to take her there on the floor.

The familiar sensation of his cock stirring in his trousers made him utter a grunt of disgust. It had been difficult enough living with the fact he couldn't have her, but *this*. This newest fabrication of hers wasn't just ludicrous, it was implausible. She'd actually tried to convince him she was able to talk to Nigel by acting as though it was his brother giving her that ridiculous name they'd had for Professor Hodge. No doubt she'd gotten that little tidbit from Nanny.

The sudden chill filling the room made him turn toward the doors leading out to the terrace. He crossed the room in several quick strides and twisted the door handles. The doors were locked. Where the devil had that draft of cold air come from? As he turned back around, he caught a glimpse of something out of the corner of his eye near the front windows, but it vanished before he could make out what it was.

Tomorrow he intended to tear the room apart if necessary to find out how Constance's visitor had gained such easy access to the salon and to the keep itself. It would please him immensely to drag her into the salon to show her she wasn't as clever as she thought. The woman had no more been talking to

Nigel than he was free of the Blakemore curse. Rubbing his hands together in the icy cold of the room, he uttered an oath of fury and strode from the salon.

ⅤⅣ

Constance stared out at the rising sun framed in a sky of pink and mauve clouds as she leaned against the wooden frame of her window. Fingertips pressing into her temple, she winced at the way her head hurt. Bruised and battered, her heart hurt worse. She'd done nothing but cry since she'd returned to her room in the dark of the early morning.

Now she had no more tears left. There was only the dull throb inside her head, and the pain sliding through every part of her body. How could she have been so dim witted to fall in love with him? She should have left Lyndham Keep that first day he arrived home. Then none of this would have happened.

But it had happened. Her visions had shown her the passion, but not once had she seen anything else. She should have known there would be nothing beyond the pleasure. If she had foreseen his rejection, his anger—would she have done anything differently?

It was always easy to reflect on what one should or shouldn't have done. Looking back wouldn't help her now. From her bedroom window, she watched two of the gardeners engaged in an animated discussion about the brilliant flowerbed in front of them. For all the bright spring colors surrounding the keep, inside it was cold and dark.

God, she'd been a fool to think she could ever help Lucien or any of the other spirits here in the keep. She buried her face in her hands as a fresh set of tears welled up in her eyes. Tears she didn't think she still possessed. What was she going to do? She loved him so much, and the thought of leaving Lyndham Keep cut through her with the precision of a sharp blade.

She turned away from the window and crossed the floor to the bed. The mattress creaked softly as she curled up into a ball amidst the sheets. Perhaps she could reason with him, make him understand she really was able to see Nigel. A derisive laugh parted her lips and caused the white pillowcase beneath her head to flutter.

Lucien's reaction had made it clear he thought her nothing more than a liar. When he'd first stormed into the salon demanding to know who she'd been talking to, she'd been so startled it had been impossible to come up with a satisfactory explanation.

He'd used her surprise to his advantage. He had his grandmother's skill for pinning an opponent into a corner from which there was no escape. Worse yet had been the way he'd manipulated her into admitting her secret. His kiss had distracted her so much she'd blithely confessed everything without the briefest of hesitations.

But it had been the depth of his anger that chilled her. Frightened her. Not for her safety, but for his. Even furious with her, he'd not made any attempt to harm her. The only danger Lucien posed to anyone was himself. In believing in the Blakemore curse, he was creating his own torment, his own pain. There was no curse. If there were, he would never have been able to restrain himself from hurting her last night. But it didn't matter what she believed.

Lucien believed it.

And she didn't know how to help free him from the demons he'd locked deep inside him. Demons that tugged at him with a strength she could only imagine. Lines from an Edgar Allan Poe poem swept through her head. *From the thunder and the storm / and the cloud that took the form / when the rest of Heaven was blue / of a demon in my view.*

The words could have easily been written by Lucien. The dark, brooding aura of the verse reflected so much of his torment. She brushed another tear off her cheek, her heart aching.

How could she convince him she wasn't lying? Was it even possible? The circumstances all weighed against her, and he had no reason to trust her. Making matters worse, she'd asked him to believe she could talk to his dead brother. She should never have even hoped he would find it possible to trust she was telling the truth.

Her gift had never brought her anything but heartache and, more often than not, rejection when she'd failed to keep her ability a secret. Even Graham, for all the affection he'd felt for her, had been uncomfortable with her gift. How could she expect Lucien to feel differently? And yet, a small part of her had hoped he would. Hoped he would come to identify the torment he bore with her own suffering.

But how could he? He'd have to believe in her ability before he could understand her personal hell. Worse still, he'd lived with his torment for so long, it might be impossible for him to believe anything she or anyone else told him about the Blakemore curse.

Lucien was a man of facts. If she was going to convince him that his family had been murdered not because of insanity, but for other reasons, she had to give him proof. But what? She only had bits and pieces of clues that made no sense at all. This was a puzzle even she couldn't put together.

Pushing herself upright, she brushed a teardrop off her lashes. What could she do to reach him? There had to be a way, but deep inside her, she knew there wasn't. There was nothing more she could do. If she'd had more time, perhaps, but Lucien wasn't going to want her here. It was only a matter of hours, minutes even, before he sent word for her to leave. Scooting off the bed, she moved toward her wardrobe.

"So that's it. You're giving up. You're reneging on your promise to help him."

Listlessly, she turned to see Nigel watching her with a frown she'd often seen on Lucien's face. Although the two brothers didn't look all that much alike, their mannerisms were remarkably similar.

"Go away, Nigel. There's nothing I can do anymore. He won't listen to me. He's convinced himself that I'm lying. I can't fight that."

"Damn it woman, the boy needs you. I'm positive of it."

"Just like you were so positive you could convince him that I can see you?" she snapped. "If you'll recall, his reaction was one of bitterness and contempt."

Bending her head at the memory, she bit back a fresh onslaught of tears threatening to wet her cheeks. Nigel coughed slightly.

"Yes, well...I admit to overestimating Lucien's willingness to believe you. However, he does need you, Constance. He's just not willing to admit it yet. This damnable curse business has him convinced that if he allows himself to care for you, he'll endanger you."

"Go away, Nigel. I'm past caring at this point."

When only silence met her statement, she lifted her head to see him staring at her with a strange expression on his face. "You love him very much don't you?"

Immediately, she turned away and moved to stare out the window. "Yes, but it changes nothing."

"But it *does*. Don't you see? Your love can save him, Constance."

"*How*?" she cried out with anguish as she whirled to face the ghost. "I can't save him if he doesn't want to be saved."

And she was certain Lucien didn't want her to save him from anything. Stubborn and defiant, he wrestled with his torment in solitude, refusing to let her or anyone else help him find safe harbor from his pain. And God knew how desperately she wanted to ease his suffering. She was willing to do anything for him. Follow him anywhere, even to hell itself, if only to be with him.

"Simply love him, Constance. It will be enough," Nigel said with a small smile as he shimmered then dissolved into a mist.

The sudden knock on the door made her heart skip a beat until she realized the sound didn't bear Lucien's authoritative mark. A moment later, the upstairs maid entered the room. The girl bobbed a curtsey.

"Good morning, my lady. Her ladyship wondered if you would be joining her for breakfast."

With a shake of her head, Constance turned away as she noted the curiosity burning in the maid's face. "Not this morning, Anna. Please give her ladyship my apologies. I'm not feeling well."

"Yes, my lady." The girl turned to leave then paused. "Is there anything I can bring you, my lady? You look like a hot cup of tea might set you right."

"No, Anna." She shook her head. "That will be all, thank you."

The soft snap of the door closing behind the maid tugged a

sigh from Constance's lips. Lady Lyndham's curiosity was going to be provoked, especially if Anna was to describe her appearance to the dowager countess. Pressing her palm to her forehead, she closed her eyes. She was so tired. If she slept for a short time, perhaps she could come up with a way to make Lucien understand she wasn't a liar or a charlatan.

∞⃝∞

The sound of crisp paper being folded and slid into an envelope barely penetrated Lucien's preoccupation as his grandmother set aside a letter.

"Edward told me Oliver is visiting him, and Mrs. Armstrong is staying nearby with a relative. I invited them for supper this evening."

When he didn't answer her, she frowned, but continued eating her meal. Pushing his plate of half-eaten food away from him, he leaned back in his chair. Across the table, Aurora arched her eyebrows as she bit into a piece of the roast chicken Cook had prepared for their luncheon.

"Appetite off, my boy? You're not coming down with something, are you?"

"No," he growled.

"I do hope Lady Westbury is all right." With a pointed look at Constance's empty chair, she took another bite of food.

"I'm sure she's fine, Grandmother." He ignored the autocratic look the dowager countess sent him.

"Perhaps, but it's so unlike her to be ill." Aurora looked down at her plate. "I don't suppose you had anything to do with her sudden indisposition?"

"*No.*" He reached for his wineglass and took a healthy swig of the red liquid. Damn his grandmother for her intuitive nature. He had no doubt he was the reason for Constance's illness. But he doubted she was ill. More likely she was hiding in shame for having been exposed as the liar she was. Although it was damned difficult to prove it when he still didn't have any evidence.

"Do you mind telling me exactly what you were thinking

when you instructed Jacobs to have the servants tear the salon apart?"

"I wanted to inspect the walls."

"The walls?" Lady Lyndham looked at him as if he were mad. "What in heaven's name are you looking for?"

Scowling at her, he shrugged. Damn, he should have known better than to agree to lunch with her. "A door to the labyrinth."

"A *what*?" Lowering her fork to her plate, she glared at him. "Whatever makes you think there's a hidden door in the salon?"

"I have my reasons," he snapped as he returned her glare.

"And do your reasons have anything to do with Lady Westbury?" She eyed him with her most imperial of looks. As a boy, he'd always known he was in trouble when she'd looked at him that way. But he was no longer a boy.

"Damn it, Grandmother, I have no doubt your spies have told you everything, why must you hound me for an explanation?" Throwing down his napkin, he pushed himself away from the table in an abrupt move.

"Because my spies, as you put it, are completely baffled as to what's going on in this house. Obviously something has happened since supper last night that has both you and Lady Westbury at odds with one another. I don't care what you do to the keep, but I won't have you upsetting Constance."

"I beg your pardon." Palms flat on the table, he leaned toward his grandmother. "How I choose to conduct business with my employees is my affair, not yours, Grandmother."

"I knew it, you've offended her somehow." Aurora reached for her cane and pushed herself to her feet. "What the devil did you say to her? I won't stand for you treating her badly, Lucien. I won't have it."

"You won't—" He straightened and swallowed the anger rising inside him as he watched his grandmother slowly walk toward him. "Your championship of Lady Westbury is misplaced, Grandmother. The woman is a liar and most likely involved with a scoundrel."

"I don't believe it. Where's your proof, boy? Prove to me that Constance is what you say she is."

"I haven't found it yet," he growled. "But it's in the salon."

"And exactly how do you know it's in the salon?"

"Because last night, I saw her—" Clasping his hands behind his back, he avoided his grandmother's astute gaze and tightened his mouth.

"I take it you saw her with another man?"

Not looking at her, he grimaced. "Not exactly. I could only hear him whispering to her."

Arching her eyebrows, Aurora braced both hands on her cane as her gaze slid over him with assessment. "And did she tell you who she was talking to?"

"Nigel."

Her silence didn't surprise him, but it was the smile of happiness on her face that did. In fact, her reaction astounded him. It was as if she wasn't surprised at all. What the devil was going on? Studying his grandmother's face more closely, he uttered a noise of disgust. Constance had already hoodwinked his grandmother into believing she could talk to the dead.

"You knew!" he exclaimed.

"What? That Constance has a wondrous gift?" With a wave of her hand, Aurora walked away from him toward the dining room door. "Yes, I knew."

"You knew, and you didn't tell me?" Following her, he gritted his teeth as he realized how well Constance had ingratiated herself with his grandmother. It was going to be difficult to send her away if Aurora had anything to say about it, and he was certain she'd have plenty to fill his ears. As she entered the main hall, his grandmother sent him a scornful look over her shoulder.

"Bah! Do you think I would throw her to you like a lamb to a wolf?"

"I'd hardly call the woman a lamb, Grandmother. She's a liar, and if the timing were right, I'm convinced she'd be a thief as well."

The moment the word thief left his mouth he knew it wasn't true. Constance might be a liar, but he'd stake his reputation she wasn't a thief. If she were, his collection would contain far fewer valuables now. Just yesterday, he'd reviewed her work to date, and everything was accounted for. He did her an injustice by calling her a thief. Something his grandmother quickly chose to reiterate.

"A thief? Quick, have Jacobs count the silver spoons." Her sarcasm echoed in the great hall, rising up to the beams high above. "It seems to me you're trying to rationalize something that's impossible to rationalize."

"No. I know what she is, Grandmother. She deceived me when she applied for the position of cataloger. She lied about not knowing Standish—"

"She's admitted she knows the man?"

"Damn it, no." He shoved a hand through his hair in frustration at his grandmother's obstinate refusal to see his point of view. "Of course she's not admitted it, but he was with her the day she took the children on a picnic, and last night—"

"Last night? Something tells me the conversation you interrupted last night was a private one." Her sharp gaze pinned him with a look of disapproval. Stiffening at the condemnation in her voice, he clenched his jaw in an effort to keep from exploding with the anger bubbling just beneath the surface.

"She wasn't talking to Nigel," he bit out.

"Then who was she talking to?" Aurora's piercing gaze met his as she waited for his response.

"I don't know, but as soon—"

"Well if you don't know who she was talking to, how do you know she *wasn't* talking to Nigel?"

"Because my brother's dead," he snarled.

The words bounced off the stone walls like a stray bullet. They reverberated in the air for several seconds before silence enveloped the anger and grief behind the sound. The sadness in his grandmother's eyes made him look away from her as she studied him with an expression of understanding on her weathered face. Gently, she patted his arm.

"Constance has a wonderful ability, Lucien—a gift. It allows her to ease the pain of others."

"Lies, even if well-intentioned, are still lies."

"You know me well enough, boy. I'm not easily fooled. When she told me William was in the room with me, I didn't believe her either." She swallowed hard, and he saw her blink back tears. "But then she said one word. One word convinced me William was in the room."

With a derisive shake of his head, Lucien met a blue-eyed gaze almost identical to his. The confidence and peace reflected in her eyes amazed him. She smiled.

"Believe what you like, boy, but Constance gave my heart back to me when she uttered one word. A word only my William could have told her himself."

Aware his grandmother was convinced beyond any doubt of Constance's ability, he expelled a deep breath of frustration. In the face of such certainty, there was nothing he could do but allow her to believe what she wanted. Leaning forward, he kissed her cheek.

"I'll have Jacobs return the salon to its original state," he muttered as he turned to leave her.

"And Constance. What will you do about her, Lucien?"

Tension shot through him, holding him rigid and stiff as he heard the second meaning beneath her question. He didn't know what to think, and he damn well wasn't going to admit that to his grandmother. She'd waste no time wearing him down, convincing him Constance was talking to Nigel last night. The disturbing thing was, he wanted to be convinced. Without looking at his grandmother, he shook his head.

"The situation with Lady Westbury is my affair. I'll deal with it in my own way."

Without waiting for her to renew her probing, he stalked away from her. Deal with it his way. Exactly how was he supposed to do that? If he'd found some sign of a hidden door in the salon or some other means of exit, it would be a simple matter of confronting Constance.

But he'd found nothing. Not one indication there was a secret means of entering and exiting the room. Not one. Then there was his unsettling visit with Nanny just before lunch. When he'd asked his old nurse about Professor Hodge, the woman had barely remembered the man. That alone told him that someone other than Nanny had given Constance the man's nickname.

There was only one other person who could have known

what he and Nigel called their old professor. And that person was dead. He winced and uttered a grunt of disgust. Either Constance had been talking to herself or she really had been—

Inconceivable. It simply wasn't possible. Even considering the possibility told him just how willing he was to let the woman ensnare him in her seductive web. He wanted to find some reason, any reason, to believe her. To know she wasn't lying to him. To know she'd not been with another man.

That was the key. It wasn't that she might have lied. Forgiving her a lie or a dozen lies would be easy compared to the possibility she'd been with someone other than him. So perhaps the best thing to believe was that she'd been talking to herself. But that didn't account for the man's voice he'd heard.

Damnation, it couldn't be Nigel. Striding through the back hall, he stepped out into the stable yard. He needed to clear his head, and the best way to do that was a hard ride across the estate. Perhaps the fresh air would provide him with a logical answer to all of this hocus pocus nonsense.

$\wp\backsim\mathscr{C}\!\mathcal{S}$

Constance sat in front of the fire, sipping on the tea Anna had brought her more than an hour ago. Breakfast, then lunch, had come and gone without her feeling the least bit hungry. The plate of cold meats on the tea tray remained covered and untouched.

It had been an effort simply to dress this morning, but she'd done so, sitting in front of the fire for most of the day. Occasionally she'd dozed off, only to wake from the nightmares that haunted her brief naps. Images from last night that made her heart ache all the more when she awoke.

The sudden intrusion of giggling and snorts of laughter in the hallway broke through her numbness. Recognizing her son's voice, she rose from her chair and crossed the room to open the door. Both Jamie and Imogene were only a few feet past her door as she poked her head out into the hall.

Heads together like conspirators, they were covered in dust and spider webs. Startled by their appearance, she gasped in dismay. Immediately the pair spun around to face her, guilt clearly evident on Imogene's face while Jamie quickly schooled his features into a cheerful expression of innocence.

"Where in heaven's name have the two of you been?" She gestured for them to enter her room, and with obvious reluctance the two of them did as she bid. As she closed the door behind them, she caught Jamie by the shoulder to hold him still as she tried to dust him off.

"Well, young man, you haven't answered my question," she said as she shifted her attention to Imogene's dust-covered dress.

When he didn't answer, she turned her head to look at him. The expression on her son's face immediately told her he'd been up to something. She arched an eyebrow and sent him a stern look as she planted her hands on her hips.

Dropping his head to avoid her questioning look, Jamie scuffed his shoe against the large floral rug covering most of the floor. When he didn't answer her, she turned a stern eye on Imogene who was standing quietly beside her friend. Despite being older, the girl always followed Jamie's lead.

"Imogene, why don't you tell me what the two of you have been up to."

The girl sent a sideways glance toward Jamie then dipped her head. "We were playing."

Not surprised, Constance frowned in puzzlement. "Yes, but *where* were you playing?"

"In the secret—" Imogene's words came to an abrupt halt as Jamie elbowed her in the ribs.

"James Percival Athelson, you will apologize at once for hitting Imogene." Appalled at his behavior, she glared at him.

"I'm sorry, Gene," he mumbled.

"And when did you start calling her Gene?" Constance exclaimed.

"She doesn't mind, Mother, do you, Gene?"

Imogene shook her head. "No, my lady, I like it."

"Well, I doubt your uncle or grandmother would approve. It's inappropriate. Jamie, in the future, you will address Imogene by her full name, is that understood?" At her firm tone, Jamie grimaced with displeasure but nodded.

"Yes, Mother."

"Thank you," she said with a nod at her son before smiling at Imogene. "Now where is this secret hideaway where the two of you were playing?"

Almost without thinking, Imogene grinned. "It's the labyrinth. We found it a couple of weeks ago."

The words sent a chill through Constance as Jamie groaned loudly.

"Awww, Gene—" He pulled a face as he sent Constance a quick glance. "Imogene, why did you have to go and tell her that? Now she'll make us show it to her."

"Do you mean to tell me the two of you have been traipsing around in dark tunnels for the past two weeks without telling anyone where you were?" She gasped in horror at the possibility they might have gotten hurt. "What if something had happened to you while you were playing? No one would know where you were."

The children stared up at her with an expression of first surprise and then guilt. Satisfied they were suitably chastened, she shook her head. "You're not to go back into this labyrinth—"

"But Mother—"

"No, Jamie. You're not to go back into it again. Is that clear?"

"Yes, Mother," Jamie said with a deep sigh.

When she swung her gaze to Imogene, the girl nodded her agreement as well. The labyrinth. They'd found it, which meant that if the labyrinth existed then the Seth statue might exist as well.

"How do you get into this labyrinth?" Eyeing her son sternly, she watched him hesitate before straightening his shoulders.

"I found the hidden doorway in the library, Mother. It's part of the bookcase."

"Then how did you get up here?" She stared at him in puzzlement as she remembered how she'd caught them passing her bedroom door.

"We found an exit in Uncle Lucien's room." Imogene's

217

words tugged a gasp of surprise from Constance's lips.

"Good Lord," she muttered. "I can't believe the two of you didn't think to tell someone what you found."

"Well we did, Mother."

"Whoever you told, obviously didn't think to order you to stay out of those tunnels," she snapped. "Who did you tell?"

Jamie grimaced as he averted his gaze again. Beside him, Imogene frowned as she took his hand and squeezed it. Then looking up at Constance, she lifted her chin to a defiant angle.

"We told my Papa. I know you told Jamie not to talk to my Papa, but I made him. I told him I wouldn't be his friend anymore if he didn't tell me what my Papa was saying."

With a sigh, Constance looked at her son as he stared down at the floor. Obviously he'd tried to do as she'd ordered, but when faced with losing his friend, he'd chosen to do as Imogene bid. She understood all to well the desire to hold on to his friendship with the young girl.

As for Nigel—the next time he made an appearance, she was going to give him an earful. The most important thing at the moment was to ensure the children didn't reenter the labyrinth. She would have to tell Lucien, but now wasn't exactly the right moment.

"Tomorrow, you're going to show me where this secret door is, and neither of you are to enter the labyrinth again. Is that understood?"

Both children bobbed their heads as if they'd just received a last-hour reprieve. For the first time that day, a smile tugged at her lips. A quiet knock on the door made all three of them jump nervously.

Opening the door, she greeted Anna who stood in the hallway. With a smile, the young maid curtseyed. "Begging your pardon, my lady, but his lordship asked me to bring you this straight away."

The chill washing over her at the sight of the envelope made her shiver as she stiffly accepted the note. As Anna walked away, heated whispers and scuffling caught her attention from behind. Her gaze pinned on the bold writing across the face of the envelope, she barely glanced over her shoulder at the children.

"I want both of you to go to the nursery, and ask Nanny to help you get into some clean clothes."

The chorus of obedience echoed softly in the room, and as they passed by her into the hall, Jamie stopped at her side. With one hand on her wrist, he stared up at her. "Are you feeling ill, Mother? You look very pale."

"I'm fine, Jamie." Forcing a smile to her lips, she gave him a gentle shove out the door. "Go on now, and remember what I said."

Closing the door behind them, she stared down at the note in her hand. Afraid to open it, she moved to the vanity and sank down onto the small stool. With mixed emotions, she laid the missive on the dressing table, her fingers smoothing across the fine linen envelope in an abstract gesture. She stared at the note for several minutes before she drew in a deep breath, exhaled it with sharp resignation and reached for the envelope. She tore it open and pulled out the single, folded sheet.

Lady Westbury,

It seems we are at an impasse. While I remain unconvinced about your dubious claim, my grandmother has interceded on your behalf. If you are amenable to the suggestion, I request that you continue cataloging my antiquities collection. Your skill and knowledge in the field of Egyptology is the one, singular truth, which I cannot deny.

Lyndham

For a moment, she simply sat there, a tremor running through her. He wasn't sending her away. The relief and joy warming her blood made her wince. The man had used her for his own pleasure, labeled her a liar and yet she was behaving as though he'd just given her the world by asking her to stay.

She shook her head. What a fool she was. If she had any pride at all, she'd pack her possessions and run as fast and as far from Lyndham Keep as she could. But she didn't have any pride where Lucien was concerned. With a sigh, she stared at her reflection in the mirror.

What had made him reconsider? Not the dowager countess. She could be quite persuasive, but while Lucien might on occasion indulge his grandmother by giving in to her whims, it was unlikely he would do so in this matter. She read through the words one more time.

He still thought she was lying, but he couldn't prove it. That's why he wasn't sending her away. The man was plotting something. He was going to try to trick her into confessing she was a liar. The paper rustled loudly as she crumpled it in her fist. God, she didn't know whether to be furious with him or grateful she didn't have to leave. She hated feeling this way. Hated being at odds with him.

A soft chime sounded behind her, and she turned to look at the clock. Supper was in little over an hour, and she'd hidden long enough. She would have to face him sooner or later. Better to do it at supper with Lady Lyndham as a buffer than alone. Looking at herself in the mirror, she grimaced.

If she arrived downstairs looking like this, Lucien was going to view her washed-out appearance as that of a guilty party. Well, she wasn't going to give him that satisfaction. She might not be able to make him believe she wasn't a charlatan, but she didn't have to look the part of someone ashamed of who they were. She had no control over her gift, but she could conduct herself with dignity and grace in spite of his angry accusations.

She was tired of feeling ashamed of her ability. Tired of walking in the shadows for fear of being ostracized or viewed as a madwoman. It was time she stopped feeling ashamed of her gift. And that's what it was—it was a gift. She had the ability to help others. It might be unorthodox and unusual, but it was a talent few others possessed. And she used it for good.

Lucien might label her a charlatan, but she knew better. She was through believing as others did that her talent was a curse or a ruse. Springing to her feet, she crossed the floor to the wardrobe. Quickly searching through her evening gowns, she reached for a dress she'd never worn before. As she pulled the satin garment from the large chest, she smiled. Tonight the Earl of Blakemore was about to discover that a Rockwood never admitted defeat.

Chapter Thirteen

The sonorous chime of the grandfather clock in the main hall had just sounded the quarter hour as Constance slowly descended the staircase. Her earlier bravado was beginning to fade as the time to face Lucien drew imminent. Worse still was her choice of dress. It was the first time she'd worn the gown and with good reason.

It might not be scandalous in Paris, but in England she'd known it would be viewed as outrageous. None of that had mattered to her when she'd seen it in Worth's showroom. All she knew was that she had to have the crimson gown. Swallowing hard, she relaxed slightly as she heard Edward Rawlings and Major Fenwick conversing jovially in the salon.

There were other voices floating out into the hallway, but she couldn't place them, although the woman's voice sounded familiar. She was two steps from the bottom of the stairs, when Lucien emerged from the salon calling for Jacobs. His cry died on his lips as he saw her.

The sight of him made her heart slam into her chest. He'd dressed more formally for the evening, and tonight he was more devastating than she'd ever seen him before. The crisp white collar of his shirt was a stark contrast to the black tie at the base of his throat.

His dark hair was swept back without the aid of any oils, and the piercing blue of his eyes swept over her with a look she couldn't decipher. Tension tightened the scar on his cheek, and she sucked in a sharp breath at the raw, untamed masculine power he exuded. The force of it sent a wicked flame of desire skimming through her blood until it heated every part of her body.

Dear Lord, the man had only to crook his finger and she would willingly submit herself to whatever torture or pleasure he desired. Afraid to speak, she remained frozen on the stairs. For a long moment, he did nothing but stare at her before he stepped forward to offer her his hand.

She hesitated for a fraction of a second before sliding her glove-encased palm against his. The connection was sharp and electric, and Lucien struggled not to pull her into his arms as she descended the remaining stairs to the hall floor. It was impossible to believe any other woman could ever compare to her voluptuous beauty.

The dark red dress she wore was the most seductive gown he'd ever seen. Not even when she'd been dressed as Isis had she looked so tempting. With only two straps of material embracing her upper arms to substitute as sleeves, her shoulders were completely bare. The gown's bodice was so low as to be almost indecent, while the large velvet bow at the valley of her breasts served as a soft edging that failed in any attempt to hide her attributes.

The gown was a bold announcement of her knowledge that she was alluring, a siren capable of seducing any man with only one look. Swallowing hard, he raised her hand to his mouth. Through the silk of her evening glove, the warmth of her heated his skin.

"If you thought to convince me of your allure this evening, you've succeeded."

"Since you are a man I cannot easily convince of anything, I must credit Monsieur Worth for this particular miracle." Beneath her sarcasm, there was a trace of pained disappointment that tugged at him. As she tried to pull her hand from his, he tightened his grasp, refusing to release her.

"The dressmaker can make the gown, but not the woman inside it." It was the best attempt at an apology he could do at the moment, given the discord between them.

He wanted to believe her, and yet it was difficult to believe something so foreign to everything he'd ever believed in. The flash of emotion in her eyes scraped tension across his skin. He'd been a brute to her last night, and he hated seeing the guarded expression she wore because of his behavior.

With a slight tug, she pulled her hand from his, but not before the shudder sweeping through her brushed across his fingertips. Jacobs's sudden decision to answer his earlier call prevented him from keeping her at his side as he turned toward the butler who had emerged from the back hall.

Acutely aware she was no longer close to him, he ignored Jacobs for a moment. Looking over his shoulder, he saw Constance hesitate briefly at the edge of the salon before entering the well-lit room to a welcoming chorus of male voices. Jealousy streaked through his blood with the speed of an out-of-control fire.

Seeing the butler's attentive look, he cleared his throat. "Jacobs, her ladyship would like the children to meet Sir Oliver and Mrs. Armstrong. Please ask Nanny to bring them down after supper."

Not waiting for the man to acknowledge his command, he whirled around and charged back toward the salon. As he crossed the threshold, he saw Constance being warmly greeted by Mrs. Armstrong. As the two women hugged each other, he noted how Oliver was looking at both women with a smile of deep satisfaction.

Constance drew back from the other woman, and Lucien frowned as Constance hesitated to accept Oliver's hand. It wasn't a noticeable waver, but he knew her far better than anyone else in the room. There was something about his cousin that troubled her. Puzzled, he started to move closer only to have Edward grab his arm and pull him aside.

"Devilishly attractive woman, your Lady Westbury," Edward said cheerfully. "Only a woman with spirit could wear a dress like that."

"A dress like what?" The cavalier note in Edward's voice grated against him as he turned his head to pin the man with his gaze.

"Why, it...it..." Edward stammered as he blanched under Lucien's fierce look. "It was a compliment, Lucien. Not every woman could wear such a daring gown without either embarrassing herself or looking like an embarrassment."

Returning his gaze to Constance, he saw Duncan had joined her. Immediately, his body strained with the urge to put himself between the two of them. He was about to move forward, when Edward's deep sigh stopped him. Politely, he turned his head toward the older man.

"Is something wrong, Edward?" he asked despite the intense need to reach Constance's side.

"Not really, I was simply wondering how accurate Lady Westbury's skills are."

"Skills? I think she's proven herself more than knowledgeable with the work she's done on the collection so far. I'm quite pleased."

"No, no, my boy. The woman's other talent. Her talent for speaking to the dead."

"Good God," he growled. "How the devil did you learn about that?"

Edward simply raised his eyebrow as he turned his head toward Lady Lyndham. Glaring in the direction of his grandmother, Lucien inhaled a deep breath as the man at his side cleared his throat.

"So you believe her?" Edward sent him an inquisitive look.

"Believe what? That she can talk to the dead? That she's talked to Nigel, to my grandfather? I don't know what to believe."

He fixed his gaze on Constance as she stood conversing with Mrs. Armstrong and Duncan. It was true. He didn't know what to believe where she was concerned. He only knew he wanted to believe her. And he was doing his damnedest to do so. It just was too fantastic an idea to comprehend as possible.

"Do you know what William said to her?" There was a hard edge to Edward's question that pulled him out of his thoughts.

"What?" he asked as he looked at the white-haired man.

"Aurora was less than forthcoming about this conversation Lady Westbury had with William." Again there was an odd note in Edward's voice.

"The only thing I got out of Grandmother is that she believes Lady Westbury has the sight." He shrugged as he looked back at Constance. "I'm not convinced."

She'd deliberately worn that dress tonight as a way of saying he could go to hell. But he already was in hell knowing he couldn't be the man who would keep her heart. Christ Jesus, what the devil was the matter with him? Things were what they were. Wishing they were different was pointless.

"You think she's lying then?"

"I don't know," he snapped. "If she's lying, then she's incredibly clever at it."

From across the room, Lady Lyndham pinned the two of them with her eagle-eyed gaze. "Lucien, were you aware that Oliver knows Malcolm Standish?"

His grandmother's nonchalant tone made him jerk his head in Oliver's direction. The man had a harsh scowl on his face, and Lucien crossed the floor to join the others with Edward close on his heels.

"I take it from the expression on your face you've had dealings with the man?"

"Unfortunately, I have indeed," Oliver said in his deep baritone. "As I was just explaining to Lady Westbury, I was one of the investors Standish secured for her husband's failed expedition almost five years ago."

With a quick look in Constance's direction, Lucien noted her pallor was distinctively wan, and he saw her eyeing Oliver with an uneasy look. Uncertainty gripped him once more as her eyes met his for a brief instant before shying away. Damnation, she made it decidedly difficult to believe her when she chose to act evasive.

"Have you had dealings with the man, Lucien?" At Oliver's question, his grandmother snapped her fan closed and used it to point toward his marred face.

"Yes, and he has the scar to prove it." Aurora declared with a touch of anger. "The man tried to kill the boy."

At his grandmother's dramatic announcement, Constance's gaze of horror flew to his face, and the expression in her hazel eyes warmed him. She was clearly troubled by Standish's behavior. Her distress made him think she cared about his wellbeing. With a slight shrug, he turned back to Oliver.

"About two years ago, Standish was disputing a claim I'd made on Aramun's tomb. I'd been digging at the site for more than a month when he showed up and declared I had superseded his claim." With the back of his hand, he rubbed the scar on his cheek. "Our argument became a bit more aggressive than I would have liked."

"Aramun," Oliver mused in the pompous tone he always assumed when he discussed antiquities. "Wasn't he one of the priests associated with Sefu and the Seth cult? They were based in the lower valley during Horemheb's reign I believe."

"Yes, Aramun's tomb is where I found the statuette of Isis." His gaze shifted toward Constance, but her expression revealed nothing more than avid interest in the conversation he and Oliver were having.

"Ah, yes, Father told me you'd found the statuette. An excellent find. If we have time, I'd like to see it, I understand it's exceptional."

"So it is, son, so it is." Slapping Lucien on the back, Edward grinned at his son and then Lucien. "And when he finds the Seth figurine he'll have the location to Sefu's tomb."

"You say that with far more confidence than I feel, Edward." Lucien shook his head as he smiled at the older man. "As I've said before, the statuette isn't here, any more than the labyrinth is."

Across from him, Constance's head was bent as if she wasn't even listening to the conversation at all. But it was the way she gripped the handle of her fan that alerted him to the fact she was listening. The silk glove on her hand was stretched taut across her skin, and her body was rigid as if under great pressure. She was listening to every word, and the fear emanating off her was almost tangible. What the devil was she thinking?

"Supper is now served, my lady." Jacobs announced in his most stately of tones.

The thick tension in the air quickly evaporated as everyone prepared to move into the dining room. Seeing Duncan making ready to move toward Constance, Lucien stretched out his hand to her.

"Lady Westbury?"

Her gaze flitted up to meet his before she accepted his hand. Over the top of her bent head, he shot Duncan a triumphant look. His friend simply scowled at him. Entwining her arm in his, he led her toward the salon door.

"What are you afraid of?" At his quiet question, she jerked

her head up, her hazel eyes meeting his steady look for a moment before she averted her gaze.

"Afraid? I think you're mistaken, my lord. I'm not afraid."

"Damn it, Constance," he hissed beneath his breath. "You're obviously uncomfortable around Oliver, and just now you looked as if the devil himself were going to sit beside you for dinner."

"I think you exaggerate."

"And you're avoiding the issue," he muttered as they entered the dining room. His time alone with her was almost up. "Why the hell won't you trust me?"

As he pulled out a chair for her, she turned her head to look at him. The pain in her gaze ripped at him. "What reason have you given that I should do so? Trust must be mutual, my lord. It isn't exclusive."

With a graceful move, she swept her skirt to one side and sank down into the chair. As he pushed her forward, he leaned down until his mouth brushed against her ear. "I don't deny my missteps where you're concerned, *yâ sabāha*, but I *am* making every effort to trust you—to *believe* you."

His fingertips drifted across the side of her neck and down over her shoulder as he left her to take his place at the head of the table. Shaken by his words, she inhaled a quick breath as she stared down at the charger plate in front of her.

What was the man thinking to suggest she should trust him? And then to say he was trying to believe her. Did that mean he was actually on the verge of believing in her ability? To do that would be an incredible leap of faith for him. She lifted her head and glanced down to where he was sitting. The complexity of the man continued to astonish her.

"Well now, Lady Westbury, what do you think of my son?" Edward Rawlings shook out his napkin and laid it in his lap as he smiled at her.

"He's quite nice," she lied as she suppressed a shiver.

Instinct had told her several months ago Oliver was anything but a pleasant man. Her opinion hadn't changed. The vision she'd had of him beating Davinia still flooded her senses every time she looked at him.

"It looks like he's quite taken with your friend Mrs.

Armstrong." Rawlings picked up his spoon to taste the soup a footman had set in front of him. "She's a delightful woman. A good settling influence on the boy."

"Davinia is obviously happy," she said politely. "And I'm delighted by her happiness."

And the truth of it was, Davinia did look happy. When her friend entered the salon earlier, Constance had been delighted to see her conversing with Lady Lyndham, although she'd been less than thrilled at meeting Sir Oliver.

It had been a blessing her gift had not stirred up any further visions when she'd been forced to shake the man's hand. No, she was delighted for her friend as long as Sir Oliver didn't raise his hand to Davinia. But there was something about the man that just made her blood run cold.

"I sense you're somewhat distracted this evening, my dear lady. Tell me what troubles you." There was a concerned note in Edward Rawling's voice, and she turned her head to smile at him.

"I think you mistake a bad night's sleep for poor spirits, Mr. Rawlings."

"What? Lost sleep over a suitor?"

Unable to answer honestly, she forced a smile to her lips and shook her head. Relief swept through her as Major Fenwick's deep voice on the opposite side of her pulled her attention away from Rawlings.

"I think you've monopolized the lady's time quite enough, Edward. Now it's my turn."

Laughter escaped her at Duncan's petulant tone. Turning toward him, her gaze slid over Lucien who was watching her from the end of the table with a frown. Uncertain what to make of his disapproval, she focused her attention on Duncan.

"Well, Major, I'm at your disposal, what shall we discuss?" Wineglass in hand, she took a sip of wine as she looked at him over the rim of her glass.

"Do you have any idea how beautiful you look this evening?" His soft whisper made her gulp with surprise as she quickly put her wineglass down.

"I don't...that's very kind...thank you." She stumbled over her words as she stared down at her soup.

"I've embarrassed you," he said with a smile. "Don't be."

Collecting her thoughts, she pressed one hand to the base of her throat as she looked at the man seated beside her. "I confess to being more surprised than embarrassed, Major, although I'm quite flattered."

"But your heart belongs to another." He briefly glanced in Lucien's direction before eyeing her with a small smile. "I've known from the beginning I suppose. It's simply that I'm not accustomed to losing."

Relieved she wouldn't have to answer his unspoken question, she arched her eyebrows and picked up her knife to butter the roll on her bread plate. Smiling, she looked at him out of the corner of her eye.

"I'm not sure if my being likened to a prize in some gaming concern is a compliment or not."

"I can assure you, Lady Westbury, even the most exclusive of London's professional beauties insist upon being a prize at one time or another."

Major Fenwick winked and sent her a mischievous smile, which was impossible to resist. Laughing, she shook her head with amusement as she returned her attention to her plate. A sudden frisson skimmed over her shoulders, and she knew Lucien was watching her.

She tried to resist looking in his direction, but failed. The moment she met his piercing gaze, she swallowed hard. The brilliant blue of his eyes blazed with a stark look of possession that thrilled and frightened her at the same time. It was only when Davinia captured his attention that he looked away from her.

Shaken by the intensity of his stare, Constance had difficulty focusing on anything for the remainder of the meal. It was with a suppressed sigh of relief that she saw Lady Lyndham rise to her feet. Although the dowager countess suggested the men remain behind for a glass of port, they refused, and the small party moved back into the salon.

They'd only been in the room for a few moments, when Imogene and Jamie appeared in the doorway. Their appearance was remarkably changed from when she'd seen them earlier, and she smiled as Jamie quickly crossed the floor to where she sat on the scrolled-back gossip seat. He greeted her with a small bow then kissed her cheek.

From across the room, Lady Lyndham called to him, gesturing for him to join her and Imogene. A tingling sensation tickled the back of her neck then skated its way down her back as Lucien sank down into the opposite side of the serpentine-shaped seat that curled away from her and faced the opposite direction. Although there was a hard surface between their bodies, the intimacy of the chair set her pulse racing. The brief glance she sent his way told her she was the object of a fierce, steady look.

"I don't think I've ever told you what a wonderful boy Jamie is. You've done well by him, Constance."

Startled by the compliment, she nodded in mute acknowledgement of his words as she watched her son greet Sir Oliver. Watching him, she tensed as Jamie shook the older man's hand. His usual charming self, her son immediately engrossed himself in an animated conversation with Sir Oliver. The end result was that Jamie had the man laughing heartily with something he'd said.

Puzzled, she frowned. How odd that Jamie didn't seem to react negatively toward the older man. Obviously his abilities were different than hers. Lucien shifted restlessly in the seat beside her. She glanced in his direction, and his obvious discomfort made her laugh.

"I think the seat you've chosen makes it quite difficult to monitor the room. Why they call it a gossip seat is beyond my comprehension."

With a smile that was devastating in its brilliance, he shrugged. "I would imagine it was designed more to keep lovers from holding hands than gossips from spreading rumors."

The huskily spoken words sent her pulse rocketing as their gazes locked. There was a haunting need in his eyes as he studied her. It was the look of a man who could never have what he desired most. Her heart ached with love as she lifted her hand to reach out to him.

The sudden impact of the vision was brutal.

Her breath was sucked out of her as if she were under cold water. The darkness swallowed her whole, and she struggled to reach the light in front of her. As she stepped into a small room lit by candles, dank air flooded her lungs.

In front of her there was a small altar with icons of Seth and Isis. Close by was a larger altar. Something lay on top of it, but in the dim light, it was difficult to make out what it was. Drawn forward by some inexorable force, she reluctantly moved toward the large stone. Whatever was on the slab didn't move, and she shivered. Something was wrong.

Then she saw him. He stood in the shadows. Although she couldn't make out his features, she could feel his hatred, his power—the essence of his evil. The sound of his laughter echoed in her head as he pointed at the slab. Oh God, Lucien, he'd hurt Lucien. Propelled forward, she stumbled toward the slab. The blood was everywhere...

The scream began as a silent cry deep in her soul. It wailed up out of her like a banshee in agony. The sheer terror of the sight in front of her filled her lungs, pressing in on her until she opened her mouth and shrieked in horror. Scream after scream poured out of her throat as she stared at the devil's handiwork.

A sharp crack rent the air, and she flinched at the stinging sensation in her cheek. Disoriented and frightened, she stared up at Lucien who was speaking to her, but she couldn't hear what he was saying because someone in the room was screaming at the top of their lungs. In that instant she knew it was her screams she was hearing—screaming Jamie's name with a shrill panic that etched agony through every part of her body as she tried to find her son in the suddenly crowded room.

Chaos reigned around her as she heard appalled cries over her head. Then a small body flung itself against her. Enveloped in Jamie's warmth, she wrapped her arms around him, clinging to him as she sobbed with relief. The cacophony of voices assaulted her like a harsh wind, and still clinging to Jamie, she fainted.

As Constance went limp, Lucien pulled her close with Jamie still hanging on to her. One arm wrapped around her waist, he gripped Jamie's shoulder. "It's all right, lad. She's simply had another one of her spells. She was frightened." Even as he spoke, he knew it was far more than that. Constance had been terrified to the point of hysteria.

"Frightened," exclaimed Edward, "the woman was screaming as if she was being murdered. Good God, Lucien, what did you say to her?"

"Actually, I don't think it's what Lucien said, so much as what Lady Westbury might have seen," Oliver mused as though having just made an interesting discovery.

Lucien jerked his gaze up to look at Oliver's speculative expression, while Edward looked at his son with irritated confusion. "What the devil does that mean, Oliver?"

For a moment, Oliver look decidedly uncomfortable before one corner of his mouth dipped downward in a bored frown. "Just something Davinia mentioned some time ago about the lady."

Mrs. Armstrong touched his arm and whispered something to him, but Oliver shrugged. "Well, if they didn't know before, they do now, don't they."

Gently pushing Jamie away from his mother, Lucien shot his cousin a look of irritation. From behind them, Lady Lyndham rapped Oliver on the shoulder with her cane, causing the man to yelp. "Now is neither the time nor place to discuss the matter, Oliver Rawlings."

"I quite agree." Edward directed a disapproving glare at his son.

"Lucien, take Constance up to her room," his grandmother ordered. "When she comes to, she'll not want to have all of us ogling her."

Throughout the incident, Duncan had remained silent, but he now stepped forward to gently pull Jamie away from his mother. The moment he did so, Jamie fought him off violently. Lifting Constance up into his arms, Lucien sent the boy a stern look.

"Jamie." The commanding note in his voice made the boy jerk to attention. Fear flashed in his eyes as he met Lucien's gaze. "Come with me, lad. Between the two of us, we'll see to it that your mother is well cared for."

Relief evident on his pale features, Jamie nodded. Over the top of the boy's head, Lucien met his grandmother's strained look. Once again, he was reminded of her fragility as she swallowed hard. "I'll have Jacobs send up tea for when she awakens."

With a sharp nod, he followed Jamie out of the salon and up the staircase. He was halfway up the stairs when she stirred in his arms and uttered a soft sigh, which was quickly followed by a shudder.

"Jamie," she gasped in fear.

"He's safe, *yâ sabâha*. He's just up ahead."

Another shudder rocked through her, and she buried her face in his solid shoulder as he reached the upper hallway. The movement brought her hair close to his nose, and he inhaled the soft scent of jasmine. Reaching her bedroom, he saw Jamie open the door for him, and he swiftly crossed the bedroom floor and laid Constance on the bed.

Jamie was at her side in a heartbeat, and he touched the boy's shoulder as he stepped backward. "Stay with her. I'll return in a moment."

Anna, the upstairs maid, appeared in the doorway with a tray of tea that she set down on the fireside table. Taking her arm, Lucien pulled her aside.

"Have Jacobs come up here immediately. I'm going to let the boy stay with her for a few minutes then Jacobs is to escort Jamie directly into Nanny's care, while you help her ladyship prepare for bed."

Not waiting for her response, he turned back toward Constance to see her sitting up on the bed, hugging her son. There was still a look of shock on her face, but color was beginning to return to her cheeks. For several long moments, she simply sat still and hugged her son close. Watching her, he knew whatever had frightened her so terribly involved her son.

A quiet knock on the door announced Anna and Jacobs's entrance. As the two servants moved into the room, his gaze met Constance's as she looked at him over the top of her son's head. She looked exhausted, and the sooner she rested, the better.

"Jamie, we need to let your mother rest. Come along now."

The boy shook his head in protest and wrapped his arms around Constance with renewed vigor. Responding to her son's reluctance, she whispered something to him. He protested for only a moment more before finally giving in to her wishes.

Jamie gave his mother one last hug then moved toward the door. When the boy reached his side, Lucien rested his hand on the boy's shoulder.

"She'll be fine, Jamie. I won't leave her alone."

The boy eyed him in silence as if searching for an answer to an unspoken question. Lucien returned his somber look steadily. With a worried frown, Jamie shook his head.

"I shouldn't leave her. She might have another...another episode." The maturity in the boy's voice reminded him of himself in the days following the deaths of his parents.

"It's all right, lad. I'll stay with her until morning. I promise you."

Jamie hesitated before nodding his head in agreement. With one last look over his shoulder at his mother, the boy left the room with Jacobs. Lucien turned to Anna and ordered her to call him back into the room when Constance was ready for bed.

In the hallway, he paced the floor. He didn't know what the hell had happened downstairs, but it amazed him how many people seemed so certain of her abilities. Edward appeared to be as convinced as his grandmother was by her skill. Even Oliver and Mrs. Armstrong hadn't been overly surprised by her hysteria.

From the interaction between the couple, it was clear Oliver's lady friend had confided her knowledge of Constance's secret on the condition he not share the information. As usual, the man's ability to be discreet was anything but. He grimaced. Oliver never had been one to behave honorably. Maybe he should just let the Set tear him to pieces. No, that he couldn't do. Regardless of his past behaviors or background, Oliver had Blakemore blood in him, and a Blakemore never deserted their own. Not even when they were blackguards like his cousin. At that moment, Anna stepped out into the hall.

"She's much better now, my lord. Shall I stay with her tonight?"

"We both will," he said. "I told the boy I wouldn't leave her, but I've no wish to compromise her reputation."

"Of course, my lord. Let me fetch my mending."

With an abrupt nod, he watched the maid hurry down the

hall. Leaving the door open, he entered Constance's room. As he approached her bed, he took in the air of hopelessness about her. It made her look pale and fragile. He wanted to take on her demons for her, but he felt powerless to do so. It was the same emotion he'd felt when Constance had been screaming with such terror. He despised himself for slapping her, but she'd been unresponsive to any other attempts to calm her.

Sitting on the bed beside her, he gently touched the red splotch on her cheek. She brushed his hand away, and her fingers were ice cold against his skin.

"I can only imagine what everyone must be thinking about my...my exhibition." A sigh parted her lips as she looked away from him.

"They're as concerned for you as I am." The dismissive shake of her head made him frown.

"There's no need. I'm fine."

"That point is debatable, but I think you need to sleep right now."

"I don't want to sleep."

"Why not?"

"It's...I...please, must you hound me like this. There's no need for anyone to worry about me, I'll be fine."

"Look at me, Constance." His sharp command forced her to meet his gaze. "I want you to tell me what happened."

Panic flickered in her gaze as she turned her head away from him. "No."

"I refuse to accept that answer," he said with frustration. "I want to know what happened to you in the salon."

"You don't have the right to ask that," she said in a brittle voice as she tugged her hand out of his firm grip.

"Bloody hell," he snapped. "You must trust me, Constance."

"I have no wish to be labeled a liar and a charlatan again." Bitterness tightened her mouth as her sharp words lashed out at him, making him wince.

Silence hung dense and heavy in the room as he struggled to say the words that would heal the breach between them. Could he honestly say he believed her? His grandmother believed her. Jamie had been emphatic about his ability to see

Nigel, and there was the issue of the nickname he and Nigel had for Professor Hodge. It was an extraordinary piece of evidence, especially given Nanny's difficulty in even remembering the professor, let alone knowing their childhood nickname for the man.

"Last night...perhaps I—damnation," he exclaimed as he jumped to his feet and paced the floor.

He was mad. What other reason explained his need to discount Constance's possible deceit, his desire to ignore every illogical thought in his head and believe her fantastic tale? There was only one way to determine whether he was in his right mind or simply mad. He wanted one more piece of evidence. One more miscellaneous piece of information that only he and Nigel knew.

If she gave him that, he'd believe. His pacing took him back to her side, and he sank down next to her. Confusion furrowed her brow as he studied her for a long moment.

"You told me you saw and talked to my brother." He paused as she nodded, her expression wary. Drawing in a deep breath, he exhaled. "I'm not certain you understand the implications of what you're asking me to believe."

She stared at him for a long moment, a small flame of hope brightening her hazel eyes. "I do know what I'm asking, Lucien. I'm asking you to believe something based on my word alone. I'm asking that you believe without any evidence you can see or hear."

"Then you'll understand why I require at least one more piece of evidence that you really can talk to...talk to Nigel."

Her eyes clouded with disappointment as she turned her head away from him. "You asked me to trust you, and yet you find it impossible to trust me. Impossible to trust that I'm not lying to you."

"Damn it, Constance." He shoved his hand through his hair, frustrated at his inability to make her understand what she asked of him. "This isn't about trusting you. It's about trusting myself. Believing this isn't the prelude to the madness I've come to accept as my fate."

"And what if you're wrong?" The gentle question whispered past her lips as she returned her gaze to his face. He shook his head in anger.

"Now you ask more of me than *I* can give," he said tightly. A sudden blast of cold air blew across his body, and he frowned. "It's cold in here. Let me find you another blanket."

She clutched his arm in a surprisingly strong grip as he started to rise from the bed. "The cold is a natural occurrence in these instances."

"Instances?" Uncertainty seized him as the cold air warmed slightly, almost as if something had moved away from him.

"Nigel."

"He's here?" he asked with a terse skepticism. "Now?"

"I'm afraid he's not very happy with you at the moment." A smile touched her lips as she stared at the empty space off to his side.

Doubt renewed itself as he glared at her. "I see."

"Actually, Nigel says you're quite unclear about a great many things. Including the curse. He says it doesn't exist...no, I won't..." she shook her head vehemently. A flush of color darkened her face. Her eyes met Lucien's for a moment before she looked away. "He said the only curse hanging over your head is your stubbornness."

The color in her face deepened as she listened to a voice he couldn't hear. She shook her head again, her mouth forming a silent gasp, then tightening into a firm line. It was a brilliant performance. One could almost believe she was actually talking to his dead brother.

The doubt stirring in him pricked at his conscience. He'd promised to believe her with one final piece of evidence, and yet here he was questioning her honesty again. Could he do so otherwise? God knew he wanted to believe her. Still, he wanted more proof than Professor Hodge's nickname. He wanted something he knew no one else would know that Nigel had told him.

"Ask him to repeat what he told me the morning of the day he died."

"No, *don't*," she said with a frown as she looked toward the empty space beside him. You'll waste your energy."

Turning her head back to him, she winced. "He's furious.

He said you know...you know *damn* well what he told you."

"I want to hear it from your lips." He leaned toward her and grasped her chin tightly as a wave of fury surged through him. It was an anger that tried to smother the tenuous belief taking root inside him. "Tell me."

With a vicious jerk of her head, she broke free of his grasp. "The two of you are the most irascible, pig-headed, arrogant bastards I've ever met."

Her response enraged him. She was lying. She didn't have an answer, and she was attempting to divert him from the fact. With a harsh glare, he leaned into her.

"And you, my dear, are avoiding my question. Tell me what my brother said to me the day he died."

One hand pressed against her throat, she flinched as if someone had hit her. Determined to end this game of deception, he grabbed her arms and gave her a hard shake. "Tell me."

"He told you...he told you about Katherine."

Frozen in place, Lucien stared at her. She knew. But how could she, unless— His fingers bit deeper into her shoulders as he struggled to believe the impossible. "What did he tell me about Katherine?"

Her eyes focused on a point over his shoulder. "They fought about it. He hit her..." She gasped, her face growing pale as her gaze jerked back to Lucien's. "He told you about her affair with Oliver."

Chapter Fourteen

Stunned, he simply stared at her. The unbelievable had happened. She'd given him the one answer he knew she couldn't have heard from anyone else. Shortly after Nigel had told him about Katherine's affair, his brother had killed his wife then jumped to his death. There wasn't anyone who had been privy to their conversation.

In proving her innocence, Constance had simply confirmed the certainty of his own fate. In his fury over his wife's betrayal, his brother had succumbed to the curse, and it would happen to him as well if he ever allowed Constance into his heart. Harsh laughter filled his head. *If?*

Deliberately, he locked his thoughts into an isolated compartment of his mind. Stumbling to his feet, he walked away from her bed. Nigel was here. In this room. He looked around. For what he didn't know. Some sign that he wasn't truly going mad. A firm, cold pressure pressed into his shoulder, and he froze.

"Lucien?" The quiet compassion in Constance's voice echoed softly behind him.

"He's really here?"

"Yes, he's touching your shoulder." Her words shot a bolt of lightning through him, and the weight on his shoulder tightened then eased completely. "He says to tell you there is no curse."

"Then how in the hell does he explain why he killed Katherine?" Shaking his head, he grimaced. Nigel was confused. There were no other explanations for Katherine's death or his brother's.

"Because he didn't kill her." The calm, serene response made him spin around to look at her.

"What the hell does that mean? I know what I saw and heard. He killed her and then threw himself from the tower." The memory of Nigel's cry as he'd jumped off the North Tower still had the power to send a chill coursing through his blood.

"The killer escaped through the labyrinth," she said quietly. "Nigel chased him up to the tower, but in the struggle, your brother was shoved off the rampart."

"*Who*?" Raw fury coiled in his stomach as he fought to cope with the rage that threatened to blind him. "*Who* did this to him?"

Empathy darkened her hazel eyes until they were almost green. With a slight shake of her head, she sighed. "He doesn't remember."

"God damn it. That's not an answer. He has to know who killed him. How could he not remember?"

"It's not unusual for spirits not to remember things from their earth-bound state, especially traumatic events such as what Nigel experienced."

"He doesn't remember because he doesn't want to know the truth," he snapped. An instant later, a cold weight pressed heavily against his shoulders. Obviously his brother disagreed.

"Nigel wants you to know he loved Katherine. Adored her. He was furious...devastated by her betrayal. But he was determined to win her heart again. When he went back to their room a short time after their fight, he found her dead and the door to the labyrinth open."

"Bloody hell," he exclaimed. Turning away from her, he strode to the wall, his hands and eyes searching for a possible opening. This had been the room Nigel and Katherine had shared, which meant the door had to be in here. Providing of course he'd not hallucinated everything that had happened in the past few moments.

"Lucien—"

"Where the devil is it? Tell him to show you where the door is."

"I can't," she said with a sigh of regret. "He's gone."

"What do you mean he's gone?" he growled, frustrated by the fact he couldn't see or hear his brother—talk to him. Now she was telling him Nigel was gone. Gone where? How could a spirit just disappear?

"It takes a great deal of energy for him to communicate. Some spirits find it hard even to show themselves, let alone speak and interact with the world we live in. He was too weak to continue."

"Damnation, why didn't he tell you where it was?" he snapped.

"I told you before, spirits don't always remember things. What happened to him was very traumatic."

The flat base of his fist slammed into the gray stone. "Then how the hell am I supposed to find his killer? There has to be evidence of some kind behind these walls. Something that will tell me what the hell is going on."

"Jamie knows where an entrance is." Her quiet words made him wheel around to face her.

"The boy knows?" Scowling at her troubled expression, he waited impatiently for her reply.

"He and Imogene have apparently been playing in the labyrinth for a few weeks now. I just learned of it late this afternoon."

"And you didn't see fit to tell me until now?" he snapped.

"I learned of it just before supper, and I didn't think you'd want me to announce the fact with so many people here this evening."

She sent a pointed look toward the open bedroom door as Anna entered with a basket filled with items for mending. As he turned toward the doorway, he acknowledged the maid's quick curtsey with an abrupt nod. The servant's return afforded them less privacy with which to continue their conversation, but a quick glance back at Constance told him she needed to sleep. As the maid seated herself near the fire and pulled out a pair of socks to darn, Lucien returned to Constance's side.

"I think we've both had enough excitement and revelations for the evening. We'll talk about the labyrinth in the morning." She nodded her agreement, but he sensed her fear returning. Immediately, he squeezed her hand in a reassuring manner. "I won't leave you alone, *yâ sabāha,* Anna and I will stay the night."

Relief swept across her face, and she sighed. "Thank you."

As she sank deeper into the bed, he pulled the bed linens up to her chin and proceeded to tuck her in beneath the covers. The action came to him naturally as if he'd done it many times before. It felt comfortable, and he relished the sensation. His destiny would not offer him any other moments like this.

The delicate scent of jasmine floated up off her skin and he longed to kiss her. Aware of Anna's presence behind him, he satisfied himself by stroking her cheek with his fingers. Dousing the gaslight beside her bed, he squeezed her hand one last time.

"Go to sleep, Constance. I'll be here if you need me."

Not waiting for an answer, he moved to the fireplace and sank down into one of the chairs facing the hearth. Anna raised her head from her mending with a curious expression on her face.

"Can I fetch you something, my lord? Perhaps a hot toddy?"

"No thank you, Anna." He turned his head to stare into the fire.

Out of the corner of his eye, he saw her nod before she returned to darning the sock in her hand. The maid might be curious about the evening's events, but she would be circumspect in her chaperone duties. Jacobs was a harsh taskmaster when it came to discreet behavior among the household staff.

He wasn't sure about others though. Something told him Oliver would be far from discreet when he returned to London. The idea of his cousin spreading stories about Constance sent a flash of anger streaking through him. He refused to let her be the topic of the moment among the Set. He'd have to make it clear to the man the folly of gossip.

And he refused to let the man do or say anything that might harm Constance. In truth, he had a lot to make up for where she was concerned. The thought sent guilt ricocheting through him. He'd been a monster to treat her the way he had. In convincing him of her special ability, he'd found it hard to believe she'd ever lied to him about anything. He'd make it up to her. He just wasn't sure how. Glancing over his shoulder, he released a sigh of relief. Good, she was sleeping. Perhaps she'd find some peace in her dreams.

For him, there would be little sleep this night. His entire world had just been turned upside down in ways he'd never dreamed possible. When she'd repeated what Nigel had told him about Katherine, everything he'd ever believed had been shattered. His brother had been here. In this very room. And that cold air. Over the years, he'd experienced similar instances of the temperature taking a distinct plunge whenever he was home. He'd always put it down to the keep's stone walls and cold drafts of outside air.

Had those moments been Nigel trying to communicate with him or were there other spirits here as well? His mother and father? He flinched as the memories of that terrible day flooded over him. It had been a horrible sight for anyone, but it had shaped his life from that point forward. Could his parents have been murdered like Nigel and Katherine? No. Nigel had to be mistaken. Constance had said that spirits often forgot things. Especially traumatic things. Perhaps his brother simply didn't want to remember his own complicity in Katherine's death or a subsequent suicide.

Lucien tilted his head back, resting it on the chair as the events of the evening cluttered his head once more. Where had Constance gone in those few short moments before her screams had ripped through the salon? One minute she'd been talking to him, then in the blink of an eye, she'd ventured into a realm where he couldn't reach her.

Worse still had been the moment when he'd been forced to slap her. Calling to her and shaking her had done nothing to disrupt her trance or silence her screams. Even after he'd slapped her cheek she'd continued to scream as if she'd not been fully aware of where she was. The stark terror in her cries had gripped him with an overwhelming sense of helplessness.

In some ways, he was grateful she'd fainted. It had provided him the opportunity to take her away from everyone's prying eyes, especially Oliver's. Clearly, Davinia Armstrong had informed her lover about Constance's gift. But it was his cousin's response to the event that puzzled him. There had been a cold, calculating assessment in Oliver's eyes as he'd observed her hysteria.

It was as if he were appraising the situation for any advantage it might bring him. Frowning, Lucien watched a large ember fall off a log and hit the brick hearth. The charred wood flared a couple of times before it simply glowed red in the dim light of the room.

Whatever his cousin had been thinking, it could only have been something to benefit Oliver. Although *what* was impossible to tell. The man never did anything that didn't serve to reward himself in some fashion. Even his latest conquest, Mrs. Armstrong, proved that point. The woman was quite wealthy from what Edward had said. And if there was one thing Oliver wanted, it was money.

Pinching the bridge of his nose between his fingers, he closed his eyes. If his grandmother knew about Oliver's affair with Katherine, she'd never let him cross the keep's threshold again. He wasn't sure why he'd never told his grandmother about Oliver and Katherine. In the days following their deaths, he'd been too grief-stricken to think clearly. There had been the inquest to deal with, and his grandmother had been too lost to even come out of her room except for the funeral. After that, it had seemed pointless to add to her grief.

Grief—it was something he'd lived with for most of his life. Tonight, simply accepting that Nigel's spirit was in the same room with him, communicating with Constance, had offered him a sense of peace. A peace he'd not experienced since he was twelve years old. Even without actually hearing or seeing his brother tonight, his personality had been evident in everything Constance had relayed to him. As always, Nigel hadn't missed an opportunity to call him stubborn or insist the curse didn't exist.

If his brother really had been murdered, then what about the curse? Had his brother been right to berate him for believing it was real? No. Even if Nigel and Katherine's deaths were foul play, it didn't change the fact that his father and great-grandfather had murdered and committed suicide because of the curse. Believing Nigel would only give him hope—false hope. He'd lost too much already. Endangering Constance's life wasn't something he was willing to risk.

The fire popped in the hearth, and he forced his heavy eyelids open to see the flames had died out to become a mass of fiery red coals. The glowing embers had a hypnotic effect, and moments later he drifted off to sleep.

ℰℭ

The corridor she was in was pitch black, and fear crawled its way over her skin. She shuddered as she stepped into the light. In front of her, she saw him. Her nemesis. He whirled around to face her. The writhing snakes that encircled the garish head of a smiling hippopotamus made her cry out in disgust. Blood soaked his hands. Dark red, the blood dripped off the ritual blade he held. Her stomach roiled at the sight. With a wide sweeping gesture of his hand, her enemy stepped back to reveal the slab. Horror sliced into her with the sharpness of the bloodied blade, and she screamed.

The sound echoed off the walls until it enveloped her like a fiery blanket of pain. Her lungs ached from the lack of air as her shrieks of terror filled her ears. Piercing through the terrifying sound, Lucien's voice called out to her as if from a great distance. Desperately, she turned toward it. Behind her the sound of her nemesis's laughter chilled her before she was hurtled forward toward the sound of Lucien's voice.

"Constance. Wake up." Lucien's hands bit into her arms as he shook her awake.

Relief swelled over her. A dream. It had only been a dream. Jamie was safe. Lucien had sent him to the nursery with Jacobs. She dragged in a deep breath as she met Lucien's worried gaze. Behind him, Anna looked on with a similar expression of concern.

"It was a dream, Constance, just a dream."

With a nod, she closed her eyes and shuddered at the horrible images she'd seen. Jamie lying on a large slab of stone. Lifeless. Butchered by the monster who'd been killing for so long. Her stomach churned at the memory. Strong arms enveloped her and pulled her close. A solid heartbeat reverberated in her ear as Lucien gently stroked her hair.

"It's all right, *yâ sabâha*. I'm here. I'll not let anyone harm you."

She barely heard Lucien's words as she fought to control the hysteria rising inside her. The vividness of her dream had filled her with stark terror. Even now, it taunted her with the life-like sights and sounds of the blood pouring from Jamie's small body. She'd learned a long time ago her visions were never fully accurate. But the possibility of someone harming her son was almost more than she could bear. A tear slid down her cheek. She needed to see Jamie. Needed to know he was safe.

Pushing her way free of Lucien's arms, she scrambled out of bed and reached for her robe. She ignored Anna's gasp of dismay and Lucien's growl of aggravation as she raced toward the door. She'd only gone a few feet down the hall, when a strong hand pulled her to a halt.

"Damn it, Constance, where the hell are you going?" Concern laced its way beneath his sharp question, but it didn't stop her from tugging against his grasp.

"I'm going to my son," she said vehemently. "Now *let me go.*"

With a vicious jerk of her arm, she whirled away from him and raced toward the stairs leading to the third floor. Reaching the nursery, she threw herself into the door of Jamie's bedroom. The lively fire in the hearth, mixed with the pink dawn drifting through the windows, created a reddish glow in the room.

The sight of Jamie sleeping in his bed pulled the air out of her lungs, and she clung to the door for support as relief washed over her. Strong hands gripped her shoulders from behind as Lucien's deep voice echoed in her ear. "He's safe, *yā sabāha*, let him sleep."

Nodding, she allowed Lucien to guide her back to her room.

"Oh, my lady, you look bone weary." Anna clucked at her like a worrisome hen as she entered the bedroom. "Why don't I bring up some warm milk so you can sleep?"

Anna's words made Constance stare at the bed with distaste. The last thing she wanted to do was sleep. She'd had more than enough nightmares for the time being. She shook her head and moved toward the fireplace to sink into one of the chairs.

"No thank you, Anna."

"Tea and toast I think, Anna." Lucien nodded at the maid

as he crossed the room to stand at the fireplace opposite her. "See to it at once, and leave the door open on your way out."

The maid bobbed a curtsey and hurried from the room. The fire crackled quietly as he stared into the flames. There was a steady strength about him that made her feel safe. His presence comforted her as did his understanding. Although his physical strength could have easily overpowered hers a moment ago, he'd not interfered with her need to see Jamie was safe and unharmed. He was capable of great understanding, and it was one of the reasons she'd fallen in love with him.

"You should sleep. You only slept a few hours last night."

"I can't...I...the nightmares..."

"I think it's time you trust me with all your secrets, Constance." The quiet steel in his voice demanded she answer him.

When she hesitated, his mesmerizing gaze locked with hers, silently commanding her to speak. With a slight nod, she looked away from him and stared into the fire.

"My gift allows me to see spirits, but it also shows me things too. My visions are sometimes things that have happened in the past or they might be things in the future."

"Are you saying you can tell the future?" he asked in an incredulous tone.

"No." She shook her head. "I see images of the future. Not all of them come true, but my experience has taught me to be cautious."

The memory of Jamie and the man in her visions made her stomach lurch with fear. How could she protect him? She could take him away from the keep, but what if that's what the devil wanted her to do? She'd fled London thinking she was safe here from Lucien. Instead, fate had guided her not away from him, but straight into his arms. If she left the keep, would she be dragging Jamie closer to danger or saving him from harm? She didn't know what to do.

"These images you refer to. You had one about Jamie." The pragmatic note in his voice indicated he didn't need an answer so much as he was simply stating a fact.

"Yes." She nodded her head, refusing to expand on the horror of her vision. Dwelling on it only intensified her fear.

"When you saw Jamie in this vision, where were you?"

"The labyrinth." Despite the unexpected nature of his question, she responded without thinking.

The moment she did so, she jerked her head up and met his gaze with a numb sense of shock. How had she known it was the labyrinth? There hadn't been anything to indicate where she was, but she was certain her response was correct. Unable to remain seated, she rose to her feet and restlessly paced the floor behind her chair.

Lucien remained by the fire, one elbow resting on the mantle as he rubbed his chin with his fingers. He didn't speak for the longest time, and just when she was about to go to him, he uttered a decisive sound. Straightening, he turned and walked to the window to pull back the heavy curtains. The sun was well over the horizon, and the light streaming into her room ushered in the promise of a warm spring day.

He dropped the curtain and moved to her side. The heat of his hands warmed her shoulders as he pulled her forward to kiss her brow. Breathing in a deep breath, she trembled at the rich, masculine scent filling her nose. Her tiny shudder didn't go unnoticed, and his grip tightened on her shoulders for a brief instant before he gently pushed her away from him. Behind her, the sound of rattling china announced Anna's return. Lucien immediately headed toward the door as the maid entered the room.

"I'll leave you in Anna's capable hands as I've business to attend to this morning." He nodded toward the tray the maid held. "See to it that her ladyship eats something."

There was a finality about his manner that worried her. He'd come to a decision about something, and she was certain it wouldn't be to her liking. Constance stretched out her hand to him as he strode toward the door.

"Lucien..."

If he heard her soft call, he ignored it. As the door closed behind him, she frowned at his sudden departure. So much had happened to him last night. Acknowledging her ability had turned his world upside down. It had changed things between them. He'd become more protective of her. But was that because he still believed in the curse, or was it something more? Was he coming to care for her? Despite the fear surrounding her, the idea that Lucien might have feelings for her, made her heart skip a quick beat. If she helped him solve the riddle of the Blakemore curse, would it be possible for things to change between them? He'd be free to love, but would he love her? That was a question she didn't have the answer to.

℘〇℃3

Striding through the front door of the keep, Lucien pulled off his riding gloves with a quick tug. When he'd left Constance earlier this morning, he'd blindly stumbled through his daily routine as he grappled with the implications of the night before. His mornings always included a ride around the estate, and today the exercise had served to help him think through a plan of action.

As Jacobs met him in the main hall to accept his riding crop and gloves, he turned his head toward the soft laughter floating out of the library. Beside him, the butler cleared his throat in response to Lucien's curiosity.

"Young Westbury and Lady Imogene, my lord."

With a nod, Lucien finished removing his gloves and handed them to the butler. The fact that the children were close by simplified matters. He'd planned on exploring the labyrinth today, and he needed Jamie to show him one of the entrances. Now seemed like the perfect opportunity. Quietly entering the library, he saw the children kneeling in the chairs surrounding the map table. It was the only table available as Constance had filled the remaining flat surface with cataloged items. Their heads close together, Jamie was drawing something while his niece looked on in fascination. His tread quiet, Lucien moved closer.

"Now look, Imogene, you know we'll be strung up if we're caught, so we have to be very careful. But those sounds we've been hearing at night have to be coming from the labyrinth. We have to find out what they are."

"Do you think we can really do this, Jamie? What if the ghosts are making those noises?"

"It's all right, Gene, I won't let them hurt you," Jamie said with bold confidence as he patted the girl's shoulder.

"But what about your mama? Won't she be angry with us for going back into the secret passageways?"

"If we're quiet, she won't be able to get angry until we've solved the mystery. Then she'll be happy, and we'll be heroes. We just need to keep it a secret, otherwise there'll be the devil to pay."

Having heard enough, Lucien cleared his throat loudly. The two children whirled around in a frenzied fashion. Jamie kept his hands behind him, clutching his drawing out of view. Imogene's guilty look didn't surprise him. She'd never been able to keep a secret. Young Westbury's expression, however, made him stifle a chuckle. With the air of a brash highwayman, the boy met his eyes with a jaunty smile. He acted as if he'd merely been playing a game of tic-tac-toe with Imogene. Admiration for the boy's ingenuity and spirit tugged the corner of his mouth up in a small smile.

"What are the two of you up to?"

The children looked at each other, before Jamie spoke up. "We were talking about my mother, my lord. Is she better? May we see her this morning?"

Damnation, he was more seasoned than half the politicians he knew. The boy hadn't actually lied, but he'd neatly sidestepped the question without revealing the true nature of their activities. He would have to stay on his toes with the lad. "Yes, she's doing much better. I'm sure she'd enjoy a visit from both of you."

"Come on, Gene. Let's go see if Cook has some strawberries we can take to her." Jamie grabbed the girl's hand in the process of dragging her out of the library.

Lucien bit back a smile as the pair skirted him on their way out of the room. The children had taken only a couple of steps past him, when he cleared his throat again.

"My lord, one moment, if you please." Behind him, he heard the rustle of paper, and he smiled to himself. Without looking at the children, he clasped his hands behind his back. "If you would, my lord. I'd like to see your map."

Silence greeted his request. He turned to see Jamie and Imogene staring at each other in helpless despair. When neither of them moved, he arched his eyebrows in a silent command.

Jamie grimaced at the inevitable and stepped forward with obvious reluctance to hand over his drawing.

Lucien accepted the crumpled paper and opened it. The schematic was impressive for a boy Jamie's age, and he looked up from the map at the boy. "Did you draw this?"

"Yes, my lord." A note of belligerent pride echoed in the words, and Lucien returned his gaze to the detailed drawing.

"Most impressive. How did you come up with all this detail? Did you copy it from another source?"

"No, sir. I did it all from memory." Indignation in his voice, Jamie straightened to his full height. At that moment, Imogene stood up for her hero.

"He's a very good drawer, Uncle Lucien. Why, every time we come out of the labyrinth he adds to the map."

"*Gene!*"

Despite his dismay that the pair of them had been exploring the labyrinth for some time, Lucien struggled hard to suppress a laugh at Jamie's appalled cry. As usual, Imogene had revealed more than she was supposed to. Obviously frustrated, the boy glared at his companion.

"I'm sorry, Jamie. I didn't mean to tell him." Regret filled his niece's voice, and Lucien shook his head.

"Never mind, Imogene. It doesn't matter, because your days of playing in the labyrinth are over. If I find either of you have entered these passages again, the consequences will be severe, is that understood?"

"But, my lord—"

"My word is final in this matter. Is that clear?" He directed a stern look at first Imogene and then Jamie.

"Yes, Uncle Lucien."

"Yes, my lord." Jamie's response was sullen compared to Imogene's obedient tone of voice. Controlling his amusement, Lucien nodded.

"Good." He looked down at the map again. "Now then, Westbury, I want you to show me where the labyrinth entrance is here in the library."

"Oh, all right." With sigh of disgust, the boy shrugged and bobbed his head in the direction of the narrowest section of bookshelves in the library. "It's over here."

Leading the way, Jamie walked to the far corner of the room and got down on his knees to reach under the bottom shelf. It was clearly a stretch for the boy, and Lucien was about to offer assistance when he heard a small click. Smooth and silent on its hinges, the bookshelf swung wide to reveal a dark passage. Exhilaration lanced through him as he stared into the dark entrance. It really did exist.

Imogene grabbed his hand and tried to pull him toward the opening. "Come on, Uncle Lucien, there are lots of different passages, and we can get to the other side of the keep a lot quicker than the usual way."

"No, Imogene. I meant what I said. Neither of you are allowed to enter the labyrinth again. Is that understood?" Disappointment turned their mouths downward, but they both nodded. Satisfied they would obey him, he smiled. "Weren't you going to ask Cook if she had some strawberries for your mother, Westbury? If she does, I'm certain there will be enough for you and Imogene as well."

The possibility of strawberries for himself as well as his mother erased the boy's disappointment as Jamie grabbed Imogene's hand and dragged her out of the library at a dead run. The moment they disappeared, Lucien quickly crossed the room to the fireplace and retrieved one of the candles on the mantle. Lighting it, he entered the dark passage hidden behind the library wall.

A sudden gust of air blew out the candle, and he muttered an oath. As his eyes adjusted to the darkness, he saw small pinpoints of light pouring through the walls from the library bookshelves. Whoever had built these passages had deliberately provided a source of light for anyone using the hidden corridors. Although it was still quite dark without the candle, it was possible to see several feet in front of him.

The excitement stirring in his blood created a familiar rush of exhilaration. It was the same feeling he got every time he found a new excavation site. But this time it was different. This was where his grandfather had supposedly hidden the Seth figurine. The narrow passage he was in suddenly became a set of stone stairs. He climbed upward until the corridor leveled out again. Ahead of him, he could make out a bright point of light.

The passageway opened up into a cross section and sunlight streamed in from the circular opening in the roof above. The engineering feat to light the labyrinth was unlike anything he'd ever encountered in all his excavation work in Egypt. The architect had been brilliant in his use of natural light to make it easy to find one's way through the corridors without candlelight. Even during the nighttime there would be enough outside light filtered in to help someone see where they were going.

Pulling Jamie's map from his coat pocket, he held it under the light. Once again he marveled at the detail and complexity of the boy's work. From where he was standing, Constance's bedroom was straight ahead, while the passage on his left led to the South Tower. The other passage wasn't shown on the map, and he interpreted that to mean Jamie and Imogene hadn't explored the labyrinth in this direction.

A soft noise echoed in the passage leading to Constance's room, and he cocked his head in an attempt to hear better. When the sound didn't repeat itself, he returned his attention to the map. He frowned slightly as he studied the unfinished map. Based on his knowledge of the keep, the unmapped corridors of the labyrinth either simply ended or pointed toward the North Tower.

Peering more closely at the map in the dim light, he grunted softly. That was odd. Why had Jamie drawn the corridor to end at that point? Puzzled, he tilted the paper at a different angle in an effort to see what Jamie had written on the map. Inhaling a sharp breath, he never had the chance to utter his oath.

The sack over his head didn't just blind him, it disoriented him as well. The map slipped from his hands as he tried to remove the hood from his head. A moment later something lashed around his neck, cutting off his air.

Instinct forced him to kick his right foot up and back to hook around his attacker's leg. It took only a slight tug of his leg to knock his assailant off balance. As his opponent tumbled to the floor with a thud, Lucien staggered forward and jerked at the cord wrapped around his neck.

His throat no longer constricted and closed off, he choked in deep breaths of stale air. A muttered oath behind him said he wasn't out of danger yet, and he didn't dwell on the finer points of breathing. If he didn't get this hood off, he'd find it difficult to get out of this situation alive. Even blind, he knew better than to keep his back to the man and he whirled around as his opponent scrambled to his feet.

The blow to his stomach forced a loud grunt out of him as he doubled over in pain. Damnation. He'd not been kicked that hard since his days fighting at Eton. It was time he taught this bastard a lesson. But first, he needed to know where the man was. With one last vicious tug, he yanked the hood off his head and came upright.

He blinked as cool air brushed over his face and he tried to get his bearings. His hesitation kept him from avoiding the shadowy figure rushing at him. Large hands plowed into his mid-section and shoved him backward. Too late, he realized he was at the top of the stairs leading down to the library. As he plunged down the stone stairs, his shout reverberated off the stone walls until his head hit sandstone and he lost consciousness.

₮CC⁃

The subtle scent of jasmine brushed across his senses as he awoke to a dull throb in his forehead. Bloody hell. The last time his head had hurt this bad, he'd been out the night before drinking and brawling with the Viscount Wiltham. With a grimace, he raised his fingers to touch the painful area. He'd barely touched the spot before someone gently slapped his hand aside. Opening his eyes, he stared up into Constance's worried features. The moment her eyes met his, a sigh of relief escaped her.

"How do you feel?" she asked softly. The mattress gave way as she sat next to him and gently applied a cool compress to his forehead.

"As if I've been in a brawl." Wincing, he pushed himself into an upright position despite her protests. In the next instant, he was forced to flop back down onto the mattress to quiet his churning stomach. The room was spinning violently, and he closed his eyes to stop the sensation.

Warm fingers grasped his hand.

"You look as if you've been in one, too." The light note of brevity in her voice made him open his eyes to glare at her. She smiled and reached for a glass of milk. "Here, take a sip of this. Cook promises it will help ease any headache you have."

She slipped her arm under his shoulders to help him sit up. Someone had removed his jacket, and the warmth of her seeped through his shirt into his skin. God, he ached all over, and yet her touch made him long for one more night with her. He quickly swallowed the milk, then pulled away from her to alleviate the sensations she'd aroused. Even the cold milk couldn't douse the fire her presence had ignited in him. Lying back against the pillows once more, he closed his eyes as the throbbing in his head took center stage again. Bloody hell, he was lucky to be alive. How he'd managed to fall down those stone steps without breaking his neck was a miracle. Even the children might have— With a grunt of pain, he lurched upright in bed.

"Imogene, Jamie. Where are they?" he growled.

"They're perfectly fine. They're in the nursery having tea." A sigh of exasperation parted her lips as she pushed him back into the mattress.

"I told them they're not to go into the labyrinth," he muttered with soft groan of pain. "It's too dangerous."

"I doubt they'll be interested in exploring the tunnels anytime soon. They were the ones who found you. Jamie forgot his drawing pencil and came back to the library. When he and Imogene found you they were quite distraught."

The sharp tap of a cane on the floor drew his attention as his grandmother entered the room. As regal as ever, Aurora stared at him down the line of her sharp nose. The strain on her elderly features worried him. He should never have gone into the labyrinth alone. It had been a stupid thing to do— something he would never have done on one of his digs.

"Well, boy. What have you to say for yourself?" Pinned beneath her formidable glare, he grimaced.

"I'm fine, grandmother. Thank you." The irony in his voice wasn't missed by Lady Lyndham, who sent her cane tip crashing against the floor.

"Don't get cheeky with me, boy. I've known you to do nonsensical things in the past, but never when it comes to your safety."

"Agreed," he muttered. "I wasn't thinking clearly."

"When Jamie told us about the hood he found beside you…" Constance's voice quavered slightly as his gaze shifted to look at her. "Someone tried to kill you, Lucien."

"But they didn't succeed."

"Not this time they didn't," Aurora snapped fiercely. She tapped her cane against the floor for emphasis. "What the devil is going on here, Lucien? The entire keep is in an uproar over what happened to first Constance and now you."

"Then there will continue to be an uproar, Grandmother. If I knew what was going on, I'd be happy to tell you. As it is, I have a much larger problem on my hands at the moment."

Closing his eyes, he remembered the sense of helplessness he'd experienced as he'd tumbled down the stairwell. At that moment, he'd realized he wouldn't be able to protect Constance if he didn't live. Worse yet, someone was in his home, uninvited. They'd tried to kill him, and for all he knew they might try to harm those he loved.

"Well, boy, are you going to enlighten us as to your problem?" His grandmother's voice was sharp with exasperation, but there was fear there as well.

"Someone knows how to get into the labyrinth from outside the keep," he said grimly.

Chapter Fifteen

His quiet words hovered in the air for a long moment, as the two women simply stared at him in stunned silence. Their expressions reflected the way he felt. It was an unsettling feeling to know that someone could enter the keep without detection.

"How is that possible?" Aurora demanded.

"Jamie's map shows a corridor that ends near the foot of the North Tower. I believe we'll find a door there leading into the orchards."

"Jamie's map?" Horror filled Constance's voice.

"Your son is quite industrious, *yā sabāha*. He mapped out his explorations of the labyrinth in great detail." He grunted as Constance gently applied another cool compress to his forehead. "I can only assume my assailant now has the lad's map."

"Then if the door is where you think it is, we'll find it and seal it off." Aurora said in an imperial tone.

"Whoever discovered the labyrinth most likely knows all its secrets by now, Grandmother. I can't believe there's only one outside entrance."

The unsettled expression crossing his grandmother's face made him heave a sigh. Aurora wouldn't take kindly to his reasoning as to why someone was exploring the labyrinth. But there could be no other explanation for someone finding the labyrinth and keeping it a secret.

"Someone is moving about the keep undetected and whenever they please. That, I will not allow," he said.

"You think he's after the statuette, don't you?" Constance met his gaze steadily. "Standish, that is."

Odd how she'd added the remark about Standish. Almost as if she was thinking of someone else. Trying to sit up, he nodded with a grimace. His movements immediately propelled Constance forward, and she pushed him back into the pillows. The action forced a grunt of annoyance from him, but she simply glared at him in return.

"Yes, I think it's Standish, but without my half of the map to Sefu's tomb and the Isis statuette in my possession, the Seth figurine is useless to him. Odd though, that he's not tried to steal the Isis statue."

"That cursed statuette again," Aurora bit out angrily. "If it's in the labyrinth, then I say let him have the damned thing. It's brought nothing but pain and sorrow to the Blakemores."

Lucien closed his eyes at the anger and pain woven through his grandmother's words. Perhaps she was right. Maybe he should find the damned thing and just hand it all over to Standish. The map, the figurines, everything. The thought lingered for a moment before he tightened his mouth with determination. When hell froze over. The man had broken into his home and had tried to kill him. God only knew what Standish might have done if Constance or one of the children had encountered the bastard in the labyrinth. He might already be damned by the Blakemore curse, but he'd be damned for sure if he let the bastard get away with his illegal activities.

"What if it's not the map he's after?" Constance's soft words made him frown, and he turned his head toward her. She was staring off into space, her expression troubled.

"Of course it's the map he's after," Aurora snapped. "And I say give it to him. I prefer to have my grandson alive for what's left of my life."

"I am *not* going to give that bastard the map *or* either one of the statuettes."

Irritated by his grandmother's outrageous suggestion, he pushed himself up into a sitting position and glared at the elderly woman. She returned his scowl with equal exasperation. His anger ebbed as a firm hand pressed against his shoulder. Unlike the touch he'd experienced when Nigel had been in the room, Constance's touch was warm, soaking its way into his body.

"Blast it, Lucien! Will you please lie still," Constance huffed as he easily avoided her attempt to keep him flat on his back. "You are the most pig-headed man I've ever met."

"If I recall correctly, you indicated my brother was equally so," he retorted.

The words tugged a small moue of surprise to her lips as she busied herself with stuffing pillows behind his back so he could sit up comfortably. At the sound of his grandmother's gasp, he turned to eye the Blakemore matriarch sternly. "You have something to say, Grandmother?"

With a gleam of calculation in her piercing blue gaze, she stared at him for a long moment. Whatever she believed about the Seth figurine, she decided not to push him on the subject. Or perhaps he'd actually surprised her for a change.

Aurora shook her head and rose to her feet. She walked stiffly to the door. "It's time for my spot of tea. If you feel up to it, my boy, I'll see you at supper, but in the meantime I leave you in capable hands. Constance, remember what I told you."

The no-nonsense look Constance received from Aurora made her cheeks flare a bright red. Intrigued, he waited until the door closed behind his grandmother before turning his head toward her.

"An interesting choice of words."

Flushing a deeper color red, she shook her head and rose from the bed. "Your grandmother is a tenacious woman, especially when she makes up her mind about something."

He grabbed her hand to prevent her from walking away. Beneath his fingers, her skin was soft and warm. He raised her hand to his mouth, and the delicate fragrance of jasmine tantalized his nose as he kissed the inside of her wrist. She trembled at the touch.

"Exactly what did she say to you, Constance?"

"It was of no importance."

"No?" His mouth brushed across her palm before he gently nipped at her forefinger. The soft sigh of pleasure that escaped her pleased him. "I've never known my grandmother to say anything insignificant."

She snatched her hand out of his grasp and moved away from the bed to the tea tray sitting on the fireside table. "Since you seem to be doing quite well, I'll take this tray downstairs and ensure the children aren't embroiled in some new adventure."

"That night at the Clarendon..."

He watched her freeze in the act of lifting the tea tray. After several seconds, she set the tray down and turned to face him. Tipping her head slightly, she silently encouraged him to continue. Satisfied she wasn't going to run away, he moved to sit on the edge of the bed, his body hurting as he did so.

"Why did you race away from me that night as if your life was in danger?" His question made her flinch as if the memory was unpleasant. Rising to his feet, he took several steps to the foot of the bed and leaned against the bedpost.

"I saw a man and a woman murdered. I thought you were involved with their deaths, but I was wrong."

"Which is why you ran from me." Relief barreled through him as her quiet words filled the air between them. She'd had a vision, but it hadn't been about him. Her special ability hadn't shown him descending into madness in a fit of uncontrollable rage. He folded his arms across his chest as he watched her.

"Yes." She nodded. "I'd never had a vision like it before. It was horrible."

"You thought I'd killed my brother?"

"No. Not Nigel, your parents."

The words drew up his sore muscles until they were knotted and shouting with pain. With a grunt, he pushed himself away from the bedpost. Christ Jesus, she'd actually seen his father kill his mother. He swallowed the bile rising in his throat as he remembered his mother's blood splattered everywhere.

"My parents. Why would you have witnessed the deaths of my parents?"

Compassion softened her features as her hazel eyes darkened to a mossy green. "There is no Blakemore curse, Lucien. Your parents were murdered, and whoever did it is using the curse to cover up their heinous actions."

The tension pulsating through him taunted his aching body

with tenacious glee. It reminded him of the first time he'd fallen off his horse as a child. There was this sense of uncertainty, a distance between the knowledge of the event and the acceptance of it. Disbelief made him shake his head.

"You're mistaken. My father murdered my mother before he took his own life."

"That's what someone wants you to believe, but it didn't happen that way." Certainty gave strength to her voice as she disagreed with him.

"Damn it, Constance, there was a bloody inquest. The investigation showed my father butchered my mother and then slit his own throat," he rasped.

Hands clasped behind his back, his fists burned from the tightness of his clench. She had to be wrong. The curse was real. His great-grandfather had killed and committed suicide. Then his father had followed the same path. Even if what she believed were true, who could possibly be responsible for so much mayhem over such an extended period of time? Not to mention the question of why. The clock on the nightstand ticked the seconds off softly in the silence of the room as he struggled to try and believe her once more. He shook his head.

"It's not possible. The curse made my father go mad. *He* killed my mother, not some phantom killer." Stubbornly he shook his head as he met her unwavering gaze. She scowled at him.

"Your mother was already dead when your father found her. He was beside himself with grief. The anguish he experienced..." She closed her eyes, and her sigh was a mere whisper. "It was a pain unlike anything I've ever felt before. He wanted to die, but he didn't kill her or himself. I saw him being murdered."

"*Who*?" He gestured for her not to bother answering his question with a wave of his hand. "Like Nigel, you don't know who the murderer is either."

"No, I don't have all the answers. I only have bits and pieces of a mystery I've been trying to unravel ever since I arrived at Lyndham Keep. However, there are some things I'm certain of." She moved to stand at his side, and her fingers dug into him as she clutched his arm. "There is no Blakemore curse. Whoever the murderer is, they made it look as if Nigel, your father and your great-grandfather killed a loved one out of madness and then themselves out of guilt."

"This is ridiculous," Lucien snapped as he glared down at her. "We're talking about a span of time that covers more than thirty years."

"I know it sounds impossible, but I can only tell you what I've seen. And there are two things that are key. Malcolm Standish is deeply involved. He knows the murderer. The second item of importance is that the murderer wants the Seth figurine."

"I'll say it again. The statuettes are worthless without the second half of the map. A prize I have no intention of giving away." He flung his hand to the side in a gesture of irritation. Damn it, why did the woman have to persist with this ludicrous train of thought?

"The map isn't what he really wants. He hates your family, and he's a devotee of the Seth cult. This man believes in the god of chaos's ability to grant him whatever he asks for, and he believes murder is how Seth intends him to achieve his goals."

"And what are these goals?" he snarled.

"I wish I knew. But this man has killed six people, and he might kill more…"

Fear made her grow pale, and he narrowed his eyes as he watched her. Did she believe her son might be the murderer's next victim? He caught a glimpse of horror in her gaze before she looked away from him. It was true then. Whatever she'd seen had shaken her deeply.

"That's why you were so frantic last night," he mused softly. "You saw him hurt Jamie."

She nodded her head and turned away from him. "He knows…I can see him. I'm a threat…he…"

The way her voice trailed off tugged at something deep inside him. Worse, he didn't like the way his gut clenched the moment she turned away from him. He knew it was a mistake to offer her comfort, but he couldn't stifle his need to console her. Gently he pulled her close and allowed her warmth to wash over him and soothe his aching muscles. He couldn't let her stay here. She had to leave the keep. The question was, how could he let her go?

Almost as if she could read his mind, she raised her head to look up at him. His heart slammed into his chest with the force of a sledge hammer. The emotion lighting her face held a promise of something he knew better than to ever hope for. He didn't move as her fingers lightly trailed along the scar on his cheek. One touch. Just one touch and she'd managed to twist his insides into knots.

He heard her breathing grow slow and labored, but he refused to act on the desire he saw flaring in her beautiful eyes. A desire that might be insatiable if he relaxed his guard. Worse, it might actually change him into a monster. A shudder ricocheted through her and bored its way into him. God, he was just torturing himself by holding her like this. He captured her mouth in a hard kiss then quickly released her. A look of puzzlement furrowed her brow as he put several feet between them. Somehow he knew she wouldn't like what was coming.

"I'll make arrangements for you and Jamie to return to London first thing in the morning. If you would, I'd like you to take Imogene with you. I'd send my grandmother, but she's not left the grounds of the keep for years and will refuse to leave."

Shock widened her eyes, and he steeled himself not to respond to her touch as she reached out to grip his arm.

"Why are you doing this, Lucien?"

"I want you safe."

"I am safe. I'm safe with you." Desperation whispered beneath her words, and he hardened his heart. He refused to answer the plea in her voice.

"We both know that's not true. I'm still not convinced my father didn't go mad, which means my own fate is sealed. Even if the Blakemore curse doesn't exist, this murderer you've seen is a dangerous threat. Either way, you and the children aren't safe here. You'll return to London on the morning train."

"*No*," she exclaimed sharply.

"This matter is not a subject for debate."

"The children can go to my brother Sebastian's home. They'll be safe there."

"As shall you."

"But—"

"I'll not discuss the matter with you any further, Constance. Nothing you say will change my mind."

"I won't leave you," she said with quiet insistence.

For a moment, her response stunned him. Didn't she understand he was trying to protect her? Keep her from harm? Especially from him. Infuriated, he gritted his teeth. The woman would try the patience of a saint. With a grunt of anger, he wheeled away from her. She could say no all she wanted, but he was putting her on the train tomorrow whether she liked it or not. He stalked toward the door with stiff, stilted movements. He needed to put some space between them. If he stayed in here much longer, he might actually consider giving in to her. And God help him if he did that. He grabbed the doorknob and twisted it with brutal force.

"I love you, Lucien."

Her words hung in the air like a pendulum halted in mid-swing before it continued toward him, pinning him against the door. She was mad. What would have prompted her to say such a thing to him?

Grandmother.

He bowed his head as he released his vicious grip on the brass knob and pressed his palms into the wooden door. He didn't want her to love him. It was dangerous for her to do so.

"I love you. Nothing you say or do will change that."

"You ask more than I can give, Constance." He dragged air into his lungs, desperate to silence her persistent declarations. "I can't love you."

"I don't believe that," she said firmly.

Too late he realized his mistake. He'd given her the hope he might change his mind. God, if only he *could* love her. A dark laugh deep in the back of his head taunted him. As much as he wanted to believe the curse didn't exist, he couldn't take the risk. He didn't see her move, but her sweet scent filled his senses as she came to a halt beside him.

The way her fingers clutched at him reminded him how stubborn she could be. He threw off her hand in a savage manner and immediately put several feet between them. There had to be some way to end this. Some way to make her understand she was wrong to love him.

"Believe what you will, Constance. I'm not capable of loving anyone."

"You're a hypocrite, Lucien. You put such stock in people telling you the truth, and yet you've lied to yourself every day since your parents died."

Her words sent a raw fury whipping through him. Who the hell was she to suggest he wasn't being honest with himself? He'd lived with the memory of his father's nightmarish handiwork for years. He knew what he was capable of. Even now, the animal inside of him snarled to be unleashed. He didn't want to hurt her, but this dark emotion inside him would be both their undoing. Taking a step toward her, he silently willed her to stop speaking. Most people would have flinched in the face of his anger, but not her. Instead she glared back at him.

"There's no curse, Lucien. There never was. You've used it as an excuse to keep from getting close to anyone."

In three strides he towered over her. Still she didn't shrink from him. If anything, she became even more defiant. He wanted to throttle her. Even worse, he wanted her. He could feel need winding its way through him and into his groin. With his body, he pressed her into the door, and his hands bit into the softness of her arms. She winced slightly at his brutal grip, but the stubborn tilt of her mouth remained the same. A mouth he wanted to taste again. Perhaps there was only one way to convince her they had no future together.

"Take care with your words, Constance."

"*Why*? Because you can't stand to hear the truth?"

"No," he growled. "Because you leave me no choice but to show you that passion and love are two different things."

He leaned into her and slanted his mouth over hers in a hard, fiery kiss. God, how was it possible for the woman to make him furious and hot all at the same time? She didn't resist him. Instead she melted into his arms as if she'd always belonged there. She gently bit on his lower lip in a hungry demand, and he eagerly gave her what she wanted. In an instant, honey and lemon exploded over his taste buds as he probed the inner warmth of her mouth.

Christ Jesus, he'd missed this. Missed the passion between

them. This wasn't love, but giving this up would be difficult. Pleasure surged through him as her hands unbuttoned his shirt and explored his chest. It was like being singed by a raging fire, except this was a fire he didn't want to put out.

Her mouth slipped away from his to trail its way down to the base of his throat. He was already growing hard, but the moment her hand brushed down over his stomach, his cock became a steel rod. As her mouth continued to inch its way downward, he released her for an instant to lock the bedroom door.

It had been too long since he'd enjoyed the sweetness of her body, and he needed her now—this instant. No seductive caresses or kisses, just the power of desire barreling through him. Despite the groan of protest from his aching muscles, he picked her up and carried her to the bed. This wasn't about anything except raw, hot need. Setting her on the edge of the bed, he firmly pressed her backward until the upper half of her body sank into the mattress. His mouth sought hers in another hard kiss as with fast and furious movements, he yanked her dress up to her waist.

He had no idea why she didn't protest his rough handling, and he didn't care. This was about convincing her that what they shared wasn't love. It was lust, pure and simple. The soft flesh of her inner thigh was warm as he ripped her silk drawers away from her skin. Fresh cream drenched his fingers as he explored the depths of her sex. Christ Jesus, touching her like this made him harder than he thought possible.

The sooner he buried himself inside her slick core, the sooner he could prove his point to her. She thought him capable of love, but he knew better. God help her if she thought this was love. This wouldn't keep her safe from harm. It wouldn't warm her in her old age. This was nothing more than the most basic of mating acts. One he needed to finish here and now. His fingers raced to undo his trousers, and his blood surged faster through his veins. As his hard rod broke free of his clothing, her hand wrapped around him snugly. It was an unexpected pleasure, and his body jerked from the sensation. The sudden heat of her palm against his chest made him pause.

"Open your heart to me, Lucien. Let me love you."

Like a rosebud unfolding under the sun, she opened herself

up to him. The emotion glowing in her face ignited a flame inside him. An answering emotion he couldn't afford to feel. His jaw flexed as he remembered why he was taking her so quickly and without finesse. Without responding to her quiet plea, he bent her legs upward and buried himself deep inside her in one hard thrust. A cry of pleasure flew from her lips, and he grunted with satisfaction. She needed no other answer from him than this one.

Embedded deep in the heat of her, he groaned as he remained motionless for a long moment. He wanted to savor this small moment, because he knew it would never happen again. Her body flexed around his cock, and he pulled in a swift breath. With just a tiny movement, she'd managed to make him so hot he was having difficulty holding his seed. She moved against him one more time, and he released another groan. Christ Jesus, he ached for her.

Desire blinded him as he began to pump his body into hers with a powerful fury. Stroke after stroke, he drove into her, desperate to prove this was nothing more than raw, unbridled passion—not love. Her body responded to him with first one ripple and then another. Pleasure and love weren't the same, but the way her body clutched at his cock was incredible.

Reason departed him as he lost himself in her completely. He ignored all the warnings his brain was screaming at him as he heard her cry out his name. She bucked against his hips as she peaked and shattered over his rod with tight, hot clenches of passion. The darkest part of him cried out against the emotion welling up inside him. Determined to stave off the feeling, he told himself this was merely a good fuck and nothing else. Then her climax pulled on him, demanding he experience the same satisfaction. With one last thrust, his body slammed into hers as he exploded and throbbed inside her.

Hands braced on either side of her head, he leaned forward, his brow almost touching her breasts as her spasms continued clutching at him.

He wanted her again.

He wanted her with him always.

The thought plunged him into the depths of hell. God help him. He'd thought to show himself there was nothing but passion between them. Instead, he'd opened himself up to the real and horrible possibility she might have been right. What the hell was he going to do? The answer to his question was immediate and harsh. Swallowing hard, he desperately searched his mind for another option. There was none.

Retreating from her, he quickly pulled her dress down and turned away from her to adjust his own clothing. Behind him, he could sense her confusion and the beginnings of fear. With his back still to her, he cleared his throat.

"As I said. There is a distinct difference between love and a good fuck."

Although he couldn't see her face, her strangled cry of horror spoke volumes as to how deeply his words had cut into her. God, he excelled at being a bastard. All the better for her. One day she'd thank him for the cruelty of this moment. He tried to turn and face her, but his courage failed him.

The bed squeaked softly, and he heard the rustling of her dress as she stood up. Straightening his jacket, he dragged in a deep breath before turning to face her. To his surprise, she'd already reached the bedroom door. Stunned, he stared after her. Was she actually going to let his brutish conduct go unchallenged? Her hand grasped the doorknob, and she hesitated for a mere fraction of a second before opening the door. Disbelief crested inside him, followed by intense despair, as he watched his life walk silently out of the room without a single backward glance.

In the hallway, Constance leaned against the wall and closed her eyes as she reeled with shock. She'd lost. He'd turned away from her, unwilling to open himself up to her love. Pain in the form of a fiery blaze engulfed her heart until it was a charred ember.

The bleak moment swallowed her until there was little reason to breathe. A sob escaped her lips as she moved down the hall, numb to any sensation. She was so devoid of feeling that she didn't even realize Nigel was present until the sound of his voice stopped her in her tracks.

"My brother is a fool." The quiet sympathy in the ghost's voice did little to comfort her as she turned toward him.

"No, he's simply unwilling to risk his heart. So many of the people he's loved have died brutal deaths. I cannot blame him for not wanting to risk loving me."

"He's stubborn and hardheaded in refusing to admit he loves you."

"Perhaps," she said with a disbelieving shrug. "It doesn't matter. He's sending me away tomorrow. He wants me to take Imogene with Jamie and me."

She saw Nigel shake his head vehemently with an expression of anger. "It's too late for that, the boy—"

The sound of Mrs. Clarke's voice interrupted them, and she saw the ghost vanish as the housekeeper's bulky figure drew near. There was a look of deep concern on her face.

"My lady, I was wondering if you've seen Lord Westbury. Nanny hasn't seen him since tea time, and she's been searching everywhere for him."

Fear scraped its abrasive fingers down her back. "Oh God."

"Now I'm sure he's quite all right, my lady. He's a good lad, just a bit high spirited at times. He's probably hiding just to give us all a good scare so he can laugh himself silly."

Constance shook her head. Jamie wouldn't do that to her. Especially given how upset she'd been last night. He knew she'd worry. Despite his high spirits, he was sensitive enough not to do something so thoughtless or mean. She closed her eyes and reached out with her senses. Nothing. Why couldn't she sense if he was in danger or not? She sagged slightly and rested her palm on the corridor's cool gray stone. The chill of it permeated her hand as she caught the wisp of an image in her head. She pushed her emotions deep and forced herself to grow quiet.

It was then she saw him. The priest turned away from the altar and she saw his thin lips twist into a cruel smile. In that split second, she knew the man had her son. Dear God, that's what Nigel meant by saying it was too late. The boy he'd referred to wasn't Lucien, but Jamie. The knowledge dragged her fear back to the surface as the vision winked out.

Without hesitating, she whirled away from the housekeeper and raced back toward Lucien's room. Her fists pounded on the door as her fear evolved into a state of panic. It was coming true. Her nightmare was going to come true. The door flew open and she pressed her hands into his solid chest. He might not love her, but he wouldn't refuse to help her save her son.

"He's taken Jamie."

"What the devil are you talking about?" he asked with a sharp edge of concern.

"Jamie's gone. No one can find him." She shuddered as she suddenly realized she couldn't feel whether her son was alive or dead. "Oh sweet Lord, Lucien, he's going to..."

Nausea swept over her as the images she'd seen swept back into her head with a vicious abandon. There had to be a way for her to find him. A way for her to save him. Oh God, why did she possess this gift if she couldn't use it to save her own son? Closing her eyes, she ignored the way Lucien was giving clipped orders to the housekeeper.

If she focused her energy and thoughts on Jamie, she might be able to see him. She might have a vision that would point her to where he was. Desperately, she tried to clear her head of everything but her son. She pictured his cheerful features in her head. Clinging to the image of his smile and jaunty manner, she silently called out his name. There was no answer, only a dead weight where her heart was supposed to be.

It wasn't working. Panic sluiced through her veins. How was she going to find him? He'd be scared. And it would be her fault. Graham had warned her not to try and help people. He'd always told her nothing good would come of it. Her eyes flew open as Lucien's strong hands gripped her shoulders. Concern darkened his blue eyes, and his mouth was a thin line of determination.

"Mrs. Clarke has gone to gather the servants. I'll have a search party organized in a few minutes. We'll find him sooner than you think."

"The labyrinth," she gasped. "You need to look for him there."

"I'm going to do that with one of the men, while I have the others search the house and the grounds. It's possible he simply lost track of time while playing outside." The grim expression on his face made her stomach lurch with a sickening jolt.

"I want him back, Lucien." A frenzied panic laced her voice

as her fingers dug deep into his arms. "I want him back safe and sound."

Warm hands cupped her face. "I'll find him, Constance. Now I want you to go to Imogene. She's certain to be frightened."

The memory of her vision returned to haunt her. She never would have come to Lyndham Keep if she'd known something like this might happen. If Jamie were harmed, she'd never be able to live with herself.

Booted feet pounded the hallway carpet behind her, and she turned her head to see two footmen hurrying in their direction. As the men came to a halt, Lucien nodded toward the older of the two.

"Lazenby, walk with her ladyship to the nursery where Lady Imogene is, then meet me and the others in the main hall." His fingers were gentle as he lifted her chin and looked down into her eyes. "I'll find him, Constance. I swear to God I'll find him for you."

A moment later, Lazenby's hand was on her arm as he walked with her to the nursery.

Chapter Sixteen

The moment Constance entered the nursery Imogene pulled away from Nanny and raced across the room to throw her small body into Constance's arms.

"Oh, my lady. Have they found him?"

"No, Imogene. Your uncle and the staff are looking for him now."

"He told me something bad was going to happen, but I thought he was just trying to get me to do what he wanted to do. I didn't believe him."

Over the top of Imogene's head, her gaze met Nanny's concerned look before returning her attention to the young girl. One hand cupping Imogene's chin, she studied the child's tear-stained face.

"Do you know where he went, Imogene?"

"No, my lady. He was very cross with me. He said he didn't like me anymore, and that I'd never see him again."

"Did he tell you what was going to happen, Imogene?"

"No, my lady." Imogene reached up to wipe at her wet eyes. "We were playing in the garden. When he got angry with me, he ran back into the house. I followed him, but I couldn't find him."

Constance's heart thudded painfully in her chest as she tried to absorb everything the child was telling her. Jamie had seen something. Something so terrible he couldn't even bring himself to tell Imogene. She hugged the little girl close and gently stroked her dark hair. It had a calming effect on the child, but her own fear didn't abate.

Swallowing hard, she struggled not to cry. The images she'd seen of Jamie filled her head, and fear wove an insidious path through her body. A warm hand patted her arm reassuringly, and she turned her head to see Nanny standing at her side.

"I think we could both use a cup of tea," Nanny said quietly. "I'll be back in a few moments."

She nodded her thanks as the nurse hurried from the room. One arm wrapped around Imogene's shoulders, Constance pulled her toward the sunny window seat. The sun was beginning to set, and she could see men searching the grounds. She knew they wouldn't find anything. Jamie was in the labyrinth with *him*. She couldn't see or feel anything, but she knew in her heart her son was in danger.

With Imogene nestled in her arms, Constance stared out at the sunset with a sense of hopelessness. How could she just sit here and do nothing to help find Jamie? She was useless. Her gift had abandoned her. Desolation crept through her to wrap a smothering hand around her heart. She was going to lose her son.

Eyes squeezed shut against the pain, a tear slid down her cheek. Imogene's small hand touched her face in a comforting gesture. A moment later the girl stiffened against her.

"Oh, my lady, do you see her? Do you see the lovely lady?"

Startled, she opened her eyes to look down at Imogene. There was a look of excitement on the girl's face as she sat upright with a sharp movement.

Turning her head, Constance saw the transparent figure of a woman shimmering in the ebbing sunlight. Tears stained the beautiful woman's cheeks, and the sadness on her face was reflected in the soft sobs she made. Sobs that reminded her of the cries that woke her every morning. Was this Katherine?

The ghost floated forward to hover near Imogene, a sorrowful smile on her face as she stretched out her hand to the child. In response, the girl extended her own hand to the ghost. The tips of their fingers barely touched when a look of horror swept over the spirit's features.

The frantic expression on the woman's face sent a chill through Constance. Their eyes met, and the ghost tried to speak. Her mouth moved rapidly, but there was no sound.

Something about the woman's agitated movements made Constance stand up.

"What is it, my lady?" Imogene grasped her hand. "What is she trying to tell us?"

"I don't know." As she stepped toward the ghost, the apparition darted toward one of the nursery's stone walls. The woman's body wavered and shimmered in the dim sunlight, her frenetic movements clearly pointing to the wall next to a tall bookcase.

Imogene gasped loudly. "It's an entrance to the labyrinth. Jamie said it was here, we just couldn't find it."

"But why is she telling us where..." Constance sent the ghost a puzzled look for a brief moment. Then, sucking in a sharp breath, she hurried toward the wall. "...unless she *knows* where Jamie is."

Relief crossed the ghost's features and she nodded vigorously while pointing to the gray stone. Constance's hands swept across the rough stone, her eyes searching for some mechanism to open up the hidden doorway. Beside her, Imogene searched the lower part of the wall. An instant later, the girl cried out her success.

"It's here, my lady. Here." Imogene looked up at the ghost who beamed at her for a brief second before urging them to open the door.

The girl pressed a small indentation in one of the square-cut stones, and the scraping sound of stone against stone echoed through the nursery. Constance leaped back, pulling Imogene with her as the stone wall turned in on itself to reveal a black hole. The ghost hovered in the open doorway, gesturing for them to follow her. Hesitating, Constance prevented Imogene from moving forward.

"No, Imogene."

"But my lady, we have to find Jamie. The lady will help us." The heartfelt protest warmed Constance's heart as she bent over to hug the child.

"I know she'll help me find Jamie, but you're not going with me. I need you to be here when Nanny comes back from the kitchen. She needs to find your Uncle Lucien and bring him here."

"But please, my lady, I want to help you find Jamie."

Desperation clenched her muscles as she saw the ghost grow more frantic. Tilting Imogene's face upward, she sent the child a stern look. "Imogene, listen to me. I don't have time to explain, but Jamie is in grave danger. If you come with me, you'll be in danger too, and I can't let that happen."

"But I—"

"No, Imogene. You're the only one who can tell your uncle how to find me."

Understanding dawned on the girl's sweet features as she nodded her head. "All right, my lady. I'll wait here."

"Thank you," she whispered as she kissed the child's forehead. Straightening, she saw a saucer-cup candle holder on the table next to Nanny's rocking chair. In seconds, she had the lit candle in her hand, and she entered the dank darkness.

❧❧

Lucien slammed his hand into the wall of the labyrinth. Another dead end. Behind him, Smyth cleared his throat in unspoken empathy. The two of them had been walking the dark passages for almost an hour without any sign of Jamie or anyone else. Thank God he'd had the foresight to have someone bring him several squares of chalk to mark their way through the dark maze.

Returning to their starting point, he grimaced as he remembered losing Jamie's map. It would have come in quite handy, as opposed to the crude line drawing he'd created a short time ago. Examining the paper he held, he sighed heavily. "All right, Smyth, let's try the passage closest to us here."

His finger pointed to a spot on the map as the man beside him nodded. "Would it be easier if we split up, my lord?"

"No." He shook his head sharply. "It's too dangerous. We stay together to cover each other's backs."

"Yes, my lord." Smyth shivered. "If I didn't know better, I'd say it was winter outside and not spring."

Lucien nodded. The air had grown decidedly colder in the last few minutes, and his senses were attuned to every little dip in temperature. Was Nigel here—trying to help him? He frowned. Even if it was his brother, Constance was the one who could see Nigel, not him. A strong icy pressure pushed him toward the passage he and Smyth had just emerged from.

With a shake of his head, he turned toward the man accompanying him and pointed to the corridor. "This is the passage we just came out of, correct?"

"Yes, my lord. You thought it would open up into the North Tower, but it was a dead end, just like all the other passages."

"Exactly," Lucien muttered angrily. "So why do I get the feeling there's something not right here?"

"I don't understand, my lord."

Holding his candle so it highlighted the makeshift map he'd been drawing, Lucien stared at the way all of the passages they'd explored pointed toward the North Tower. Inconceivably, not one of them opened up into any part of the tower itself.

Something was wrong. No builder in his right mind would have all of these passages leading nowhere. Unless— God almighty, there was another secret entrance at the end of one of the passageways. It was the only possible explanation.

Another icy weight pressed into his shoulders and tried to push him toward the passage he'd just explored. He'd felt a similar weight before, when Constance had told him Nigel was standing beside him. Was his brother with him now? Swallowing his trepidation, he deliberately took a step in the opposite direction. A cold weight hit him powerfully in the chest and he staggered backward.

"All right, all right, I'll go back the way we came."

"I beg your pardon, my lord?" Smyth eyed him warily.

"Smyth, follow this corridor back to the library and see if Major Fenwick has arrived." Lucien pointed toward the passage that led down to the library. "As soon as you can, bring the Major back here and follow my markings down this corridor. Make sure you're both armed."

"But we've already been down that passageway, my lord," the man protested with a frown.

"Don't argue, man. I'll use double X's this time. Now hurry."

With a nod, the servant disappeared down the dark tunnel, his candlelight vanishing as he turned a corner. Alone, Lucien turned back to the dead end passage. Again the cold pressure bit into his back, and he nodded.

"Nothing's changed with you, has it?" he muttered. "You're still as autocratic and dictatorial as ever. Being ten years older than me didn't make you my father."

This time the cold pressure became a sharp jab in the side of his arm. Grimacing, he moved back down the corridor. Now that he was alone again, he worked hard not to make a sound as he moved deeper into the heart of the labyrinth. And the North Tower was the heart of the keep's extensive passageways. If he'd been thinking more clearly earlier, he would have realized that in the labyrinth the North Tower was like the hub of a wheel with all the corridors leading outward.

Marking the wall, he continued moving forward. He'd not gone far when a faint sound made him pause. It was coming from up ahead, and he strained to hear it. Cautiously, he moved forward, keeping his back against the wall of the passage to make it more difficult for anyone set on attacking him. He'd only gone a short distance, when he heard the sound again. This time it was louder, and he recognized it as the sound of heavy stone scraping across stone. There *was* another door.

Pulling his pistol from the waistband of his trousers, he remained where he was for a moment. He needed the advantage of surprise. Without thinking twice, he blew out the candle he held and set it on the floor of the dark corridor. It took only a moment or so for his eyes to adjust to the near darkness and the faint pinpoints of light that lined the passageway from above.

If he'd estimated correctly, the light filtering in from above was part of the open rampart of the North Tower. He'd only gone a few more feet when he saw it. Where the passage had earlier been a dead end, it now revealed two new passageways. Hesitating, he debated which way to go. The firm cold pressure on his back pushed him straight ahead.

Grateful for the ghostly signal, he nodded a silent thank you and continued forward. How the hell had he and Duncan not found the labyrinth when they were children? For that matter, how had Nigel and Oliver not discovered these corridors? In the next brief second, every thought fled him as he heard Constance scream. Stunned, he barely had time to wonder how or why she was in the labyrinth before he charged forward.

Moments later, he tumbled into a heap as he tripped over a flight of stairs leading upward. The fall sent a numbing pain from his elbow up into his arm, while his ribs pressed viciously into his side. Grunting softly, he suppressed a groan of pain as his already-sore body loudly protested this current abuse. He winced as he realized how lucky he was his pistol hadn't fired.

Not cocking the bloody thing had probably saved his life. If the damn thing had gone off, it would most likely have caused the bullet to ricochet off the walls of the narrow corridor. Worse, it would have announced his presence loud and clear.

As it was, he couldn't be sure he'd not already lost his advantage with the noise he'd made already. Pressed against the damp, moldy stairs, he lay still. Better not to move for a moment than charge forward and lose any possibility of surprise. At the top of the stairs, he could see a faint glimmer of light, and he could hear voices floating downward.

The sweet sound of Constance's voice made him briefly close his eyes in relief. She was alive. About to rise, he saw a shadow move in the light at the top of the stairs. Not daring to breathe, he froze. Was it possible for the person at the top of the stairwell to see him lying prone over the first few steps? The shadow stood still for several long moments before retreating back the way it had come.

In a silent whoosh of air, he released some of his tension. Christ Jesus, one more misstep like that and he'd be of no use to Constance at all. Patient, he needed to be patient. Damned difficult to do when the woman he loved was in danger. He closed his eyes at the revelation. Hell of a time to admit such a thing now, but he did. He loved her, and he was damned if he'd allow anyone to harm her if he could help it. He just hoped he would get the chance to tell her how much she meant to him.

Quietly, he moved up the flight of steps, continuing to hug the wall. The corridor stretched out a few feet past the stairs before it made a sharp left. Light flooded the small landing, and he pressed himself flat against the stone wall. Inching his way along the damp formation, he took a quick look around the corner then jerked back out of sight.

Bloody hell, who the devil was wearing a death mask of Sefu? It couldn't be Standish. The man was a common foot soldier, nothing more. He didn't have the knowledge needed to act as a high priest of the Sefu order. And the man he'd just seen wore the distinctive robe of a leader of the sect.

The markings embroidered on the long sleeves and floor-length garment proclaimed his high ranking within the cult. From the sinister mask that covered half of his face to the elaborate robe, the man was a Sefu priest, and a dangerous one. The worshipers of Seth in Sefu's order believed in blood sacrifices.

And Jamie's slender form on top of the room's stone altar illustrated how far this madman seemed willing to go to satisfy the Egyptian god of chaos. Somehow, Constance had managed to get within a few feet of the giant slab of rock. But she was still too far away to save the boy. Despite her calm demeanor, he knew she was terrified. Plan. He needed a plan of action. Somehow he needed to distract the priest.

He took another quick look, his eyes focused entirely on the man wearing the black hippopotamus mask framed with writhing snakes. The man suddenly spoke to Constance, a sneering laugh in his voice, and Lucien froze. It was a familiar voice.

Edward.

The shock of it held him rigid. It wasn't possible. He remembered all the times the man had sat at his table. All the times the man had comforted his grandmother, comforted him. Solicitous and caring every time death had darkened the keep's doorstep.

The son of a bitch. His grandparents, his own parents, had welcomed the man into the family. That Edward had been from the wrong side of the blanket had meant nothing to any of the Blakemores. He had their blood. He was one of them despite society's ridiculous rules. A slow, burning anger gripped him. It spread its way through every inch of him, until his fingers ached with the need to choke the life out of the man.

The invisible weight of his brother's hands pressed against him, trying to hold him to the wall. He shook his head. Waiting for help wasn't going to save Constance or Jamie. There was no telling how long it would take Duncan to reach this part of the labyrinth. His pistol cocked, he propelled himself around the corner. Leveling his weapon on the man he'd come to see as a father figure, he strode purposefully into the small room.

"Let them go, Edward."

It was the soft click of another weapon being cocked that drew him up short. The cold metal of a gun barrel pressed into the side of his head. Closing his eyes, he uttered an expletive of fury. He was a fool. In his rage, he'd completely forgotten Standish.

"Your weapon, my lord." There was a sadistic glee in the man's voice as Lucien lowered his arm.

Beneath the mask on Edward's face, Lucien saw the man's mouth curl into a menacing smile. Lucien's gaze shifted quickly to Constance, and the relief in her eyes renewed his determination not to fail her. On the slab, Jamie lay still, and for a moment, he thought the boy might be dead. Then he saw his chest rise and fall with a slow rhythm. Drugged no doubt. Beside him, Standish took his pistol from him.

"Well now, what a delightful family gathering. So reminiscent of old times, if I do say so myself." Again the man smiled with malicious pleasure. "I suppose you don't truly understand the meaning of that statement, do you Lucien?"

Glaring at the man, he struggled not to leap forward, all too aware of the gun Standish still held to his head. "I'm not going to let you hurt Constance or the boy."

He suppressed his emotions as he watched the man who was threatening everything he held dear. Cruel laughter suddenly reverberated off the stone walls of the small room, and he tensed.

It was unlike any laugh he'd ever heard, and it sent a river of ice splashing through his veins. It was the laugh of a madman. Beside him, even Standish seemed to find the man's laughter unsettling as he softly cleared his throat. The laughter died away as the priest's eyes studied him with a gleam of insane hatred.

"Come now, Lucien, do you really think that after all this time and effort I'm going to let you stop me?" A savage contempt twisted the man's mouth into a thin line. "I didn't let your brother stop me."

"What the hell is that supposed to mean?" Narrowing his eyes, Lucien sent Edward a hard look.

Satisfaction curved the madman's mouth as he shook his head. "My word, I really outdid myself with that story about the Blakemore curse. Nigel didn't believe it, but you did, and apparently still do."

"You seem to know quite a bit for a by-blow."

The man's malicious grin vanished into a hard, thin line. "And you're a fool for thinking some ridiculous curse killed your family. I slit their throats. *I'm* the curse."

The words washed over him with a surreal calm. Constance had been right. His parents had been murdered. And his grandfather? Had Edward killed him? He didn't realize he'd spoken until he heard Edward's cold laugh.

"Thomas, William, your father, all of them. It was vengeance. Simple vengeance for the woman who loved a Blakemore. She left everything to be with him. Her home, her family, and for what? To bear a bastard who would never inherit even his father's name."

"If you're referring to Maibe, she was well cared for. She wanted for nothing. My father saw to that."

"She didn't want money," Edward snarled. "She wanted the man she loved to marry her like he promised to do. Instead he pushed her aside and married one of his own kind. Then he put her in a lovely cage to visit her whenever he had the urge."

"And so you justify killing innocent people as retribution for something that only affected you from the standpoint of your birth."

The bizarre sight of the mask's hippopotamus snout and the man's feral grin created a grotesque picture of evil. "There are no innocents. Maibe taught me that. She showed me how the god Seth could give her justice if I followed the practices of his high priest, Sefu. She showed me how I could avenge her."

Desperate for time, Lucien realized Standish had shifted his position again. With the gun barrel no longer aimed at his head, he might be able to gain the upper hand. If he could throw the man off balance without the gun going off—of course it would fire, and he'd most likely be shot. But the odds of him reaching Edward in time were better if he did something now than if he waited.

"And the boy? Constance? How do they come into this? They're not Blakemores." He swallowed hard at the thought of losing her. He was going to lose Constance the same way he'd lost everyone else.

"True, but I need an innocent's blood for my sacrifice, and the boy's power is such that Seth will be greatly pleased with me. As for the woman—" Edward extended his arm as he pointed at Constance, "—she's seen too much."

"You're a fool." Constance's voice rang out strong and certain in the small, windowless room. "Seth will desert you."

"Silence," he thundered as he turned to face her. She shook her head as the back of her neck tingled. The familiar drop in temperature confirmed she was no longer alone, and it was evident to her that Nigel wasn't alone either. The temperature was far colder than anything she'd ever experienced.

"He's already deserted you," she said quietly. "Don't you feel it? The cold?"

"You lie!" Panic echoed in his voice as he stepped toward her.

"You know I have the soothsayer's gift, and yet you doubt my words." Constance tried not to flinch as he moved forward, her heart skipping a beat with terror as he pulled a familiar blade out of the long sleeve of his priest's robe. "Seth has already deserted you. The heat of Egypt and the mother sun will never grace this temple or shine on you."

Through the mask she could see the fiery hatred glowing fiercely in his eyes. But his hatred slowly gave way to fear as the air between them grew icy, and her words blew out between them in small crystallized clouds. Out of the corner of her eye, she saw a white mist forming, and she pointed to it.

"Look for yourself. Would Seth let them come for you? Would Seth let them seek their vengeance on you if he'd not deserted you?"

The mist began to take first one shape then another until six specters hovered in the space around her. She'd expected Nigel and the woman, but the other ghosts startled her. At the sight of them, he emitted a shout of rage and turned toward the altar. Horror swept through her as she saw his mouth twisted into a grotesque snarl.

No. Not Jamie. Racing forward, she threw herself past the madman and over her son's small body as the blade sliced downward. The knife pierced her back with the force of a hard blow. The shock of it stunned her, and she swallowed hard to control the nausea welling up into her throat. Why didn't it hurt?

She expected it to hurt more, but the only thing she really felt was a sickening sensation in the pit of her belly. The nausea fluttered through her—growing stronger. It even suppressed the sudden throbbing pain of the wound itself. With her body still shielding Jamie's, she waited for another stabbing pain to slice through her back.

When it didn't come, she looked over her shoulder to see the ghosts circling her attacker. Their white, misty forms swirled around him as their unseen strength prevented him from striking her again. With an inhuman screech of fury and fear, the man lashed out at his spectral attackers. Over and over again, he sliced the air around him only to have his serpentine blade hit nothing solid.

Still clinging to the stone slab, Constance watched the glistening blade slash through the air with a sense of detachment. Her blood. It was her blood making his knife shine so brilliantly in the half-light. The sight of it suddenly made her stomach roil, and the altar stone beneath her fingers grew warm and clammy.

God help her. She couldn't pass out now. She couldn't leave Jamie unprotected. As her legs wobbled, she fought to keep her grip on the altar. The sudden move sent pain knifing through her, and she whimpered softly. The sound of a scuffle off to her right made her turn her head, and she saw Lucien struggling to wrestle the gun from Standish.

Blood trickled down the stocky man's chin from a split lip as they fought for control of the weapon. With a grunt, Lucien drove his fist into the other man's face once more. Standish responded by crashing the butt of the pistol against the side of Lucien's head.

Pain ricocheted its way down into Lucien's neck from the blow. A growl of fury blew past his lips as he slammed his fist into Standish's jaw one more time. The punch forced a loud whoosh of air from the man's lungs, and he gave way enough for Lucien to wrestle him down to the floor. With one knee pressed into Standish's back, Lucien risked a quick glance in Constance's direction.

The ever-widening circle of blood on the back of her gown made his mouth go dry with fear. The size of it grew quickly as she sagged against the stone altar in her effort to continue shielding Jamie. Christ Jesus, if she died— No. He wouldn't consider that possibility. He wasn't about to lose her now. His gaze flitted toward Edward.

Enveloped in a dense white mist, the man seemed to be struggling with someone as he fought to raise his arm to strike another blow at Constance's back. Bloody hell. A violent strength ripped through him as he yanked the revolver out of Standish's hand and took aim.

The weapon fired, and the noise of it reverberated like a cannon blast in the small confines of the room. Unfazed, Edward continued to fight an unseen enemy in the white mist in his effort to attack Constance. Sweet Jesus, he'd missed. Desperation made his fingers clumsy as he struggled to cock the gun one more time. He raised the pistol to fire again just as Edward's blade sliced downward. Before he could shoot, a second shot rang out. For several seconds, Edward stood frozen in place before the knife slipped from his fingers and clattered loudly against stone. A grotesque gurgle bubbled out of the man as he sank to the floor.

Out of the corner of his eye, Lucien saw Duncan entering the room. It was about bloody time. Releasing his hold on Standish, he didn't bother to acknowledge his friend's arrival as he scrambled across the floor to reach Constance. Less than two feet away from her, Edward lay on the floor with his mouth contorted like a dying animal. The strange mist settled around him, engulfing him as he uttered one last death cry.

With a soft moan, Constance slid toward the floor. The blood seeping through her gown wet his hand as he caught her in his arms. He bit back a shout of fear as he realized her injury might be worse than he expected. Gently he eased her downward until she was cradled in his arms. Her eyes fluttered open, and she released a gasp of pain.

"Jamie?"

"He'll be fine, *yâ sabâha.*" Tenderly, he brushed a stray lock of hair away from her face. "Everything is going to be just fine."

A hand touched his shoulder, and he looked up into Duncan's worried expression. "Let me take a look at her wound."

Carefully, Lucien lifted Constance into an upright position as his friend knelt behind her. Fabric screamed a protest as Duncan ripped her gown apart at the wound's entry site. The man's gentle prodding of the area pulled an agonized moan from Constance.

"For God's sake, Duncan." Lucien glared at him.

"I'm sorry, but there's no easy way to do this."

Duncan sent him a grim look as Constance went limp against his chest. Relief surged through him. At least unconscious she wouldn't feel anything. He watched his friend's expression as Duncan sank back onto his heels and tugged at his shirt.

"It's a deep wound, but she'll be fine as long as we staunch the bleeding. The real danger is if she loses too much blood," Duncan said grimly as he ripped a strip of material off the bottom of his shirt and folded it into a flat bandage. "Here, hold this against the wound and keep constant pressure on it."

"And the boy?" Lucien jerked his head toward the altar. With a nod, Duncan rose to his feet and stepped around the altar to check on Jamie.

"He's been drugged, but I'm sure he'll be fine. He's breathing easily enough," Duncan said with a note of relief in his voice. Clearing his throat, he sighed. "Sad thing that, a father having to kill his own son."

Stunned, Lucien turned his head to see a grief-stricken Edward gingerly lifting the Sefu death mask off Oliver's face.

Chapter Seventeen

Moonlight dusted the gardens below as Lucien stared out the window of Constance's room. His shoulder pressing into the wooden framework, he shifted his position slightly and winced. The move tugged at his sore ribs and back. Straightening, he turned his head to look at the bed where Constance was sleeping. It had been several hours since the doctor had left, but the laudanum he'd given her was still working. A small fire burned behind the firebreak as he sank down into one of the large chairs facing the hearth.

Elbows resting on his thighs, he pressed his chin against his interlaced fingers as he stared into the flames. The past few hours had been charged with emotion. Shock from Oliver's betrayal, guilt over his mistaken thoughts about Edward, fear for Constance and the subsequent horror of watching Oliver try to kill her.

There would be another inquest. He welcomed the thought with a sense of relief. The Blakemore men would no longer be considered deranged madmen suffering from a family blood curse. And it would set him free. Free to love Constance.

He reclined back in his chair. For the first time since he was a boy, he actually felt a sense of wonderment and hope. The Blakemore curse didn't exist.

The freedom the thought gave him was so new he kept expecting someone to say it was a mistake. To think he wouldn't sink into madness made him feel as though a great weight had been lifted off his chest. A weight that had been present from the moment he saw his parents lying dead in the library. Murdered by his cousin.

The idea still staggered him. God, how had his cousin managed to keep everyone in the dark for so long? Even Edward had been blind-sided by Oliver's murderous insanity. In the space of only a few hours, Edward had aged more than twenty years. He looked old and beaten down. Guilt twisted his insides as Lucien remembered how he'd thought Edward had been the one threatening Constance.

He wasn't the only one experiencing guilt. Edward was struggling with the fact that he'd been forced to shoot his own son to save Constance. They said losing a child was devastating because one should never outlive one's children. For Edward, he'd not only outlived his son, he'd been forced to kill him as well.

With a sigh he rubbed the underside of his chin. His cousin had hid his murderous tendencies so well, not even his father suspected. He couldn't have been more than twelve or thirteen when he'd killed the first time. The thought of a child committing such a heinous crime didn't occur to anyone. Ironically the statue of Seth everyone had looked for over the years had been in Oliver's possession all along. He'd killed his grandfather and uncle to possess the damn thing. But it wasn't just the statue of Seth or the papyrus he'd wanted.

No, Oliver had wanted retribution for his grandmother's dishonor and shame. Vengeance for the one thing he could never own—the Blakemore name. Maibe had done her work well with her grandson. She'd filled Oliver with hate and her own desire for revenge. But when had his hatred become insanity? And it could only be labeled madness simply because of Oliver's conviction that a human sacrifice would gain him magical powers.

The man might have been insane, but even insanity was hard to forgive when it had destroyed so much of his life. He couldn't forgive Oliver for the pain and suffering his actions had inflicted. The man could rot in hell for all he cared.

Sparks flew up in the fireplace as several embers popped loudly and flared up into flames. Half expecting the sound to wake Constance, he turned to look over his shoulder at the bed. She didn't move, and he slowly relaxed and turned back toward the fire.

When she was well, the constable had expressed a wish to

speak with her. He was certain it was merely a formality, but if he could spare her the trial of reliving those terrible moments in the tower, he would. Tomorrow's inquest would not require Constance's presence, and if possible he hoped to persuade the constable not to question her at all.

His testimony and Duncan's had provided the official with more than enough information to resolve the inquest quickly. As for Standish, his confession had filled in a great many pieces of the puzzle where Oliver was concerned. The two men had met in Egypt when Oliver had saved Standish's life during a bar fight. In turn, the man had become Oliver's confidant.

Behind him, he heard Constance utter a small sound, and he immediately sprang to his feet. Carefully, he checked the pillows the doctor had instructed them to place around her. The physician had left her on her stomach to help ease the pain of her injury and aid in the healing process. He flinched as he recalled her scream when the doctor had started to sew up the wound. Her fingernails had dug into his skin as he'd held her hand during the procedure. Not even the laudanum had managed to completely eliminate her pain.

Finished adjusting the pillows around her, he gently pulled back the neckline of her nightgown to check her bandage. Satisfied the wound wasn't bleeding, he brushed a stray curl off her cheek then returned to his seat at the fire.

Leaning back in his chair, he closed his eyes as he recalled the sight of Constance leaving his room shortly before Jamie was discovered missing. There had been a hopeless air about her as she passed through the door. The fact she'd not even bothered to argue with him said she'd given up. Would she be willing to take another chance on him? Could he convince her of his love despite all the cruel things he'd said to her? What if she didn't let him? The thought sent a chill through him. He refused to let that happen. Somehow he'd find a way to convince her of his sincerity, just as she had convinced him about her special gift.

And what of her talent? How did he handle that? Blakemore brides were known for their eccentricities, but Constance's ability would far surpass anything the keep had seen before. Would he be comfortable with that? The question made him irritable. He didn't have a choice in the matter. He'd have to make himself comfortable with it.

He frowned. Comfortable with ghosts. That would take some getting used to, but he'd manage. Anything to ensure she stayed with him. A sudden cold breeze blew across his neck, and his eyes flew open. Rising to his feet, he looked around the room.

"Nigel?" he whispered.

When there was no answer, he frowned. Why could Constance see his brother, but he couldn't? There was a faint sound close to the window, and he quickly crossed the floor to see if there was a change in temperature. The moment he stepped into the cold spot, he knew it wasn't simply a draft in the keep.

He spun around, looking for another sign, something he could see, but there was nothing. If he didn't know better, he'd consider himself mad. But there had been nothing insane about his brother's presence in the labyrinth or the way Nigel had led him to where Constance was. Why couldn't he see what she saw? He wanted to share everything with her, but this was the one thing he couldn't. Frustrated, he prowled the floor.

There was a steady beat to his pacing. His footsteps soft yet audible against the wood floor as he moved back and forth like a caged lion. The sound of it gently rocked its way through the foggy haze wrapped around her head.

Jamie. The memory of how she'd thrown her body over Jamie's smaller frame made her sigh with relief. She'd saved him. That much she remembered, although most of what followed was a blur. There had been a gun shot, then Lucien holding her. Beyond that, all she remembered were obscure images. But Jamie and Lucien were both alive.

She wanted to sit upright, but the agonizing pain in her shoulder warned her not to move. With her cheek nestled against her pillow, she opened her eyes to see Lucien's shadow large and strong against the stone wall of her room. Viciously shoving a hand through his hair, he cupped the back of his neck in a gesture of angry frustration.

"Bloody hell, I can't live this way. All these ghosts between us. Never seeing or knowing when they're hovering over us. I don't want to share her," he growled.

The shock of his words rolled over her with the same force as the knife blow to her back. Had he suddenly realized he loved her? The thought made her close her eyes again. What a fool she was. He didn't love her. He'd made it perfectly clear the only thing that existed between them was passion.

Even if he did think himself in love with her, it was simply his mistaking passion for love. Just now his words clearly illustrated how her gift would come between them. He didn't want to live with the ghosts and visions that would always be a part of who she was. Loving someone meant you accepted them for who they were. You didn't try to change them into someone different. Lucien would never be able to do that.

She'd thought Graham would overcome the same attitude as well. But his silent disapproval had made her bury her gift deep inside her. She'd been afraid to speak about it or do anything to help others simply because Graham had thought it best she not acknowledge her gift. If he'd lived, she would have eventually come to resent him for not loving her enough to accept her as she was. She refused to live like that.

She suppressed a sob as a teardrop slipped out from beneath her eyelid to slide down her cheek. The pain she'd woken up to was nothing compared to the hot agony burning its way into her heart now. She wanted to slip back into the pain-free, white fog she'd awoken from a few short minutes ago.

Nothing mattered there. Nothing hurt. Here, there was nothing but pain. A pain she only wanted to escape. Swallowing her tears, she hiccuped quietly. In a fraction of a second, Lucien was at her side. How could he have heard that small sound?

"It's all right, *yā sabāha*," he murmured as he knelt at the side of the bed, his piercing blue eyes meeting hers. "I know it hurts, but you saved him, sweetheart. Jamie is just fine."

She didn't answer him, and when she tried to turn her head away, the movement sent fire speeding through her body. Gasping from the pain, she grew still and closed her eyes. The touch of his fingers against her damp cheek made her wince.

"What is it, sweetheart? Would you like some more laudanum for the pain?"

"Yes," she whispered. Anything to return to that peaceful

white mist.

Several moments later he gave her the unpleasant-tasting drug, then offered her a sip of wine. The vintage erased the unpalatable taste of the drug, but she could still feel the heartache as he took her hand in his.

"I thought I was going to lose you, *yâ sabâha*."

His voice was tight with emotion, and another tear escaped as she kept her eyes closed. He cared for her. But she'd heard the frustration in his voice a few moments ago. He might love her, but he wasn't able to love her for who she was. A woman with a gift to help people. A woman who could see the dead. Another tear slid down her cheek. Gently he wiped the drop away.

"It's going to be all right, sweetheart. Don't cry. It's all over now. Everything is going to be just fine. We'll talk when you're well."

She shuddered, the pain in her shoulder like a fire, but it didn't compare to the agony tearing at her soul. Slowly, the anguish eased in its intensity, ebbing away as the drug made her grow woozy. Sleep tugged at her, offering her the numbing peace she craved as she drifted back into the fog.

ॐ

Standing at the window of her room, Constance barely paid any attention to Anna's quiet movements as the maid packed her trunk. From the window she saw Jamie playing with Imogene in the garden. Today would be the last day he would do so, because they were leaving on the afternoon train for London.

She turned away from the sight, her shoulder causing her to wince. It had been almost a month since Oliver had stabbed her, and her wound was healing nicely. But it still ached if she moved too quickly or stretched the wrong way.

The door to her bedroom suddenly crashed open as Lucien strode into the room. She'd expected his anger, but his entrance was still enough to make her jump.

"Leave us, Anna," he said with a quiet fury that brooked no

argument. The maid glanced at her with a look of concern, and Constance nodded at her.

"You can come back in a little bit and finish, Anna. Thank you."

As the maid closed the door behind her, Constance waited quietly for him to speak. Glaring at her, his eyes blazed with icy anger.

"For almost four weeks you've avoided me. Refused to have any type of conversation with me, except in the presence of others. And now I have to learn from my grandmother that you're leaving. I want answers, Constance, and I want them now."

"I've been called back to London on family business. My work on the collection is fairly well completed. The few artifacts left are ones you can do yourself."

"I don't believe you," he snapped.

"What you believe is of little consequence, Lucien. I'm leaving on the afternoon train." Moving toward the vanity table, she flinched as he closed the distance between them and blocked her way.

"If you think I'm going to just let you walk out of here, you're wrong, *yâ sabâha*. I have no intention of letting you go."

"You don't have much choice," she sighed softly. "I won't change my mind."

His hands grabbed hers, and it was like an electrical pulse charging its way through her body. Trembling, she fought not to feel, not to crave him the way she'd longed for him over these past few weeks. It had been agony to be near him, seeing the tenderness in his expression, all the while knowing they'd never be together.

"Not long ago, you asked me to open up my heart to you. I'm doing that now, *yâ sabâha*, I'm telling you I love you. I need you."

Closing her eyes, she turned her face away from him. Oh God, this was going to be more difficult than she'd thought. The depth of emotion in his voice was far more potent than she'd ever dreamed possible. She swallowed hard, struggling to keep her emotions buried as deeply as she could, reminding herself that her gift would always come between them.

"Please don't do this," she whispered.

"Don't do what? Tell you how much I adore you? How I love everything about you?" His words sliced into her with the same viciousness as Oliver's blade. It stiffened her resolve as she yanked her hands out of his, ignoring the pain shooting through her shoulder.

"I'm sorry, Lucien, too much has happened." She shook her head as she moved away from him toward the window.

"What the hell is that supposed to mean?" he growled, his gaze following her every movement.

She still looked pale, but it was clear she was almost fully recovered. Now she was being as evasive as she'd been when she first came to the keep. Frustrated by her behavior, he wanted to shake her until she lost that cool, reserved expression she was wearing.

"It means I'm leaving."

"Then have the decency to tell me why." The fierceness of his voice matched the anger boiling inside him.

They'd barely spoken two words to each other in the past month. Every time he'd come to check on her progress, she'd managed to avoid any conversation. Whether it was to plead fatigue or pain, she'd deflected any attempt he'd made to confess his heart to her. To apologize for his cruelty.

Well, he was done accepting her excuses. He wanted to know what she was thinking, and he refused to let her avoid answering him. She turned to face him, her expression unreadable. Even her hazel eyes had a lifeless look about them. Fear made his muscles grow tight with a tension that quickly coiled its way through his body.

"Too much has happened. There are words and events that have passed between us that can't be mended." He took a step toward her, but she raised her hand to stop him. "No let me finish. We have the passion, but it's not enough for me."

"Then tell me what you want. God knows I'll give it to you. I'll give you the world if I can do so," he said hoarsely. Christ Jesus, she was serious. She honestly thought he only felt passion for her. She was wrong, and he had to find a way to convince her she was wrong.

"I never wanted the world, and what I want you can't give me."

"Don't you think I should be the judge of what I can or can't offer you?" he snarled.

"I'm sorry, Lucien." Sadness seemed to grip her as she shook her head. "If I could make you understand, I would, but I can't. It's not possible."

"So, you're simply going to walk out of here, away from *me*, away from *my love.*"

"Yes."

The quiet word ripped through him with a force that threatened to tear him apart. The resolution in the tightness of her lovely mouth only reinforced the determination in her response. He wasn't going to change her mind. The reality of it numbed him. Tormented him. She'd said she loved him, but something had undermined her love.

Not something. Him. The way he'd made love to her the afternoon Oliver had kidnapped Jamie. That was it. He'd been brutal in his treatment of her. Taking her like a barbarian and then demeaning their passion in the crudest manner possible. Shame swept through him. Somehow he had to undo the damage he'd inflicted.

He stepped toward her again, but the moment she flinched, he froze. The look of anxiety and panic on her face made him grow cold with dread. Had he hurt her so deeply she wouldn't forgive him? No, he refused to believe that. So why would she draw back in fear? Bloody hell, she'd had another vision. She'd seen something about him. Something that made her afraid of him. How the hell was he supposed to fight something like that? He watched her turn away from him to stare out the window.

"Would you send Anna back in to finish packing my trunk? I don't want to miss the three o'clock train."

The flat, emotionless words sent despair slashing through him. What the hell was he going to do without her? He needed time. Time to convince her how much he loved her. There had to be a way to stop her from leaving. But the rigid, stubborn line of her posture told him it was impossible to change her mind. He would have to let her go for now, but he'd follow her to London. Giving her up wasn't a choice he was willing to live with. She was going to discover that a Blakemore could be every bit as stubborn as a Rockwood.

⁋❧

"Well, it appears you might have actually succeeded in your efforts to rid yourself of the earl, Constance." Lady Patience Rockwood sent her a look of disgust. "A man can only take so much rejection before he flees town."

"Could we please find another topic to discuss other than the Earl of Lyndham?" Constance waved her black-feathered fan in front of her face in an attempt to cool herself in the stuffy confines of the ballroom they stood in. "Surely there are any number of subjects we could talk about other than the earl."

"But he's the most interesting."

"Perhaps for you."

The sound of someone calling her name gave Constance the perfect excuse to turn away from her sister. At the sight of Davinia Armstrong, she smiled with pleasure. The last time she'd seen her friend was the night before Oliver Rawlings's death. A shiver skimmed down her back. It had been more than three months since and the terror of that night still frightened her.

"Constance, oh my dear, how lovely it is to see you."

Delighted to see her friend, she hugged the other woman. "Davinia, how wonderful to see you. You remember Patience, don't you?"

As her sister and Davinia exchanged greetings, Constance noted her friend looked radiant. It was unexpected given her recent attachment to Oliver, but perhaps her friend hadn't been quite as enamored with the man as she'd thought. Pleading a parched throat, Patience excused herself and moved toward the buffet. The moment Davinia turned back to her, Constance lightly tapped her friend's arm with her fan.

"Where have you been? I came to see you when I returned to London, but your house was closed."

"I went to Europe after that...that terrible night." Davinia's face paled slightly as her expression became troubled.

"Oh, Davinia, I can't imagine what you must have gone through when you learned about Sir Rawlings."

"It was a bit unsettling to think that I...that we..." Her friend shook her head. "The fact of the matter is, I'm the one who should apologize, and I can only hope you'll forgive me."

"Forgive you?"

"For telling Oliver about your gift." Davinia winced. "If I hadn't told him about your ability, he might never have kidnapped Jamie or hurt you."

"You aren't to blame, Davinia. There wasn't anything anyone could have done to stop him. The man was mad."

The memory of those terrible moments in the North Tower of Lyndham Keep made her skin grow cold. She tried never to think about it, but it was impossible not to remember. Even now there were moments in the early hours of the morning when she lay terrified in her bed. Shutting the terrible memories out of her thoughts, she forced a smile to her lips as Davinia squeezed her hand once more.

"I have a favor to ask of you."

The question made Constance stare at her friend in puzzlement. "A favor?"

"I should have listened to you about Oliver, and I've learned my lesson."

"Oh dear, you met someone in Europe." She couldn't help but laugh at the blush filling her friend's cheeks.

"Yes, I did, and I want you to meet him." Davinia turned slightly and beckoned a tall, plain-looking man toward her. "He's so thoughtful, kind and sweet, Constance, but if you think he's not right for me..."

"Davinia, I don't think—"

"I trust you, dearest. I know you'll tell me the truth."

Her friend didn't wait for a response; instead she stretched out her hand to the man walking toward her. As the man reached them, Constance reached out with her senses, but could feel nothing. As he kissed Davinia's hand, she found herself liking the stranger simply because of the tenderness he displayed toward her friend.

"Albert, I want you to meet Lady Westbury. Constance, this

is Albert Fowler from America."

"How do you do, Mr. Fowler." She extended her hand to him, and with all the finesse of a British aristocrat, he gallantly kissed her hand.

"Any friend of Davinia's is a friend of mine, Lady Westbury."

The smile he sent her was pleasant, and as her hand slipped from his, she saw an image of him with a child. Oh Lord, the man was married. Dismayed by her brief vision, she struggled to hide her alarm behind a smile.

"Davinia says you met in Europe."

"Yes, we literally bumped into each other as I was trying to get a better look at a painting in the Musée du Louvre." Fowler sent Davinia a look of open admiration, and once more the image of him with a young child flashed before her. Refusing to jump to any conclusions about the man, she opened her fan and stirred the air in front of her.

"You're an art lover then, Mr. Fowler?"

"Sculpture mostly, but I enjoy portraits as well. My first task after convincing Davinia to marry me is to have Frank Miles paint her portrait."

The brash comment eased some of her concerns as she saw the wild color flooding her friend's cheeks. So he wasn't married. Now the only question was the child she'd just seen. Perhaps he was a widower.

"I've told you before, Albert." Davinia patted the man's arm. "I'm not ready to marry anyone."

"I'm a patient man, my dear, but perhaps I can call on Lady Westbury to persuade you to accept my suit." He turned his head toward Constance with a hopeful expression on his face.

"I fear I have little sway over Davinia." Constance shook her head and laughed. Despite her inability to sense more about Fowler and his character, she couldn't help but like him. There was something about his pleasant mannerisms that said he'd treat Davinia well.

"Don't be too sure of that, my lady." Fowler said as he placed his hands behind his back and met her gaze in a forthright manner. "Something tells me that Davinia introduced us because your opinion means a lot to her."

Constance's gaze flickered toward her friend with a frown of consternation. Wide-eyed, Davinia shook her head as their gazes met. A deep chuckle rolled out of Fowler.

"Forgive me, Lady Westbury, but I wouldn't be a successful businessman if I didn't know how to read people. The man smiled jovially at the two women. "I'm here because Davinia wants a second opinion."

"Albert," Davinia gasped as another wave of color flooded her cheeks.

Startled by the man's straight-forward comment, Constance couldn't contain her laughter. "Are you always this plain-spoken, Mr. Fowler?"

"I'm in the steel business, Lady Westbury, and coming straight to the point has made me successful." Fowler's expression softened as he looked at Davinia. "But I've yet to be successful in convincing this wonderful woman to marry me."

His words made Davinia blush once more, but it was the look of adoration in his gaze that spoke volumes. It was an expression she'd longed to see in Lucien's eyes, and his strong features flashed through her head. Pain lanced through her, and she forced herself to focus on Davinia and Albert Fowler. Something told her the man wanted her blessing simply because he knew it would make Davinia happy. It was an admirable quality, but it still didn't account for the child she'd seen with him.

"You're most persuasive, sir. I'm surprised Davinia hasn't already said yes."

"She's rather gun shy about marriage I think, but she's particularly worried my son might not take to her."

"Your son?" Constance studied his expression carefully.

"I'm a widower," Fowler said quietly. "I lost my wife to childbirth five years ago."

"I am sorry, sir. That must have been a terrible blow."

Her senses told her his wife's death had affected him deeply, but that his grief had ebbed until all that remained was a bittersweet sadness. He nodded at her statement then took Davinia's hand in his and raised it to his lips.

"I never thought I'd be happy again until the day I met Davinia. She's changed my life, and I know Harry will love her too."

The simple declaration touched her as she saw the expressions on both their faces. She didn't need her gift to tell her this couple was meant to be together. Davinia simply needed to overcome her fear and take that leap toward happiness.

"I've a feeling you're right, Mr. Fowler. Davinia has many wonderful qualities, and from what I can see, so do you."

Her friend gave a start of surprise as she turned to face Constance. The smile on Fowler's face widened into a beam of delight. "Thank you, Lady Westbury. I'm grateful for your endorsement."

"Constance, are you—"

"Trust your heart, Davinia." She leaned forward and gave her friend a quick hug. "Be happy."

Davinia sent her a brilliant smile as Patience walked toward them. The moment Constance saw her sister studying Fowler's profile, she grew uneasy. She wasn't ashamed of her ability to help others, but she knew better than to startle people with her gift. Patience on the other hand was far less discreet. The sooner she sent Davinia and her beau on their way, the better. She didn't want Patience inadvertently interfering with Davinia's happiness. With a quick movement, she offered Fowler her hand.

"Mr. Fowler, it was a pleasure meeting you," she said with a smile. "But if the two of you will forgive me, there's someone I need to see."

"But of course, Lady Westbury. I hope we'll see each other again."

She nodded at the man as she turned to her friend. "I shall be quite upset if you don't call on me in the next few days."

"I'll do so day after tomorrow," Davinia said as she clasped Constance's hand in hers. "I have a feeling there will be much for us to talk about."

With another smile at the couple, Constance quickly moved to intercept her younger sister. Irritation marred Patience's features as Constance blocked her way.

"One would think you didn't want me talking with Davinia and her fiancé."

"Blast you, Patience," she snapped in a low tone. "You know good and well they're not engaged—yet."

"*Yet* being the important word to stress. I'm sure Davinia will make a good mother to his son and the other three children they'll have."

"Good Lord," Constance muttered. "When are you going to learn it unsettles people to say things like that completely out of the blue?"

"And when are you going to credit me with some common sense? That stubborn nature of yours blinds you to far more than you're willing to admit."

"Exactly *what* is that supposed to mean?"

"It means you're too stubborn to admit you're in love with Lyndham."

Her sister's words washed over her like a bucket of cold water, and it took a moment to recover. Inhaling a deep breath, she opened the black feathered fan in her hand and tried to move it in a leisurely fashion. Patience wasn't deceived by her efforts to create a nonchalant appearance.

"See, you're not even willing to admit to me how you feel about the man."

"I can't admit to feelings I don't have."

"Liar," Patience said with sisterly frustration. "I know you're in love with him. I hear you sobbing your heart out almost every night. You barely eat, and now Sebastian has taken notice of your lethargic behavior. He's already summoned Percy and Caleb into his study to discuss the matter."

A sudden rush of anger surged through Constance. Jerking her head around, she glared at her sister. "Blast you, Patience, what have you told them?"

"I didn't tell them anything." Her sister arched an eyebrow at her in typical Rockwood fashion. "I didn't have to. And we both know what will happen if our brothers decide to interfere."

Turning away from her sister, Constance stared out at the dancers circling the ballroom floor. Patience was right. If Sebastian, Caleb and Percy interfered, heaven knew what mischief they would cause. Perhaps she should go abroad. Traveling through Europe would end any possibility of a chance meeting with Lucien. For the past two months he'd found some way to attend every social event she did.

Whether it was a simple dinner party or a ride in the park, he always seemed to be close by. On the one or two occasions he'd asked her to dance, her refusals hadn't stopped him from pursuing her. Worse yet, she knew people were starting to talk. Lucien had made it clear he was determined to press his suit with her, which made it difficult to avoid him. Any hostess who invited one of them to a social event would ultimately invite the other.

She knew what he was doing. He meant to wear her down until she gave in to him. But the man didn't understand the tenacity of the Rockwoods. She might love him with all her heart, but she couldn't change who she was to be with him. Her marriage to Graham had taught her how important acceptance was when you loved someone. Lucien might think he loved her, but he didn't love her enough to accept her gift as an essential part of who she was. No, tomorrow she'd look into the possibility of taking Jamie abroad.

She winced at the thought of her son. He missed Imogene greatly. Not a day went by that he didn't mention the little girl or their stay at the keep. He'd even mentioned Lucien once or twice, to her dismay. Although he remembered little about his brush with death, he still had the occasional nightmare. Visiting Europe would do more than simply enhance his education. It would help him forget. It would help both of them forget. A mocking laugh echoed in the back of her mind. She would never forget.

Her gaze refocused on the dancers, and she watched Prince Edward swing Mrs. Keppel around the dance floor. Despite his devotion to the Princess, the future King of England was renowned for his affairs, and Mrs. Keppel was the current favorite. It could not be easy for the Princess. Constance's gaze shifted to Princess Alexandra and the look of resigned pain in the woman's face. It was a sensation Constance knew well.

Loving Lucien yet knowing they could never be happy together left her numb. Although she tried hard not to be aware of him, it was impossible for her not to experience a frisson every time he entered a room. She should be grateful he'd finally chosen to leave her be, and yet the knowledge pained her more than she cared to admit.

Still, the past week had provided some relief for the constant scrutiny he'd placed her under. Whether it was an affair at Marlborough House or some other event, she could feel his gaze on her continuously. On several occasions, he'd flaunted one of London's professional beauties on his arm. The sight of him with another woman had filled her with intense jealousy.

Deliberate and overt, his behavior was designed to provoke a response in her, and he'd achieved his goal. But she'd utilized every ounce of willpower she possessed to suppress the Rockwood propensity for impulsive behavior and go to him. The sudden familiar frisson dancing across her skin signaled his presence. Desperately she fought to suppress the urge to search the room for a glimpse of his tall, handsome figure.

"You've never said why."

"What?" Constance turned her head toward Patience.

"You've never said why you won't have anything to do with the man." Her sister's quiet words made her wince.

"He'll be like Graham, and I can't live like that again. I can't bury who I am anymore, Patience. We have the sight for a reason. Hiding it because it makes him uncomfortable isn't something I'm capable of doing."

Patience touched her arm in a loving gesture, and Constance saw the light of understanding in her younger sister's eyes. "Have you told him this? Does he know this is what stands between the two of you?"

"I tried to explain it to him before I left Lyndham Keep, but I didn't know how to make him understand."

The sudden ripple of surprise and astonishment sweeping through the room made Patience turn toward the door. Gasping, she tugged at Constance's arm and tipped her head toward the room's entrance.

"Good Lord, it's Lady Lyndham. The woman's been in self-imposed exile for almost twenty years." Patience looked back at her with a twinkle of mischief in her green eyes. "I do believe your Earl of Lyndham has decided its time to bring in reinforcements."

The observation made her heart sink as she turned to see Aurora entering the ballroom on her grandson's arm. The Prince immediately moved forward to greet her. Their conversation wasn't audible from this distance, but whatever Lady Lyndham said amused Prince Edward greatly.

After several moments, Lucien slowly guided the elderly woman along the edge of the dance floor in her direction. Although several people tried to greet her, it was clear the dowager countess had no intention of being diverted from her ultimate destination. Constance swallowed hard as she realized Aurora was heading straight for her.

"Oh dear Lord," she murmured.

"It would appear you're about to be subjected to an inquisition, dearest." Patience released a low chuckle of amusement. "From all the stories I've heard about the lady, I doubt she'll avoid the topic of you and her grandson."

A moment later, Lady Lyndham's piercing blue eyes met Constance's as she and Lucien halted in front of her. Immediately offering the woman a curtsey, she flushed as the formidable dowager countess looked her up and down with disappointment.

"Surely, you can greet me better than that, Constance," the old woman huffed as she offered up her cheek.

Touched that the dowager countess thought their relationship close, Constance didn't hesitate to kiss the woman's weathered cheek. Satisfied, Lady Lyndham beamed at her then settled her hawk-eyed gaze on Patience.

"I take it you're a Rockwood as well. You look like your sister." Not giving Patience an opportunity to answer, Lady Lyndham turned her head to look at her grandson. "Ask this young lady to dance, boy. I'll stay here with Constance."

Beside her, Patience sent her an amused look, then accepted Lucien's arm. Constance tried to avoid looking in his direction, but her gaze was inexplicably drawn to his face. The determination and love she saw reflected in the blue eyes so like his grandmother's warmed and dismayed her at the same time.

He'd deliberately brought Lady Lyndham to town, knowing it would be impossible for her to refuse to see the woman. Which in turn meant he had access to her whenever his grandmother was in her company. It was his way of wearing her down, and a shiver sped down her spine as she realized this latest tactic of his might actually work.

"Come, I want to sit down. These old bones of mine aren't used to so much travel," Aurora said in a blunt tone of voice.

The dowager countess accepted the arm Constance offered her as the two of them moved toward an empty bench against the wall. Once seated, Lady Lyndham turned toward her.

"Well, what do you have to say for yourself?"

"I'm not sure what you mean, my lady," Constance denied, knowing full well what the dowager countess was referring to. Obviously the woman realized it too as she narrowed her gaze at her.

"The boy is miserable without you, Constance. And the keep has become silent as a tomb. It was a mausoleum before you came, but it's worse now that you're gone."

"It can't be helped, my lady."

"Are you worried I'll expect you to produce an heir? I admit a great-grandchild would be welcome, but Lucien's happiness is my first priority. I'd almost given up hope of him ever marrying."

"I'm sorry, my lady, but—"

"Blast it, girl. If you've had a vision about your future with Lucien, it can't be as bad as everything else you and the boy have been through."

"I beg your pardon?" Constance stared at the older woman in confusion.

"Lucien's convinced himself you've had another vision. One that's responsible for driving you away from the keep. However, I don't think that's it at all." Aurora sent her an astute look. "I think you're afraid the boy's going to have difficulty adjusting to your gift."

Startled by the woman's shrewd insight, Constance looked out at the dance floor. Her gaze immediately landed on Lucien skillfully guiding Patience in a fast-moving waltz. Dressed in formal attire, he was the most magnificent man in the room. But it wasn't the black tails and white tie at his neck that set him apart from other men. It was the raw and potent aura he exuded. It was the way he moved with animalistic grace around the room. He was powerful and masculine in the most primordial sense of the word. He looked dangerous. As dangerous as he'd looked that night at the Clarendon.

"Well, am I correct?" The dowager countess's voice broke through her thoughts, and Constance turned back to face the older woman.

"Did Lucien bring you here or did you insist on him bringing you?" She deftly avoided answering Aurora's question by asking one of her own. A smile lightened the woman's still-attractive features.

"Come, take a walk with me. This room is far too hot and stuffy."

"Are you certain you're up to doing so, my lady?" Constance frowned with worry. The question brought a fiery look to the woman's face as she shook her head.

"I'm not so decrepit that I can't enjoy a small stroll," Aurora snapped.

Biting back a smile, Constance rose to her feet and offered the older woman her arm. Together they walked toward a row of French doors that opened up into a long gallery. With a quick glance in Lucien's direction, she saw he was deeply involved in conversation with her sister. It was their second dance together, and jealousy nipped at her when she realized he was so absorbed in his conversation that he didn't even glance in her direction.

The dowager countess seemed to know exactly where she was going, and as they entered the corridor that adjoined the ballroom, she smiled. "William proposed to me here at Marlborough House."

Startled, Constance sent the woman a curious look. "Was his proposal unexpected?"

"No," Lady Lyndham shook her head, her smile widening, clearly enjoying the memory. "But the way he proposed was. He kidnapped me out of the ballroom and proposed to me in one of these rooms up here."

With a wave of her hand, the woman pointed toward several doors lining the hallway. "Come along, I'll show you."

Slowly they made their way to the third door. As they reached it, Aurora's hand rose to her throat. Hesitating, Constance touched her arm as the woman stared at the closed door, a look of longing on her face.

"Are you all right, my lady?" she asked quietly, afraid the

woman was close to tears.

"What?" Lady Lyndham sent her a puzzled look then nodded. "Oh yes, I'm fine. Would you mind checking to see that we're not interrupting someone, girl?"

"Of course," Constance said with an understanding smile.

Moving forward, she knocked quietly. When no one answered, she carefully opened the door and looked inside. Not seeing anyone, she opened the door wider and stepped into the room. The small sitting room was softly lit by gaslights on the wall. In many ways, it reminded her of the room at the Clarendon, the night she and Lucien— No, she refused to think about that night.

A soft sound behind her made her spin around. Lucien's powerful frame filled the doorway and blocked any possibility of escape. Over his shoulder she saw Lady Lyndham's self-satisfied expression disappear behind the closing door.

In mute dismay, she saw him lock the door and put the key in his trousers. She'd been lured into a trap. But did she really want to escape? The silence in the room buzzed with raw tension, and she struggled not to show how much his penetrating look was disturbing her.

"I'm going to ask you a question, *yā sabāha*, and I don't want anything except a yes or a no. Is that understood?" The autocratic note in his voice said he wouldn't be thwarted, and in truth, she didn't have the ability to defy him at the moment. Remaining silent in the face of his stern expression, she nodded.

"Do you love me?" The question surprised her slightly, but not in an alarming way. She'd already confessed her love to him. That wasn't the point in question where he was concerned.

"Yes."

He closed his eyes for a brief moment before pinning her beneath his blue gaze. The intensity of his look made her shudder, and she furtively glanced around the room, hoping to find another means of escape. A taunting voice in the back of her head chided her for being unwilling to face him.

"Yes or no. Do you believe I love you?"

"I can't—"

"God damn it, Constance, just say yes or no."

"No." She bowed her head. It was a true answer. She didn't believe he loved her the way she deserved to be loved.

"At least that's an answer I can deal with." The terse note in his voice caused her to jerk up her head with surprise. His eyes narrowed as he met her gaze. "Come here."

She shook her head sharply and took a quick step backward. God help her, the last thing she wanted was to find herself in his arms again. She'd forget everything then, and when she woke up from the pleasure of it, she'd find that nothing had changed. He still wouldn't love her for who she was.

"As you wish," he said grimly. In three long strides he was standing inches away from her, and yet he didn't touch her.

Trembling, she tried to suppress the gossamer frisson layering its fine web across her skin. With each breath she took, the scent of bergamot and leather flooded her senses. The tension in him was evident from the way his scar had tightened to a thin white line. Closing her eyes, she tried to block out the sight of him, but his image was still crisp and vivid in her head.

"Look at me, *yâ sabâha*." The soft command forced her to meet his gaze.

For a fleeting instant, she saw a tortured look in his blue eyes before he reached for something in his coat pocket. Slowly, he pulled a square jeweler's box out into view. Bewildered, she looked at the box and then back up at him as he offered the blue velvet package to her.

"I don't know what made you think I don't love every part of you, *yâ sabâha*, but I do." She flinched as the tips of his fingers singed hers when she accepted the box. "I don't care that you can see things others can't. All I know is that I can't live without you. I love you, and I don't know how else to prove it to you, except with this." He tipped his head toward the box she held.

He was speaking all the right words, but did he really mean them? Uncertainty gripped her as she studied his face. His somber look of apprehension made her want to reassure him, and she resisted the impulse to reach out and touch him. Slowly, she opened the box and stared at the gold calling-card case. Perplexed, she frowned at the small accessory.

"I don't understand," she murmured with confusion.

"Open it up." The tension in him was almost palpable. Again, she had to suppress the urge to touch him, ease the note of worry she heard in his voice.

The gold case was cool to the touch as she popped up the lid. Inside there were several calling cards already prepared. Shock held her rigid as she stared at the inscription on the cards.

The Right Honorable Countess of Lyndham

Helping Others Communicate with Lost Loved Ones

Lyndham House, Mayfair, Park Street

She saw the words, but she didn't believe they were real. It couldn't be real. Could it? Raising her head, she stared into his blue eyes. The troubled light in his gaze indicated his uncertainty as to how she would respond to his gift. And it was exactly that. It was a gift of love. His love. The cards were his declaration to the world that he loved her for who she was and would never expect her to hide her true self from him or anyone else. A shudder raced through her, and she swayed on her feet. A tear slid down her cheek, and then another as she stared into his apprehensive expression.

"For the love of God, *yā sabāha*," he rasped. "Say something."

Unable to speak, she simply flung herself into his arms and sought his mouth in a passionate kiss. Clinging to him, she eagerly drank in the heady scent of him as she kissed him with all the love and passion that was in her heart. His response was immediate and fierce. Strong arms locked around her in an embrace she would never be able to escape from, even if she wanted to.

His mouth left hers to gently kiss her damp cheeks. Still holding her close, he raised his head to stare down at her, while his fingers wiped away her tears. "I take it this means you'll marry me."

"It seems I have no choice given the earl has already printed up my calling cards." She uttered a laugh mixed with a sob of happiness.

"I couldn't think of any other way to make you understand how much I love you."

"And you're sure?" she asked with just a hint of

trepidation. "There may come a time when you'll regret saying you love me as I am."

"Never," he said firmly. "Although I have no doubt there will be moments when I'll want to shut the ghosts out just to spend a quiet hour with my wife."

"I love you, Lucien." Her words tugged a sigh from him as he feathered a kiss across her mouth.

"Not half as much as I adore you, *yā sabāha*," he whispered in her ear. "I'm never going to let you leave me again."

Capturing her lips in a hard kiss, he breathed in the familiar honey-jasmine mix of her perfume. He'd almost lost her, and God knows what would have become of him if that had happened. He owed his grandmother and future sister-in-law a debt of gratitude he'd never be able to repay. Cupping Constance's face in his hands, he probed the inner sweetness of her mouth as the familiar surge of desire and need plowed through him. Beneath his hands, the silky softness of her skin reminded him of other parts of her that were equally soft. Parts he wanted to explore without the constraints of clothing. With a groan, he released her to put distance between them. The disappointment on her face made him shake his head.

"Don't look at me like that. I want you more than you know, my love."

Daring flared in her eyes as her mouth curled in a come-hither smile. Her expression made his cock grow hard as iron in a brief second. He watched in disbelief as she reached behind her back to undo her gown.

"Damn it, Constance, this is hardly the Black Widows Ball at the Clarendon."

"But it is a locked room," she said with a seductive smile.

With a quick movement, the bodice of her gown slipped off her shoulders and fell to her waist. Unable to do anything but watch, his body hungered for her as she slowly untied the front of her corset. It was unmitigated torture to see her undo each ribbon with exacting care, when all he wanted to do was rip the damn thing off her.

Her movements were sensual and seductive as she slowly undressed in front of him. God, she was the most beautiful creature in the world. And she was his. His to love without fear of madness. The dress she wore pooled at her feet. Clothed only in a transparent chemise, she slowly inched it up over her thighs then her hips as she revealed the delicious nest of curls at the apex of her thighs.

Seconds later the chemise crested over her hard nipples before it landed on the floor with the rest of her clothing. An alluring smile on her lips, she stepped forward and undid his tie. Past the point of caring what might happen if they were caught, he didn't stop to think as he quickly removed his clothes. She moved away from him toward the room's sofa. Sinking into the cushions, she stretched out her hand to him.

It was the most enticing offer he'd ever received, and she knew it. She knew the power she had over him. Desire barreled through him, and he reached the couch in two quick steps. With a quick tug of her arm, he pulled her up onto her feet, and he saw the look of surprise on her face. He smiled. She wasn't the only one with the power, and he was about to show the future Countess of Lyndham that two could play this game of torturous seduction. Bending his head, he trailed his mouth along the side of her neck and down her shoulder. She smelled heavenly and tasted even better.

As he nibbled at her, he heard her soft pants of desire. Each one more heated than the last as his mouth moved to caress the top of one voluptuous breast. An instant later when his tongue flicked over a hard peak, a soft mewl poured out of her. Taking her into his mouth, he heard her cry out with pleasure.

God she tasted good. Hot and sweet like honey. And he'd missed the way she purred for him when he suckled her. He wanted to take his time with her, but his cock wasn't going to wait any longer. Pulling her with him, his knee forced her legs apart as they sank down onto the cushions of the couch.

She went willingly, her mouth seeking his as she straddled him. The hard heat of his erection pressed against her hot core and she shuddered. It would always be like this with him. The raw passion, the blinding desire. Shifting her hips slightly, she pressed down on him until he slid up inside her, filling her, expanding her. She didn't suppress her moan of pleasure, instead she reveled in it.

Passion and need darkened his face as she looked down into his eyes. The intensity of his gaze heightened the sensations flooding her body as she moved slowly over his hard thickness, intent on drawing out the pleasure. His eyes narrowed as he dragged in a ragged breath at her slow, measured strokes.

"Ride me, *yâ sabâha*," he said hoarsely. "Ride me now."

Obeying his command, she quickened the pace of their joining, her bottom crashing into his thighs with increasing force as she rode him. In seconds, her body tightened around him in her first spasm of pleasure. A deep growl rolled out of him as he urged her to rock against him with feverish abandon.

Inside her, he stiffened and exploded at the same instant she shattered over him. It was a blinding moment of clarity. This was what she'd sought all her life. This acceptance. This knowledge that she was at one with the man she loved. Leaning forward, she rested her forehead against his. For several moments, the only sound in the room was their heavy breathing as they slowly recovered from the intensity of their mating. A strong hand slid up her stomach and between her breasts to caress the base of her throat.

"First the Clarendon and now Marlborough House," he said with a satiated smile. "What will you propose next, I wonder."

"Are you saying you don't like living dangerously?" Wiggling against him, she elicited a sharp groan from him as she returned his smile. He shook his head and trailed his fingers down her cheek.

"Not as long as I'm with you, my love. Wherever you go, so goes my heart," he whispered.

"I love you, Lucien," she murmured as she lowered her head to kiss him. The dangers of the past were gone, leaving only a bright future ahead of them. Her mouth brushed across his, and for just a moment, she thought she heard the sound of someone knocking on the door. She ignored it. For once, the spirit world could wait.

About the Author

To learn more about Monica Burns, please visit www.monicaburns.com. Send an email to Monica at monicaburns@monicaburns.com or join her on her Bulletin Board at www.monicaburns.com/bulletinboard to join in the fun with other readers as well as Monica! For her announcements only Yahoo group, visit http://groups.yahoo.com/group/MonicaBurnsAnnouncements.

Free Dangerous Epilogue

If you enjoyed Constance's and Lucien's story, it doesn't have to end here. Visit Monica's website (www.monicaburns.com) and download your FREE copy of the Epilogue to Dangerous.

Come Enjoy the Ahh...Sensation

*An ancient prophecy. A sheikh's passion. One woman will
ignite the flame that fulfills them both.*

Mirage
© 2007 Monica Burns

A man without a country…

Half Bedouin, half English, the Viscount Blakeney has
always been Sheikh Altair Mazir in his heart. A victim of
prejudice from both cultures, he's learned to trust no one. But a
feisty American archeologist and the heat she ignites in him is
about to change all that. And more.

An independent woman hunting for a Pharaoh's treasure…

Alexandra Talbot is used to men questioning her
intelligence simply because of her sex. But the mysterious
Viscount isn't like other men. He never questions her ability to
find the lost city of Ramesses II, only her resistance to the sinful
pleasure of his touch.

An ancient prophecy…

Bound by a Pharaoh's prophecy, desire flares between them
beneath the desert stars. But murder and betrayal turn their
quest into a deadly game, pushing their fragile trust to the
breaking point.

Their survival hinges on rebuilding that trust.

Available now in ebook from Samhain Publishing.

Enjoy the following excerpt from Mirage...

His tall figure filled the doorway as she flung the door open. She fought to keep breathing. There was only one word to describe him. Magnificent. Unable to take her eyes off him, she struggled to calm her erratic heartbeat. Somewhere in the back of her mind, curiosity made her question why he was dressed like one of the natives. The thought was a fleeting one as she fought to keep her senses from responding to his commanding presence.

Dressed in the dark blue, flowing garment of the Mazir, he looked as if he had been born to wear the desert clothing. No longer the English lord, he was as lean and predatory as a leopard. A utility belt filled with rifle cartridges crossed his chest, while a pistol was tucked into a belt around his waist.

His entire appearance emanated a sense of danger and excitement. Beneath his eyes, Mazir tribal symbols stained his brown cheeks. His wavy brown hair, no longer restrained by a ribbon, tumbled down over his shoulders. The image of spiking her fingers through the dark, glossy curls sent a stream of liquid fire through her.

Good lord, she barely knew the man, and yet here she was ready to offer herself to him. She drew in a sharp breath, as she looked up into the warmth of his brown eyes.

"Good morning," he murmured. Alarm bells went off in her head at the sound of his husky greeting. If she were to open her mouth, she was certain more than a dozen butterflies would flee their captivity in her stomach.

"Good...morning." The breathless quality of her voice dismayed her. Oh God, she sounded as flustered as she felt. The sudden glint of satisfaction in his eyes made the fluttering wings in her stomach stir restlessly. Her voice had revealed far too much about the effect he had on her. Desperate to regain control of her senses, she swallowed the sensual urges threatening to take control.

"I...you...you look so different. Not like yourself at all."

"And how do you think I should look, Alex?" His eyes narrowed slightly as he studied her intently.

The dark, disturbing expression in his gaze sent her heart slamming into her chest. Tiny frissons caressed her skin as his gaze slid over her. Aroused by the mysteriously hungry look in his eyes, she shook her head as if doing so would help clear her thoughts as well as the desire curling inside her.

"It's just that you surprised me. I wasn't expecting to see you dressed like a Mazir."

"I find the *gambaz* cooler and more comfortable than my English clothes."

She nodded at his explanation. Oddly enough, he did look comfortable. Far more so than when he was wearing the starched shirt and tie he usually wore. The *gambaz* enhanced the dangerous edge of his darkly handsome features.

Did the man have any idea how devastating he was dressed like a Bedouin? There was a wicked savagery about him that tantalized her senses and made her breath hitch. Trying to suppress the urge to reach out and touch him, she inhaled a deep breath.

"Is something wrong, Alex?" The gleam in his eye made the palms of her hands damp.

"No, not at all." She forced the words past her lips, alarmed by the need building inside her.

A brown finger traced the outline of her lips as he leaned toward her. Cedarwood and sweet fennel tempted her senses. "Liar," he whispered, as a smile of satisfaction curved his mouth. "Your heart is beating as if you were a jerboa caught in the claws of a leopard."

His analogy was ironic given she'd likened him to a leopard earlier. Especially when she really did feel just like a mouse trapped beneath his masterful gaze. The dark brown eyes holding her gaze hostage glittered with a dangerous light. Drinking in the masculine scent of him, her lungs tugged in a sharp breath of need. She wanted him to kiss her. Appalled, she tried to find a footing on the slippery path she was treading. Diversion. That's what was called for—a diversion.

"I...I...why do you wear the Mazir marks on your cheeks?" She almost blew out a whoosh of air as she asked the question with great relief. That would help lessen this tension between them.

"They reflect the sunlight and protect my eyes. But they're also a sign of my respect for the Mazir." He arched an eyebrow at her as his finger trailed along the edge of her jaw in a slow, seductive stroke. The touch singed every nerve in his path. "But that's not what you really wanted to ask me, is it?"

"I don't know what you're talking about." She took a quick step back from him.

"Ah, so you didn't want to ask when we were to visit the Pyramids. As you wish." As he turned away from her, she sprang forward. The man was tormenting her by making her think he wouldn't take her to the Pyramids. Determined to halt his departure, she clutched at his arm. How soft the material of his robe was beneath her fingers.

"Don't you dare tease me like that!"

A quick flame came to life in his dark eyes as he turned and looked down into her face. The slight smile curving his lips made her heart race. The man was far too attractive for his own good.

"How would you like me tease you, Alex?"

She took a quick step backward at the surprising question. With an abrupt shake of her head, she pressed her hand against his chest as he followed her.

"I don't...I meant...I want to visit the Pyramids."

"I see. So you weren't hoping I'd find some other way to tease you?"

"I don't know what you're talking about," she spluttered.

His dark hand reached out to caress her cheek. No. If he kissed her again, she wouldn't be able to control the desire shooting through every part of her body. She took another step back. Once again, he followed her. Now the space between them was almost nonexistent. He lowered his head. Dear Lord, he smelled wonderful. He had an earthy male scent that tormented her senses. A shiver pulsed through her as the warmth of his breath stirred the wisps of hair at her ear.

"Don't you? That's disappointing because I'm finding it increasingly difficult to get the image of your luscious body out of my head."

She gasped at the seductive heat of his words. He nipped at her ear lobe and reason slipped out of her head.

"Do you know what I dreamed about last night, Alex? I dreamed I was sucking on those beautiful, dusky nipples of yours."

"Oh, God," she whispered, unable to say anything else.

"Can you imagine what else I dreamed about? Shall I tell you?"

Don't moan, Alex. Whatever you do, don't moan. She swayed into him, her fingers splayed across the upper part of his chest.

No.

No. This wasn't good at all.

GET IT NOW

CPSIA information can be obtained at www.ICGtesting.com
Printed in the USA
BVOW020254190612

293071BV00001B/87/P